Stor

GW00393313

Davina Elliott ha... ...ety of jobs from dresser to small time producer. None of them include performing. She lives in London with no children, no pets and is inseparable from her laptop called Leo.

Storming the Stage is her third novel, and is a sequel to *Chewing the Scenery* and *Climbing the Curtain*.

Praise for *Chewing the Scenery*:

'I laughed out loud while planning which part I should try for when the inevitable film is made!!!' – Amanda Holden

'Oh dear, she knows us thesps far too well. It's a sparkling, wicked book & frighteningly accurate. Read & be delighted.' – Miriam Margolyes

'Theatre folk picked apart with the forensic wit of a vulture after a couple of gin and tonics. Damn good fun.' – Nigel Planer

'Hugely entertaining tale.' – AS Magazine

Praise for *Climbing the Curtain*:

'Are actors really like this? Yes, guilty as charged - my only regret is that I've finished it!' – Susie Blake

'This is a dangerously funny book - dangerous because I will never trust a dresser again. Davina knows all our secrets and knows how to exaggerate them to great comic effect.' – Harriet Walter

'Some fantastic writing, laugh out loud comedy and moments that could easily provoke tears.' – British Theatre Guide website

Also by Davina Elliott

Chewing the Scenery
Climbing the Curtain

Storming the Stage

Davina Elliott

PUCK BOOKS

Published by Puck Books
www.puckbooks.com

First published 2012

British Library Cataloguing in Publication Data
A catalogue record for this book is available
from the British Library

ISBN 978 0 9560960 2 9

Typeset in Bookman Old Style 11pt

Printed and bound in Great Britain
by CPI Group (UK) Ltd, Croydon, CR0 4YY

ACKNOWLEDGEMENTS

Firstly, and most importantly, a huge thank you to my fabulous editor Kathy Kerr, without whom my books would be full of howling grammatical and technical errors, and who is always there for me. Thanks also to Caroline Baron for her patience in listening to every word, slashing my overuse of adverbs and giving helpful advice, as did Cynthia Millar and Verena Elliott. Additionally, I'd like to thank my agent Judith Chilcote; Ken Brown for his invaluable knowledge of all things Broadway and for getting me backstage access to the St James Theatre; Vicky Scott for information on quadriplegia and Su Gilroy for being almost as excited about reading and commenting on my books as I am about writing them, and for pointing out that in my passion for the city I was in danger of turning *Storming The Stage* into a New York Guide book.

For all those 'Judith Gold' fans who inspired
me to produce a further novel

and

In memory of
The Empire Diner, the Rainbow Room
and Tavern on the Green,
New York City

WESLEY BARTLETT
AND
IRENE UBRONSKI
PHIL DAWSON, HANK PERRY
PRESENT:

ALL ABOUT EVE

A new stage version

By Owen Brady

Based on the 20th Century Fox film

Cast in order of appearance:

Addison DeWitt	Rupert Blake
Eve Harrington	Mindy Blue
Margo Channing	Judith Gold
Young actress	Paige Parker
Birdie	Alyce Gilmore
Bill Sampson	Digby Weston
Karen Richards	Jennifer Hoffman
Lloyd Richards	Kyle Henderson
Miss Caswell	Paige Parker
Phoebe	Paige Parker
Director	Aubrey Henson
Miss Gold's dresser	Tim Coates

PROLOGUE

August

The hot summer's sun was slowly disappearing over New York's Times Square, and the theatres' neon signs were beginning to flicker into life. The queue around the half price ticket booth had slowed to a trickle from the earlier surge, with only a few last minute bargain hunters remaining.

On 45th Street an elderly woman with black bobbed hair, a handsome younger man and a fraught looking man with glasses were walking slowly, but with purpose, staring up at the theatres' facades.

"The Music Box is a good theatre for a straight play," said the man with glasses.

"Well, it's a fucking stupid name for a theatre hosting a straight play," the woman retorted. "Besides, Wesley, it's got a lousy hoarding. There's no room for my name to go up in enormous lights. I want it to say: Judith Gold is Margo Channing in *All About Eve.*"

"If we have to put all that we'd have to hire the whole of Times Square," the other man said.

"Fuck off, Rupert," Judith said, amicably. "Don't you want your name up there too? After all, you've never done a show on Broadway, have you?"

"No. But that's exciting enough. I'm not so bothered about the billing thing. Besides, if they hate me I'd rather my name wasn't hanging

9

around to remind them."

"Why would they hate you?" Judith demanded. "You're a perfect Addison DeWitt. The critics in the London version adored you. Why wouldn't they feel the same here?"

"Because I'm not American and they might feel I'm poaching their roles, especially when it's such a classic Hollywood movie."

Judith made a dismissive gesture with her hand. "Rubbish. I dare them to find anyone to play the role as well as you do. Besides, judging from the popularity of your plethora of movie appearances you'll doubtless bring in more audience than I will."

"No, I won't. People want to see Judith Gold, The Queen of Theatre, live on Broadway. As producer, Wesley, don't you agree? Judith's the one going to be making you rich."

"I hope so," Wesley said, frowning. Staging a show in London was child's play compared to doing so on Broadway. Most shows here had more producers than cast members, a veritable essay of them before the title, whilst Wesley was used to being a one-man band. He stopped and pointed to another theatre, the Booth, on the corner of Shubert Alley. "This is a good theatre for plays and it's in a perfect position."

Judith rejected it immediately. "That awning makes it look like an apartment block. The audience will be looking for a doorman, not an usher." She walked along Shubert Alley and stopped for a minute in front of the Helen Hayes Theatre on 44th Street.

"It's a nice size for a straight play and next to Sardi's for those late night meals," Wesley tried.

10

Judith gave him a withering look. "You can't imagine I'm going to perform in a theatre named after some American actress when no fucker has ever named a theatre after me." The lack of a Gold Theatre had always been one of Judith's bugbears. Behind her rigid back Rupert grinned at Wesley. Wesley gave him a look of deep despair. He was rapidly losing his nerve for this project.

"How about this one?" Judith pointed to the St James Theatre, a few feet further along from the Helen Hayes on 44th Street.

"It's a musical house," Wesley said. "It'll be too big for *All About Eve.*"

"Don't think so small. I'm sure we could fill any theatre, judging by our success in London and how eager they are to transfer it here. And I like the outside of this one. It has the perfect old-fashioned appearance. I could easily envisage Margo Channing acting in such a theatre."

"Margo Channing's producer almost certainly didn't have to pay such exorbitant rents," Wesley pointed out.

"Stop being so tight," Judith snapped. "I want this theatre."

"I don't suppose it's even available," Wesley said. "That musical has been running for years."

"Then it's about time it closed, or they can move to another theatre. We're talking about next year, so they've got at least six months to organize something. I've made my choice and if they want me so badly they can fix it."

Wesley made another attempt. "We haven't looked at the American Airline Theatre on the renowned 42nd Street."

Judith gave him such a fierce look he felt as if he could melt from the heat. "Do I look like a fucking air hostess?" She gave an exasperated sigh at his expression of bafflement. "Keep up, Wesley." She strode off towards the St James Theatre.

"American Airlines – air hostess," Rupert muttered to Wesley. "I think we can take that as a no."

Wesley groaned. "Why can't theatres just have numbers? Then we could be Theatre No 6 on 45th Street. Surely Judith couldn't object to that?"

Rupert watched Judith peering at the photographs outside the St James Theatre. "Don't you think she'd insist on being in number one?"

"Yes, you're probably right." Wesley removed his steamed-up glasses, wiped and replaced them. "Now where's she going?" Judith had pulled open a door to the right of the theatre, and disappeared. The two men followed her down an indoor and then outdoor corridor and found themselves backstage. Here a bemused stage door keeper, after enquiring if they were with that rather alarming lady, pointed them towards the stage. Judith was standing on it, staring out into the auditorium, much to the surprise of the crew who were setting up for that evening's show.

"Judith!" Wesley hissed from the wings, glancing around nervously. Judith ignored him and marched from one side of the stage to the other, her face a picture of concentration. Without seeming to be aware of a large piece of scenery being carried directly at her she ducked with perfect timing and then neatly stepped over a rolled up carpet before striding back out of the theatre.

"Yes, that will do nicely," she told a harassed Wesley. "Although we must make sure they improve their security. Anybody could have walked in there. I don't want some stalker accosting me in my dressing room, or Rupert's drooling fans camping outside his. Oh, dressing rooms!" she exclaimed, in an annoyed tone. "I must inspect them." She turned back to the stage door, but Wesley quickly stepped in front of her.

"No," he said firmly. "Enough is enough."

"You'll scare the life out of some poor actor if you burst in on him when he's half naked," Rupert commented.

"He should be so lucky." Judith scowled and then shrugged. "I suppose we can deal with that once we have the theatre," she conceded.

Wesley looked at Rupert, silently pleading for his support.

Rupert shrugged. "I'm sorry, Wesley, I can't do anything when Judith has her heart, or whatever passes for that organ, set on something."

"Bastard." Judith gave Rupert one of her glares.

Rupert, who'd received many worse looks, ignored it. "And I agree it's a lovely theatre," he said. "Still, maybe we should leave the vicinity before the management call the police to report suspicious visitors."

"So?" Judith asked Wesley.

Wesley put up his hands in surrender. "OK,

I'll look into it, but don't get your hopes up. I'm not in a position to re-arrange the Broadway theatre scene. Now I'm going to a meeting with my co-producers. I can't see them being overjoyed with your latest request." Wesley wandered mournfully towards Times Square.

Judith gave a smile of satisfaction as she regarded the St James. "This is Margo Channing's theatre. I've known that since I came here before, when we were rehearsing for the London production."

Rupert eyed her suspiciously. "You mean you always intended to demand this theatre?"

"Naturally."

"So why did you let Wesley research half the theatres on Broadway? And I could've spent my evening doing better things than traipsing round them. In fact, why did we even bother coming?"

Judith opened her eyes innocently. "I wanted to make Wesley feel he was a little bit in charge. And that you had a say too. Besides, we can see a few shows, check out some prospective actors, soak up the atmosphere, that sort of thing. How often does one get an all expenses paid trip to New York?" She gave Rupert a wicked smile. "Come along, let's find somewhere decent to celebrate our new theatre."

"We don't have it yet."

Judith gave him a pitying look. "Don't be silly, Rupert. Of course we do."

The St. James Theatre has been named as the venue for the transfer of the Olivier Award winning London production of *All About Eve*, based on the Bette Davis movie, adapted by Owen Brady and directed by Aubrey Henson. Judith Gold and Rupert Blake reprise their award winning roles as Margo Channing and Addison DeWitt. Further casting to be announced. The production currently at the St. James Theatre will be transferring to the Al Hirschfeld Theatre. Judith Gold has already appeared on Broadway in *An Ideal Husband,* while Rupert Blake will be making his Broadway debut. This show promises to be a hot ticket. The box office will be open to American Express Gold Card holders from Monday and for the general public from November 7th. The production previews from March 1st with a press night of March 20th.

CHAPTER ONE

"That woman should not wear short skirts," Judith commented as a large lady in a skintight mini skirt and high heels tottered past the Starbucks on 42nd Street. She and Rupert were sitting in the window there, having a coffee, on Friday evening following the first week of rehearsals.

Rupert regarded the woman. "She certainly looks underdressed for the weather. It's barely above freezing out there and they're forecasting blizzards for next week. I'm seriously thinking of buying a pair of UGG boots."

"You can't!" Judith said, horrified. "They're for women."

"Why should women be the only ones to have warm feet?"

"You buy a pair of those and you can go out for coffee on your own."

Rupert leapt to his feet and got out his wallet. "Right, where can I get a pair?"

"You bastard!" Judith glowered at him. "And sit down before that couple clasping coffee cups and eyeing our seats grab yours. The last thing I need today is strangers pinning me against the wall and asking why they recognize me."

Rupert sat back down, grinning at the idea of anyone pinning Judith against anything and surviving unscathed. Not that he'd mind being pinned by the girl of the couple, a stunning blonde who managed to make a fairly silly woolly hat look attractive.

"How's Holly?" Judith asked, making Rupert start guiltily. Judith smirked. "You're so obvious, Rupert. Like all bloody men – thinking of nothing but sex."

Rupert started to protest but Judith cut him off. "How long have you been with Holly?"

"Just over a year, as you well know."

"Try and make it another year before you start screwing around. You might even make it into the Guinness Book of Records under Casanova: unusual celibacy of."

Rupert scowled at her. "I have no intention of screwing around. I adore Holly and would never intentionally hurt her. I can still appreciate other women though, especially since I'm not going to see Holly for months."

Judith shrugged. "That's the problem with theatrical relationships. It's virtually impossible for them to work when both halves have jobs which keep them apart."

"We're going to make it work," Rupert stated firmly, before pointedly changing the subject. "Rehearsals went better today, don't you think?"

Judith slammed her coffee cup down. "Are you crazy? It's a disaster. I wish I'd never agreed to the whole idea. If I didn't have a contract I'd be tempted to walk out this minute."

Rupert nodded at Judith's, by now familiar, threats and settled back to listen to her complaints. As far as she was concerned none of the other actors were up to scratch or understood Judith's concept of the play. Technically it was Aubrey Henson's concept of the play since he was credited as director but, as was Judith's way, the final product had more to do with her than with any nominal director.

Judith's vision had made *All About Eve* a huge West End hit and in spite of her reservations about the Broadway transfer, Rupert was fairly certain it was going to be as successful here. The bookings were highly promising with most of the previews already sold out, an impressive feat for a straight play in such a large theatre. Yet to keep the production on track meant keeping Judith happy, and Rupert was one of the few people who could do that. So for an hour he listened, commented, cajoled and pacified.

The root of the problem lay in Judith's not being responsible for any of the American casting, as she had been in London. For while Judith and Rupert's international star status allowed them to recreate their roles, Equity rules would not permit the other British cast to join them. Although Wesley's Broadway producing partners had politely listened to Judith's opinions, they insisted on having the final say.

The leading role of Eve Harrington, for example, was being played by a 25 year old Hollywood actress, Mindy Blue, who had absolutely no theatre experience. While she was talented, her gestures and vocal ability were accustomed to the intimacy of filming and unlikely to read from the back of a large theatre. Even the ineffectual Aubrey was aware of that and working hard to try and enlarge her performance, while a vocal coach had been brought in to give Mindy lessons in projection.

The roles of Lloyd and Karen Richards,

the writer and his wife, and that of Margo Channing's dresser, Birdie, were cast with experienced theatre actors, and causing fewer problems, while a very keen young actress fresh from summer stock and one Off-Off Broadway play was playing the dual roles of Miss Caswell and Phoebe.

It was the actor playing Bill Sampson, Margo Channing's love interest, who was the cause of most of Judith's grievances. Digby Weston was originally a Broadway actor, before making his name in the TV comedy series, *Allow Me, Sir,* playing a pompous butler. When ratings fell following six successful seasons, the series was axed and Digby found himself washed-up in Hollywood. Declaring his undying love for stage work he returned to New York where he belittled the falseness of the television industry while constantly phoning his West Coast agent pleading for more TV work.

"The pompous fool considers he's a better actor than he is," Judith grumbled. "If only he'd drop that attitude he might be bearable. As he is, he's impossible to work with. I'm supposed to be in love with the man and I can't abide being within two feet of him. I was more attracted to Richard in London, and he's gay!"

"It's only the first week," Rupert said. "I'm sure you'll manage to get a good performance out of him, in time."

"Why should I? I'm not a fucking acting coach. My job is to act, and maybe give a few directing suggestions. A <u>few</u> directing suggestions," she repeated with emphasis at Rupert's sardonic expression. "This is supposed to be a professional production, so why am I given unprofessional actors to work with?" Judith scrunched up her empty paper coffee cup in her fist and scowled out of the window as if everybody on 42nd Street was to blame.

The couple Judith had pointed out earlier went out of the door, letting in a blast of cold air. As they walked past the window the girl looked back in and gave Rupert a seductive smile through the glass. Rupert returned the smile in kind and then felt, rather than saw, the expression on Judith's face. "What?" he demanded. "I was only being polite."

Judith stood up, pulling on her scarf and camel-hair coat. "Since you're obviously more interested in flirting with half of Manhattan than worrying about our play, I'm going back to the hotel."

"Judith, wait." But Judith had already stormed out. Rupert flung on his own coat and threw their empty cups in the bin, before heading outside. Halfway along the street he could see people scattering as Judith ploughed through them, head down. Experience told him to leave her alone for the present and make amends later.

He wandered along the streets running west off Times Square, studying the different theatres. That he'd soon be appearing on Broadway was an exciting prospect. Much as he enjoyed making movies, the theatre provided an exhilaration which standing in front of a camera could never rival. Judith, he knew, felt the same. It was one of the reasons they got on so well. That, and Rupert's laid-back attitude and refusal to be upset or angered by anything, an approach which Judith claimed was exasperating while secretly relishing it.

Few people understood their relationship, some even reading it wrongly as sexual which convulsed Rupert with laughter and even faintly amused Judith. Rupert described it as a friendship, while Judith, who claimed not to need friends, commented that he was a good actor and went so far as to admit he made her laugh. Much to her astonishment she'd found herself confiding in him – an entirely new experience for Judith.

The audiences were beginning to pour into the theatres now. In London they sort of trickled in, Rupert thought, but here there were long queues through the doors and stretching down the streets. The theatres were so close to each other that the back of a queue for one theatre would meet the front of a queue for another. The more enterprising theatres had staff working the queues selling their merchandize. He hoped *All About Eve* would be a hit, for his sake, for Wesley's as producer, but above all for Judith. The entire show had been her baby, from her discovering the author who'd adapted it from the film, to casting, to unofficially directing, to almost killing herself by performing her role with pneumonia.

He went into the Theatre Circle shop, next to the St James Theatre, and bought a musical snow globe of Broadway theatres for Holly. Judith had made him feel guilty about her simply because he'd smiled at a blonde. As he left the shop his eye was caught by a T-shirt in the window which read: 'What I really want is to direct', and he doubled back in to buy one in small.

When Judith opened the door to her hotel room shortly after, she found Rupert proffering a bag. She pulled out the T-shirt and read it. Giving Rupert one of her famous glares which had been known to cause panic in many a young actor, she demanded, "Are you suggesting I'm a megalomaniac?"

"Yes."

Judith's lips began to twitch, rather to her annoyance. Rupert leant over and pulled the sides of her mouth up into a rather grotesque grin. "I was going to say that was better," he commented, "but actually it's a bit gargoyle like. Maybe we should suspend you from the top of St Patrick's Cathedral."

Judith gave up the fight and started to laugh. "You are such a fucker, Rupert. I suppose you'd better come in. In fact, go and get some ice and we can have a drink."

When Rupert came back from the ice machine Judith had changed into the T-shirt and was pouring two glasses of whisky.

Rupert eyed her admiringly. "That suits you."

"The T-shirt, or the message?"

"Both. I've never seen you in such casual attire. You should wear more clothes like that, instead of hiding yourself under black blouses and sweaters."

"At my age? Don't be ridiculous; 55 year old women don't wear T-shirts. The next thing you'll suggest is my buying a pair of running shoes."

"If you did you'd fit right in as a New Yorker,"

Rupert said, wondering for how long Judith had claimed to be 55. It had certainly been for as long as he'd known her which was getting on for four years now. "We should give one of those to Aubrey," Rupert continued, gesturing at the T-shirt. "He's been trying to direct this play for two years!"

Judith gave a slight smile at Rupert's remark. "Well, he gets the acclaim for all my hard work so he should be grateful." Her face fell and she reverted to looking thoroughly depressed. "And when it's a huge flop here and we close overnight he can get the blame for that too."

Rupert reached over and touched her arm, but her natural instinct against physical contact made her pull away. "It's not going to be a flop." Rupert's voice was gentle but confident.

"What, even with that bloody Digby?"

"Yes, even with that bloody Digby."

Judith felt strangely comforted, though that could have been the two large glasses of straight whisky she'd thrown back before Rupert had arrived. Unusually for her she felt she ought to explain her outburst in Starbucks. "You see, Rupert, I'm quite fond of Holly." Quickly she amended her comment. "At any rate she's an improvement on your ex-wife."

Rupert hid a smile at Judith's dread of displaying anything that could be considered sentiment. "Considering what you think of Miranda I'm not sure how great a compliment that is. I know you're fond of Holly though, and I appreciate your loyalty to her, but I'm not going to do anything, I swear. I'm a reformed character." Judith gave a derisive snort. "I am," Rupert insisted. "I merely can't resist a bit of window shopping occasionally." He dug the snow globe out of another bag beside him. "Look, I bought this for her." He turned the key at the bottom and it started to play rather a distorted version of *New York, New York.*

Judith regarded it doubtfully. "How are you going to get it to her? If you send it by post it'll most likely be blown up as a suspect package, sent by one of America's sworn enemies bent on wreaking revenge by murdering their music."

"I'll give it to Wesley. He's going back to England next week and I'm sure he wouldn't mind popping it in to Holly's theatre."

"Why is Wesley going back?" Judith's eyes narrowed. In her opinion Wesley should be constantly on call to solve any problems for her, from complaints about the play, the cast or theatre, down to whether her sheets were being changed enough at the hotel.

"Apparently he's missing Blythe so much that he's going home for a few days to see her," Rupert explained.

"Thereby leaving us in the lurch! If he must get all paternal, why doesn't he bring Blythe out here? After all, she's my god-daughter."

Rupert threw his hands up in the air in exasperation. "No, she's not! You merely keep telling everybody she is, especially Wesley."

"Well, she ought to be. Just because I don't care for children is no reason not to ask me to be godmother. After all, I came up with her name. In any case, he could still bring her over. I'm sure Henrietta would like a trip to New York; it must be terribly dull being stuck at home with a baby day and night."

"Blythe's not exactly a baby anymore; she's just started at nursery so I don't think either Wesley or Henrietta want to upset her routine by bringing her over here in term time."

"Fucking children," Judith retorted.

"Oh no, even I wouldn't go that far," Rupert drawled.

"Oh, get out!" Judith grabbed a pillow off the bed.

Rupert got out, laughing.

CHAPTER TWO

In Joe Allen's restaurant the other cast members of *All About Eve* were also dissecting that week's rehearsals, from a rather different standpoint.

"I've never been treated in such a manner in my entire career," Digby Weston said. "I'm not some nobody that Judith Gold can walk all over. She may be important in England, but over here I'm more of a name than she is and I won't put up with her behaviour."

"It's the feeling of hostility," Mindy Blue said, slowly. "I try to do what she wants and yet I sense she considers my performance to be sub-standard. I have an aversion to hostility."

Digby stabbed at a piece of his pasta with his fork. "Why the hell is she directing the play any-way when we have Aubrey Henson on board? He has a superb directing résumé, everything from Shakespeare to Tennessee Williams. I was so energized about working with him, yet he never opens his mouth unless he's asked that dreadful woman's permission first."

"She does seem to know what she's talking about though," said Jennifer Hoffman, who was playing Karen Richards. "Her notes to me are right on the nose and she's great to act with. She gives so much back."

"Aren't you the lucky one; I get nothing back from her," Digby snapped.

The rest of the cast looked embarrassed. It was obvious that Judith had taken an utter dislike to Digby. It was quite understandable – the man was intolerably arrogant – but equally they felt sorry for his discomfort, especially since Judith had the reputation of destroying any actor she didn't consider up to scratch. Even in those she didn't actively dislike she could produce such terror that many actors and directors never recovered.

"So, it's not normal to have the big star directing the play?" asked Paige Parker, who was playing the double role of Miss Caswell and Phoebe. "It sure never happened in summer stock, or Off-Off Broadway, but then we didn't have many stars."

"No, it certainly is not normal," Digby retorted, conveniently forgetting that he used to do exactly that on his TV show, much to the annoyance of his fellow actors and his directors. "That woman is a complete bitch."

Jennifer looked at Alyce Gilmore, who at fifty four had been acting longer than any of them, and was playing Margo's dresser and confidante, Birdie. "What do you think, Alyce? Have you worked with anyone like Judith before? Do you think she's going about it the wrong way?"

Alyce played with a piece of bread. "I kinda like her. I'm sorry, Digby, I know she's tough, but I have to agree with Jennifer. She does know what she's doing and it is wonderful to act with her. In that scene we did today, she made me feel I'd actually been her dresser and friend for years."

"And you think that makes up for her disrespect for us as actors?" Digby demanded, loudly enough for people at the neighbouring tables to look towards them.

Paige glanced around in embarrassment. Wasn't that Bernadette Peters over there? And behind the pillar, surely that was Harry Connick Jnr? What would they think about Digby's behaviour? Having been working on the perfume counter in Macy's for the last few months, spraying unsuspecting shoppers with the latest, and in her opinion rather unpleasant, fragrance, Paige was determined to make the most of this break and impress anybody she could. Being mortified by her fellow actor in the middle of Joe Allen's was not part of her game plan. She cast around for a change of topic and yet in keeping with the subject in hand. "Rupert's very nice, isn't he?"

"Oh sure, because no doubt you want to sleep with him," Digby retorted.

"No!" Paige was horrified that anyone might think that.

"Don't tell me you don't fancy him, the great British heartthrob?" Digby sneered.

"No, I mean yes, he's very handsome and all but..." She came to a halt.

"Don't worry hon," said Alyce. "I wouldn't mind a bit of him myself."

"That's disgusting," said Digby. "You're old enough to be his grandmother."

"You are such a prick, Digby." Kyle Henderson spoke for the first time since putting in his order with the waiter. Kyle, who was playing Lloyd Richards, was happily married with two small children and completely uninterested in theatrical bitchery, gossip and backstabbing, preferring to simply do his job and go home.

He'd only agreed to attend this meal in the interests of company relations and would far rather be eating dinner with his family. But nor would he allow this kind of vitriolic attack of Digby's.

Digby was temporarily silenced by Kyle's remark. Kyle quietly continued to eat his burger. Then Digby slammed his fist down beside Kyle's plate, causing several French fries to jump off it and into Kyle's lap.

"How dare you speak to me like that?"

Kyle carefully removed the fries and placed them on the edge of his plate. "I don't appreciate your speaking to Alyce in that manner. It's very disrespectful."

"What, you think it wouldn't be gross: her and Rupert?"

"Why? There are plenty of successful relationships with age gaps. My wife is several years older than me for starters. And if I wasn't already spoken for I would be very flattered to have a sugar mummy like Alyce." Alyce gave a loud guffaw. "And I agree with Paige, Rupert seems a nice guy."

"Right, if you like toadying," Digby snarled. "He's all over Judith. Talk about major arse kissing. He knows which side his bread's buttered."

Kyle regarded him calmly. "Actually, if anything I'd say she needs him."

"Oh please!"

"Think what you like, but I believe you'd find that if Rupert wasn't here we'd be having an even tougher time with Judith. Haven't you noticed how carefully he diffuses situations when they're about to get out of hand?" There was silence as everybody digested this notion.

"You're right," Jennifer said. "When Judith started screaming yesterday that we were all incompetent, he calmly suggested we take a coffee break and she agreed. If anybody else suggests a break she goes nuts."

"Exactly." Kyle got out his wallet and put some dollar bills on the table. "I've gotta go say hello to my kids before they're asleep. See you guys Monday."

There was an uncomfortable silence after his departure, broken by Digby. "What the hell's the matter with you all? We should be on the same side against these Brits coming in and taking over our heritage. *All About Eve* is a landmark American movie so we should be in charge."

Jennifer continued trying to play mediator. "But the Brits came up with this stage adaptation. If it wasn't for them making it a hit in London it wouldn't be on Broadway and we wouldn't have jobs."

"I'd always have a job," Digby said, having not had one in over six months. His agent had actually had the nerve to suggest he apply to play Santa Claus at one of the out of town department stores last Christmas, since he had the perfect look. If anyone seriously thought that he, Digby Weston, star of *Allow Me, Sir*, was going to have a whole lot of drooling, disease-ridden children sitting on his lap whining about what they wanted for Christmas, they were insane. And out of town too. He informed his agent haughtily that if that was how he saw Digby's career he would be seeking other representation, although so far other representation seemed not to be seeking him.

"OK," Jennifer said, appeasingly. "So you'd be fine, Digby. But I wouldn't have a job."

"Me neither," said Paige, keen to show her appreciation.

Alyce held up her hand in agreement.

"And if I have to kowtow to Judith a bit, even when I don't agree with her, then I will," Jennifer continued. "What about you, Mindy?"

Mindy, who had been playing with her salad throughout the entire conversation and argument, looked up. "It's the hostility," she repeated and went back to dissecting a small tomato.

"Right," said Jennifer, not sure what other comment she could make and wishing Kyle hadn't deserted her. The two of them were hitting it off well in rehearsals and she felt they had a similar attitude to their work and their fellow cast members. She gave a bright smile, which she didn't feel, and said, "Shall we get the check?"

Mindy paid her for her barely touched salad and asked a surprised but smitten waiter to hail her a cab. Since the producers had provided Mindy with an apartment opposite the Lincoln Centre, she could have walked it in the time it took for the cab to crawl up traffic-filled Broadway. But Mindy didn't feel safe walking anywhere; nobody in LA walked. There if people wanted to walk they used the treadmills at the gym. She found it strange to watch the hundreds of people striding up and down the roads with great determination and disappearing down steps into, for her, the unknown and terrifying world of subways.

As the taxi dropped her off at her exclusive

apartment block, the doorman leapt forward to open the front door with a flourish. Mindy got into the elevator and watched the floor indicator illuminate as it shot up to the tenth floor. Inside her sanctuary she removed her shoes, curled up on the sofa and pushed a button on her Dictaphone. The tones of her vocal coach echoed around the room, and dutifully Mindy copied each breathing and vocal exercise until the tape finished. Then she lay back and started her visualization exercises. "I am Eve Harrington, I am Eve Harrington," she repeated over and over. When she got up she continued the rest of her evening in the role of Eve Harrington; doing everything the way she believed Eve would. Method acting was Mindy's passion and it saddened her that Judith didn't seem to feel the same.

Alyce and Jennifer, both living on the Upper West Side, got the subway together, while Paige got the Flushing train out to Queens and her four room-mates, dreaming of a time she could afford to live in Manhattan – and with fewer people.

"You did well tonight," Alyce said to Jennifer as the train made its way uptown. "Trying to please everybody is hard, especially against such negativity as Digby's."

"I'm not sure I succeeded, but I had to try." Jennifer sighed. "I want this to be a great experience. I can't bear it if it gets spoilt by bad feeling. It's so rare to get a great job in a straight play on Broadway, because believe me I'm never gonna be in a musical. Tone deaf was an expression created for me."

Alyce smiled. "I managed to get by playing Aunt Ella in *Oklahoma!* for a year without being able to sing. I just kinda croaked it. The critics thought it was a directorial decision! But I'm with you; I'm definitely happier on a straight play. And I think this is gonna be a very exciting ride, if rather a rough one."

The train stopped at 72nd Street where a disembodied voice announced that the local train had now become an express. Reluctant to stop this conversation, Jennifer opted to stay on and walk back to her local stop.

"I don't know anything about you, Alyce." Jennifer said, as the train moved off again. "About your personal life, that is. Actors are always so busy talking about their careers and the job in hand. Sometimes we forget there is another life outside, a real one."

Alyce grimaced. "There's nothing very exciting about me. I've been married to the same man for thirty years. We live in a very squashed apartment which we've been talking about moving out of for twenty-nine years, but it's rent controlled so we keep it. My career has been fun, but spasmodic like most actors, so it's all we can afford."

"What about your husband?"

Alyce didn't reply.

"I'm sorry, I didn't mean to pry," Jennifer said, embarrassed, imagining Alyce's husband as some kind of bum who lived off his wife and drank every night.

"You're not prying. And you'll meet him on first night anyway. Only it's hard to know how to put it without receiving waves of pity in return.

33

My husband is a quadriplegic as a result of a car accident twelve years ago when he was driving up to his parents' house in New England: a drunk driver coming the other way. He has very limited movement below his neck. His medical insurance paid for the apartment to be adapted for him and for a carer when I'm working, but the drunk driver had no insurance so there was no large pay-out there and my wages go towards the general cost of living. So the condo overlooking Central Park is never going to happen. End of story."

The subway train pulled into 96th Street and Alyce and Jennifer got out, Alyce to walk north and Jennifer south.

"Do you fancy a coffee?" Jennifer asked, eager to continue talking.

Alyce looked apologetic. "I'd love to, but I ought to get home. Nate will worry, bless him."

"Nate? That's your husband?" Jennifer asked, over-brightly to cover her disappointment.

"Yes." Alyce hadn't been fooled. "How about you and I go out for the lunch break together on Monday? We can escape from our feuding fellow actors for an hour – or however long Judith allows us!"

Jennifer smiled. "That would be great."

"And I can find out about your life outside the theatre."

"Sure." Not that there was much to tell, Jennifer thought, as she started walking back to her apartment. She had no Nate to worry about her. She had remained single after an acrimonious break-up two years ago, when she'd been forced to change the locks, get new phone numbers and buy a high-tech security system. If she'd rented the place she might have moved but, thanks to a long run in a Broadway play seven years ago, she had managed to buy a studio in a building of walk-up apartments and she refused to lose that. However, it had made her wary of men in general, and she was considering remaining celibate from now on. After all, she was approaching forty and surely her sex drive must be diminishing.

Jennifer's passion was for England and anything English. She religiously watched every British TV show on PBS, spent hours practising her English accent for any roles in America which might require one, and visited London whenever she had a vacation. Being such an Anglophile was one reason she was so excited to be working with two English actors. She longed to talk about their country and dreamt of being invited to stay on her next trip across the Atlantic. Having met Judith, she could hardly imagine such an invitation would be forthcoming, yet she might make headway with her during the run.

She wouldn't mind making headway with Rupert on any level. He was gorgeous, and his English accent was incredibly sexy, but even if she wasn't celibate he was unlikely to be interested in her. She didn't even know if he was available. While Rupert seemed easy going on a casual level, he kept his private life immensely private. Although it was general knowledge that he'd split up with his glamorous actress wife, Miranda Flynn, there was a definite lack of knowledge apropos any current relationships.

She poured a glass of wine and started working through her *All About Eve* script, looking for any hints about her character which she might have missed. Karen wasn't an easy role: friend to Margo, wife to the writer of Margo's play; it was probably the most thankless role, yet Jennifer didn't care. She was going to make the very most of it.

After the rest of his dining companions had left Joe Allen's, Digby moved to the bar area and informed anybody who would listen of Judith's outrageous behaviour and of his despicable treatment at her hands. By the time he left, several hours and a great many drinks later, he felt sure there wasn't a diner in Joe Allen's who wasn't aware of what a monster Judith Gold was. He might even have mentioned it to a newspaper reporter who was present, conducting an interview with another actor. Yes, all in all, a rather good evening's work.

CHAPTER THREE

Rupert returned to his room, threw himself down on the bed and started playing with Holly's snow globe, watching as snow descended on Broadway. A few minutes later the hotel phone rang. "Problem solvers anonymous," he answered, presuming it was Judith with yet another complaint about Digby.

"Oh dear, has it got that bad already?"

"Holly! I was just thinking about you, but thought it was too late to phone."

"I'm on my way to bed. I tried to call you before but there was no answer."

"I was in Judith's room."

"Is she being a nightmare?"

"No more than usual."

"Is she still being vile to Digby Weston?"

"Oh yes."

"Poor man."

"I'm not sure that's exactly how I'd describe him. I guess anyone on the end of Judith's tongue deserves some sympathy, although I can't say I care much for him either. But I've had enough of my show; I've got two days off rehearsals and intend to forget all about it."

"What are you going to do?"

"There's a tennis club I want to check out. I ought to get in some practice in case *All About Eve* is a flop and I have to return to my former career."

"Hmm. And when exactly did you last play

professionally?"

"I don't know – nearly twenty years ago?"

"And you think <u>now</u> you could beat Roger Federer?"

Rupert chuckled. "You know how to hurt a guy, don't you?"

"Well, I couldn't be a tennis player's girl-friend. It would be too stressful watching you from the players' box with a camera shoved up my nose every time you lost a shot."

"I might win one very occasionally," Rupert protested. "Admittedly not against Federer. All right, entirely for your sake and nothing to do with my dwindling prowess on court, I'll simply play for exercise and to keep my mind off the show for a couple of days. I'm amazed Judith didn't want to rehearse all weekend – probably couldn't face the idea of working with Digby for any longer than necessary."

"I hope that situation won't spoil the play."

"At the moment I don't care. Tell me how your play was tonight."

"OK. No, actually it was pretty good. We got cheers at the curtain call, really loud ones."

"I'm sure they were all for you."

"Rupert!"

"Well, you are the best thing in it. And that's not only me being prejudiced, because Judith thinks so too and she's never wrong." Rupert sighed. "Still, I hate the fact that our plays clash, especially when they're in different continents."

"That's what happens with acting couples."

Rupert thought back to what Judith said earlier. "I don't want us to be like other acting couples. We have something special."

"Really?" There was no mistaking the pleasure in her voice at this remark.

"Really," Rupert said truthfully.

"That's so lovely." She gave a sudden yawn.

"Charming," Rupert said. "You pay a girl a compliment and she yawns in your ear!"

"So it's all about you and nothing to do with it being 2am," Holly teased. "In fact, I ought to go to bed, or I'll be useless for two shows tomorrow. Only, there's one other thing." Holly cleared her voice shyly. "I've been nominated for an Olivier Award as best actress. The producers came in and announced it after the show tonight."

"Bloody hell, Holly, that's fantastic. I can't believe you kept that until the end of the conversation. I'm so proud of you."

"Thanks. I don't suppose I'll get it - I'm up against people like Juliet Stevenson and Harriet Walter. Still, I'm thrilled simply to be nominated. When I heard I ran into my dressing room and did some kind of weird Irish jig!"

"I wish I could have seen that."

"I wouldn't give Riverdance much competition."

"You really deserve it. I can't wait to tell Judith."

"That won't impress her; she must have tons of those statues!"

"Of course she'll be impressed, although knowing her she'll merely say that it's about time and then personally attack the judges if you don't win. She was saying earlier how fond she was of you." There was a silence down the other end of the phone. "Holly, are you still there?"

"Yes, I'm trying to take it in. Judith never admits to such things."

"Well, she did."

"Why did I even come up in conversation?"

Rupert couldn't help smiling at Holly's amazement that she could be interesting enough to be talked about. He paused for a minute, wondering if he should tell Holly the truth. If it had been Miranda he certainly wouldn't have or she'd have given him hell, but then his relationship with Holly was very different from that with his ex-wife. "She believed I was eyeing up some girl in Starbucks and told me to behave myself," he explained eventually.

"Were you?"

"Behaving myself?"

"Eyeing up a girl in Starbucks?"

"I might have glanced at her."

"You'd hardly be you if you hadn't."

"You don't mind?" Rupert still found it hard to be living with somebody who didn't scream and berate him for even the most harmless flirtation.

"Rupert, I can hardly expect you to walk round New York wearing a blindfold for seven months. Besides, there's nothing wrong with admiring beautiful things, whatever or whoever they are. I just like that you're honest about it."

"You're amazing. So tell me, when are these awards? Will I be able to fly back and escort my amazingly talented girlfriend?"

"They're next month, so you'll be in the middle of technical rehearsals."

"Damn. You'd better take your parents then or a female friend otherwise I'll be insanely jealous."

Holly giggled. "No you won't; you don't get jealous. Actually, I was thinking of asking Victor. Since you and Judith are together in New York, I thought your abandoned partners could seek consolation together."

"OK, I officially approve Victor as your escort. I shall issue him with a list of exactly what he is allowed to do and not to do, and that he has to have you back by midnight."

"Otherwise will I turn back into a one-shoed, rag-wearing kitchen maid?" Holly enquired.

"That's an adorable picture."

"Does Judith talk about Victor much?"

"No. And if I've brought up the subject she's cut me dead."

"You don't suppose they've had a row, or split up?" Holly's voice was full of horror.

"Over Victor's dead body. He's waited over thirty years for Judith, and there is no way he's letting her escape this time. Judith merely refuses to admit to any kind of intimacy. I imagine she doesn't want anyone here to know she has an 'other half' in case they see it as a sign of weakness. It's a shame as it might make her seem more approachable, which wouldn't be such a bad thing."

"Do they all hate her?"

"I don't think they hate her, well, apart from Digby, but..." He paused. "Let's say I can't visualize many jolly get-togethers with Judith as hostess."

"They like you though, don't they?" Holly asked.

"I'm in a tricky position with trying to keep

Judith happy and not alienate myself, but I'm sure it'll work out. It's only the first week and we've got another three to go before we even get to the theatre." There was a pause before he added, "Oh Lord, that prospect's made me really depressed!"

The phone woke Rupert early on Monday morning, a good hour before he had intended waking up for rehearsals. He reached for the receiver, wincing as he did at the stiffness in his right arm and shoulder. He'd played tennis for two hours yesterday with another ex-professional and been forced to pull out every stop to win the match two sets to one.

"Hello?" he muttered.

"Rupert, it's Wesley. Did I wake you?"

"Not really," Rupert replied, politely if untruthfully.

"I'm sorry, but I wanted to give you the heads up before rehearsals."

"What's Judith done now?"

"Nothing, yet, but she may do something if she reads the *New York Post*. It's run a piece about how unpopular she is with the American *All About Eve* cast. A secret source claims Judith is utterly vile and has everybody in tears during rehearsals. Apparently, experienced Broadway actors are having their confidence broken and Mindy Blue is considering returning to Hollywood under the pressure from Judith. The article's headline is: IT'S ALL ABOUT JUDITH GOLD."

"That's not so far from the truth, but only because she cares."

"But nobody has cried, have they?" Wesley sounded worried.

"It's only the first week; there's plenty of time yet!"

"You don't seem to be taking this seriously. Don't you think Judith is going to be furious?"

Rupert considered the question. "You've worked with Judith for longer than I have, but I don't think she particularly cares what people say about her. She's aware of her reputation for being merciless, and almost enjoys it. It is, after all, fairly accurate. If, on the other hand, this so-called secret source had maintained she was a lousy actress, I would have suggested the *New York Post* request police protection from her wrath."

There was a nervous clearing of Wesley's throat. "There is one other allegation."

"Yes?"

"It insinuates that you and Judith might be an item."

Rupert chuckled. "That's not the first time I've heard that."

"Oh." Wesley was obviously taken aback. "I'm glad you think it's comical. I've had half of New York on the phone to me this morning demanding to know if it's true, and my co-producers are practically apoplectic at the very notion. They want you and Judith to go on some TV chat show to deny it and talk about your real-life partners. Americans are very big on the façade of moral behaviour."

"Judith won't do chat shows even to publicize the play, as you well know, so I can't see her going on to talk about her love life. She'll barely

43

admit Victor's existence, even to herself, let alone discuss him. And while I have no problem admitting Holly's existence, she's not public property to be paraded on air. Private lives are called private for a reason."

"What about going on simply to deny that the company is unhappy and hate Judith? You could both tell some funny anecdote about rehearsals to show the camaraderie."

"Can you seriously imagine Judith doing that? I'm not sure I could go on there and blatantly lie either. Sorry."

There was a sigh from Wesley's end of the line. "I thought that'd be the answer. At least I can tell them I tried."

"You can tell them they shouldn't have employed Digby Weston in the first place."

"You think it was him?"

"I'm certain it was him. He's the real problem in this company, not Judith. And she'll know it was him too, with the consequence she'll make his life even more miserable, if that's possible. What am I saying? Of course it's possible."

"Good luck today. I'd be there only I have an appointment with... with..." Wesley's imagination failed him. All he knew was that he didn't intend to be anywhere in the vicinity of the rehearsal room.

"Coward!"

Rupert bought a copy of the *New York Post* and scanned it quickly over breakfast at the local diner. It said nothing that Wesley hadn't already told him. Once he reckoned Judith would be up he returned to the hotel to show her. As he'd anticipated, she shrugged off the comments about her lack of popularity, and produced one of her rare smiles at the notion of an affair between her and Rupert.

"They'll have a field day when they see the play and discover we've added a previous affair between our characters," she commented. "The *National Enquirer* will doubtless manufacture a photograph of the two of us in a passionate clinch, or, even better, naked in bed together. I only hope they give me a younger body-double!"

"That'll kill our moralistic producers off altogether."

"Fuck them. Rupert, be a dear and get me a strong black coffee. I've a feeling I'm going to need it today. I suggest we don't arrive until the last minute this morning to allow the rest of the company time to discuss the article and get it off their chests. No doubt that fucking Digby will have bought copies for everybody."

Digby hadn't bought enough copies for everybody, but had bought several and, arriving at the rehearsal room so early the stage management were still setting up, he left them scattered obviously around the room with the appropriate page open. Those actors who hadn't already read the article did so now, although Kyle took one glance, threw it down in disgust and went back to studying his script.

"She's gonna go nuts," Jennifer said. "And we don't hate her. And nobody has cried. Who would have said such a thing?"

"Guess, hon," said Alyce, looking pointedly at Digby.

"You didn't, did you?" Jennifer asked him,

appalled.

Digby shrugged. "I only mentioned it to somebody at Joe Allen's – who would have guessed she was a reporter?" He took in their cynical expressions. "You should be pleased. I'm only telling the truth."

"But we don't hate her, and nobody has cried," Jennifer repeated.

"Not yet but I'm sure she'll eventually get to somebody." He gestured at Mindy, who was poring over her script, muttering lines with an anxious expression.

At exactly 10am the door opened and Judith and Rupert came in and were regarded by the rest of the cast with a mixture of worry, fear and, in Digby's case, defiance.

Judith marched into the middle of the room, crossed her arms and looked around. "Last week's rehearsal was a farce; you were all truly pathetic. I've never had to work with such a bunch of amateurs. I've spent the entire weekend working on what needs to be done, and I don't want to waste a minute putting it into action. Is our director here?"

Aubrey, who'd been surreptitiously reading the *New York Post* in the corner with great enjoyment, leapt nervously to his feet. "Yes, Judith."

"This is what I want to rehearse today." She handed him a piece of paper covered in her scrawl.

"Yes, Judith." Aubrey frowned as he tried to decipher it. "Right, everybody, let's do the second part of scene three. Judith, Mindy and Alyce stand by please. Stage management set up for Margo Channing's apartment."

"What about me?" Digby enquired. "I'm in this scene."

Aubrey glanced at Judith's list. "We're going from after your exit – apparently."

They rehearsed this scene for an hour with Judith constantly pushing Mindy to produce an emotion visible to anyone further than a foot away. Next on the list was the Miss Caswell audition scene. Paige and Rupert began and two pages later Judith and Kyle joined them. Digby stood by to make his entrance, but as they reached his cue Judith called a stop. The next scene didn't involve him at all.

By the time they broke for lunch Digby hadn't done anything. When Judith and Rupert left to eat he complained to Aubrey about the waste of his time.

Aubrey looked down Judith's list. "I'm sure it's merely coincidence, Digby. Look, Bill appears in most of the scenes scheduled for this afternoon. You must be used."

Aubrey had made one error in his speculation: these scenes were ones in which Bill didn't appear throughout. As they rehearsed them Judith either called a stop as he was about to enter, or started after he had make his exit. Digby had sat there from 10am – 6pm and done absolutely nothing. He was furious. As the stage manager called the end of rehearsals he stormed across the room to Judith.

"How dare you waste my time like this? You deliberately cut me out of every scene. Don't try and deny it."

Judith regarded him disdainfully. "I wasn't intending to deny it." She turned to leave but

Digby grabbed her shoulders and yanked her round to face him. Rupert moved quickly across the room, prepared to pull him off, but Judith was more than capable of looking after herself. The "let me go" was uttered in such a terrifying tone of voice that Digby instantly dropped his hands. Judith narrowed her eyes. "How could I possibly rehearse such a sensitive actor? You might cry. That's right, isn't it? You are the cast member you were talking about? Unless the rest of you have been crying in private, because if so please tell me. I'd much rather you did so in public; it's more fun for us monsters to watch." Judith's eyes swept round the room. Nobody spoke. "No, I thought not." She collected her coat and bag and then turned back. "There was some improvement today, but I suggest you all go home and do a lot more work before tomorrow."

"Will I be permitted to participate then?" Digby demanded of her.

"I don't know. I'll see how I feel. Presuming you know the film of *All About Eve*, you'll be aware we have already removed one character from it for the stage version – that of Max, the producer. Perhaps I should have the writer eliminate the role of Bill too."

Digby stared at her, briefly speechless, before stammering out, "You can't! He's an integral part of the story."

"Really? Is the play called All About Bill?"

"No, and it's not called All About Margo either."

"That," Judith said, with great emphasis, "can be changed."

"No!" Mindy exclaimed. The title belonged to her character. If they changed it she'd have to find a whole new motivation and weeks of work would go for nothing. "You can't change it. It's in my contract. I'll... I'll sue."

"Don't be so fucking dramatic," Judith snapped. "And so American, a culture who'd sue over a paper cut."

"Now try telling us nobody hates you," Digby said.

"I don't care if everybody hates me. At least I can act."

Digby took a step towards her, his hands clenched into tight fists. "Are you suggesting the rest of us can't?"

"There's no question of suggesting in your case. I reserve judgement on everybody else."

Digby had gone almost purple with rage. Judith appeared perfectly cool, but Rupert was fully aware she could explode at any moment. "Judith, can I cadge a lift back to the hotel in your car?" he interjected. "I'm shattered."

"Get your own fucking taxi. I'm in the middle of something here."

There was a shocked silence from the American contingent at Judith's response to the one actor who always seemed in favour. Digby's eyes gleamed with excitement at the idea of a showdown between these two English interlopers. To his disappointment Rupert merely shrugged and tried another approach. "But darling," he growled sexily, "all these electrifying vibes are seriously arousing me. I'm not sure how long I can contain myself."

Everybody held their breath at the thunderous expression on Judith's face, including Rupert who hoped he hadn't gone too far. Finally she turned her back on Digby. "Come along then, fucking Romeo," she snapped at Rupert. "Let's get the hell out of here." Then, deciding to get a little of her own back, she added, "It's my turn to tie you up tonight, isn't it?" With that she swept out of the room. A highly amused Rupert said a brief goodnight to an even more stunned room and followed. Judith's car, provided by the producers, was waiting outside. The driver opened the door and Judith and Rupert climbed in.

After ten blocks Rupert finally wiped the tears of laughter off his face. "You are evil. God, their faces were a picture."

Judith shrugged. "You started it. I merely wanted the final word." She put her head back against the seat and stared out of the window.

Rupert contemplated her as they drove towards their hotel. "That article bothered you, didn't it?"

"Not especially, I've had worse things written about me. That odious man bothers me though. I had to teach him a lesson. Watching him desperately trying to make an entrance and never getting the chance was the most fun I've had since we started rehearsals here."

Rupert couldn't help but agree. It wasn't helpful to the production, but it had been funny. "Digby apart," he said, "I have to say you've certainly opened my eyes to something today."

"Yes?" Judith couldn't think what she'd done that Rupert hadn't already experienced.

"All that talk of tying me up. I've got a completely different picture of your sex life with Victor now."

"What? No! Don't be ridiculous." For once Judith was almost embarrassed. Rupert raised his eyebrows at her, quizzically. "I was simply trying to shock everybody," she expounded.

"So you say. However, in the light of this development, I'm not certain I should allow Victor to escort Holly to the Olivier Awards. She's such an innocent in many ways. I don't want her corrupted."

Judith gave him a sceptical look. "She may have been innocent originally, but I very much doubt she is after living with you for a year. By now I expect she's an expert in the Kama Sutra."

"Kama Sutra? We use the Kama Rupert – it's far more pleasurable."

Five minutes after Rupert had left Judith at the door to her hotel room and returned to his, the phone rang. "I shouldn't have snapped at you in the rehearsal room," said Judith's voice and the phone went dead again. Judith was not big on apologies.

"I felt quite sick," Jennifer said, as she and Alyce rode the subway home. "Digby was wrong to talk to that reporter, but the feeling of hostility was awful. I sound like Mindy, don't I, going on about hostility, only I was so excited about the play and it's all turning rotten."

Alyce patted her hand. "It'll be fine, hon. Judith strikes me as someone who can cope with conflict. Today probably got it out of her system and tomorrow it'll have blown over."

"You figure?"

51

"Sure. Don't worry, hon."

When Jennifer got home she poured herself a glass of wine, microwaved a packet of popcorn and munched her way through it as she went over the day's events. In spite of the row between Judith and Digby it was Rupert she kept thinking of. How he'd jumped in to stop it escalating any further when it wasn't his problem. And although he'd appeared unconcerned at Judith's reaction, she thought she'd seen a brief anxious look on his face. What if Judith was seriously angry with him? That would be awful. She had to find out. Resolutely she phoned his hotel hoping, since she didn't know his room number, that the front desk wouldn't think her a fan and refuse to put her through. To her relief, within seconds she heard Rupert's wonderful English tones. "Hello?"

Suddenly she found she was tongue-tied.

"Hello?" Rupert repeated.

"Sorry, Rupert, it's Jennifer. Jennifer Hoffman from *All About Eve*."

"Hello, Jennifer Hoffman from *All About Eve*." She heard the amusement in his voice. What a stupid thing to say, of course he knew who she was. Her mind went blank again. "Is there anything I can do for you or are you phoning to perform heavy breathing?" Rupert enquired. "Because in that case you're not very good at it; I can barely hear you."

"Sorry," she said again. "I wanted to say... I mean to check... Judith wasn't too mad at you, was she? You were so brave stepping in there because you really didn't have to."

"Jennifer, that's terribly sweet of you to worry, but no, Judith isn't mad at me. At least, no more than usual. I'm pretty used to her by now."

"Yes, of course, how stupid of me."

"It's not stupid; it's very thoughtful. Are you OK? As I said, I'm pretty used to Judith but I realize she can be pretty intimidating if she's a new experience. And rehearsals have been no picnic."

Jennifer felt a glow inside at his question. He was concerned about her. "Yeah, I'm good, thanks. I guess today was a bit scary. Still, I'm sure we'll get used to it. And she is a wonderful actress."

"Yes, she is. But then, as the expression goes, it takes one to know one." Jennifer felt an even warmer glow at Rupert's praise. "Can I tell you something in confidence?"

"Yes. Oh yes please." She must stop sounding like an overgrown schoolgirl. "That is, if you'd like to."

"Yes, I would like to, because I think you'll understand."

Jennifer's hands were sweating so much with excitement at the way this conversation was going that the phone almost shot out of them when she gripped it harder. "OK, shoot."

"The reason Judith is so difficult is because she cares too much. Most of us actors love our work, but it isn't our entire life the way it is for Judith. This play especially means everything to her, and if it's not going the way she wants it to she needs to take it out on somebody. And that somebody is going to be the weakest link."

"Digby."

"Digby."

There was silence as Jennifer tried to think what else to say. She longed for him to refute the claim about his and Judith's sexual relationship without having the nerve to ask. She'd love to go into rehearsals tomorrow and tell everybody, especially Digby, that it was total nonsense. "I don't suppose you'd like to go out for dinner," she blurted out. "It must be lonely for you here, away from your friends. I know some great restaurants, which aren't too touristy."

"Thanks, that sounds lovely, only could I take a rain-check? I already have dinner plans with Judith and Wesley. Wesley's going to London tomorrow and there are things we need to sort out before he leaves."

"Sure. The offer stands anytime."

"Great. I'll see you at rehearsals tomorrow. And thank you again. It's nice to have friends in a strange city."

Jennifer hung up with a whoop. Rupert considered her a friend. That was all she wanted – wasn't it?

Rupert had a tense dinner with a furious Judith and an exhausted Wesley. He didn't blame the producer for wanting to return to England, if only as a temporary respite from the pressure. Judith had such a long list of grievances on arrival at the restaurant that she refused to let the three of them order until she'd finished. Then, ten minutes after their food arrived, she was complaining of exhaustion and demanding Wesley pay the check. If he and Wesley continued eating meals with Judith when she was in this kind of mood, they were both going to get ulcers or, at best, chronic indigestion.

When Rupert got back to the hotel there was a message on his room's voice mail from Holly, who had taken to reading both the *New York Times* and the *New York Post* online since Rupert had been there.

"I cannot believe what I'm reading. All this time I trusted you and you've been having an affair with Judith. How could you? Was I merely your toy-girl while you were seeing an older woman? Whatever will Victor say? How can you break both our hearts?" Holly's dramatic and tearful tones gave way to a giggle. "Oh, rats, I spoilt it. I wanted you to think I really believed it. I'd written it all down too, and spent ages trying to get the right tone of disbelief and distress." There was a sigh and another giggle. "Anyway, I'd better go to bed, it's horribly late here. Oh, and I googled the name Digby, and one of the hits was the movie, *Digby, the Biggest Dog in the World.* So if you get really fed up with your Digby, picture him very hairy with huge paws and enormous floppy ears. Jim Dale was in it, but I don't think he was the dog. I love you. Goodnight."

Rupert felt instantly cheered. All the same, as he climbed, exhausted, into bed he wished he could sleep through the next three weeks' rehearsals and wake in time for the first performance. Maybe if he pricked his finger he could do a Sleeping Beauty and sleep for one hundred years. But Judith would probably still be there, 155 years old (or whatever she was admitting to by then) and going strong!

CHAPTER FOUR

Wesley and Rupert's only real success over dinner had been to persuade Judith to allow Digby to rehearse, with both producer and actor pointing out that if he was the weakest link he needed more rehearsal, not less. Thus the list of scenes Judith gave Aubrey on Monday consisted entirely of Digby's key ones. However, Judith refused to acknowledge him other than in character and gave any notes to Aubrey to relay. Aware how much Judith loathed her stage lover, the other actors were full of admiration for her convincing performance. In the emotional reconciliation scene, Judith held Digby tightly with an expression of utter ecstasy. Immediately the scene finished she shot away from him as if electrocuted, told Aubrey to call a break, and disappeared.

When she hadn't returned after ten minutes, Rupert went to investigate and discovered her huddled outside in the street, slowly exhaling on a cigarette.

"I thought you'd given those up," he said, frowning as Judith took another puff.

"I had, but I needed one after rehearsing that scene. The great thing about New York is you're never far from a shop."

"Victor is going to be furious if he finds out."

"He's not my fucking warder; I can do what I like." She stubbed out the cigarette and took another from the packet. Rupert turned to go back inside. "Where are you going? The least you can do is stay here and tell me I did brilliantly in there."

"You did do brilliantly in there; you amazed the entire cast, including me. However, I'm not going to stand here and watch you kill yourself. You nearly achieved that last time we did this play, remember?"

"That was pneumonia."

"Yes, with cigarettes being a strong contributory factor to your contracting it. Do you really want to go through that again this time? And even if you do I certainly have no intention of passive smoking." He made another move towards the door.

"Wait!" Judith put the cigarette grudgingly back into the packet and slid it into her bag, glaring at Rupert, daring him to comment further. "Now you can tell me how wonderful I was." Before Rupert could say anything she added, "But what the hell's the point when I get nothing in return. I couldn't have been more passionate, embracing him, and touching his oily skin until I felt utterly nauseous, while he was rigid and cold. It was like playing a love scene with a fish at attention. What the fuck are you laughing at?"

"At the notion of Digby as a fish at attention, clad in a bearskin hat and carrying a gun."

"God forbid. He's so incompetent he'd probably shoot his foot off. Actually, that might be an improvement. If he played Bill on crutches or in a wheelchair I wouldn't have to get so close to him. I wish Margo and Addison's affair in the play hadn't been years earlier; it would be easier to emote passion with you."

Rupert bowed deeply. "I'm highly flattered."

"Don't be; I only said it would be easier, not easy."

"Go on, admit it, you fancy me rotten," Rupert said, proceeding to give her a weird selection of winks and suggestive gestures with his head.

"Stop it! You look as if you're having some kind of seizure. It's most unnerving." Judith was impressed at her ability to keep a straight face at Rupert's antics. Perhaps Digby had completely destroyed her capacity for humour. "We'd better get back to rehearsals. Only, I cannot act with that man again today."

"That's going to limit us. We're supposed to be working on the party scene, which does need it, and the pianist is arriving this afternoon to be fitted into it."

As soon as he'd said this, Rupert wished he hadn't. In London the actor playing Bill had been an expert pianist so they had incorporated his playing into the scene. Digby couldn't even manage chopsticks, which made his performing out of the question so a professional pianist was being employed to play live on stage. Digby would do nothing which, as Judith had pointed out, was much as usual.

Judith's face darkened at the thought of sharing a stage with a non-actor. Before she could go into another diatribe, Rupert pointed across the street and said, "Isn't that Al Pacino?"

"Where?" There was something almost resembling excitement in Judith's voice. Al Pacino, as Rupert knew, was one of the few American actors Judith respected, since he delivered excellent work on stage in addition to film.

Rupert pretended to study a small man, whose size was the only thing he had in common with Pacino. "No, my mistake. Shall we go back inside?"

"Bastard!"

On the Saturday afternoon of the second week of rehearsals, Victor Lewis disembarked from a plane at JFK, and made his way to the rehearsal room. He could hear Judith's voice shouting as he climbed the stairs. Home sweet home! He took a seat in a waiting area and started to read a copy of the *New York Times* he'd picked up from a paper stand. Ten minutes later the door to the rehearsal room opened and an elderly man, who in Victor's opinion might once have been handsome but now looked decidedly worse for wear, strode out shouting "screw you" over his shoulder.

Victor concluded this constituted a break and went inside. Judith was standing facing him, screaming obscenities at the open door, presumably at the man who had just left. As she saw Victor she stopped dead, an unreadable expression on her face. "What the fuck are you doing here?"

Victor grinned. "It's good to see you too, Judy. I thought I'd come and see how you were getting along." He gestured towards the open door. "It appears everything is progressing as normal."

"That's all I need, something else to distract me."

Victor gave a small bow. "I'm highly complimented that you consider me a distraction."

Judith gave him one of her famous looks, which never had any effect on Victor who turned to his right and stuck out his hand. "Rupert, it's good to see you."

Rupert shook hands. "You too, Victor, believe me."

Victor glanced at his watch. "What time are you breaking? I can come back then or hang around."

"We may as well finish now," Judith snapped. "I can't work with that incompetent clown any more today. Besides," she glared at Victor, "you've totally thrown my concentration. You'd think as an ex-actor you'd know better than to interrupt a rehearsal."

"But as a reporter I know it's when to get the best stories."

"You're a fucking war correspondent; you don't need theatre stories."

"I may not need them, but I do enjoy them." Victor gave Judith a lazy smile and then picking up her coat, he held it out. Ungraciously Judith slid her arms into the sleeves, gathering it around her as if it was a safety blanket and stalked out of the room. Victor picked up his small travelling bag. "It was nice sort of meeting you all," he said to the astonished company. "See you later, Rupert?"

"I expect so."

There was a buzz in the room as Victor left, half at the prospect of finishing early and half at the extraordinary entrance of this unknown man.

Rupert picked up his own jacket. "Does anyone fancy a coffee since we seem to be unexpectedly free?"

Jennifer, Alyce, Paige and even Mindy accepted. Kyle declined on the grounds that this was a good opportunity to spend some extra time with his children. "They've seen me so little recently I'm worried they'll start calling our doorman Daddy," he commented.

"As long as you've seen your wife enough so you know that's not true," Rupert retorted.

Kyle gave a good-natured laugh, half sorry he wasn't going out with such good company.

"Mindy and I are the out-of-towners, so we're in your hands," Rupert said to Jennifer, Alyce and Paige, "Where do we go?"

Jennifer tried to think of somewhere around the rehearsal rooms which would impress Rupert. Did he like smart places? Or exclusive? Or seedy bars? Could they get into Soho House which was THE place to go but normally only open to residents or members?

"You know what's real fun and only a few blocks away?" Paige broke in keenly. "The Empire Diner. Have you been there, Rupert?" Rupert shook his head. "It's like a proper old diner and we can have a drink, or eat or have a shake. And it's open twenty four hours."

"I wasn't intending to stay quite that long." Rupert's eyes twinkled at her. "Or are you planning an all-night orgy?"

Paige, unsure if Rupert was teasing her, played her answer safe. "Not unless you want to. I just meant... well, it shouldn't be that busy at this time anyway."

"Sounds good to me, how about the rest of you?"

"Sure, I haven't been there for years," said Alyce. Mindy consented on the proviso that if she was accosted by weird fans they'd go elsewhere. Jennifer would have preferred a quiet, dark bar, or one of the quaint English tea rooms which were dotted about Manhattan, but not wanting to appear contrary agreed with such fervour that Rupert regarded her with slight bemusement.

Settled into a booth inside the diner, the five of them made general conversation for a while, until Paige eventually burst out, "I'm just gonna pop if I don't ask soon – who was that guy in the rehearsal room?"

"Victor's a friend of Judith's," Rupert said, having been expecting this question since they'd left the rehearsal room.

"It's a funny way to treat a friend. She was like real rude to him."

"In case you hadn't noticed, Judith didn't graduate from charm school." There was general laughter at this remark; even the serious Mindy smiled. This was followed by a silence as the Americans waited for Rupert to expand on the subject. He didn't.

Paige tried again. "Judith said he was an ex-actor. Did they work together?"

"Yes."

"When?"

"A long time ago. Thank you." This last remark was addressed to the waiter who'd brought him a coffee and a piece of apple pie.

"He called her Judy." Paige was nothing if not persistent.

"Yes." Rupert took a sip of his coffee.

"Couldn't we call her that too? It would be so much less daunting than Judith."

Rupert smiled wryly. "I wouldn't advise it."

"So how come this Victor can? Were they like an item once?"

Rupert looked around at the four curious faces. "Judith is an immensely private person and I respect that. So if you only came out with me for gossip pertaining to her then I'm afraid you're going to be disappointed."

"Oh no, we came because we wanted to get to know you better," Jennifer said quickly. "We get so little chance during rehearsals."

"Ah. OK." Rupert leaned back, crossed his arms and took a deep breath. "I was born in England to my mother, I was rubbish at school, great at tennis – me and Tim Henman were inseparable – I switched to acting because the girls had fewer muscles and I've been conning everybody into thinking I could act ever since." He exhaled. "Now that you know absolutely everything about me should I leave?"

"No!" Jennifer almost squealed. Then added in a less desperate tone, "I mean, you can't insult America in general by not finishing a slice of apple pie!"

Rupert grinned at her. "Well, we can't have that!"

"Were you and Tim Henman really inseparable?" asked Alyce, who was passionate about tennis.

"I think we used the same locker once."

"Really?"

"Yes. Sadly it was at different times. It was also in different years."

Alyce punched him playfully on the arm. "And there I was thinking you were going to introduce me to my tennis heroes."

"I still have a few contacts. Most of my contemporaries are coaching on the circuit now. I'm aiming to catch the US Open while I'm here. Why don't you come with me and I'll see what I can do?"

"Try and keep me away." Alyce picked up a paper serviette and fanned her face with excitement.

"How did you switch from tennis to acting?" Paige asked. "It's so different."

"I slept with a models' agent. She wanted me to model; I didn't, so we settled for acting."

"Seriously?" Paige wondered if this was the quirky sense of humour the British were supposed to have.

"Seriously. She's the best agent too. I'm one of only two acting clients she has, and the other is female, so I get plenty of attention. Plus, I'm surrounded by beautiful models every time I go to her office."

"But you are a good actor," Jennifer said, hoping she didn't sound too sycophantic. "So she must have seen some potential – apart from... from..."

"My body? No, I don't think so. To be honest she didn't know a thing about the acting business, but she was a quick learner and a fantastic negotiator." He left a pause for effect before adding, "And pretty good in bed."

Paige giggled and Jennifer blushed. Alyce looked thoughtful. "I wonder if I could get better jobs if I slept with my agent," she said. "Al-

64

though, there are so many of them at my agency it might take a while. And I'm not sure how my husband would feel."

Jennifer wanted to get back to Rupert. "What was the first acting job you got?"

"Some TV comedy you wouldn't have heard of. Now you know my life story I want to hear about you four. Alyce, I know you're now considering a mass orgy at your agency and that you're married, but I want to know more." Alyce started to list her acting credits but Rupert stopped her. "I know what you've all done, job wise."

"You do?" Jennifer asked, thrilled that he'd bothered to find out.

"Judith insisted the producers send her every detail of your work, even down to college productions, I think. Once she'd read them, I was then summoned to give my opinion."

"And did you approve?" Alyce asked, smiling.

Rupert eyed her. "I was a bit doubtful about your tennis groupie credentials, though so far you don't seem too creepy."

"Wait until you find me hanging around your practice courts waiting to smell your sweaty T-shirt."

Mindy stared at Alyce with a shocked expression. "That's totally gross, and so unhygienic. Don't you know how many germs you could pick up?"

Rupert spluttered into his coffee. "Oh dear, I'd better start showering in bleach to combat all those bacteria," he said.

"I didn't mean..." Mindy started.

Rupert cut her off. "No, I know you didn't." He

grinned at her. "And I rather hope Alyce wasn't serious about her T-shirt smelling desires either or I might be withdrawing my consent for her casting."

"Did you really have a say in our casting?" Paige enquired. That was the good thing about Paige, Jennifer thought. She asked all the questions Jennifer wanted to, yet hadn't the nerve.

Rupert shook his head. "No. Neither did Judith. The American producers had their own ideas."

"Did you have a say in London?"

"Judith did, yes."

There was a silence as the Americans digested this information. No wonder Judith was so unhappy when she'd been presented with actors if she was used to selecting her own.

Paige finished her second beer. She was not as sober as when they'd arrived. "So what's your relationship with Judith?" she asked.

"Paige, that's none of your business," Alyce said.

"Come on, everybody's gonna be asking after that article in *The Post*. Don't you want to know?"

"No," Alyce replied, simply.

Jennifer, pretending to be shocked by Paige's question, was secretly praying Rupert would answer. Mindy looked up from her plate, but whether that was curiosity or because she'd finished eating it was hard to tell.

"Judith and I are good friends and that means good friends and not a euphemism for anything else. Right, I am heartily sick of talking about myself. It's your turn. I want to know at least three interesting facts about each of you before we leave."

Over the next two hours Rupert gradually drew out his four fellow actors. Even the reserved Mindy opened up enough to admit how much she missed her LA beach house, the Californian lifestyle and her director boyfriend who was too busy directing a new TV series to come and visit her in New York. "It's as well, I guess," she added. "I get real involved in my roles and it can be hard to live with. When I was playing an anorexic on a TV movie he got mad that I threw out all the food in our house and wouldn't let him bring home any more."

"You didn't eat the entire time you were filming?" Paige asked, impressed by Mindy's dedication to her art.

"Only enough to stay alive. I lost like 20lbs."

"You must have been a stick," Alyce commented, looking at Mindy's tiny figure. "Didn't it do you any harm?"

"I had a nutritionist with me constantly who gave me pills to ensure I got the vitamins I needed. But they nearly had to take me into hospital by the end," she added, with great pride.

"If I ever needed to play a truly skinny person I'd stipulate they only filmed me from the neck up and used a body double for long shots," Rupert said. "I don't think they've invented a pill yet that tastes like a juicy steak and chips, sorry, fries."

Mindy shook her head. "Then you can't feel the part. Don't you need that?"

Rupert sighed. "No, I'm afraid I'm not a very

intuitive actor. It's all technical. Besides, if I had to feel every role I've played I'd be pretty screwed up by now. Daniel Day-Lewis, a great method actor, had a sort of break-down when he played Hamlet because he saw his own dead father instead of the one in the play. Quite an alarming thought really. I don't suppose he could say, 'Dad, there are 1,500 people out there who've paid to see me and not you, so bugger off'."

Jennifer, Paige and Alyce laughed. Mindy didn't.

"I'm sorry, Mindy," Rupert said, seeing her expression. "We all have our own ways of working and it's wrong of me to laugh at yours. Besides, Daniel Day-Lewis is a bloody good actor, far better than me, so I shouldn't scoff."

"Didn't he insist on riding to the set on a horse when he was filming *The Crucible*?" Alyce said.

Rupert laughed. "That sounds like fun; maybe I should ride in to rehearsals tomorrow."

"What would Judith say?" Paige asked.

Rupert thought for a minute. "She'd probably take one look at the horse and say, 'Finally, a decent actor'."

The response to this comment was so raucous that the few other diners looked over at their table. Mindy immediately ducked her head towards her plate, in case she should be recognized, and ended up with mayonnaise on her nose. Alyce delicately pointed it out and passed her a napkin.

"Didn't you play Hamlet once?" Jennifer asked Rupert.

"Yes. But I wasn't as good as I should've been.

I hadn't enough stage experience at that point. I wouldn't mind another crack at it now but I think I'm a little too old."

"You wouldn't see your father's ghost though?"

"That would be exceedingly unlikely." Rupert's tone of voice was unusually terse. Yet a second later he was smiling. "OK, I'm going to head off. Thank you for taking pity on a stranger far from home and sharing your evening with him." He signalled for the waiter to bring the check and, before anybody could protest, handed over a wad of notes. "Goodnight all. Have a good day off and see you Monday."

Rupert's departure broke up the party, although Paige was all for going on to a proper bar. But Alyce wanted to get home to Nate, Mindy to work on her role and Jennifer wasn't sure she fancied being left with only Paige for company. It wasn't that she didn't like her, but Paige's youth and enthusiasm made her feel rather jaded. Instead she decided to rent a movie, some British classic like *Kind Hearts and Coronets* or *A Matter of Life and Death*, and microwave some popcorn to eat with it.

Rupert took the opportunity which Victor's presence allowed to stroll around the city for a couple of hours without having to worry about Judith. He ended up at a movie – it was always a pleasure to watch other actors working and know they'd have been slaving away doing crazy long hours to produce this piece of celluloid – and didn't return to the hotel until nearly midnight. A couple of minutes later there was a knock on his door and Victor stood outside.

"That was good timing, I've just got back," Rupert said.

"I know."

"I shan't even ask how. If you ever give up investigative journalism you should try working for MI5," Rupert remarked, peering into the corridor behind Victor. "Isn't Judith with you?"

"No, she's asleep."

Rupert waved Victor in. "Ah, you've exhausted her after an evening of passion. I'm glad I went out; I'd hate to have heard you from along the corridor."

"I should be so lucky."

"Don't tell me she's angry with you for flying over? Or was it because you turned up unannounced at the rehearsal room?"

"Neither – well, both actually – but I think she's got over them. I'm not certain but she might even be a little glad to see me, even if I did break the rules and visit during the rehearsal period. An action which I realize is unacceptable and punishable." Victor sat down on the chair and gestured for Rupert to sit on the bed. Rupert complied, wondering whose room this was. "Now, we need to talk."

"You've no idea how many women I've known who've started a conversation like that," Rupert drawled.

"Don't worry, I'm not about to make a pass at you or complain about a lack of sex."

Rupert grinned. "That was never the problem; a lack of commitment maybe."

"Talking of which I went out to lunch with Holly last week. It's great about her Olivier nomination, isn't it?"

"Yes it is, and would you and Judith stop with the guilt trip. I'm being good, I swear. I take it that wasn't what you wanted to talk about?"

"No." Victor reached into his pocket and brought out a notebook. He flipped it open. Rupert could see a list, all neatly numbered down the page. "Right, I have some questions."

"I hope it's multiple choice," Rupert remarked. "I prefer the odds. Otherwise I'll be sure to fail."

Victor glowered at him. "Behave." Rupert gave a mock salute. Victor started to say something and gave up. He returned to his list. "First…"

"Is this question one?" Rupert enquired, grabbing the pad and pen from beside the phone and writing a large 'one' on it, then circling it for good measure.

Victor put down his notebook and crossed his arms. "I've got all night."

"Sorry. It's been a stressful week. I needed to let off some steam." Rupert laid down the pen. "Go ahead."

"Digby Weston: is he as bad as Judy says? Or does she merely hate him because he's obnoxious and ignores her direction?"

Rupert made a face. "He isn't terribly good, no."

"Is he going to ruin the play?"

"I doubt the audience or critics will be aware of it. Bill is a biggish role but not a particularly significant one in comparison to Margo, Eve and Addison."

"But he has a lot of scenes with Margo. Can he spoil it for Judy?"

Rupert considered the question. It wasn't as

if he hadn't already thought about it, but he'd been trying to put it to the back of his mind since there was little he could do to resolve the matter. "Judith totally loses herself on stage," he said eventually. "So perhaps if he's just about believable she can accept him as Bill. She was utterly convincing playing opposite him in rehearsals. Nobody would have guessed there was even the slightest animosity between them. I know how good Judith is, yet even I was impressed."

"Still, Judy can't do all the work herself; she needs to get something back. I do recall that much about acting." Victor looked down at his pad. "What about rehearsals? What does he do that winds Judy up, other than not doing what she says?"

"Isn't that enough?"

"But he's incensing her."

"There's always somebody she takes against; she needs a scapegoat. That's the way Judith works. Without that I'm not sure she'd be happy. You must know that by now."

"I certainly do. I've been that scapegoat in my time and it's not pleasant. But this is different. It isn't simply moaning or bitching. It's more of an obsession. A kind of hysteria. She's done nothing but rant about him since I arrived. That's why she's asleep now because it's exhausted her. If Judy admitted to tears I'd have said she was almost crying with frustration." He looked back down at his notebook. "Is he incompetent?"

"He knows his lines, says them with something resembling emotion, and stands in the right place, so not really." Rupert struggled to put his finger on the problem. "He's perfectly adequate, only he doesn't have that certain extra something that makes actors stand out. There's no spark."

"So we couldn't get rid of him on those grounds?"

"If that were the case, half the actors Judith has ever worked with would have been fired within two hours. Beside, he and Mindy are the American names the producers brought in to protect their investment. They're not going to let him go simply because Judith doesn't like him."

Victor scribbled something down. "Alternatives?"

Rupert gave a helpless shrug, wishing he had an answer.

"Could he do extra work with Aubrey?"

"I thought you wanted him to get better, not worse."

Victor drew an arrow linking two notes on his pad. "How's the understudy?"

"Terrified, I would imagine. Judith won't let them into rehearsals."

"So an accident to Digby wouldn't help?"

Rupert's mouth fell open. "Are you serious? You're considering sabotage? Don't tell me you carry a souvenir hand grenade in your suitcase."

"Absolutely, every war correspondent is given one as a memento of our holidays in hell! Mine says: 'Greetings from Baghdad, proudly twinned with Bognor', and the pin is all swirly like a stick of rock. It's my prized possession."

Rupert moved further away along the bed, feigning alarm. Victor laughed. "Actually, I had something in mind more along the lines of providing a dodgy prawn sandwich or leaving a banana skin on the stairs."

"I'm sure Judith would love to visit you in Sing-Sing. I don't think Digby not being an especially good actor is any reason for you to be arrested for attempted murder."

"I always keep a 'get out of jail free' card on me – just in case."

"Good, because I can't see Judith baking you a cake with a file enclosed."

"Heaven forbid. With Judith's cooking skills the cake would be more lethal than the file. All right, no sabotage. I'm fresh out of ideas. I suppose I shouldn't interfere; Judy would be furious if she knew. But she sounded so despondent over the phone which is why I flew over now, risking her wrath. It's only that she cares so much for this play – far too bloody much. It's unhealthy. I don't want her making herself ill for a second time. Talking of which..." He tapped his fingers on a number at the bottom of the page. "Is she smoking again?"

"Can I take the fifth amendment on that?"

"No, you can't. I'm waiting. Yes or no?"

Rupert held up his hands in surrender. "Christ, Victor, do you interrogate all your informants like this? No wonder you're such a good reporter. It's terrifying."

"I shall take that as a 'yes.' Right, I'll soon put a stop to that."

"Good luck!"

Victor tossed his notebook down. "So much good those did me."

"I suppose I could offer to work with Digby

privately, without telling Judith," Rupert said. "I have a pretty good idea what she wants by now. Of course, the man is so pigheaded I don't know whether he'd agree. In his opinion he's far superior to any of us."

Victor shook his head. "I don't think it would be a good idea anyway." Rupert looked at him, surprised. "If it stayed secret fine, but if Judy found out – and knowing Judy she would – she'd feel you'd let her down. And right now that's the last thing she needs. She's more reliant on you than she'll ever admit."

Rupert rolled his eyes upwards. "No pressure on me then!"

"Sorry." Victor climbed to his feet. "Thanks for being a sounding board, Rupert, and I'll try and give you a break as chief whipping boy while I'm here."

"How long are you staying?"

"I'm supposed to have a piece filed on the failure of the Middle East peace talks by the middle of next week, but I can write and email it from here if necessary. Perhaps I should change it to a piece on the failure of the Judith/Digby peace talks instead. It'd probably sell more papers."

When Victor had gone Rupert crossed the room and put his head against the window, watching the tiny people in the street far below. He felt exhausted mentally and physically and, for the first time in his life, homesick.

He turned on his laptop and found yet another email from Miranda, who had expressly learnt enough about computers to be able to send him long, complaining missives while he was away.

He supposed he should be grateful she used that method rather than reversing transatlantic phone calls, an act which had cost him a fortune over their eleven years of marriage. She seemed not to understand the 'ex' part of the word ex-wife and still considered Rupert should be there for her at any point, in spite of the fact she was now living with her present co-star, Robert Collins.

A four paragraph, error covered message (Miranda's computer knowledge didn't go as far as working out the spell and grammar checker) described the problems she was having on her TV show, *NHS: The National Hope Service*, and what she wanted Rupert to do about it. He hit reply and typed: Talk to Mike. That's what agents are for. Rupert. He clicked send and watched it disappear into cyberspace, imagining Miranda's furious reaction. Then he put in Holly's email address and sent a message which she'd receive when she got up in a few hours time. It consisted of just one word: AHHHHHHHH.

Two minutes later, concerned that the first message might make Holly worry, he added another. Sorry, just emailed you a copy of Judith's orgasm cry – my mistake. Or should I say my success!!!! You were right, there's nothing like age and experience. Love R. PS See – two can play at that game.

Next morning he got a reply. You should have heard me with Victor last night. We had complaints from the neighbours. Love H.

Rupert chuckled – he was definitely going to win this one. Victor must be impressively well endowed to stretch that far. He arrived in New York yesterday. Love R.

Holly's reply came almost instantly. So who was I with last night? I must find out and invite him back. Please stop, I give in! I can't cope with the jealousy.

CHAPTER FIVE

Mindy was up at 7am on Sunday morning. Filming, her natural habitat, usually involved very early starts and she was finding it difficult to break the habit. Besides, that hour, especially on a Sunday, was one of the few times New York was relatively peaceful. She enjoyed walking into Central Park before it filled up. She'd enjoy it more when the weather got warmer. After California's mild climate she was struggling with the East Coast's icy winds and snow. Snow was something she'd only ever experienced from a machine on a movie set and, although it was very beautiful, she completely failed to understand the peculiar activity of throwing lumps of the stuff at other people.

But today she didn't have time for Central Park; she was on a mission. After lunch, Krystal Moon, her drama coach and mentor, was flying in from LA. Mindy couldn't wait to enlist her help with the role of Eve Harrington. Since starting rehearsals, surrounded by stage actors, she'd felt at a loss and was longing for help from one who understood.

She bought a huge bouquet of fresh flowers for Krystal's room; grateful that her agent had insisted the *All About Eve* producers provide a two room apartment. She didn't want Krystal staying in a hotel when their time together was precious. Krystal's services were in huge demand in LA and she could only spare three days in her busy schedule to visit Mindy.

Mindy had booked Krystal first class on a plane arriving mid-afternoon at JFK. An individual of Krystal's importance didn't travel coach.

She checked over the apartment for the millionth time. She'd paid the cleaner (also provided by the producers) overtime to clean again yesterday so the place was sparkling. Krystal's bed was made with sheets of the most natural cotton while the refrigerator was packed with tofu, bean sprouts and Kabala water. Krystal was a health fanatic, and Mindy tried to follow her example, although last night at the diner she'd had a BLT and fries. She hoped Krystal wouldn't be able to discern this reckless behaviour from something in her face or attitude.

While she waited for a limo to drive her to the airport, Mindy ran through Eve's character once more. Krystal would expect her to be completely au fait with every trait and she must ensure she didn't let her mentor down.

Waiting in the arrivals hall Mindy felt a frisson of excitement as a figure appeared wearing a white trouser suit, high heeled boots, dark glasses and a fur coat. Mindy had often wondered how Krystal could be a vegan and wear fur, but obviously there was a finer distinction about wearing and eating that she'd failed to grasp.

Krystal kissed Mindy lightly on both cheeks. "Blue, you appear stressed." It was a trait of Krystal's to call her pupils by their surnames, claiming Christian names were too personal. To immerse oneself thoroughly in a character involved a blank canvas on which to start; nothing should remain of the original performer.

"I'm fine, Madame," Mindy said. None of Krystal's pupils called her anything but Madame. "I'm longing to work with you. I'm feeling so out of my depth here."

Krystal regarded her gravely. "What have I told you about feelings?" Krystal always spoke slowly, as if every word she uttered was of the utmost importance.

Mindy hung her head. "That I shouldn't have any of my own; that they should all come from my character."

"And what would Eve Harrington feel? What are your key words?"

"Ambitious, confident, determined, driven."

"Precisely, but it's not good enough to know this; you have to truly feel it."

"Yes Madame."

"We had better start work as soon as possible; there is obviously a huge amount to get through. Is there a car?"

Mindy took Krystal's case and led her out to the limo. In the apartment Krystal looked around with the appearance of a person expecting to slum it. In the spare bedroom she stared in horror at the bouquet of flowers. "Are those carnations?" she asked in a quiet voice, pointing to a few pink flowers nestling in the middle.

Mindy, being more of a beach girl than a country girl, regarded them uncertainly. The expression on Krystal's face told her it was a rhetorical question. "Are they bad?" Mindy queried.

"Bad? Carnations are considered extremely unlucky by many. Marcel Marceau the mime artiste, for example, would never permit them in his dressing room."

"Sorry, Madame," Mindy flew to remove the offending flowers and throw them in the trash.

Krystal took off her shoes and lay on the bed. "I must rest; these long flights are damaging to my concentration. When I am fully restored we will commence work. I trust you will be prepared." She closed her eyes and Mindy quietly left the room and spent yet another hour working on her character in a frenzy of anticipation.

Mindy entered the rehearsal room the following morning full of new found confidence – and with Krystal in tow. Krystal was wearing a tight T-shirt with the words BARE ALL written across her chest. Judith glanced up from the *New York Times* crossword. "Who is this?" she demanded of Mindy.

"This is Krystal, my acting coach and mentor."

Judith slowly looked Krystal up and down. "Why doesn't that surprise me? Is the sentiment on your breasts an open invitation because, fun though that sounds, it's too fucking cold?"

"To bare your souls, not your bodies," Krystal explained. "Release your inner feelings."

"Heaven help us." Judith stabbed the crossword savagely with her pencil. "Well, Miss Bare All, I'd love to say it's been delightful meeting you, but it hasn't, so goodbye."

"Krystal is staying for rehearsals," Mindy jumped in.

"No, she's not."

"She's helping me with my performance."

"God knows it could do with it, but she's not doing it in my rehearsal."

"Funny, I thought it was Aubrey's rehearsal what with him being the director," Digby commented from his seat on the opposite side of the room to Judith's.

Judith ignored him. "I do not permit anybody in rehearsals who is not essential. I don't even allow understudies, so I am hardly going to allow acting coaches. Fuck off."

Krystal glared at Judith. "Blue! I do not appreciate being spoken to in this manner."

"I'm sorry, Madame." Mindy looked from Krystal to Judith.

"Madame?" Judith appeared faintly amused for the first time. "Are you the owner of an up-market brothel?"

"I most certainly am not. My pupils call me Madame out of respect."

Judith gave a snort of what could have been considered laughter. "And people think I'm pretentious," she said. "At least I've never expected anybody to call me Madame, although I've often thought Goddess, Queen Judith would do nicely." Judith's eyes were sparkling and Rupert and Kyle, who'd been discussing the upcoming baseball season, started to laugh. Judith, unable to resist playing to an appreciative audience, began a hilarious improvisation between a maid and her mistress, playing both roles, which convulsed everybody with laughter, with the exception of Mindy, Krystal and Digby.

"Right, entertainment over," Judith said finally. "We need to rehearse the play we're actually employed to perform. Madame here needs to go."

"Blue!" Krystal managed to make Mindy's

surname sound as if it had at least three syllables.

"No, she stays," Mindy insisted, standing in front of Krystal as if to physically protect her from Judith.

Judith's good humour vanished as fast as it had come. "Get out!"

"Blue wants me here," Krystal swung her hair dramatically.

"Why does she use her surname?" Jennifer whispered to Alyce.

"Do you want me to have you thrown out?" Judith demanded, looking over to where their camp, elderly stage manager was wondering if the building had security guards he could call upon.

"You wouldn't dare throw me out." Krystal's eyes narrowed as she faced Judith. "Blue is the star of your play. She is the big Hollywood draw, brought in to save your show from insignificance. If she wants me here then she'll have me."

"Really?" Judith's voice was remarkably self-controlled. Most of the cast had expected fury in response to this last remark. "In which case, please stay here and rehearse your protégée." She gave a condescending smile. "I'm obviously superfluous to requirements so I shall take a well deserved day off. Aubrey, I leave it in your capable hands – or, at any rate, in your hands." Aubrey dropped the cream cheese bagel he'd been eating on to his trousers at the notion of being in charge of rehearsals. Judith swept out of the room.

There was total silence, broken by Digby

giving a loud clap. "Congratulations, Krystal. You've succeeded in doing what we've wanted to for the last two weeks."

"No we haven't," Jennifer retorted. "Aren't you going after her?" she asked Rupert.

Rupert shook his head, wearily. "I may be a masochist but I don't have a death wish."

"She didn't seem that mad," Paige said.

Rupert gave a faint smile. "Believe me, she was." He turned to Krystal. "I hope your coaching is worth it because antagonizing Judith is not going to make Mindy's life any easier."

Krystal eyed him coolly. "I am worth every cent. Trust me."

"Then we'd better make the most of today." Rupert stood up and stretched. "Let's do the scenes which involve Mindy and not Judith."

"You mean the scenes which include Eve and not Margo," Krystal said.

"Whatever." Rupert rubbed his temples with his fingertips. "Aubrey, can you be parted from your coffee and bagel long enough to give us your input? I need to make a quick call."

"How cute," Digby sneered. "Is it a lover's call to our recently departed so-called leading lady?"

Rupert didn't even deign to reply. He moved out of general earshot and phoned Victor to impart the morning's events. It was a brief conversation as Victor was anxious to contact Judith.

Rupert turned back to hear Aubrey say, "Let's do Eve's first entrance."

"But isn't Margo in that?" Paige asked.

"Yes, of course." Aubrey flipped through his script. "I mean the second scene, the one with Birdie. Margo isn't in that one." He looked doubtful. "Is she?"

This was going to be one hell of a rehearsal, Rupert thought.

The only people who got anything out of the day were Mindy and Krystal. Even Aubrey, initially excited by the prospect of being in charge, found Krystal was using the occasion as personal training time for her client. Any suggestion he made, Krystal would nod slowly, proclaim huskily, "I see where you're coming from," - and then ignore it. Since Eve's most important scenes were with Margo, who was now absent, Krystal threw herself into the role, playing it so differently the rest of the cast were utterly thrown. Mindy, in contrast, was in her element. She'd never felt more confident.

When they broke for lunch Krystal insisted she and Mindy take some air, even the New York air which she deemed polluted, to rejuvenate their minds for further achievements that afternoon. Digby left in their wake, hoping to be included in their excursion. Having Krystal Moon as a drama coach was a significant Hollywood status symbol, and if she'd take him on it would hugely improve his profile there. After tailing them for three blocks with no result, he gave up and sat grumpily on his own in a restaurant, taking his foul mood out on the young waitress.

The rest of the cast were left in a state of shock, bordering on hysteria. "Is that woman for real?" Alyce asked.

"Not much of her," Kyle commented. "I've seen less plastic in Toys R Us."

"The breasts don't even move," Alyce said.

85

"Even when she was jumping around playing Margo, they were completely static."

"Don't you mean 'being' Margo, not playing?" Rupert said. "Remember, 'Madame' said we must be, not act, our characters or they would lack realism."

"If her Margo is realistic I'll go for acting anytime," Jennifer said. "She was hyper."

"Margo on acid," Kyle said. "I was afraid to go near her in case her head started spinning."

"She'll certainly make us appreciate Judith," Jennifer said. She turned to Rupert. "When do you think she'll come back?"

"Once Krystal has gone, I would imagine."

"I hope that's soon," Kyle said. "I'm struggling with that first dressing room scene and could do with Judith's advice."

"Excuse me," said a voice behind them. They turned to find Aubrey, brushing some cookie crumbs off his shirt and looking eager. "Perhaps I could help. I am the director."

"Of course," Kyle said, politely, fairly sure that he couldn't. "That would be great. Perhaps we could talk about it if we do that scene this afternoon."

"Right," Aubrey said, mollified. "I'm going to get some lunch."

Rupert gave Kyle a nod of admiration behind Aubrey's vanishing back for his tactful handling of their ineffectual director.

"Did Aubrey direct any of the play in London?" Paige asked Rupert.

"What on earth do you mean?" Rupert sounded quite cross. "Aubrey Henson is the highly acclaimed and award winning director of *All About*

Eve."

"Oh." Paige felt she'd been thoroughly chastised.

"And anybody who says different," he glared severely at her and then gave a sudden grin, "would be entirely correct. However, that's only between us."

"Doesn't Judith mind if she does all the work and Aubrey gets the credit?"

"Not as long as the play's a success."

"So why doesn't she officially direct it?"

"Because everybody would be super-critical; it's crossing that forbidden line. Actors act, directors direct. If some renowned director does something peculiar with a play they'll be praised as adventurous. If an actor does it they'd call it ill-advised. Besides, Judith never admits to directing. Now since we have no directors, official or unofficial, or acting coaches, how about we order in food and do some work on our own?"

"Only if I can play Margo," Kyle said, proceeding to execute a perfect impersonation of Krystal's earlier performance.

"Bags I play Eve then," Rupert said, jumping in with the correct line. Alyce, Paige and Jennifer all switched roles and everyone was too involved in this piece of improvisation to notice the door opening. Eventually they became aware of the figure standing watching in the doorway and the room felt silent.

"If that's a realistic imitation of my performance please shoot me," Judith said.

"It wasn't," Jennifer broke in quickly. "Kyle was impersonating Krystal's portrayal of Margo."

"That Californian guru was playing Margo?"

Judith's voice was icy. Jennifer could have kicked herself.

"In a way that made us miss you desperately," Rupert said, lightly.

"You are such a fucking creep, Rupert."

"Isn't that why you employ me?" Judith gave a sniff. "Please tell us you're coming back this afternoon," he added.

"No. I left my notes here from last week's rehearsals and I want to study them." She crossed to the table and picked up a notebook. "Actually, I'm going to the Botanical Gardens this afternoon. I thought I'd look at things which are even more wooden than some of the actors in this play."

Realizing the lunch break was almost over and that none of them had eaten, Rupert said he'd walk down with Judith and then buy some food. In the street Victor was leaning against a cab. As he saw Judith and Rupert approaching he opened the cab door. "Are you going AWOL too?" he asked Rupert.

"He most certainly is not," Judith snapped. "Somebody has to keep an eye on rehearsals. Mindy's performance had better be one hundred percent better after this." She clambered into the cab and slammed the door shut. Victor gave Rupert a sympathetic look and then walked round to get in the other side. Rupert watched them drive off before going in search of pizza.

Mindy was greatly relieved when Krystal accepted her first choice of restaurant that evening and, following her mentor's lead, she chose the brown rice and vegetable stir fry. As their waiter brought it to their table and then moved away, Krystal asked, "Would you fuck that waiter if it could lead to the achievement of your deepest desires and ambitions?"

"Excuse me?"

"Your problem, Blue, which was obvious at rehearsal, is you are failing to live the most important part of Eve's scheme. How does she persuade Lloyd to make her the star of his new play instead of Margo? Why does Addison endorse her? And how does she believe she can get Bill to direct her? What is her strongest weapon?"

"She has an affair with Lloyd, she tries to have one with Bill and she'll end up having one with Addison."

"Exactly. It's the power of sex."

Mindy furiously prodded her rice with the fork. "You're saying I should have an affair with Kyle, and Rupert? And proposition Digby?"

Krystal looked her severely. "With whom?"

"Sorry, with Lloyd, Addison and Bill."

Krystal nodded approvingly. "Of course you don't have to have an affair with them." Mindy began to relax. "It's entirely your choice."

"I'm not sure I could and, besides, they might not want to."

Mindy received another severe look. "Am I talking to Eve Harrington or to Mindy Blue?"

Mindy took a deep breath and held herself up proudly. "Eve Harrington."

"Good. The sexual act isn't important; it's your desire for it that is. Your second failure is your trepidation of Margo Channing. When she attempted to ban me from attending rehearsals your support for me lacked confidence. Are you afraid of her?"

Mindy thought of Judith's constant screaming and berating of her. "A little, I guess," she
admitted. "She's kinda awesome."

"Wrong answer. You must merely appear to
be in awe of her. You, Eve Harrington, are the
dominant force. Your star is in the ascent while
hers is waning. You must remember that. That
is the key. Moreover, it is essential you imitate
her behaviour; every mannerism, every odd
quirk, even her speech pattern. Remember, Eve
imitates everything about Margo, which is why
she's the perfect understudy – she has under-
studied her life in addition to her role. Do you
comprehend?"

"Yes, Madame." Mindy felt as if a cloud had
moved away and suddenly everything was clear.
Krystal was a genius. Up until now she, Mindy
Blue, actress, had held the wrong perspective about this role. Eve was the powerful one,
not Margo. She gazed at Krystal, eyes shining.
"Thank you, Madame. You are such an inspiration to me."

"Good." Krystal beckoned the waiter over.
"Do you have vintage champagne? If not bring
us the best you have. Money's no object, correct, Blue?"

"Correct, Madame." Mindy didn't mention
that she didn't usually drink. If Madame considered that was the way to celebrate this break-
through then who was she to object? Besides,
Eve would like champagne.

CHAPTER SIX

After two days of driving the majority of the *All About Eve* Company almost insane, Krystal returned to California and Judith returned to rehearsals. Though she'd never acknowledge it, Judith had enjoyed her time off under Victor's guidance. When she'd previously performed on Broadway Judith had done nothing more than travel between her hotel and the theatre. She hadn't even been aware that New York had a botanical garden, or that there was a Zodiac light display at Grand Central station, and she'd certainly never considered ice skating in Central Park. When Victor took her there she initially refused point blank to try. "I haven't skated since I was young. I might break my leg and then where would the show be?"

"We used to skate together," Victor said. "Don't you remember that run-down rink with the dodgy skates?"

"As I said, that was when I was much younger. We both were."

"I won't let you fall, I promise," Victor assured her, and added, "Don't tell me you're afraid." This remark achieved precisely the reaction Victor had anticipated as Judith instantly marched off to collect a pair of skates. And he kept to his promise, holding her arm and helping her avoid the more erratic skaters.

At the end of an hour exhausted, but elated, Judith rolled off the ice and demanded a drink and something to eat. Victor bought her a can of soda and a pretzel from a food stand.

Judith regarded the items disdainfully. "Oh joy, salmonella in a paper bag."

"Don't be a snob, Judy."

Judith had been forced to admit, although not to Victor, how good it had been. As she walked back into the rehearsal room the following morning she could still recall the saltiness of the pretzel. To her surprise the cast, with the obvious exception of Digby, appeared pleased to see her. Maybe she should play hooky more often.

Most surprising of all, Mindy said, "I'd like to thank you for allowing Krystal to work with me. I'm so in awe of your work that it was vital she coached me to achieve your high standards, and she's helped me to understand that I can learn significantly from you."

"Christ." Judith wasn't sure if she liked this open heroine worship. She started to take off her coat and immediately Mindy was there helping. Judith pulled away. "I can undress myself; I'm not that past it yet."

Mindy gave a sweet smile which turned Judith's stomach. "I'm sorry; I was merely trying to assist."

"Well, don't!"

"Whatever you wish."

"What's with the Pollyanna act?" Judith muttered to Rupert as she put her own coat and bag down. Rupert shrugged. Judith eyed him. "You look terrible."

"Thanks! The last two days haven't exactly been a picnic, with Aubrey thinking he's a director and Mindy's mentor thinking she's God's answer to the acting fraternity. I've been attempting to keep the ball rolling in the correct direction and not let the whole project sink without Gold."

"Ah." Judith tapped her fingers for a few seconds before demanding they do some intense work, since they'd lost two perfectly good rehearsal days. Aubrey opened his mouth to point out there had been rehearsals, changed his mind and popped a piece of cheesecake in there instead.

Judith certainly meant intense and by the end of the day the actors felt utterly drained, but, certainly in Kyle, Jennifer and Alyce's cases, back on track.

As Aubrey announced the schedule for the following day, given to him by Judith, Rupert was surprised to find he wasn't called. When, in the cab on the way back to the hotel, he asked Judith why, she told him she wanted to spend extra time working with Mindy to break her of certain bad habits that Krystal had installed. While Mindy had improved slightly, the fact she'd started persistently calling Judith Margo, in and out of rehearsals, was unsettling. Besides, her gestures, although perfectly acceptable, were still too small. Judith was threatening to take her to Times Square, stand on one side of it and make Mindy perform the role to her from the other.

"And you don't want me there for moral support?" Rupert enquired.

"Yes, I bloody do. However, I am attempting to be pleasant and give you a break." She cleared her throat, preparing for the difficult task of apologizing, Judith style. "I should have checked on your progress instead of swanning around the city like some tourist. So now it's your turn."

"Are you sure?"

"Yes, so explore New York, play tennis or spend all day being nauseatingly soppy on the phone to Holly, I don't care. Just stop harping on about it or I'll change my mind." Rupert leant over and kissed her on the cheek. Judith recoiled and Rupert laughed.

"You're not so bad, Gold, whatever they say."

"Fuck off."

Kyle was sharing a bottle of wine with his wife, Lauren, after their children were in bed on Saturday night, when the doorman rang up to announce that Mindy Blue was downstairs.

Kyle's heart sank. He didn't want his home life invaded by his job. Next time he wasn't putting his address on the contact sheet. "Anything I should know?" Lauren enquired with a mischievous expression.

Kyle kissed the top of her head. "I'll go downstairs; it'll be easier to get rid of her that way."

"Now I'm really worried." Lauren smiled up at him. "If you're more than ten minutes I shall be contacting my lawyer."

Kyle ruffled her hair. "I consider myself warned, but I'll be back in five."

Kyle got downstairs to find Mindy huddled against the wall. Her face was stained with tears and she was shaking. The doorman was attempting to be impassive whilst unable to keep his eyes averted. Kyle hesitated. They couldn't stand in the lobby with an audience and yet he didn't want to take her back to the apartment. In the end he led her outside and then realized it was below freezing and he hadn't got any kind of coat. "What's wrong?" he asked through chattering teeth.

"I'm sorry to disturb you, but I didn't know who else to turn to. I don't know anybody in this city and you always seem so kind."

"Thank you. So what's wrong?"

Mindy gave a sob. "There was a man. He followed me down the street when I was coming back from the deli and started coming on to me, like heavily. It was awful and nobody tried to help. I was so scared."

Kyle felt dreadful for his previous lack of sympathy. "I'm so sorry, Mindy. Did he do anything? Are you hurt?" He studied her face and clothes for signs of an assault.

Mindy shook her head. "No. I shouted at him real loud to leave me alone and he ran off. I guess I was lucky. But I didn't wanna go back to my apartment alone. So I jumped in a cab and came straight here. It wasn't easy to get a cab to come to Brooklyn," she added.

"No, they're not keen on leaving Manhattan," Kyle said, wondering why, of all the cast, she'd chosen to come out here.

"I guess I'm being pathetic, but I didn't know what else to do."

Kyle tried not to wish that Mindy could be somebody else's problem. "Don't you have any friends in the city?" he asked.

"I don't know anybody except in the *All About*

Eve Company." Mindy looked at Kyle with eyes full of fear. "And I know it sounds stupid but I wanted to be around somebody male. It makes me feel safer, like protected. I did consider Rupert, only he might be with Judith and she scares me." She sniffed loudly. "I miss my boyfriend so much." She gave another shiver and hugged her coat closer to her. Kyle was beginning to lose sensation in his fingers and toes.

"You'd better come up to the apartment," he said. They rode the elevator in silence. On hearing Mindy's tale, Lauren insisted she stay the night. She moved their daughter in with her younger brother so Mindy could have the third bedroom and lent Mindy a pair of her pyjamas. She was about to send Kyle to buy a new toothbrush when Mindy produced a complete overnight bag. She never travelled without one, she told them.

"I might lie down now if that's OK," she said, even though it was barely 9pm. "Thank you both for being so kind."

"Poor girl," Lauren said, after Mindy had gone into their daughter's room.

"I suppose so," Kyle said. "It just seems weird that she's come all this way. Most of the company live much closer. And if you'd been assaulted by a man wouldn't you rather go to a girl for comfort? It feels wrong somehow."

Lauren laughed. "What, you think she's stalking you? I didn't realize I'd married somebody so irresistible."

Kyle threw his head back against the chair and groaned. "You're right. The play has obviously gone to my head. I'm seeing conspiracies

96

everywhere."

At 1am Kyle woke to the sound of crying. Lauren was asleep, so Kyle rolled out of bed and automatically moved towards his son's room. When he peered in he saw both children were also asleep and realized the noise was coming from the other room. Briefly he considered waking Lauren and getting her to check on their guest, but he could imagine the ribbing he'd get. Besides, Mindy wasn't Lauren's problem. Gently he knocked at the door, calling out Mindy's name, and went in. The nightlight, bought to ward off the green monster of which his daughter had recently developed a fear, was on, lighting up Mindy's silhouette on the bed.

"Who's there?" Mindy asked; she sounded terrified.

"It's only me, Kyle. Are you OK?"

Mindy sat up. "I'm sorry, did I wake you?"

"No problem." Kyle would have felt uncomfortable sitting on the bed and the only chair was sized for three year olds, so he opted to lean against the wall with the tail of his daughter's toy monkey dangling on to his head from the shelf above. "Can't you sleep?"

"I was, but I had a nightmare. People were chasing me down the street, shouting at me – I think one of them was Judith."

Kyle gave a quiet chuckle. "A nightmare I imagine we all share. However, I can assure you there are no shouting people and no Judith in my apartment." He corrected himself quickly. "In Lauren and my apartment."

Mindy nodded, but Kyle got the impression she was barely listening. "I get a lot of nightmares," she continued, "only in LA my boyfriend sits up with me when I have them and soothes me. I guess his not being here to do that made me miss him more, and I got tearful. I'm sorry. I just feel awful lonely here. And then what happened tonight was scary. I keep picturing the guy getting nearer and nearer. What if he hadn't run off? What if he'd followed me inside my apartment and..." her voice trailed away into a sob. She put her arms round her body and hugged herself, rocking back and forth.

Kyle took a hesitant step nearer, causing the toy monkey's tail to swing back and knock him sharply from behind. "Mindy, New York isn't that dangerous, in fact we've a much lower crime rate than LA. I'm sure such an incident won't happen again. Besides, you have a doorman on your building, right?" Mindy nodded. "Well, he'd have stopped him, and called the cops if necessary. And as for the loneliness, you'll settle in. Once the show's up and running you'll feel like you've known us forever. Theatre companies can become a second family." As he said this Kyle thought about Judith and tried to visualize her as the mother of the *All About Eve* family: it didn't really work. Neither did Digby as a member of any family. "At any rate some of us will be like a family," he amended. "Just give us a chance."

"Thank you." Mindy leaned up on her elbow and the first button on the pyjama jacket came undone, revealing the top of her breasts. Kyle instinctively jumped back, thinking his worst fears were about to be realized. But with an embarrassed "sorry" Mindy instantly drew the jacket together and for further good measure pulled the duvet up over her. Suddenly Kyle felt a total idiot. Lauren was right – what on earth made him think he was so irresistible to womankind?

"Thank you for checking on me," Mindy said. "I'll be fine now. You should go get some sleep. Goodnight." Mindy reached over and squeezed Kyle's hand before curling up under the duvet and closing her eyes.

To restore some sense of normality to the night, Kyle checked on his children, taking a few minutes to watch them sleeping peacefully before bending over and kissing them. His daughter stirred, turned over, and was asleep again immediately. His son never moved a muscle.

Eventually feeling calmer he climbed back into bed beside Lauren "Did the kids wake up?" she muttered, snuggling up against him.

"No. Mindy did."

"Don't tell me she wanted passionate sex with you?"

"NO!" Kyle's vociferous response made Lauren open her eyes to stare at him. "Actually she was very sweet. She'd had a nightmare. Maybe I misjudged her."

"Oh, I don't know, perhaps I did. The old nightmare trick. Didn't she throw off my pyjamas and jump on you as you comforted her?"

"You're joshing with me."

Lauren looked thoughtful. "Weren't you even a little tempted, alone together in a bedroom in the middle of the night? She is very attractive."

"But shallow. I like my women with character and brains."

"And stretch marks."
"And stretch marks."

CHAPTER SEVEN

"Where are my gloves?" Judith demanded on Wednesday as they finished rehearsals. "I know they were here earlier." After a general search turned up no gloves the ASM was dispatched to buy some. On his third attempt he procured a pair which Judith deemed acceptable. Victor was taking her to the Metropolitan Opera House later to see *La Bohème* and she was not arriving wearing gloves from the Army surplus shop.

Rupert had been asked to join them but declined on the grounds that a woman endlessly singing whilst supposedly dying of consumption was not his cup of tea. Instead, at the end of rehearsals, he walked to the subway and was climbing down the steps to the turnstiles when he heard his name. Turning around he found Jennifer and Alyce behind him.

"Where are you going?" Jennifer asked, surprised that a big star like Rupert would get the subway.

"I'm not actually sure," Rupert admitted. "It's such a lovely evening I thought I'd find somewhere on the water to appreciate it."

"As long as you've got a thick coat," Alyce commented, hugging her padded one to her.

Jennifer clasped her hands, getting up the nerve to make a suggestion. "How about Battery Park? It's on the harbour and you can even ride the Staten Island Ferry for a great view of the Statue of Liberty. I... I could show you around

101

if you like."

Rupert smiled at her. "I'm sure you have better things to do than act as a tour guide."

"Oh no, nothing at all. I'd enjoy it – that is if you'd like me to, but not if you'd rather be alone, of course." Jennifer realized she was babbling. "Alyce could come too," she added with sudden inspiration, so it sounded less like a date.

"That sounds like fun, but I have to get home, thanks," Alyce said. Jennifer sent up a silent prayer of thanks.

"Well, if you're sure, then I'd love it," Rupert said. "Lead on."

On the subway two giggling young girls sitting opposite asked for Rupert's autograph. As he obligingly signed Jennifer felt a surge of happiness that she, Jennifer Hoffman, was with this famous English actor. She glanced around the carriage to see how many other people were watching them, and to her satisfaction there were quite a few.

At Battery Park Jennifer and Rupert bought hot dogs and coffee and consumed them looking out over the water.

"Damn," Jennifer said, as some mustard squirted out of her hot dog and on to her coat.

Rupert passed her his paper napkin. "I'm glad to see you're following the lead of our revered director."

"He does seem to wear rather a lot of his food." Jennifer tried to choose her words carefully and not be too impolite.

"Be grateful it's winter. If you get downwind of him in summer it can be most unpleasant," Rupert remarked, causing Jennifer to almost drop her entire hot dog.

Later, walking briskly around the park which was buzzing with locals and tourist entertainers, Jennifer pointed out Castle Clinton and tried, but failed, to look offended when Rupert commented that it might be an acceptable fort, but as a castle it was a little wanting. When compared to those wonderful old English castles Rupert had no doubt grown up with, it did seem pitiable.

A five foot tall female human Statue of Liberty offered a photograph of herself with Jennifer and Rupert for the cut rate of $5. Rupert politely refused, although Jennifer, while knowing it was tacky, would have paid ten times that for such a memento.

Having inspected the park to Jennifer's satisfaction she and Rupert joined the dash to board the Staten Island Ferry for a return trip. They were almost the only people on the outside deck, wrapped up against the cold, watching the impressive sight of the Statue of Liberty growing larger as they neared it on the way out, and the lights of the Lower Manhattan skyline twinkling on their return.

"I love this view," Jennifer said. "Whenever I do this trip I get a tingle of excitement that I live in this city."

"Do you do this trip a lot?" Rupert enquired, enjoying the look of pleasure on her face. Jennifer had a boundless enthusiasm, which was endearing.

"Quite often, the fact that it's free helps when you're a struggling actress." Jennifer replied, watching the wind whipping through Rupert's hair. "I like to imagine how the immigrants must have felt arriving and seeing the Statue of Liberty for the first time and then landing at Ellis Island to be vetted. It must have been both exciting at the prospect of a better life, and terrifying that there'd be a chance of being turned away."

Rupert considered her. "You remind me of somebody else I know, always imagining other people's lives. It's a lovely quality." Rupert didn't notice Jennifer's delight at this compliment; he was thinking of Holly. She would love this. Only three more months and she'd be able to join him. He could envisage her riding back and forth on this ferry all day, thrilled that she wasn't costing him money and imagining she was an immigrant.

"Thank you for a lovely evening," Rupert said, half an hour later as he stood up to get off at his station.

"Anytime. I love being able to share my city with out-of-towners." Rupert gave her a peck on the cheek and then disappeared among the throng of subway riders. Jennifer went back to her apartment in a dream. An hour later Alyce called her to ask how it had gone. Jennifer told her, finishing with, "It was wonderful."

"That's great, hon, only be careful. Don't get too involved unless you know what you're getting involved in."

"Alyce, he's only a friend."

"Uh huh."

Jennifer laughed. "Yeah, uh huh! And don't you have a husband to go be with? I'll see you tomorrow. I'm gonna go do some work on the play now so I don't get in trouble with Judith."

"Judith's gone out tonight, so maybe she won't have prepared such a tough schedule for tomorrow."

"Yeah right!"

"That woman should not have been allowed to wear such a dress," Judith said, as she and Victor left The Met after the opera. "Don't opera designers have any taste? And there was some terrible blocking. At one point the leading man was totally upstaged by some bit part singer. I'd never have allowed that."

Victor grinned. "No, I'm sure you wouldn't."

"Also, was that set supposed to represent Paris? It bore more of a resemblance to Blackpool. At any moment I expected them to wear 'Kiss-me-quick' hats and offer donkey rides."

"But what did you think of the opera?"

"Oh." Judith looked surprised, as if she'd already answered this question. "It was OK. You know what I liked the best?"

"No. Please, tell me."

"The way the chandeliers in the auditorium rose up towards the ceiling as the houselights went down. What a superb theatrical effect."

Victor sighed. "I don't know why I bothered to pay a fortune for our seats. We could merely have sat there until the curtain went up and then vacated them for somebody who would have appreciated the opera."

"Yes," Judith said, without paying attention. She gave a little gasp. Victor waited expectantly. "I wonder if we could get chandeliers in our theatre which could do that. Wouldn't it be perfect? Eve and Addison would take their usual seats among the audience and up would shoot the chandeliers. What do you think?"

"I think next time I'm going to the opera on my own."

Judith frowned at him. "Never mind that! Honestly, you've got a one track mind."

Victor gave a half chuckle. "I've got a one track mind?"

Judith ignored him. "What do you think about our having chandeliers? I'm going to talk to Wesley this minute." Judith reached in her bag for her phone only to find it seized from her hand. "What are you doing?" she demanded of Victor who was placing it in his pocket.

"We," Victor said, with strong emphasis, "are having an evening out, like normal people. We've been to the opera and now we're going out for dinner. We are not going to talk about rehearsals, actors, theatres, ascending chandeliers or anything else to do with *All About Eve*. Is that clear?"

Judith made an ineffectual attempt to reach her phone, before Victor grabbed her arm and held it in a lock behind her back, ignoring her cursing and claims of brutality. "Now, are you going to come nicely," he asked, "or do I have to drag you?"

Judith considered saying he wouldn't dare, but with Victor there was always the chance that he would dare, and being dragged across the road and into a restaurant was simply too degrading. Instead she went, sat down at the table and announced her decision not to eat until she'd talked to Wesley about chandeliers.

Victor's response was merely to shrug and order for her.

"I trust you're not going to force feed me?" Judith said, to which Victor didn't reply. However, the smell of the lemon sole the waiter placed in front of her weakened Judith's resolve. "I do hate you, sometimes," she snapped, picking up her knife and fork.

Victor reached across the table and squeezed her hand. "Only sometimes? I must be doing something right."

On returning to the hotel two hours later, Judith changed into one of the provided bathrobes, picked up her rehearsal bag and started rifling through it. Victor came out of the bathroom and looked at her in exasperation. "What are you doing? It's nearly two o'clock in the morning."

"I wanted to go through the notes I made at rehearsals today, only I can't find the damn things." She turned her bag upside down on the bed, flinging its contents around but failing to find the notebook.

Victor picked up a large hat pin. "What on earth is this for?"

Judith gave a wicked grin. "Ah yes, I borrowed that from the costume department. I'm intending to use it to get some kind of reaction from that so-called actor I'm lumbered with. One prod with that and he'll be reacting all over the place."

"Don't come running to me if he sues."

"Imagine what a fool he'd look in court: Your Honour I was stuck with a hat pin. See this tiny prick on my buttock."

"That would certainly be an interesting place to see a tiny prick."

Victor was rewarded for his remark by a howl of laughter. Getting laughs out of Judith made him feel like he'd won some major humanitarian award.

"I've totally revised my opinion of where to stick it now," Judith spluttered.

"Don't even think about that, Judy. He could claim major damages."

Judith fluttered her eyelashes at him innocently. "I don't know what you mean." She turned back to fruitlessly rifling through the contents of her bag. "Damn, I must've left them at the rehearsal room. Now what shall I do? I'm not in the least tired." Victor ran his hand down her back. "For fuck's sake, don't men ever think of anything else? Get off. No wait... Oh... Well at least turn the lights off first."

Judith got to the rehearsal room early the following morning, intending to go through her notes before rehearsals started but she couldn't find them there either. Mindy, being the next to arrive, found Judith still searching. "Can I help?" she asked.

"I've lost my notes from yesterday."

"That's too bad. When did you last see them?"

Judith shook her head in disbelief. "Why do people always ask that stupid fucking question when an item has gone missing? If people knew where they'd lost things they'd know where to find them."

"Sorry. I'll help you look."

"Forget it, they're not here."

"Who aren't here: the cream of British acting talent? Yes, disappointing, isn't it?" Digby said, walking into the room.

"Margo's lost her notes," Mindy explained.

"It's Judith," Judith said, through gritted teeth. She was not in the mood for method actresses today.

"Losing her gloves yesterday and her notes today – don't tell me our so-called star is losing her marbles too," Digby sneered, as he took his coat off and grandly handed it to the stage manager to hang up.

"At least I haven't lost my talent, you debauched troll," Judith retorted. "Presuming you had any to start with."

"Welcome to another fun-packed day at the *All About Eve* rehearsals," Rupert drawled, as he strolled in exactly on cue, with Alyce and Jennifer on his heels.

Judith glowered at him, but dropped the subject – regretfully. If Victor hadn't insisted on removing the hat pin from her possession, she might have been tempted to use it on Digby at that very moment.

With only one week to go before they moved into the theatre, Judith was driving the actors harder and harder. Even Rupert was struggling to keep up with her demands, in addition to trying to maintain a bearable atmosphere.

"I feel I've been mangled and spat out again," Jennifer said to Alyce over the very short lunch break they were now permitted by Judith, who cared little for Equity rules. Digby ignored this decree and continued to take the official hour, which hardly bothered Judith who would be happy if he'd take a permanent lunch break.

"I don't even know if I'm improving or dis-improving," Alyce said, having been berated by Judith for a full fifteen minutes that morning.

Wesley popped in occasionally, but mostly kept clear since Judith was cold shouldering him after he'd refused her demand for ascending chandeliers. The fact that the St James Theatre would have to be structurally altered to accommodate such an effect was not an acceptable excuse in her eyes. Rather than face Judith's hostility, Wesley received the lowdown on rehearsals from Rupert or Aubrey. It never ceased to amaze the producer how much the two reports varied.

Mindy seemed to be the person least affected. In spite of Judith's constant tirades she would merely smile, accept the criticism, and move on. She even brought in her lunch so she could work without a break if Judith so required, or late into the evening when everyone else had gone home. Nothing, it seemed, was too much trouble. This had the consequence of irritating Judith intensely. She was used to reducing young actresses to tears and found Mindy's attitude incomprehensible.

"You are supposed to pass me the letter on the line before," Judith shouted at her on Tuesday afternoon.

Mindy looked surprised. "Yes, originally, but you changed it yesterday when we stayed late." She picked up her script and showed it to Judith. "See, I wrote it down by this line as soon as you told me to alter it." Noticing Judith's expression of rage, Mindy added hastily, "I'll change it back, no problem."

"Do what you fucking like! I've had enough for today. Aubrey!"

Aubrey spilled half the contents of his can of coke down his jumper. "Yes, Judith."

"I want to break for the day, now."

"Now?" Aubrey repeated. His mouth opened and closed in astonishment. "But we're scheduled for another two hours."

"For fuck's sake will somebody please clarify the word 'now' to our renowned director? It obviously escaped him at director school." Judith stormed out and hailed a cab off the street without even waiting for Rupert.

"I'm real sorry I upset her," Mindy said. "I'm sure that's what she said."

"I was right first time," Digby said, with great glee. "The great Judith Gold has lost her marbles."

Rupert regarded him with utter disdain. "God, you're an odious man." He grabbed his belongings and walked out.

Jennifer ran down the stairs after him. "Rupert, are you OK? Can I buy you a coffee or something? I feel I should apologize for my fellow American."

"No, thanks, I'm fine. I'm going back to the hotel to get some rest while I can. If you think it's hard now, wait until we get to the theatre! And you don't need to apologize for Digby – you can hardly be held accountable for every American. Besides, if he really gets annoying we could always check out the unsubstantiated rumour that he was once a rent boy."

"No!" Jennifer gasped. "Really?" Rupert grinned at her. "Oh, you're kidding me again!"

"I'm afraid so. It would be a good rumour to start though!" Jennifer could see a sort of crease of exhaustion down Rupert's forehead as he leant over to give her a quick kiss goodbye. She stood watching him go until a voice behind her made her jump.

"Just friends huh? I bet you won't wash your face for a week."

"Oh Alyce! Stop already! It was a brotherly kiss."

"Sure, but do you feel like his sister?"

"Yes. Absolutely."

"Hmm," Alyce said.

When Judith returned to the hotel she lay down and shut her eyes. Rupert, arriving back shortly after, knocked on her door but she ignored him. He tried another three times until she shouted at him to piss off. Half an hour later Victor came back from visiting the Guggenheim, and was taken aback to find Judith prone on the bed.

"Judy, are you all right? Don't you feel well?" He sat down beside her.

"I'm perfectly fine, thank you."

"Are you indeed?" Victor settled back on the bed and crossed his arms.

"What are you doing? Go away."

"No. I'm staying right here until you tell me the truth."

Judith gave a shrug of indifference as if to say should Victor want to waste his time it wasn't her problem and that he'd get bored soon enough.

That was reckoning without Victor's resolute nature and after half an hour he hadn't moved, his eyes boring into her. "Oh, for fuck's sake, if you're going to hang around get me a drink."

Victor climbed off the bed, got some ice from the machine outside and poured two glasses of whisky. Judith took a gulp of hers and savoured the moment the alcohol hit her system. It took another two glasses to relax her. She sank back with a sigh. "Maybe I should leave rehearsals entirely to our director. Maybe I'm not up to dealing with it anymore."

"Ah."

"What do I need all this hassle for at my age?"

"Mm."

"I should be allowed to simply act."

"Uh huh."

"Good grief, it's like being at a fucking shrink's. They let you talk and never say anything useful."

"Have you ever been to a shrink, Judy?" Victor was fairly confident of the answer.

"Certainly not. But I've seen it in the movies. It's very irritating. They get paid a fortune and never give any advice."

"Sometimes people only need to talk – like you do now."

"No, I don't."

"OK." Victor poured them each another whisky, he was only on his second, and waited.

Judith swished her drink around in the glass, and some of it splashed out on to the bed. "Damn it, now I've got the fucking shakes as well as going senile."

Victor nearly chocked on his drink. "Senile?

Is that what you're worrying about?"

"What if it is?" Judith's voice was defensive.

"Judy, you are the most un-senile person. There are new born babies more senile than you."

"Fine, don't take me seriously."

"I am taking you seriously. It was just the last thing I was expecting. You have the most amazingly sharp mind. Tell me why you're worrying about it." Judith said nothing. "Judy, please. I don't think you're the slightest bit senile, but there has to be a reason you're concerned." He took Judith's free hand, the one which wasn't clasping the glass and, ignoring her initial resistance, held it tightly.

Judith sighed and reluctantly told him about the gloves, the notebook and giving Mindy the wrong cue. "I have absolutely no memory of changing it," she finished, draining the last drop of whisky. "I've never forgotten anything like that before."

Victor removed the empty glass from her hand and turned her face to look at him. "Judy, you've been working so damn hard I'm amazed you're still in one piece. Forgetting that you've changed one thing is only human. Most people under that sort of duress would be forgetting a lot more than one cue, and in all probability suffering a nervous breakdown to boot. And as for losing things, we all do it."

"I don't."

"Welcome to normality."

"I don't want to be normal."

Victor laughed. "Don't worry, I doubt there's actually much chance of that."

"There are other things I've forgotten. For example, it took me over twelve hours after we'd been to the opera to remember to ask Wesley about those chandeliers. How could I forget that? Not that it did any good."

Victor ran his fingers over Judith's hand. "As I recall, I distracted you in other ways."

Judith almost blushed. "You're too distracting full stop. When are you going back to England? Isn't it this week?"

"Actually, I'm going to stay a bit longer."

"Why?"

"I like it here. Don't worry, I know you'll be frantically busy getting *All About Eve* into the theatre, so I'll keep out of your way."

"Don't you have work to go back for?"

Victor gave a non-committal shrug. "I can do it from here. New York is an inspiring city. My only concrete engagement is escorting Holly to the Olivier Awards and that isn't until Sunday week. What?" he added, as Judith eyed him with suspicion.

"If you find New York so inspiring, go and walk its streets and get me a decent coffee. I need to sober up so I can work on tomorrow's rehearsals."

Victor returned ten minutes later bearing a cardboard cup and a muffin to find Judith sitting straight backed in the chair, obviously irate. Victor vaguely scanned the room, half wondering whether Digby had called round in his absence. He held out the coffee.

"I don't want it."

"OK." Victor put it down on the table.

"I wanted you out of the way."

"I see."

"Don't start that shrink business again or I swear I'll throw the coffee at you. I'm furious enough with you as it is."

"All right. Why did you want me out of the way and why are you furious with me?"

"I know I'm going senile and all that..."

"Judy..."

"Shut up." Victor put his hands up in surrender. "Senile or not, I did recall Rupert mentioning an interview you were very excited about: a disillusioned army general who's agreed to give you an exclusive. I meant to mention it before but it went out of my head. Anyway, I just phoned Rupert and he confirmed that it's scheduled for this Thursday. Since today is Tuesday, you need to be on a plane tomorrow at the latest."

Victor could have kicked himself for not telling Rupert to keep it quiet. No doubt he presumed Judith knew. Judith was glaring at him, tapping her foot. "I changed my mind. It wasn't as noteworthy as I'd thought," he lied.

"Really? You told Rupert it was the kind of interview that journalists dream of."

"Maybe I thought that at first, but it's lost its novelty."

"Bollocks. You're staying because of me, aren't you?" Victor tried to speak but Judith cut in, "Don't lie to me, Victor."

"All right, I won't lie to you. Yes, I'm staying because of you. Strange as I know it seems, to both of us, I love you and I want to be with you."

"And now I'm going senile you've decided you'd better look after me in my dotage."

"For the hundredth time, woman, you are not senile. But yes, I am worried about you. You're overworking, incredibly stressed, not eating properly, smoking again, and in serious danger of committing murder by hatpin. I don't want to be three thousand miles away."

Judith spoke in an icy tone. "I've managed on my own for most of my life. I am perfectly capable of managing now. I cannot, will not, tolerate anyone feeling sorry for me. Nor do I want people organizing their lives around mine."

Victor tried to hide a smile at this blatant piece of misrepresentation. Judith caught the look and gave an exasperated sigh. "All right, I do expect people to organize their lives around mine occasionally, if it's to do with work. But I won't let you lose the interview of a lifetime. Support within relationships can work both ways."

Victor crouched beside Judith's chair. "I appreciate that, I really do. But it's my choice and I want to stay."

"Have you cancelled the interview yet?" Victor didn't reply, so Judith repeated the question in a manner which demanded an answer. At Victor's finally admitting he was intending to pass the assignment to another journalist tomorrow, Judith sighed and sat back. "Suit yourself."

Victor was surprised how easily she'd given in, but relieved because after tonight's conversation he had no intention of leaving her. Or that's what he thought. Since Judith was too tired to go out, Victor picked up an Italian takeaway. When he returned he found his travel bag neatly packed and sitting outside the door to the hotel room. When he tried his key card it merely flashed the red no entry light. There was an envelope on top of his case. He tore it open and pulled out a note scribbled in Judith's handwriting on hotel paper.

Victor,

There's a late plane out of JFK tonight. You have a seat booked. If you aren't on it I shall never speak to you again and you know me well enough to realize that's not an idle threat. Don't try and get into the room. I had the front desk change the code. As I told you before you're too distracting anyway and I need to concentrate on nothing but the play.

Judith.

PS Leave the food outside and go quickly. I abhor cold pasta.

CHAPTER EIGHT

On the Thursday morning of the last week of re-hearsals, Judith announced a full run-through after lunch to establish which problems needed to be ironed out before two final run-throughs on Saturday. Victor had left under coercion two evenings before and Judith was throwing her-self into her work to fill the void she unexpect-edly found in her life.

"Sorry, no can do," Digby said. "I have a cast-ing for a TV pilot this afternoon." He looked at the outraged faces of his fellow cast who obvi-ously had no regard for his status as a Holly-wood star.

"You had better be joking," Judith said.

"I never joke about work."

"Then you'd better cancel it."

"No way. It's in my contract that I can have time off for TV or movie work."

"And what happens to this play if you get this amazing role?" Judith's voice was almost a hiss.

"Then I'll have to miss some shows for the actual shoot. It's only a pilot so it shouldn't be more than a couple of weeks. No biggy."

"No biggy?" Judith repeated. "Not only is that appalling English, but it's a huge fucking biggy."

Digby regarded her coolly, arms crossed which had the effect of increasing Judith's rage and for five minutes she let rip, calling Digby every name under the sun, mostly on the sub-ject of unprofessional behaviour, with a few personal slights for good measure. The angrier she became the smugger Digby became until Judith grabbed the elegant cane which Rupert used in the play and started towards him. This alarmed even the arrogant Digby and, with a yelp, he put up his arms to protect his face. Luckily for him, before Judith could inflict damage Rupert grabbed her, wrestling the cane from her hand.

"Let me go," Judith shrieked.

"No. I'm not having you arrested for assault and battery." Rupert held firmly on to her, trying to avoid being elbowed in his rib cage. "Digby, if you're going to your casting I suggest you leave now."

Slowly Digby got to his feet and strolled to the door. Then he turned back to Judith. "You're lucky your boyfriend," he gestured towards Rupert, "stopped you in time. If you'd harmed my looks I'd have sued you for every penny you've ever made."

"You haven't got any looks left, there are scarecrows more attractive than you," Judith spat at him from Rupert's grip.

Paige gave an involuntary giggle at Judith's snub and then wished she could disappear into the ground as both Judith and Digby glared at her.

"Obviously the casting people today don't agree with you," Digby retorted, waving a script at the room in general and subsequently tapping it for extra emphasis. "The role is that of a handsome police captain. My agent says it'll be a walk-over. The meeting is a mere formality." Digby gave Judith a condescending smile and sauntered from the room.

Once Rupert judged Digby had left the building he released Judith who sprung away from him, literally shaking with rage. She strode across the room, collected her coat and bag and left without a word.

"Oh dear," Aubrey said, with obvious glee in his voice. "It looks as if I'm in charge of rehearsals again."

"What exactly do you suggest we rehearse without a Margo or a Bill?" Rupert asked.

"There are scenes which don't involve either of them. Let's start with the one where Eve realizes Addison has total dominance over her. That's very powerful."

Rupert started to say they'd have to work without him too, but what was the point? Judith was going to be too angry to talk to, so he may as well stay and help her by trying to stop Aubrey re-directing her play.

Aubrey was getting into his stride now. "Actually, I'd like to do the last scene with Eve and Phoebe. It's such a significant part; the crux of the entire matter; the heart of the play's theme. The..."

"Well, it's the end, anyway, so we and the audience will be able to go home," Kyle cut in, finding Aubrey fairly nauseating.

Paige giggled again and this time earned Aubrey's wrath. "Perhaps you could manage to stand by, rather than behaving like a simpering schoolgirl," he said to her. "It's hardly like your work is particularly satisfactory. Mindy, I'm sorry, Eve, could you join us too? Let's start some proper work." Aubrey was gesturing wildly like a demented traffic controller.

Paige took her place, curled up on the rehearsal chair which represented the armchair in Eve's apartment. Mindy made her entrance, Paige leapt up, opened her mouth to say her lines, and burst into tears. Mindy stood there bemused, not recalling this part of the direction, while Alyce and Jennifer both rushed over to Paige.

"I'm so sorry," Paige wept. "It's stupid of me, but everything is so tense and we're going into the theatre on Monday and I don't feel ready because I seem to do everything wrong. This is my first proper Broadway show and I'm useless. I don't want to go back to spraying perfume at Macy's, or having to dress as a bagel to promote some food store."

Alyce put her arm firmly around the younger girl's shoulders. "Rubbish, hon, you're doing great. We all feel the same way. But it'll be fine. Judith's just..." she struggled to find the right words.

"A pain in the arse on occasions," Rupert finished. "Aubrey, here's a challenge for you. Find a scene to rehearse which doesn't involve Margo, Bill, Addison, Miss Caswell or Phoebe. The bagel and I are going to walk round the block."

"I wasn't even a good bagel," Paige wailed. "I got fired."

Rupert held out her coat. "You know, I cannot think of an appropriate response to that, but I'll work on it as we walk – if you promise to give me a full description of exactly what bad bagels wear!"

"Oh, honestly," Aubrey muttered as they left.

"I bet Trevor Nunn never has this problem."

Rupert and Paige came back half an hour later. Paige looked positively cheerful; Rupert completely shattered.

Two hours later Wesley burst into the room, cutting Aubrey off in the middle of a story about when he'd worked with Diana Rigg. "Where's Judith?" Wesley demanded.

"She walked out – again," Aubrey said. "But don't worry, we're going ahead with rehearsals. It's coming along nicely. I'm in charge," he added, in case there was any doubt.

"There's not much point having rehearsals if you don't have a leading lady," Wesley snapped. Nobody had ever seen their mild producer so uptight.

"It's only temporary, Wesley," Aubrey said, as if to a small child. "She's making a point."

"Do shut up, Aubrey, you have no idea what you're talking about," Wesley said. Aubrey took consolation for yet another slight in a large chocolate muffin. Wesley held up his mobile phone and addressed the full company. "I just received this text from Judith: 'If moron stays in play I don't. This is not an idle threat. Good luck finding another Margo'." Wesley turned to his leading man. "Rupert, do you think she means it?"

"Yes. I'm very much afraid she does."

Victor was in the process of feeding Judith's two cats on Friday morning when the phone rang. "Good, you're there," Judith said, from the other end of the line. "I need you to pick me up from the airport. I was going to get a taxi, but there's

123

a queue around the block and then the drivers will want to talk. I'd rather wait for you."

"Heathrow airport?" Victor queried.

"No, Abu Dhabi airport. Yes, of course fucking Heathrow."

Victor didn't ask questions, simply got in his car and headed down the A4. When he arrived, Judith was standing outside Terminal 3 puffing on a cigarette. He scowled but refrained from rebuking her. The expression on her face told him that would be a mistake. Judith gave a final puff and stubbed the cigarette out. She dumped a small travelling bag into the back, climbed in the passenger seat and slammed the door shut. Victor started the car and they drove back to Judith's house in silence.

As Judith opened the door the cats came to greet her. She bent down and stroked them as they pushed against her legs. The cats, the tenth and eleventh she'd owned, all of whom were named Max, were the only living beings to be shown any real emotion by Judith.

Judith picked up Max XI, the cat Rupert had given her, and hugged it closely for a while, while Max X stalked around her feet. Eventually she picked up her bag and headed upstairs. "I'm going to bed. I didn't sleep a wink on that bloody overnight flight." Victor followed her into the bedroom and she glared at him. "Don't even think about it, I'm far too tired."

Victor gave a half smile. "Much as it may amaze you, I wasn't. I was hoping you'd tell me what you were doing here. I'd love to think it was because you missed me so much, but somehow I doubt it."

"I've left the play. End of subject." Judith headed for the bathroom.

"What?" He went to follow her but Judith slammed the door in his face and locked it. Victor returned to the bedroom to hear Judith's mobile ringing. He glanced at the caller ID. It was the voice mail. Apparently Judith had a quantity of messages.

Judith came back from the bathroom in her pyjamas and climbed into bed. Victor passed her the phone, suggesting she check her messages, but she switched it off and threw it across the room. "Now go away," she instructed. "And draw the curtains and turn the light off."

Victor did as he was bid. Then he leant over Judith and kissed her. "I love you." Judith gave a sort of snort and turned away. Victor went downstairs to await further developments.

An hour later the landline rang. Victor snatched up the receiver, knowing Judith would be furious if it woke her. It was Rupert trying to sound nonchalant but wondering if Victor had heard from Judith. "There's nothing to be anxious about or anything," he added.

Victor laughed. "It's OK, Rupert, you don't have to worry about panicking me. Judy's here."

"Oh, thank God. I've been up half the night trying to find her. I never thought of checking the airport – she must have been on the first flight out."

"Could you fill me in?" Victor asked. "Judy hasn't said a word except to say she quit."

Rupert did so. "Wesley is about to jump into the East River," he finished. "His whole project is about to disintegrate in front of him."

125

"Wesley's project? It's Judy's project. If it goes ahead without her it'll kill her."

"I know."

"I'll talk to her when she wakes up."

Victor had to wait less than an hour before Judith stomped down the stairs, fully dressed, declaring she'd been unable to sleep. Victor made her a cup of coffee and tried to broach the subject, but was met by a brick wall. Judith flatly refused to do the play while Digby was in the cast. When Victor wouldn't drop the subject, Judith marched out of the room. Victor had to phone Rupert and report total failure.

Rupert hung up and stared out of the window. The sun would be coming up soon on whatever this day was going to bring. He'd wait a few hours in case Wesley was asleep and then phone him with Victor's report. He needn't have bothered. Wesley had been in a meeting with the American producers most of the night and was far from asleep. Rupert's call didn't make him feel he was going to get any for a while either.

Digby was also not sleeping much. He was too angry with his agent and the whole TV industry. The role in the pilot had not been the handsome policeman, but the trusty old sergeant, who had only ten lines. He wasn't ready to play old sergeants yet, especially those in supporting roles. Informing the casting people exactly what he thought of them, Digby stormed out. At 7am the following morning he was woken from a fitful doze by a phone call from the *All About Eve* producers requesting a breakfast conference. There was no doubt in his mind, as he arranged to meet them at a nearby diner, that they were going to apologize for Judith's behaviour.

Wesley and a female American producer were already waiting, drinking coffee, when Digby arrived. He ordered French toast and bacon. "So," he said, as the waitress poured him coffee, "I presume you're here to make amends for that bitch's atrocious behaviour." He took a sip of his coffee and waved at the waitress. "This coffee is disgusting. Bring me some that hasn't been sitting in the pot all night." He turned back to his companions. "Well?"

"I'm afraid we're going to have to let you go," the American producer said. "It's not working out as we'd anticipated."

Digby didn't even notice his coffee being replaced as he stared across the table. "Excuse me?"

"You're fired," Wesley said. It wasn't the most diplomatic way to impart the news, but he'd had no sleep, was cranky and not in the mood for niceties.

"You can't do that. I've got a contract. I'll sue you."

The female producer opened her briefcase and produced a piece of paper. "This document states that you do not feel comfortable in the role of Bill Sampson, and are being released from your contract by mutual agreement. If you sign it you will receive your full wage for the six months you were contracted for. You'll find it hard to sue with such an offer."

"I won't sign it."

"We will still pay you for those six months and you will still be replaced. But if you refuse

127

to go without a fuss then we'll be forced to announce that you were totally inadequate and have been fired for incompetence in the role."

"I'm not incompetent."

"You're not good enough," Wesley said.

"That's only what that bitch says. She hates me because I don't hang on her every word like everyone else. You're scared of her and I'm not. She may not like what I do but she's stuck with it." The waitress brought Digby's breakfast and made a hasty departure before he could complain about that too. He was the kind of customer she could do without first thing in the morning.

"Actually she's not stuck with it," Wesley said, finding the smell of Digby's bacon was making him feel sick. "She's refusing to do the play if you continue in the role."

"Good. Then you can find a decent American actress to play Margo Channing. We don't need her."

"Yes, we do. *All About Eve* is Judith's project from start to finish. Without her it's nothing."

Digby turned to the American. "I'm the name in this country. People will come to watch me."

The woman shook her head. "Actually, our research shows that people want to see the actress who created the role in London play it on Broadway. And she's hardly unknown here. She's the biggest draw for *All About Eve*, followed by Rupert and Mindy. You come in fourth. Since we have been forced to make a choice, you have to go."

Digby looked down at his congealing bacon. This could not be happening to him. He'd never come in fourth in his life. "The play moves into the theatre next week. Who are you going to get to replace me at such short notice? No actor could learn the lines, the moves and play the role to Judith's satisfaction over one weekend."

"That's no longer your problem." The American producer brandished the paper at Digby. "Are you going to sign or are we doing it the hard way?"

"I wish to consult my agent."

"Feel free to do so, although I would imagine they'll recommend you sign rather than lose face over a public firing. Once we've received the signed document we'll pay you your full six months salary and put out a press release." She stood up and threw some money on the table. "Enjoy your breakfast."

"Are you screwing Judith?" Digby asked Wesley who was also getting to his feet.

"What?"

"Why else would you put up with all her shit?"

Wesley regarded Digby with disdain. "I put up with Judith for many reasons, none of which are sexual and not least because I'm actually fond of her in a strange way. But mostly it's because I admire her as a person and because she's an exceedingly good actress."

"And she makes you a lot of money."

"She has done in the past, but with Broadway overheads and now this situation, I'll be lucky if I break even. However, I'm still happy with my decision."

"You're going to lose a lot more than my pay when you have to cancel at least a week of performances while you find a replacement."

Wesley and the American producer left the restaurant with Digby's embittered laughter in their ears.

Richard Gresham's phone rang on Friday evening as he was rearranging his furniture – for the second time. Although he had recently recorded two radio plays and made a guest appearance in *Foyle's War*, he was currently one of the eighty percent of actors out of work at any one time. The fact that this call was an availability check from Wesley Bartlett, for whom he'd previously worked twice, started his brain racing as he tried to recall hearing anything about a new production for which he might be suitable. It wasn't like him to miss something on the theatrical grapevine.

"Thank God," was Wesley's response, when Richard pronounced himself extremely available. "I need you to recreate your role as Bill Sampson on Broadway. We've lost ours and have no time to rehearse a new one before we move to the theatre on Monday. Can you be on a plane to New York tomorrow?"

"Absolutely, I'll swim the Atlantic if necessary." Richard prided himself on his laid-back attitude to work, but this was something else.

There was a tired sounding laugh from Wesley's end. "Thank you for your enthusiasm but that might take more time than we have."

"But will American Equity let me do it? I thought they wouldn't allow any of us except Judith and Rupert."

"Yes, they've agreed." Wesley didn't go into details of how long he and the other producers had spent debating the subject with Equity. Only by illustrating how many people would lose work if *All About Eve* was pulled because of the lack of a leading actor had they persuaded the reluctant union. "I'll organize a flight for the morning and talk money with your agent, but as far as per diems and accommodation go you'll be on the same deal as Judith and Rupert."

Two hours later, in the midst of imparting his news to every theatrical acquaintance he could think of, Richard received a further call from Wesley telling him his work visa would take another day and that he'd have to wait until Sunday to fly out. That certainly made it tight the other end. It began to hit Richard what he was taking on. He hadn't played this role for nearly a year, and now he was about to play it on Broadway, with a cast most of whom he'd never met who'd been rehearsing for a month while he'd had no rehearsal and, far scarier than any of that, he had to live up to Judith's terrifyingly high standards.

Victor let himself into the house on Friday evening, laden with bags from Waitrose, to be greeted by a pacing Judith. "There you are," she said. "I need to get on a flight to New York first thing tomorrow and all the business seats are full and I cannot go economy. Pull some strings, will you? You're good at things like that. If necessary get somebody unimportant bumped off."

Victor put down the shopping. "You're not staying then?"

Judith had the grace to look a little shame-faced. "Well, you can freeze anything you can't

131

eat. Or feed it to the cats. Now get me a flight."

Victor saluted. "Yes, Madam. I take it the Digby situation has been resolved?"

"Yes." Failing, for once, to suppress her emotions, Judith's whole face lit up. "Digby's been fired. Fired," she repeated, relishing the word. "And Richard is coming to replace him. Isn't that wonderful?"

Victor put his arms around her and to his surprise she yielded into them. She really was happy. "Yes, Judy, that is truly wonderful." He held her until she pushed him away and gestured towards the phone. "OK, I'll get on to it. Is Richard flying with you?"

"No, he has to wait for his visa and I have to get back before Aubrey starts thinking he's a director, and Mindy takes her method acting to such extremes she ceases to exist in the real world."

Victor picked up the phone. "If I am successful in my mission may I cook you a celebratory supper?"

"You most certainly may. Suddenly I'm starving. And make me something for the plane too. Even in business the food is inedible."

Richard's visa took longer than anticipated and he didn't fly into New York until Monday morning, and even with the official documentation the grilling he received at immigration was intense. When he finally exited the customs hall he found Rupert hanging over the rail holding a large sign which read: *OUR HERO.*

"Should I be wearing underpants over my trousers and spinning round in a telephone

132

box?" Richard said, as he and Rupert shook hands.

"Believe me, Superman wouldn't be more welcome. None of us can thank you enough for coming to our rescue."

"Are you serious? I'm so tickled to death about the whole situation I could barely chat up the very cute steward on the flight."

Rupert laughed, knowing with Richard it was all talk; that after the death of his long-time boyfriend from AIDS Richard had remained loyally celibate. "Well, you may end up regretting it," he told Richard. "It's pandemonium here."

"It was good of you to come and meet me."

"It's the least we could do. Judith and Wesley would have come but they were busy at the theatre. They're finishing the get-in today and Judith is determined to be there regardless of the fact she knows little about technical matters. Wesley has to be there to stop her from being murdered by stage hands furious at being given orders by a bossy, meddlesome and foul-mouthed actress. Actually, Wesley and I drew straws over who was to meet you and who stay with Judith. Wesley lost."

"I'm rather glad. Wesley's a nice chap, but I'm dying to get the lowdown and I'm sure you'll fill me in better on the juicy bits. How on earth did you lose your Bill? It seems terribly clumsy."

By the time their car had reached Manhattan, Richard had the general picture, commenting that it was better than any soap opera. He was stunned by Digby's attitude and audacity. Not that he was complaining.

"Do you mind if we go to the theatre first

before you check into the hotel?" Rupert asked, as their car drove through Times Square. "Otherwise Judith will be furious."

"I'd prefer that. I'm longing to see it. Wow!" Richard had spotted the St James where the *All About Eve* signs were being erected. He and Rupert clambered out and stood on the pavement.

"Wow indeed," said Rupert, as his name was hung above the front of house doors, next to Judith's and Mindy's. "It seems we're really doing it."

"Ooh look, I'm being appended!" Richard pointed to where a man was carefully adding 'And Richard Gresham' to the bottom of *All About Eve's* billing board.

"It should read: 'And thank God for Richard Gresham,'" Rupert said.

The two men stood silently for a while watching the sign people at work, before going in search of their producer and leading lady. They had little problem locating Judith who was marching about the stage, in grave danger of being knocked unconscious by moving scenery.

Hearing the door open as they entered, Judith turned, annoyed at being interrupted. As she saw Richard her expression changed to one which was almost recognizable as joy. "Well," she said, "it's about fucking time you got here."

CHAPTER NINE

When the cast arrived at the theatre at 10am on Tuesday, the set was still being put up. Since they only had until the first preview on Saturday to carry out the complicated technical and the dress rehearsals, this did not improve Judith's mood. She'd stayed at the theatre until all hours the night before trying to persuade the crew to work later, but precisely at their assigned time they stopped, leaving Judith standing centre stage swearing at their departing backs.

Accepting there was no likelihood of getting on stage for the present, Judith announced a meeting in her dressing room suite which comprised an ante-room with a bathroom off it, and the main dressing room with make-up table and bed. Always one to enjoy a dramatic effect, Judith sent Richard into the bathroom until everyone else had assembled and then called him out. "This is Richard Gresham," she said. "He played Bill in London and now he will be reprising his role here."

"Thank God," Alyce said, shaking Richard's hand. "We were going nuts wondering what was going on. I kept having this nightmare that I was going to have to play either Margo or Bill depending on who came back. I'm Alyce, by the way. I'm playing Birdie."

"So Digby's gone?" Paige asked.

"That man is completely gone," Judith retorted. "I'd say he'd been that way for some years."

135

"They actually fired him so you'd stay?" Paige continued.

Judith regarded Paige as if she were the village idiot. "Of course."

Jennifer gave Richard a huge smile. "Hi, I'm Jennifer Hoffman. I'm playing Karen. Welcome to New York."

"Thank you. I'm delighted to be here."

Jennifer, thrilled to have the opportunity of adopting the formal English style rather than the American habit of self-introduction, personally introduced the rest of the cast to Richard. Richard, taking his cue from her, politely bowed to each person and shook hands.

Judith regarded this performance with faint amusement. "Christ, we've strayed into an Edwardian drawing room comedy. All we need is a young man with a croquet mallet, a butler serving afternoon tea and a stuttering Vicar." She looked at her watch. "We may as well do a line run if we can't get on stage. Where's Aubrey?"

"I saw him sitting in the orchestra," Paige said.

"Best place for him."

"In the orchestra?" Richard queried. "Are we doing a musical version? I didn't bring my tap shoes."

"What the British call the stalls seats, we Americans call the orchestra," Jennifer explained, overjoyed she could use her expertise of things English.

"So what do you call the place where the orchestra plays?"

"The pit."

"How very appropriate."

136

"And we normally call them the band rather than the orchestra. Orchestras play more classical music at like Carnegie Hall."

"Do you think we could stop the translation and tourism service and get on with the fucking line run?" Judith said.

Jennifer blushed. "Sorry."

Richard blew her a surreptitious kiss. Jennifer was so busy thinking how charming he was that Kyle had to nudge her to say her first line.

At 12pm the stage manager informed the cast that the stage would be available at two. This meant they needed to get lunch and be back at one to get into costumes, wigs and make-up.

While Judith demanded food be brought in for Rupert, Richard and herself, and Kyle and Paige ate previously prepared sandwiches, Alyce and Jennifer dashed next door to the Pizzeria.

"Richard is adorable," Jennifer said, as they shared a large pizza. "He's like the perfect English gentleman. I imagine him as the Lord of the Manor riding around an English county on a huge horse visiting his estate workers."

Alyce laughed. "You've read too many Thomas Hardy or Jane Austen novels. In case you haven't noticed, Richard is an actor."

"Maybe he's the black sheep of the family and there's an estate he'll inherit one day. In which case I shall insist on marrying him and becoming Lady Gresham, or is it Lady Jennifer? I always get muddled about that."

"Hon, don't get too overexcited. Even apart from the fact that he's doubtless only a struggling actor with no estate, he's also gay."

Jennifer stared at Alyce, a piece of pizza half way to her mouth. "No, don't say that, it's just his Englishness."

Alyce gently shook her head. "Look at Rupert. He's English through and through too, but compare them. Richard is definitely gay. Trust me."

"Damn it. All the best ones are."

"Besides, he's a little old for you."

"That's no problem – I just love that English manner. We could have a platonic marriage. That could have its merits, right?"

"That's not all it's cut out to be."

"Oh, God." Jennifer remembered about Nate in his wheelchair. Could he and Alyce have sex? "I'm such a klutz."

"It's fine. But you don't want a platonic marriage."

Jennifer sighed, knowing Alyce was right. "But he's gonna be a great Bill, isn't he? Even from the line run I could see why Judith hated Digby so bad. Richard has exactly the right quality. And he's gonna be able to actually play the piano in the party scene instead of using a musician. Maybe he's our lucky mascot. Now he's here it'll be perfect."

Alyce cut the last piece of pizza in two and took one half. "Amen to that."

Richard felt far from being a lucky mascot as he returned to the hotel that night. He'd forgotten exactly what working with Judith was like, and there was no doubt she was worse here than she had been in London. Presumably bringing an acclaimed show to Broadway was adding extra strain. She had to prove what all the fuss was about. When stage management had called a stop to rehearsals at 10pm, Judith demanded they continue. As far as she was concerned they were seriously behind schedule. It took all Rupert's tact and slight force, to persuade her to leave the theatre. On arriving at the hotel she marched from the car to her room without even saying goodnight.

"Welcome to Broadway," Rupert muttered to Richard, as he staggered to his room.

Richard, totally jet-lagged, could barely keep his eyes open. What was it in London now, 4am? There was an authoritative knock on his door. "Who is it?" he enquired with a slight apprehension, half-wondering if his visa had been revoked and he was about to be deported.

"It's Eve. Could we go over a couple of things?"

Eve? Richard thought drowsily. The only Eve he knew was the title character in... Then he remembered Rupert's mentioning Mindy's method acting. He peered through the peep hole and indeed there stood Mindy. Regretfully he opened the door. "Mindy, um, hello. Look, I'm not sure what it is you want but I should warn you I'm totally bushed and won't be much good to you. Could it wait until another time?"

"I'd prefer to do it now, Bill."

"Richard."

"I'd rather call you Bill. And I'd appreciate it if you could call me Eve."

Good grief, Richard thought, gesturing towards the chair. "Please sit down." He sat on the bed, wondering if he could fall asleep sitting up. "I'm sorry I can't offer you anything, but I'm afraid my cupboard is bare."

Mindy waved this aside as if eating and drinking were an irrelevance in life. She fixed her eyes on Richard. "You see, Bill, we can have a special bond; a bond which you and Margo don't have. I can take you places you've never been. Give you experiences you've never had."

"Um, OK. Thank you. That sounds..." Richard couldn't think for the life of him what it sounded. He made another effort. "I've never been to Brooklyn when I've been here before, or Queens or Long Island. Any of those would be pleasant."

"I had other experiences in mind."

"Boston?" Richard hedged. "Cape Cod?"

Mindy moved swiftly from the chair to join Richard on the bed, putting her hands on his shoulders and gazing into his eyes. "No, Bill. My career as an actress is about to take off on Broadway. I'm going to be the biggest star around. And you're hugely respected in the theatre. Together we can achieve great things, things which Margo can never provide. Just give us a chance to create magic. Margo is a has-been. I'm the story now. We could make a great team."

"Right."

"What do you say?"

Richard stared at her, having absolutely no idea what to say. "Could I tell you in the morning? I'll sleep on it."

Mindy moved her body against his. "If I slept with you, I could make it clearer."

"Christ no!" Richard pushed her away in revulsion. What kind of a crazy woman was this?

Mindy got off the bed and went to the door,

seemingly unperturbed by this rejection. "OK. I'll see you at the theatre, Bill." After she'd let herself out, Richard leapt up and put the chain across the door. What had he got himself into? He crawled into bed and pulled up the bed-clothes. He'd worry about it tomorrow. Tonight he was going to sleep. Within thirty seconds he was out cold, having forgotten to ask for an alarm call.

It was Rupert, banging on his door at 8.30am the next morning, which woke him. "I thought I'd check you were up. Judith's already left for the theatre. I'm afraid I chickened out of going in early too. Twelve hour days seem quite long enough without adding any more. How did you sleep?"

"I slept fine, but I had a very odd experience."

"Do I want to know?"

Richard recounted his encounter with Mindy, acting out the whole scene in great detail. "I think it actually happened but it was so surreal maybe I jet-lagged it."

"I'm sure it happened. Mindy is getting too into character. It's a bit worrying. But her per-formance is spot on, if still a little small."

"She knows I'm gay, doesn't she?"

"Ah, but you're not."

"I'm fairly sure I am."

Rupert laughed. "Yes, Richard Gresham is, but Bill Sampson isn't."

"Good grief. But she didn't seem bothered when I spurned her advances."

"No, well, Bill spurns Eve, doesn't he? You played the scene quite correctly."

"She wants an answer though. I said I'd give

it today."

"An answer to what?"

Richard shrugged. "I haven't the foggiest idea. It was something to do with us being a team. We don't have to do competitive sports, do we? Or go on those outings to the middle of some barren wasteland, to perform company morale boosting exercises?"

Rupert pulled a face, as if breaking bad news. "Yes, I'm afraid we do, it's some damn Broadway tradition." Richard's expression registered total horror. Rupert, trying not to laugh, added, "Judith's insisting on it. In fact, she's leading us all in a paintballing session after the rehearsal tonight in the middle of Central Park."

"You sod, Rupert. You had me going there for a second. Still, in case you're not joking, I want to be in Judith's team. I'd hate to be her enemy."

"Mindy will be disappointed when she asked you so nicely – and even offered to throw in sex. An offer I doubt Judith will match."

Richard clasped his hand to his head. "Lord, I'd almost forgotten about that. Please, don't leave me alone with her."

"I'll do my best. Now do you want to join me for breakfast? There's a great diner down the block if you can get ready quickly."

"Sure."

"I'll meet you in the lobby in ten minutes."

Judith let herself into her dressing room and ran her hands along the familiar costumes. She wished she'd insisted Wesley bring Fred, her English dresser, over. At least that way she'd feel confident about her costume changes if nothing else. The elderly female dresser she'd been given yesterday had walked out after Judith had screamed at her for being useless during every quick change. The wardrobe supervisor had promised to find another dresser for Judith to interview before the 10am call.

She held her favourite, a dark green silk dress with a full skirt and off-the-shoulder sleeves. "It's a beautiful frock," said a voice, from the open doorway. "Pure silk I'd say from here. A bugger to maintain, and specialized dry clean only, but classy. And the design is pure 1950s."

Judith regarded the grey haired man with glasses who had spoken. "And who are you?"

"I'm Tim. I've been sent to you for dresser inspection."

Judith sniffed. "How are you at quick changes?"

"I've never had any complaints. How are you with them?"

"I'm brilliant at everything. Have you dealt with divas before?"

"Did you know avids is an anagram of divas? Singularly appropriate I think. Most actors are avid about their careers."

"Can you go out and get me a coffee?"

"How do you take it?"

Judith nodded and reached in her bag for her purse, but Tim waved it away. "My treat. You won't have gotten the money right yet."

"Have you worked at this theatre before?"

"Sure. It's got quite a history. It was built in 1927, I think, but don't quote me. And it's been home to stars like Marlene Dietrich and Yul Brynner. When Shirley McLaine got her big break in *The Pyjama Game* from chorus girl to leading lady she was in the dressing room under the stage with all the other ensemble girls. The room your Rupert Blake is now occupying, in a single capacity. You see that window?" He pointed into the corner of the ante-room. Judith nodded, intrigued. "Yul Brynner's dresser used to help Marlene Dietrich to climb through that on to the fire escape outside for her secret trysts."

"Will you do the same for me with all my lovers? I warn you I have quantities of them."

"On condition you don't damage the costumes. One rip and you're grounded."

Judith slowly nodded. She liked Tim's dry humour. She got out a $20 bill. "I'm getting pretty good at this money thing, even for a stupid Brit. Get me that coffee, black, and get one for yourself. Then we'll go through the costume changes. You're hired."

The relief of finally working in the theatre produced a much needed boost for the cast, even though the size of the St James was daunting. There was an enormous distance from the stage to the very back of the balcony and, unlike musical shows where voices were amplified with microphones, straight plays relied on the actors' projection. Judith, whose projection could in all probability have filled a sports stadium, was the only person not to be personally worried, but she was worried about her fellow cast. On Wednesday she sent Aubrey to sit in the back row of the theatre to test their audibility. Aubrey listened to a few lines and then drifted off into a fantasy world of personal critical acclaim and Tony Awards. He returned to the real world only when Judith called up occasionally for a sound check, when he'd give affirmation of audibility before drifting off again.

The technical rehearsal was successfully completed by Thursday night although the Friday afternoon dress rehearsal was not so successful. Mindy, unused to theatre quick changes, missed two entrances while struggling into new costumes, refusing to let her dresser help. Apparently, since Eve didn't have a dresser neither could Mindy. Props were dropped or forgotten to be brought on, and at one point several lights started flashing giving the impression of a tacky disco.

The incident which brought the dress rehearsal to a complete standstill however, was the failure of the party set to come on at the correct time. The actors took their positions on stage, holding party drinks, and then had to dodge sofas and a massive grand piano as they belatedly whizzed on around them.

"Maybe I should enter draped on top of the piano," Richard said, as they were forced to stop. "I could play hanging down and distract from the flying scenery."

"You'd be like Michelle Pfeiffer in *The Fabulous Baker Boys*," Jennifer said.

"Ooh, do you think so?" Richard flicked back imaginary long hair, pouted and started to croon *Makin' Whoopee* in a high voice.

"That's more like Danny La Rue," Rupert commented.

"I know who that is, he's that English female

impersonator," Jennifer exclaimed.

Everybody jumped as a tray of party glasses was hurled towards them, courtesy of Judith. "We're supposed to be doing a fucking dress rehearsal not watching Richard present his cabaret act," she shrieked. "Or does nobody except me care that we open tomorrow night."

"It's not the official opening, Judith," Aubrey called up from the orchestra seats where he was making notes on the rehearsal, which Judith would doubtless ignore. "It's only a preview."

Judith swung round to glare at him. "And are those people tomorrow paying for their seats?"

"Well, yes."

"Full price?"

"Yes."

"But there aren't any critics in. Is that what you're saying?"

"Yes." Aubrey's voice expressed relief that she'd understood what he'd meant. "So you don't have to worry."

"Aubrey, let's drop the subject," Rupert said, having a good idea where Judith was heading and preferring not to go there.

"No, it's fine, Rupert. Judith understands." Aubrey gave a condescending smile. "Don't you, Judith?"

"Yes, I understand. I understand that you're a complete, utter fucking moron. I don't care about the critics. I care about giving the best show I can for whoever is out there. How dare you suggest that people who come to a preview don't deserve perfection? If I thought this show wasn't good enough to perform tomorrow night then I'd insist it was cancelled. And there's a

146

very good chance of that happening at present."

Aubrey shifted uncomfortably. If Judith insisted on the performance being cancelled then the producers would be furious and he would get the blame. He spoke very gently and slowly. "OK, Judith. I'm very sorry. I was wrong. Of course preview audiences are important."

"Don't patronize me, you cretin." Judith discovered a plate of food which had quietly slid on stage courtesy of the ASM now crouched behind the sofa. One by one a selection of canapés were hurled in Aubrey's direction.

"Judith, that's enough." Rupert said calmly, after Aubrey had been struck by several delicacies.

"No it's not. I haven't even started yet." Judith had run out of canapés and was eyeing the set for any other throw-friendly prop items. Luckily most of them were stuck down.

"Stage Management needs to re-set the party scene so they can try and bring it on correctly this time. I suggest we adjourn for fifteen minutes while they do so." Rupert placed his hand firmly on Judith's arm. After initial resistance she allowed him to guide her back to her room, where she sank down on to the bed.

"Jesus, Rupert, what's wrong with me? How could I have thrown those glasses? It's unforgivable to risk smashing props."

"You knew they were plastic. You wouldn't have thrown them otherwise."

"Wouldn't I?"

"No."

"It's all going wrong."

"It's only our first dress rehearsal. They're

147

supposed to be bad, remember: 'A bad dress rehearsal is the sign of a good performance'."

"That's such bollocks. It's some slogan invented by theatre managements to cover their fuck ups."

Rupert laughed. "Maybe, but it's going to be fine. Tonight's dress rehearsal will be much better."

"I don't want to talk about it anymore."

"OK." Rupert sat down in a chair, put his head back and closed his eyes. Judith did the same and neither spoke for the rest of the break.

While Aubrey spent the time demolishing what he could rescue of the rather good canapés Judith had lobbed at him, the American actors clustered around Richard in the wings as stage management worked on the set. "Was she that fearsome in England?" Paige asked.

"No, I think she's even more formidable this time – though it's a close call. In London we had the problem that she and our Eve were permanently at war. There were times I considered wearing a hard hat to avoid flying shrapnel."

"Why on earth did you agree to do it again?" Alyce asked. "Even presuming you're kidding about the shrapnel."

"I suppose working with Judith is a bit like giving birth – or so my female friends tell me. Once it's over you forget the pain and go back for more. Anyway, this is Broadway; I'd practically sleep with Judith to work here."

Rupert's optimism proved correct and both the dress rehearsals on Friday evening and Saturday afternoon went well, or, according to Judith, adequately. There was an hour before the first preview which most of the cast spent holed up in dressing rooms running through their lines. Rupert and Richard went out for some air and found the queue to get into their theatre stretching around the corner on to 8th Avenue. There was another queue, for return tickets, stretching the other way along 44th Street to the Helen Hayes Theatre next door.

"I know you have nerves of steel, Rupert, but aren't you even a little nervous about your Broadway debut?" Richard asked. "I certainly am."

"I'm wary, simply because there's so much riding on this, especially for Judith and Wesley."

"Don't you worry about forgetting a line or something going wrong?"

Rupert thought about it for a second. "Not really, I always imagine I'd improvise something. But I'm sure my laid-back attitude means I'm missing some special actor gene which would improve my performance."

"No, I think it means you're a lucky bugger."

Rupert's mobile rang. He answered it, listened for a few seconds, hung up and turned to Richard. "I'd better go back. Judith sounds borderline hysterical."

"I withdraw my comment about you being a lucky bugger."

In spite of Judith's pessimism the first preview went perfectly and the audience gave an ecstatic response with all of them on their feet as the curtain came down. The stage manager wanted the actors to take an extra bow but Judith refused. "Never milk it. Imagine if we went back on to find half the audience with their backs to us dashing up the aisle."

Tim had a large whisky waiting in Judith's dressing room. Even though she desperately wanted to go home, she sent him to invite the whole company to join her for a drink. That's how the leading member of a company behaved and Judith did everything by the book. "Well, that wasn't bad," she told them as they perched in her room clasping tumblers which Tim had conjured up. "But we have a long way still to go. I won't give notes before the matinee tomorrow, but we will be working during the days next week so don't make any plans."

Jennifer picked up a spoon and tapped it against her glass. "I'd like to make a toast to Judith for giving us the chance to be involved in *All About Eve*. Judging by the audience reaction tonight, I'm sure she'll make it the hit here she did in London. To Judith."

"To Judith." The company clinked glasses.

Aubrey made a sort of coughing noise. Jennifer blushed and hastily added, "And of course to Aubrey for his direction."

"To Aubrey," the company said, with less enthusiasm. Judith's glass remained resolutely on her dressing table.

As Judith picked up her coat five minutes later, a clear hint that the evening's socializing was at an end, the stage manager explained the leaving procedure. Metal barriers were placed in lines outside the stage door, so the actors could sign autographs in an orderly fashion. It didn't normally take more than five, maybe ten, minutes.

"Cool," Paige said. "Do you think they'll want mine?"

"They'll have to settle for it because they aren't getting mine," said Judith. "I have no intention of standing outside in the freezing cold signing for people who should get lives. I don't do autographs."

"But it's expected on Broadway," the stage manager almost stuttered, taken totally aback. "For a lot of the audiences it's part of the whole experience."

Judith gave him one of her looks which caused the man to take a step back, catch his foot on Richard's chair and nearly sprawl in the actor's lap. "I am not an exhibit, or a trained seal," Judith said. "I am an actress. I get up on stage and give an audience the best performance I can. It's not part of my job to perform in the street as well. And if you try to force me, I will do a Marlene Dietrich and climb down the fire escape with the help of my trusty dresser. End of discussion."

The throng of people behind the barriers, clasping *All About Eve* playbills and Sharpie pens, was massive. It stretched along the pavement and out into the road. There was even a policeman keeping a watchful eye on the crowd. As Judith emerged a cheer went up which turned into a disappointed groan as one barrier was pulled back to allow her to step straight into her limo and be driven off. Their patience was rewarded when both Rupert and Richard came out and signed for a good fifteen minutes.

"It feels surreal," Richard said, as they eventually finished. "We always had fans in London,

151

but this is like being a pop star."

"Come on then, Cliff Richard, do you want a lift?" Rupert offered. "Now the play's started I'm provided with my own chauffeured car."

Richard clasped his hand to his chest in mock horror. "Cliff Richard? I thought more Madonna, but yes please."

At the hotel they discovered Judith at the front desk, requesting another key card. "Are you expecting company?" Rupert enquired.

"No, I lost mine. I forget things. Is that a problem?" She snatched the new key card from the receptionist and stalked off towards the lift. She let herself into her room, threw down her bag and collapsed on to the bed where she fell almost instantly asleep, only waking when she kicked her left shin with her right shoe. As she pulled the offending shoes off, she concluded that there had to be an easier way to make a living.

CHAPTER TEN

Following the next day's Sunday matinee, the last performance before a well deserved Monday off for the exhausted company, the stage manager called into Judith's room as she was removing her make-up. "I'm not signing autographs," she snapped.

"Actually we have another problem. I thought you should know."

"Yes?"

The man looked wary and took several deep breaths before he spoke. "There were complaints from the balcony about inaudibility. Several people demanded a refund."

Judith spun away from the mirror to look at him properly. "Was it me?"

"No, not at all. You could be heard anywhere."

"Who was it? Or was it more than one?"

"I wasn't sure if you were the person to talk to." Judith glared at him, leaving him in no doubt that she was. "It was Mindy. Apparently they could hardly hear her at all."

"Damn it!" Judith slammed her fist down on the dressing table. "Get me Rupert, Aubrey and Wesley, now. I don't care how you get them here, just get them. And do you have contact details of the audience who demanded their money back?"

"We always ask for a phone number when people book seats."

"Good. Get their addresses. I want a letter of

apology to go out to every one along with an invitation to come again for free."

"But there are hardly any seats left for the entire run."

"Find some. Sling hammocks from the ceiling if necessary. I won't have anyone going away dissatisfied from any play I'm in."

"What about the audience from last night?"

Judith gripped her cleanser tightly, tempted to throw it at this excuse for a stage manager. "There were complaints last night too?"

"A few, but I didn't want to bother you on your first preview. I thought it might get better."

"Get out!" The bottle of cleanser flew across the room, catching the stage manager on the arm. He gawped at Judith, amazed. He'd had to deal with some temperamental actors in the past but nobody had ever thrown things at him. He left hastily in search of Rupert, Wesley and Aubrey.

Rupert, being already on the premises, was there within a couple of minutes, still pulling on his own clothes. Wesley, having watched the performance, was only a couple of blocks away, while Aubrey, who was supposed to be watching the performance but instead had slipped across the road to watch *The Phantom of The Opera,* arrived last. God, he hoped Judith didn't know he hadn't been watching her play or there'd be hell to pay.

"About fucking time," Judith shrieked at him as soon as he entered.

Aubrey looked nervously at Wesley for a clue. The producer ignored him. "Is there a problem?" Aubrey hedged.

"No. We have a leading actress who can't be heard, but why should that be a problem?"

"You can't be heard?" Aubrey was amazed. How could anybody not hear Judith?

"Not me you simpleton, Mindy."

"Sorry, you said leading actress so I presumed..."

"Why did I even bother summoning you? I'll sort it out myself. Tim!" Tim, who'd been in the ante-room, emerged. "Get Mindy in here."

"Judith, I don't think that's a good idea," Rupert said. "Wait until you've calmed down a bit."

"Calmed down? I doubt I'm ever going to calm down. Tim, go." Tim went.

"Rupert's right," Wesley said. "We're all exhausted and stressed. Let's go home, get some rest and work on it next week. We'll get Mindy some more voice coaching."

"Do you actually believe I'll be able to get any rest in these circumstances?" Judith glared around at the three men. "You're all fucking useless."

There was a knock at the door and Mindy came in. "You wanted to see me, Margo."

"It's Judith! Judith! Judith!" Judith's face was directly against Mindy's. "If you spent a little less time method acting and more time being comprehensible to the audience it would be most beneficial."

"I'm sorry, I don't understand."

At this point Rupert's mobile rang, displaying his London landline number. He answered it quickly, putting his hand over his other ear in an attempt to drown out Judith's tantrum.

"Holly, can I call you back? We're in the middle of a slight crisis."

"Oh." He could hear the disappointment in her voice. "Yes, of course."

Rupert hung up and went back to trying to act as arbitrator.

"I am trying real hard," Mindy was saying. "But I don't feel it's in Eve's nature to shout."

"Fuck Eve! And it's not about shouting – it's about projecting. That's what actors do. I can whisper on stage and still be heard in every seat in the theatre."

"I'm sorry if I'm letting you down."

"It's not me you're letting down, it's the paying audience who can't follow the play because, to them, you are playing the role as a mute. Perhaps we can sell the balcony to lip readers only."

Rupert frowned as his London number flashed up again on his ringing mobile. "Holly, I'm sorry it's still a bit crazy..."

"It's not Holly, it's Victor. And I don't care what crisis that woman of mine is demanding you deal with, you need to talk to your girlfriend now."

Rupert felt a sudden panic. "What's wrong? Is Holly OK?"

"I do realize Judy brainwashes everybody around her, but think. It's Sunday night, I'm sitting with Holly in your house having just escorted her to a major theatrical event. Mean anything?"

"Oh bugger, bugger, bugger."

"I'll pass you back to Holly, shall I?" Victor said wryly.

There was a clunk and then Holly's voice.

"Hello?"

"Sweetheart, I cannot believe I forgot. I am so, so sorry. I'm a complete bastard. What happened?"

Holly cleared her throat. "Your best actor Olivier statue now has a best actress one to keep it company."

"You won?"

"Apparently, although I keep expecting somebody to tell me there's been a mistake and I have to take the award over to Harriet Walter's house immediately."

"Holly, that is fan-bloody-tastic. I'm totally over the moon. And proud beyond belief and gutted I couldn't be there. I want to hear every single detail. I feel like a total shit that I didn't remember."

"It's OK. I can hear you're in the middle of something. I wouldn't have minded waiting, but Victor insisted on calling you back."

"I'm very glad he did. How long ago did you get the award?"

"About two hours. It's 11pm here now."

"And you waited until now to call me?"

"Yes."

Rupert sighed. "Because you were hoping I'd call you."

"Not really. Anyway it doesn't matter when you know. You know now."

"It does matter. It was unforgivable."

"Will you get off the fucking phone? We've got a catastrophe to deal with." Judith was shouting down his other ear.

"Hang on a second, Holly." Rupert put his hand over the mouth piece. "Judith, thanks to

157

this play I forgot about the Olivier Awards and when Holly called to try and tell me the result I hung up because I was too caught up with yet another problem. So I would appreciate it if I could talk to her without your demanding my attention for a few minutes."

"Oh." Judith didn't appear in the least contrite. "I trust she won?"

Rupert's face broke into a delighted grin. "Yes, apparently we've got his and hers Olivier Awards."

"Most people settle for matching towels. And take that smug expression off your face. You didn't win an award. And if this play goes on like this you're not going to stand a chance of doing so. We need to resolve this matter."

"I'm sure you will, but at present you'll have to do so without me." Rupert replaced the phone to his ear and left the room.

"Well, really, that's not very helpful," Aubrey said, hoping he could get into Judith's good books while Rupert was out of them.

Judith eyed him contemptuously. "Oh, do be quiet, you miserable little worm." She turned to Mindy. "I want you in the theatre first thing tomorrow and we're going to work on your projection until they can hear you at *Phantom of the Opera*. Perhaps that way Aubrey would be able to comment."

Aubrey opened his mouth to plead ignorance of Judith's accusation but Judith held up her hand to stop him. "You should realize by now, I know everything." Judith had actually simply seen the playbill for *The Phantom of the Opera* poking out of Aubrey's coat pocket, but she didn't think she'd spoil the illusion of having spies everywhere. It might stop him playing hooky again on further previews. Technically his attendance made no difference to her, but it was the principle. Directors should attend every performance up to, and including, press nights and odd performances after that too.

"Judith, the theatre isn't open on Mondays," Wesley said. "It's everybody's day off."

"Then open it. Now piss off the lot of you. I want to send some flowers to Holly."

Judith worked with Mindy for five hours on Monday, alternating between sitting in the balcony shouting that Mindy couldn't be heard, and standing on stage trying to demonstrate how she could improve her projection.

"It's not going to work, is it?" Judith hissed to Wesley. They were both wandering around the theatre listening for any sound dead spots. "I can't teach her something in one day the rest of us have been working on for years."

Wesley rubbed his chin. "We could mic her," he suggested and then moved away as Judith told him exactly what he could do with that idea. "Just one of those small microphones they use in musicals. It could go in her wig and nobody would see it."

"Yes, they would. The battery packs are worn around the waist and the leads go up the back and neck. In case you haven't noticed, Eve has several dresses with low backs. If there's a fucking great wire clinging to her spine the audience will either realize she's wearing a microphone or think we're using her as a human lightning conductor. I won't have it in my play. It's too humiliating."

"What about float microphones on the front of the stage? We could disguise them somehow."

"Oh wonderful, so the audience will finally be able to hear Mindy, but they'll be deafened by the rest of us. Or do you suggest we all go down to her level? Try it again," she screamed at Mindy.

Mindy did it again, and again. She never gave up. Wesley was amazed at her tenacity. Judith found it plain creepy.

Judith looked around her. "Where the hell's Rupert? There was no answer in his room earlier and I've been leaving messages all day. I want his input."

Wesley said nothing, silently envying, and admiring, Rupert's refusal to work on his day off. "If Judith asks where I am," he'd said to Wesley earlier, "tell her I've had an overwhelming desire to go skydiving."

Kyle's phone rang early on Monday evening as he was playing dominoes with his children. Much to his surprise it was the dreaded Krystal, calling, thankfully, from California. In her slow deliberate drawl it took so long to discover what she wanted that his children had built a domino road between his feet by the time he'd hung up.

"Who was that?" Lauren asked, as he carefully extracted himself. "You don't look happy."

"Mindy's acting coach. Apparently, Judith's had Mindy in the theatre all day working on her projection and she's exhausted and in a terrible state but wouldn't give way in front of Judith.

Mindy told Krystal that I was the only person to have been kind to her."

"That'll teach you. Next time be a total bastard. So what does she want you to do about it?"

"She's worried Mindy is getting close to a breakdown. She wants me to go over there."

"Are you going?"

"I don't want to, but I'm not sure I have much choice."

Lauren frowned. "Can't someone else go? What about this Rupert guy. You said he solves everything?"

Kyle shook his head. "That wouldn't be fair. He has enough on his plate already. It's everybody's night off so I'd feel bad passing the buck."

"Honey, please don't go. We never see you at the moment. And I promised the kids you'd put them to bed tonight."

Kyle seeing the two pairs of hopeful eyes gazing up at him agreed to call Jennifer, who didn't have a family, lived nearer to Mindy and was sensible and kind.

Jennifer agreed, hoping she didn't sound too reluctant. Kyle's assurance that he owed her one merely made her wish it had been Rupert who'd asked the favour.

The doorman at Mindy's apartment block had to repeat Jennifer's name twice into the phone to Mindy, which did little for Jennifer's enthusiasm for her mission. Perhaps Mindy was disappointed that it wasn't Kyle, although she opened her door with a smile and led Jennifer into the living room. Jennifer couldn't believe the size and elegance of the place. What it was to be a famous movie star and have people

161

provide luxury apartments for you.

"It's very good of you to come," Mindy said. "But I feel real bad that Krystal called. She worries too much about me, though that's kinda nice."

Jennifer wasn't sure whether Krystal worried too much about Mindy as a person or as her illustrious client. "I'm sorry you've had such a bad day with Judith," she said, carefully sitting down on a cream chair and hoping she didn't knock something on to it. "It must be pretty scary being alone on stage with only her."

Mindy hugged her arms around her. "It's OK. Only I hate the idea of her disapproval. I want to please her so much, learn so much, but nothing I do is good enough. Could you help me, Karen? Help me to please her?"

"I'll try," Jennifer replied, still finding Mindy's insistence on using characters' names disconcerting. "What can I do?"

"You could be my friend."

"Sure."

Mindy reached over and squeezed Jennifer's hand. "Thank you. Perhaps you could help me with my projection too. I've done all the vocal exercises but Margo says I still can't be heard. It's all about breathing, right?"

For two hours Jennifer patiently worked with Mindy, and without Judith's vociferous criticism she did make progress, but there was still no question of her voice reaching the back of the St James Theatre.

By Tuesday afternoon Judith had to admit defeat and Mindy was issued with a microphone. But to ensure the audience's ignorance of this unspeakable aid, Judith insisted that those costumes in which the lead would show be covered with shawls.

"They're not very period," Tim commented as he and Judith looked through an assortment the costume supervisor had managed to acquire with no notice. "Or very Hollywood. They look more like Mexican national costume."

"What do you suggest?"

"Fur stoles. Paige wears one as Miss Caswell for the party and another at the audition. Why can't Mindy have those for the present? Paige doesn't have a wire to hide so can wear the dress only for the party and a full fur for the audition."

"But I wear a full fur for that scene," Judith protested. "We'll look like fucking twins."

"Hmm. You know, I think I can lay my hands on an authentic fox fur, which you could put over your coat."

"Should I ask how?"

"It's probably better if you don't."

Judith gave a glimmer of a smile. "Just ensure it's been dead at least twenty four hours. If it's still moving I'm not touching it."

The sound operator, brought in at exceedingly short notice, was given a script with Mindy's lines, entrances and exits marked. With no time to rehearse and no knowledge of the play his only option was to turn the microphone up as Mindy entered and off as she exited. It was hardly ideal, but it would have to do.

Wesley sat in the mezzanine with his fingers crossed as the curtain rose, but, to his great relief, everything seemed to work perfectly. Mindy's amplified voice reached every seat in the theatre at the same volume as the other actors. Unfortunately, this system began to unravel during the fourth scene when Eve starts to ingratiate herself into Margo's life and consequently into closer proximity to the cast. As Mindy leant over Judith, handing her a letter, Judith projected her lines within an inch of Mindy's microphone, which obligingly picked Judith's words up and resonated them around the theatre. Judith, hearing her voice echoing back from the auditorium was completely thrown. Glancing into the wings she could see Rupert motioning at her. Leaving a surprised Mindy standing over a now empty chair, Judith wandered casually over to the wings while she spoke her next line.

"You're being picked up on Mindy's mic," Rupert hissed. "Don't get too close to her."

Judith played the rest of the scene, and the rest of Act One, at a sizeable distance from her co-star.

"Jesus," she swore as she came off in the interval, "I cannot work like this. Now everybody is going to think I'm wearing the bloody mic."

All assurances that they'd iron out the problem did nothing to appease Judith. The very notion that anybody might believe she was being amplified was horrifying to her.

"We could take out a page in the *New York Times* denying it," Aubrey said, attempting to be helpful. Judith stared at him, shook her head in disbelief and walked away. Aubrey watched her go, puzzled. "What did I say?"

"What didn't you say?" Rupert replied.

*   *   *

"At least there were no complaints about inaudibility tonight," Wesley said, standing in Judith's dressing room after the show.

Judith stared gloomily at her reflection in the mirror. "That's all right then. We all look completely stupid, but at least Mindy can be heard. Super duper! The fact that Eve resembled a pariah because nobody dared go too near her obviously didn't matter." She slapped cleansing cream on her face and started to rub it in.

"Judith, it will get better."

"Will it? Why can't things ever go right? Why am I stuck with a cast of incompetents? I had one who couldn't act and now one who can't be heard. Doesn't anybody check these things? Or is a pin merely stuck at random in the idiot's guide to casting?"

There was a knock on the door. "Fuck off," Judith shouted.

"OK."

"Oh, Rupert, come in. I thought it was Aubrey, although he's probably off watching fucking *Wicked* tonight."

Wesley gratefully took Rupert's entrance as his cue to leave. Rupert stood directly behind Judith so he was looking at her in the mirror. "Nice clown make-up," he commented, at her white face.

"So now I'm a clown who appears to be using a microphone." Judith wiped the cleanser off with angry sweeping motions.

"It wasn't that bad."

"Yes it was. It was awful. I've never been so humiliated."

"Judith, you can't be responsible for your co-

165

stars' failings."

"I'm responsible for everything about this play."

"You shouldn't be. Let other people help."

"They'll only fuck it up." She sighed and leant her head forward on to the dressing table. "But honestly, I'm so tired of everything being a battle."

Rupert perched on top of the dressing table and started to rub her shoulders. Immediately Judith tensed and started to sit up. "Relax," Rupert instructed, pushing her back down. "It's like steel in there."

Judith started to say that was none of his business, but decided she was too tired to fight. Besides, it was fairly pleasant. "Another one of your bloody talents," she muttered, turning her head towards him.

"Will you keep still and enjoy it." Rupert stood up so he could work on the tension in her back better. His massage expertise was more on the sensual side than the medical, but even he could feel Judith was incredibly tense. He pulled her shoulders up and then released them, expecting them to flop back down. They didn't.

"What makes you think I'm enjoying this, anyway?" Judith demanded.

Rupert gently pressed her shoulders back down and continued kneading them with his thumbs. "I've never had any complaints."

"Now there's a surprise. But don't think that means I'm as easy as your usual conquests!" Rupert laughed and carried on working. There was silence for a few minutes.

"Just imagine if that odious Digby could see

this," Judith said eventually, sounding half asleep. "Then he'd really believe we were having an affair."

"So I shouldn't send him a copy of the video footage I'm taking?"

"What?" Judith sat up violently to find Rupert grinning. "You bastard!"

CHAPTER ELEVEN

Richard had just got out of the shower on Thursday morning when there was a knock on his door. Rupert was standing there, wearing a dressing gown, and waving an open copy of the *New York Post*, which he thrust into Richard's hand, before throwing himself down on the bed and closing his eyes while Richard scanned the article.

New York Post: Entertainment Latest. Following stories of backstabbing, bitchery and the mysterious departure of one cast member on *All About Eve,* the latest UK theatre import to hit our shores, there is now a question as to the use of microphones. Unlike musicals this is not usual practice for a straight play, yet in recent previews audiences have reported occasional volume swings as if a microphone was being switched on and off. Could it be renowned English actress Judith Gold cannot project to the back of our Broadway houses? A spokesman for the production refused to comment.

"Jesus," Richard said.

Rupert raised himself up on his elbow. "My thoughts exactly. I was thinking of leaving the country when I first read it."

"I didn't know you were a *New York Post* reader."

"I'm not, but Holly devours it online in case there's a mention of any of us. With the time difference she reads it at lunch time when it's just coming out here. She phoned to warn me, and I in turn phoned Wesley."

Richard eyed Rupert's attire. "And you popped out to buy a copy of it dressed like that? I had no idea nightwear was an outdoor fashion statement in Manhattan."

"No, strangely I had the front desk send up a copy."

"Ah, you see us plebs aren't used to such grand accommodation. You're lucky to get loo paper in a B & B in Bognor."

"Have you ever actually stayed in a B & B in Bognor?"

Richard laughed. "Maybe not in Bognor but I've certainly stayed in some pretty grim digs on tour." He glanced at the paper again. "Judith is going to be livid."

"Yes."

"What?" Richard demanded, noticing Rupert eyeing him with a thoughtful expression. "I don't have to tell her, do I? Please don't make me. I've finally made it to Broadway – I don't want to die before I can enjoy it!"

Rupert chuckled. "No, I'll tell her. But I was hoping you'd go on David Letterman's show with me."

"David Letterman, as in *The Late Show with David Letterman*?"

"That's the one. We must scotch the rumours about Judith wearing a mic otherwise it'll destroy her. A retraction in the *Post* won't make much difference, nobody ever reads those, but Letterman's show is hugely influential. They've been asking me and Judith to appear on it since we arrived, but Judith won't, so I thought you could make up the English contingent."

"But they wouldn't know who I was. They'd announce my name and the audience would all be muttering 'who?' That would make lousy TV."

"You were brought over to save the show. That would make great TV."

"What would I say about that? I wasn't even here when it happened."

"We'll work out answers to everything they might ask. There's a pre-interview to run through the basic line of questioning. But it's not like being interviewed by Jeremy Paxman. It's basically a comedy show, and they want entertainment. You're entertaining."

"You know how to flatter a chap. When would we do it?"

"Ah." Rupert regarded Richard with a slightly guilty expression. "Actually, they're pulling something to fit us in tonight. Our producers wanted any damage done by the *Post* kept to a minimum by a quick defence."

Richard swallowed. "Tonight? After the show?"

"No, it's pre-recorded late afternoon and aired after the show." He glanced at his watch. "So we'd have to be there in about four hours. Are you interested?"

"Just try stopping me. It gets broadcast in England too, doesn't it? Where's my phone?" He grabbed it from beside the bed and waved it at Rupert. "I'm going to make some old queens over the pond insanely jealous."

In spite of their prepared answers and the pre-

170

interview before the recording, Richard felt a sudden panic as David Letterman wound up the interview with his previous guest: a TV actress plugging an exercise DVD she'd made. He took a deep breath and shivered. This was partly nerves and partly because it was kept purposely cold in the studio as apparently comedy worked better in a cool environment. For the pre-interview he and Rupert had kept their coats on. Richard prayed he wouldn't let the show down by being horribly dull. He glanced at Rupert standing calmly beside him and was grateful it had been agreed that Rupert would answer any awkward questions. He could relax and be himself.

What Rupert and Wesley had kept from Richard was how opposed CBS and Letterman's production company had been to his appearance on the show. Since Judith had turned them down flat they'd requested Mindy, but under the circumstances that seemed a less than good idea, and Rupert flatly refused to do it on his own, which was their third preference. Finally the programme's researcher turned up a small piece of information which persuaded the network that Richard could prove a satisfactory guest.

"Please welcome, Rupert Blake and Richard Gresham," David Letterman's voice echoed back to them and the floor manager gave them their cue. Richard followed Rupert on to the Letterman set to the cheers of the studio audience. They sat side by side in small arm chairs, Rupert next to David Letterman's desk, with the New York City backdrop behind them. The interview started in safe waters: How had the play come about? How did it feel performing on Broadway as opposed to London? Were the audiences different? Rupert answered most of the questions, since he'd been involved since the very beginning in both London and New York. Letterman cracked a joke about the English taking over Broadway. Then he looked directly at Richard.

"How do you feel about replacing Digby Weston? Those are big shoes to fill. At least a size twelve I'd guess."

Richard briefly considered the *All About Eve* producers' carefully worded answer: how sad it had been that Digby Weston had felt uncomfortable in the role and how humbled he was to get the chance to appear on Broadway. But then he thought, to hell with it. This was supposed to be entertainment. "Well, I believe I'm an American size thirteen so you could say I out-shoe him. And while I'm absolutely over the moon to be here I think the man is a complete idiot."

There was a gasp from the studio audience and Rupert gave him a quizzical glance. "And I thought the English were a reserved race," David Letterman commented, removing his trademark glasses in one smooth movement and tapping them on his desk. "So let's review. Digby Weston has been quoted as saying Judith Gold treated him appallingly which is why he left, but you're saying he's an idiot."

"It appears that way, doesn't it? Am I going to get dragged off the show for bad behaviour?"

"No!" yelled out a member of the audience, causing David Letterman to hold up his hands in mock surrender, before continuing the interview.

"But Richard, I believe I'm correct in saying you weren't actually around when Digby Weston quit, so on what are you basing your very candid opinion?"

"I know Judith, and I know how she works, and if Mr Weston was unwilling to follow her lead then I'm afraid I do think he's an idiot."

"You don't consider Judith Gold could be in the wrong?"

"No. Her vision of this play is the reason it's been such a success. If one person in the cast tries to fight that vision, it throws the entire play out of kilter."

"Surely the director is the one who has a vision, not the leading actress? Certainly all the directors I know think they're in charge," David Letterman quipped.

"Ah, I notice you said 'think they're in charge'," Richard quipped back, receiving a laugh from the audience and a nod of acknowledgement from David Letterman.

"So you're saying your director," David Letterman replaced his glasses and glanced at his notes, "Aubrey Henson, is merely a puppet whose strings are pulled by Judith Gold."

"You might think that, but I couldn't possibly comment," Richard said. Wesley, watching from off camera, put his head in his hands.

"Judith and Aubrey have an excellent working relationship," Rupert broke in.

"Yes, she tells him what she wants and he does it." Richard was flying.

"And vice versa," Rupert added, surreptitiously kicking Richard's foot.

"Oh, yes of course. Aubrey's a real rock. Completely solid and always hanging around when there's a crisis. And he's very much loved – especially by the hot dog and pretzel vendor outside the theatre who is about to retire to Florida on Aubrey's kind donations."

This was too much for Rupert's restraint and he grabbed one of the blue Letterman mugs filled with water from the desk beside him and took a mouthful to try and hide his laughter.

"Since you and Judith Gold get on so well, might she purposely have made life miserable for Digby Weston in order that he would resign and you could replace him?" David Letterman was going off script and enjoying this interview enormously.

"I'd adore to think that; it's every gay actor's dream."

"So you're gay?"

Richard looked around the studio. "Am I not allowed to mention that on network TV?"

"No, that's fine. It's just unusual for such an open declaration."

"Have you never met Ian McKellen?"

"So even though you're gay, Judith Gold doesn't have a problem with you playing her lover."

Richard leant over Rupert and put his elbow on David Letterman's desk as if to privately confide in him. "It's called acting," he whispered loudly enough to be picked up by the whole studio.

"Now there has been some speculation regarding the use of microphones," David Letterman said, returning to his prepared questions.

174

"Is there any truth in this?"

Richard leaned back in his chair and let Rupert answer the question. "Yes, we have had to temporarily resort to using a microphone," Rupert said. "But we're talking about a microphone, singular. Unfortunately, Mindy Blue, our Eve Harrington, strained her vocal cords during rehearsals. Being a true professional, she didn't want to miss any performances, so it was deemed best that she use a microphone until she is fully recovered, rather than risk further damage to her voice."

David Letterman was disappointed. There wasn't much fun to be had with such a dull explanation. He tried to probe further, enquiring why Judith's voice had been the amplified one, and Rupert ran through the explanation stating, truthfully, that the technical issues had now been resolved.

"And do you agree with Richard's opinion that Digby Weston was an idiot?" David Letterman asked Rupert.

"I think it was a shame he felt unhappy," Rupert replied, carefully. "But I believe he did make some bad choices."

"And you're enjoying working with Richard instead?"

Rupert grinned at his co-star. "It's certainly entertaining."

"That I can imagine." David Letterman turned to the audience. "Now, Richard has a special talent which he uses in the role, isn't that correct, Richard?"

"None which I think I should mention on TV," Richard said, unsure what was being referred to, but winking at the audience anyway who roared with laughter.

David Letterman gestured to where a piano was being pushed into the centre of the studio. "During one scene Richard's character, Bill Sampson, plays the piano with great aplomb." David Letterman hadn't actually seen the play, relying on his researchers to provide information. "It seems Richard is a talented pianist and singer. So for the show's usual musical slot we'd like Richard to perform live for us."

Richard stared at the piano and then at Rupert, who shrugged at him. This had not been mentioned in the pre-interview. Oh well, what the hell. He took off his jacket and rolled up his sleeves. It wasn't that he couldn't play with a jacket on and his sleeves rolled down, but he felt it was the way a pianist was expected to behave.

Next there was the question of what to play, since recreating the number from *All About Eve* seemed uninspired. Since he was a Brit on Broadway perhaps it should be music with a British flavour. A few years earlier he'd appeared in *Noel and Gertie*, a musical based on the relationship between Noel Coward and Gertrude Lawrence, for which he'd received excellent reviews ('Richard Gresham is as like Noel Coward as he can be, considering he bears him little physical resemblance: *The Stage Newspaper*'), surely this was the ideal opportunity to recreate a part of that show. So, sat at a piano in a TV studio on Broadway, Richard gave his rendition of *Mad Dogs and Englishmen*, *Some Day I'll Find You* and *Don't Put Your Daughter on the Stage, Mrs Worthington.*

Enjoying the acclaim these songs brought to an audience mostly unacquainted with them, Richard progressed to a different musical British genre – the pantomime song sheet, specifically *My Bonnie Lies Over the Ocean.*

Having got the bemused yet enthusiastic audience word perfect Richard turned to his co-star. "Rupert, could you split the audience into two groups?"

Rupert, having given up any pretence of normality in this interview, divided the delighted audience, trailed by a bewildered cameraman.

A battle then ensued, with each side trying to prove they had the stronger voices as they took turns to sing. For a nation unacquainted with pantomime but steeled in competitiveness, they cottoned on quickly.

Richard had one further challenge for them. "On every word beginning with the letter 'B' you have to stand up, and on the next 'B' you sit down again," he explained. "You too, Dave," he called to David Letterman.

The audience started with confidence; with only one word per line starting with a 'B', it was a piece of cake.

"My Bonnie lies over the ocean,
My Bonnie lies over the sea,
My Bonnie lies over the ocean,"
Richard grinned as he played on.
"Oh bring back my Bonnie to me." There was a mad scuffle to leap up and down.
"Bring back, bring back,
Oh bring back my Bonnie to me, to me.
Bring back, bring back,

Oh bring back my Bonnie to me." The audience were bobbing up and down in increasing hysteria realizing, as many English pantomime audiences had realized before them, that on standing their seats flipped shut, making it virtually impossible to sit down before jumping back up.

As Richard finished the last chord with a flourish and Rupert clapped an exhausted, but euphoric audience, David Letterman came out from behind his desk and shook both their hands. "Thank you for coming on the show tonight. I can confidently say it's been an evening unlike any other."

The audience applauded, cheered and stamped their feet as Rupert and Richard walked backstage. Rupert collapsed into the nearest chair, almost unable to speak with laughter. "Remind me why we spent four hours preparing for this interview," he finally managed to say.

Richard grimaced. "Do you think that's the end of my Broadway career?"

"Judging by that response it's most likely the start. You'll doubtless get your own cabaret spot somewhere. Or you could be the person to establish pantomime here."

"I could do a mean dame."

"That I don't doubt."

"What about *All About Eve*? Do you think the producers will fire me?"

"Possibly – if we had another Bill Sampson waiting in the wings."

"Oops!" Richard looked only slightly shamefaced.

In the studio David Letterman was winding

up the show before the CBS Orchestra struck up the closing theme.

"Wasn't there another guest on after us?" Rupert asked one of the Letterman floor managers.

"There was, but they left once Richard started playing, claiming he was an impossible act to follow. Can't say I blame them, it was... remarkable. It's going to make a great show tonight. There's a car outside to take you to the theatre when you're ready."

"We're ready," Rupert said, before Richard could suggest anything else.

The programme didn't go out until eleven thirty, after *All About Eve* had finished. Suggesting they watch it together, Jennifer invited the whole cast back to her apartment. Judith declined on the grounds that she disapproved of the whole interview concept, and Mindy declined on the grounds that if Margo wasn't going then Eve couldn't either.

The others threw themselves into the evening. Jennifer produced bowls of popcorn and potato chips, while Kyle, Alyce and Paige brought wine and beer, so by the time the establishing shot of The Ed Sullivan Theater appeared on the screen everyone was distinctly merry.

"Get off, we want Rupert and Richard," Paige shouted, throwing popcorn at the screen where the TV actress was holding her DVD up to the camera and fluttering her eyelids at David Letterman. Kyle was busy blowing up inflatable sticks, normally used for cheering on sports teams, and as Rupert and Richard joined David

179

Letterman the sticks were waved around while each of their answers were received with more waving and cheers.

"You Americans are crazy," Richard said. "I love you all."

Another cheer went up as Rupert praised his American co-stars. "You just wait," Rupert told them "You ain't seen nothing yet."

"How do you feel about replacing Digby Weston? Those are big shoes to fill. At least a size twelve I'd guess." David Letterman asked Richard on the screen. The room fell silent.

"Oh dear," Richard muttered in the slight silence before his answer was broadcast. "Well, I believe I'm an American size thirteen so you could say I out-shoe him. And while I'm absolutely over the moon to be here I think the man is a complete idiot."

"Oh my God," Paige squealed, before she was shushed by the others agog for the rest of the interview.

"Oh dear," Richard said again, in the first commercial break. "I thought they'd cut more than they did."

"They did bleep over a couple of your more choice phrases," Rupert pointed out.

"You were wonderful," Alyce said. "They obviously thought so too which is why they haven't cut much."

Kyle was laughing more than anyone had ever seen him. "I loved the remark about Aubrey and the pretzel vendor. It's a classic."

"Do you think he's watching?" Jennifer asked, with a frown. "He might be awfully hurt."

Rupert squeezed her arm. "Don't worry. He'll

180

survive. In fact he'll doubtless be thrilled to have been mentioned at all."

Paige pointed at the screen. "The show's starting again. Why are they pushing on that piano?"

Richard put his head in his hands. "I'm not sure I can watch."

"That has to be the best edition of David Letterman ever," Alyce said, wiping tears of laughter from her eyes sometime later, as the end credits rolled.

"Hear, hear," said Jennifer.

Kyle stood up. "I must get home. My wife has been on single parent duty all day and night. But you were completely brilliant, Richard. In future I shall regard you in a different light."

"I've been told I look my best in a complete black out," Richard said.

"I'd heard it was in red light," Rupert retorted.

"That all depends on who you talk to."

"You guys are like a comedy show," Jennifer said. "Both on TV and off."

"He's Morecombe and I'm Wise," Rupert said.

Jennifer waved her inflatable stick excitedly. "I love them. They're so whacky."

Kyle bade a general farewell, and Alyce also excused herself and left with him. The others continued drinking and chatting until Rupert and Richard too called it a night. They insisted Paige join them in their cab and, once they'd reached their hotel, paid the driver to take her on to Queens.

At the front desk a message was waiting for them: *My room, now. Judith*

Richard looked at Rupert. "Lord, I feel I've

been summoned to the headmaster's study to get six of the best. I suppose that means I'm showing my age and you have no idea what I'm talking about."

"You'd be surprised," Rupert said, so curtly that Richard was taken aback. Almost immediately Rupert was smiling again, "Come on, let's get it over with."

"She's hardly going to be angry with you. You behaved perfectly."

"I did conduct the audience in a song sheet," Rupert pointed out as they reached Judith's door.

Judith opened the door, glaring at the two of them. "What did you think you were doing?"

"Mea culpa," Richard said, falling to his knees in the corridor. "I got carried away."

"Get up," Judith snapped.

"I might need a hand; I'm getting too old for these gestures."

"Oh honestly," Judith snapped, as Rupert helped Richard to his feet. "And come inside before somebody sees you."

The men sat down on the bed catching each other's eyes like school boys. Judith went to the fridge, opened it and a few seconds later there was a pop and Judith was waving a bottle of champagne at them and holding out glasses.

"What on earth's this for?" Rupert enquired, taking a glass and passing another to Richard.

"Fuck knows," Judith replied, pouring out the champagne. "This was supposed to be a damage limitation exercise, with your responses carefully worked out, and yet Richard starts improvising. You should be shot." She gave a brief smile. "But I took great pleasure in what you said about Aubrey. It made my night, although I would imagine it ruined his. So I suppose it's my way of saying, you know, thank you." Richard was about to reply, but Judith pointed her finger at him, "However, if Rupert had gone off script like you did the whole thing would've been futile, so don't make a habit of performing in such a manner."

"I doubt any chat show would have me now," Richard said.

Judith's mouth twitched. "I rather think they might, but you are not participating. Is that clear?"

"Yes, Judith."

Judith sank down on the chair and they drank in companionable silence for a few minutes before Judith started talking about the play. Half an hour later, when the bottle was empty, Rupert and Richard got up, slightly drunkenly, to leave. "Did you know I worked with Noel Coward?" Judith suddenly asked Richard.

"No. That must have been incredible."

Judith studied him, drumming her fingers on the table beside her. "He would have approved of your impersonation tonight. It was spot on."

"Thank you. That's amazing praise." Such a compliment on top of the high of David Letterman, plus the amount of alcohol he'd consumed was making Richard feel distinctly emotional. He bent over to kiss Judith but she pushed him away.

"For fuck's sake don't get sentimental on me. Now go away so I can work on tomorrow's rehearsals."

Rupert tapped his watch. "It's 3.30am, Judith. You should get some sleep."

"What are you, my father? Fuck off and let me do what I want."

However, finding the script was blurring in front of her eyes, Judith was forced to admit that Rupert was right and she fell gratefully into bed. If anyone should ask though, including that sanctimonious Rupert, she'd worked most of the night.

CHAPTER TWELVE

Wesley, arriving early at the theatre on Tuesday morning of the following week, was surprised to hear Judith's lines coming from the stage. That wasn't surprising in itself, except it wasn't Judith's voice. Peering on to the stage from the wings he discovered the lines were emanating from Mindy – with faultless projection. Fascinated, Wesley watched as Mindy ran, word perfect, through every scene. He even crept up to the balcony where Mindy's voice reached him clearly.

He'd returned to the wings, wondering whether to interrupt Mindy, when Judith's voice hissed in his ear. "What's going on?"

"I have no idea, but I do know she can be heard from the back of the balcony."

"But only apparently if she's playing my role." Judith marched on to the stage. "What the fuck do you think you're doing?"

"Margo, I'm sorry, I didn't realize you'd arrived."

"Why are you speaking my lines?"

"I'm your understudy. It's my job to know and practice them."

Judith stared at her, confounded. "What are you talking about? You're not my understudy."

Mindy smiled at her sweetly and spoke slowly. "Yes, I am. Eve is Margo's understudy. Lloyd and Bill give me the role. Even Addison approves."

Judith turned on her heels and virtually ran back to her dressing room. Her hands were shaking so much she could barely open the door.

Mindy turned to Wesley. "I'm sorry, I didn't mean to upset her, but I have to rehearse her role."

Wesley was at a loss. He sank down on to an on-stage sofa and beckoned for Mindy to sit next to him. "Mindy..."

"Eve."

"I'm sorry. Eve. I appreciate you're a devotee of method acting, and you're giving a terrific performance, but you must understand that it's only a role. And the role is not Margo Channing or Margo Channing's understudy. However, if you can project her lines, I see no reason why you can't project your own."

Mindy frowned. "But as Margo's understudy I'm emulating her exactly. When I'm simply Eve I'm true to her personality."

Wesley fingered his chin as an idea started to form. "But surely if Margo wants Eve to project she should do so. Eve will do anything Margo wants; she's ultra-accommodating. That's how she gets her claws into her."

Mindy considered this, nodding slowly. "Yeah, maybe."

"So if Margo were to project Eve's lines, you could emulate that?"

"I guess."

Wesley thought he'd strike while the iron was hot. "Shall we try that now?"

"OK."

Judith was less than happy to have any dealings with Mindy at present, yet if there were the slightest chance Mindy's microphone could be dispensed with it was worth a try.

Two hours later, when the rest of the cast arrived for that afternoon's rehearsals, they were greeted by Judith speaking Eve's lines, copied by a very audible Mindy. Wesley welcomed them with a beaming smile. "I've been making magic," he said, proudly.

"Most impressive," Rupert said. "Judith'll be happy."

Judith was far from being happy. While it was a huge relief that Mindy would now be microphone-free, hearing her performing Margo's lines earlier had been unsettling. When Rupert went to her dressing room to congratulate her on helping solve the problem, she pulled a face.

"What's wrong?" Rupert asked. Judith didn't reply. "Judith, I'm not going until you tell me."

Judith sighed. "It sounds absurd."

"Go on," Rupert prompted as Judith stopped again.

"Fine. The girl scares me, OK?" She glared at him. "Don't tell anybody I admitted that."

"Would I dare? I don't think you need to worry though. I admit she's rather odd, but she's harmless."

Judith's eyes narrowed. "How would you feel if she'd been performing your lines?"

"Delighted, then I could have the night off."

"Oh you're a big help."

"Sorry."

"There's another thing."

"Yes?"

187

Judith gave a brief shake of her head. "Nothing. Let's get on with rehearsals."

Judith had been about to tell Rupert that on Saturday she'd seen Mindy wearing a pair of identical gloves to those she'd lost in rehearsals, but realized she wasn't confident enough in her suspicions. If she was wrong she'd look a total fool. Her imagination was doubtless running away with her.

Rupert, seeing Judith wasn't going to be any more forthcoming, went to leave but Judith called him back. "Incidentally, what were you up to yesterday? I didn't see you at all."

"Ah." This was information Rupert had been dreading telling Judith, since he'd spent the day looking at apartments. Pleasant though the hotel was, Rupert wanted more independence than it provided and his contract had stipulated an apartment. Richard had suggested he and Rupert might share a place and find somewhere really decent, but Rupert had politely declined.

"I've got Holly arriving in a couple of months," he'd explained. "And..."

Richard had held up his hands to stop him. "Say no more. I don't want to be a gooseberry on your sex life."

"Rupert," Judith demanded now. "What were you doing yesterday?"

Rupert watched her face fall as he told her. He'd found the perfect apartment on the Upper West Side, with a six month lease, into which he could move the week after press night. It had a double bedroom, a large sitting room with a pull-out sofa bed and a view of Central Park. "I'll be less than a ten minute cab ride away," he

188

told Judith.

Judith gave an indifferent shrug. "You can move to New Jersey for all I care as long as you're at the theatre on time. Now go on stage and get everybody ready to rehearse. I'll be out in a minute."

When Rupert had gone Judith slammed her hand down on her dressing table and then swore as she hit a bone. She'd got used to having Rupert living down the corridor from her – for the good of the show, of course. Well, she'd just have to get unused to it. As she was always telling Victor, she didn't need anybody. Taking a couple of deep breaths she walked downstairs to the stage where she proceeded to tear the entire cast apart for the appalling show they'd given on Saturday night.

"Did you by any chance tell her you'd found an apartment?" Richard muttered to Rupert, as Judith screamed at Paige.

"Not my best timing, was it? For God's sake don't tell the others – they'll lynch me if they realize I'm responsible for Judith's ferocity."

In spite of Judith's constant berating, the play was in great shape. Wesley felt almost as proud a father as he did when his daughter was born, both events having been somewhat traumatic. The word of mouth from the rapturous audiences meant the entire run was virtually sold out before they'd officially opened – an unusual event on Broadway – and furthermore Mindy was now audible without the use of a microphone. Wesley couldn't say if this cast were better than that in London, but they were damn good.

Five days before the official press night Wesley was watching from the orchestra seats with Aubrey, who was supposed to be making notes, beside him. The director's head was turned away from him and Wesley wasn't sure if he was actually awake. Wesley himself had to admit the theatre was warm and he too was feeling drowsy.

Abruptly, he was jolted into full alertness. Jennifer and Kyle had been playing a tense scene and as Jennifer rose from a kneeling position she caught her foot in the hem of her full skirt, tried to free it, lost her balance and careered towards the front of the stage. For a moment it appeared she was in danger of falling into the auditorium, but as she plunged downwards she managed to grab the end of the stage with her hands, so only her head and neck hung over the edge, her face dangling inches from an astonished couple in the front row. The rest of the audience gasped, and stood up or leant forward for a better view. Kyle ran to her, yanking her dress free of her heel and helping her to her feet to tumultuous applause. By that time Wesley was already on his way backstage, standing on Aubrey's foot as he left his seat, and leaving the previously slumbering director wondering what he'd missed.

As he shot through the pass door Wesley found Judith standing in the wings hissing in the direction of the stage, "Keep going."

"Is she OK? She took one hell of a fall." Wesley said. "Shouldn't we stop the show?"

Judith swung round. "Don't be so fucking

stupid. The show never stops. She's fine. Look."

On stage Jennifer was manfully continuing with the scene, her face ashen, subconsciously rubbing her right wrist which had taken the brunt of her fall. She wasn't sure whether it was the pain from that or the shock which was making her feel dizzy and sick. Finally she exited, sinking down on a prop chair in the wings. "I'm so sorry," she muttered.

"Are you all right?" Wesley asked. "Should we call a doctor?"

Jennifer shook her head. "No, I'm only a bit shaken and completely humiliated. I'll be OK."

Tim, who had been in the wings preparing for Judith's next change, sat on the floor at Jennifer's feet stitching up the offending hem since she had to reappear in the same outfit.

As Jennifer made her re-entrance, a few minutes later, she received another round of applause from the audience which only increased her mortification. She barely remembered how she got through the rest of the play and she was fairly certain she hadn't done a single one of the notes Judith had given at rehearsals that day.

As the curtain came down the cast buzzed around her, eager to offer help with anything from arnica to Advil to a ride to the emergency room. Jennifer was touched, but politely declined everything, declaring there was nothing wrong with her. "I feel such a fool. I just want to go home, have a long soak in the tub and fall into bed. I'm so sorry I messed up, Judith."

Judith sniffed. "It can happen to any of us, but you need to recover quicker. Ad-lib so the audience believe it's part of the scene. Never let them realize there's anything wrong."

"Charming," Kyle said, as Judith disappeared to her dressing room. "I think you did great to continue at all. I had visions of having to carry you off stage."

"Are you sure you don't want a doctor?" Wesley enquired.

"I'm sure. Don't worry, I won't sue if I get a black eye or anything."

"I wasn't actually thinking of that," said Wesley, having not been brought up with the American suing culture. "I was merely concerned."

"I'm sorry. That's very kind of you, but I'm OK."

Kyle and Alyce insisted on walking her up to her dressing room where she said goodnight with pointed determination. Five minutes later there was a knock on her door. "I'm good, I don't need anything," she called out. "Honest."

The door opened and Rupert stuck his head in waving a bottle of wine and two glasses. "Does that include alcohol?" he asked. "Even though it's probably not the best remedy for shock or injury."

"There's nothing really shocked or injured except my pride. I'm just utterly humiliated. So alcohol would be great."

Rupert poured them both a large glass and handed one to Jennifer. "Every actor has their own humiliation story and doubtless a lot are worse than yours. At least you didn't end up in somebody's lap. I've heard stories of that happening."

Jennifer regarded him ruefully. "I'm not sure

that couple in the front row didn't think I was about to. I don't know which of us was more surprised. So do you have a truly embarrassing story?"

"Hundreds."

"I bet you've never made such a fool of yourself as I did."

"I'm fairly certain I have, but on the whole I tend not to let things bother me. If things go terribly wrong I'm notorious for laughing." He leant over and topped up her glass. Jennifer took another gulp and started to feel better.

"What would you have done in my position tonight? Judith said I should have gotten out of it better."

"Well, if I was wearing that skirt I would already be in trouble." Jennifer laughed and drained her glass for the second time. "I suppose if I'd fallen like that and found myself looking directly at the floor of the auditorium, I'd have said something like, 'We really must fire that cleaner, the dust down here is appalling.' It does rather depend on the play. If you're doing Shakespeare it's a bugger to ad-lib."

"Did anything go wrong when you were playing Hamlet?"

Rupert gave an impressed whistle. "You really have done your homework." Jennifer blushed. "Actually, there was this particularly hot night, and when I held the skull of poor Yorick it slipped right out of my sweating hand and bounced across the stage."

Jennifer gasped. "What did you do?"

"I continued with the speech, while picking up the skull and returning it to the gravedigger, who was hunched down in the grave, laughing his head off. And Horatio wasn't much better. As far as I recall, I played half the scene facing upstage so the audience couldn't see my face. At least I could get away with that, unlike the poor actress playing Gertrude who had to die at the front of the stage. One night she heard this old lady in the audience saying very loudly 'Oh dear, look at her shoes, they're quite worn out. It don't seem right for royalty.' Instead of a tragic death, Gertrude's corpse was shaking with unsuppressed hilarity."

Jennifer gave a laugh combined with a hiccup. She loved stories like these and she loved the man who was telling them. And she was pretty keen on the wine too. She was about to ask Rupert for more anecdotes when, to her annoyance, there was another knock on her door and Alyce came in, obviously disapproving of both the wine and Rupert's presence.

"I was gonna see if you wanted to share a cab home rather than go on the subway if you're still feeling shaky," Alyce offered.

"Oh..." Jennifer hedged.

"I'll give her a lift," Rupert broke in much to Jennifer's relief. "So you don't have to worry."

This had the exact opposite effect on Alyce, but there was little she could do, short of giving Rupert a lecture which she doubted Jennifer would thank her for. "OK. Call me if you need anything, hon."

"I will. Thanks, Alyce."

Fifteen minutes later, when the bottle was empty and they had exchanged a variety of theatre horror stories, Rupert suggested they left. The autograph hunters were still waiting outside and Jennifer was touched how many of them enquired how she was. "Fine, but embarrassed," she told each enquiry.

"Should we get a cab?" she asked, as the autograph hunters drifted away, she and Rupert having been the last actors to leave.

Rupert pointed to his car and driver waiting at the kerb. "Your carriage awaits, Cinderella."

On arriving at Jennifer's apartment block Rupert took her arm to help her out of the car and Jennifer grimaced as a pain shot through her wrist. Quickly she turned it into a smile so Rupert wouldn't notice. "I'd better make sure you get upstairs in one piece, or I'll be in terrible trouble with Alyce," Rupert said.

Jennifer was impressed by how easily Rupert took the number of steep stairs to her apartment, which wasn't called a walk-up for nothing. The night of the David Letterman party there, Richard had demanded an oxygen mask half way up.

"I think I'm a little drunk," she muttered as she made a second attempt to unlock her door. "How much of that wine did I drink?"

Rupert laughed. "Most of it, but you deserved it."

"God, how rude of me. Got it!" Jennifer had finally succeeded in her task, which had been made harder by the pain in her wrist, and the door swung open. Rupert followed her in, turning down her offer of more wine and settling instead for a cup of tea, which Jennifer assured him was imported from England.

While Jennifer was in the kitchen, Rupert

strolled over to the wall and looked at a large framed photograph hanging there. Two little girls wearing baseball caps and laughing at the camera stared out at him. "Who are they?" he enquired, as Jennifer brought in his tea and some English shortbread.

"My nieces; I adore them, but they live in Arizona so I don't see them much. I wish I did."

"Do you want children of your own?"

"It's getting a bit late for that now."

"Hardly."

"It's not like I could give them much of a life: a single mother scraping a living as an actress. Besides, I'm old-fashioned. I believe kids should have two parents not one and a test tube."

"I like old-fashioned. So there aren't any prospective fathers on the horizon?"

"No. I'm celibate." She must be drunk to say things like that to Rupert. What was she thinking?

Rupert raised his eyebrows. "I see."

"At least I have been for the last two years. I don't know about the future." She took a sip of her tea, hoping it might sober her up before she made a complete fool of herself.

"So what happened two years ago?" Rupert asked. "Did you get badly hurt?"

"A guy went crazy on me," Jennifer said. "It kinda freaked me out."

"Go on."

"No, it's boring."

"Was he an actor?"

"No."

"OK. Policeman, fireman, lawyer, dog walker, chef, builder, Olympic athlete...?"

Jennifer held up her hands, "Stop already! I don't know why you're interested, but he was the manager of one of the English tea rooms here. We got talking about our mutual love of England, and I guess that kinda clouded my judgement. He moved in pretty soon and that was when I realized he had serious mood swings. Within a month he'd lost his job for being unreliable, and then the one he started after that. Then he began getting paranoid if he didn't know exactly where I was and insisted I regularly checked in with him. And he hated that I kept such anti-social hours. People who aren't in the theatre don't understand that you're not gonna be able to go to a party at 8pm on a Saturday night or get the afternoon off to go to a ball game."

Rupert nodded. "Dating outside our business isn't easy."

"But it's hard inside it too, mostly since you get separated so often by work. I was in one relationship when I didn't see my boyfriend for nine months because we were both on the road in different shows."

Rupert nodded again. "Yes, I know that feeling too."

"How did you manage? You were married for years."

"But we are now divorced," Rupert pointed out. "And our relationship had its fair share of problems because, even apart from the separation, there's also a certain amount of competition. However much you love somebody it's incredibly tough if their career takes off and yours doesn't."

"Surely you can't ever have worried about

that. You've had a brilliant career."

"Yes, I've been lucky. It wasn't always easy for Miranda though. It's not that she hasn't been successful too, she's one of the leads in a popular TV drama at the moment."

"*NHS: The National Hope Service,*" Jennifer broke in and then blushed, realizing what a groupie she sounded.

"Indeed, top of the class Miss Hoffman. However, it was always her dream to be a big movie star and she's never quite made it."

"And you did?"

"I'm not sure about big star, but yes, I've had a movie career. At the same time I've turned down movies for theatre work, something Miranda never understood!" He grinned at the recollection.

Jennifer watched his expression wistfully. "You sound like you're still fond of her."

"You can't be married to somebody for eleven years and not be fond of them, unless the relationship turns very antagonistic. And even then there should be good memories."

"I can't believe you could ever be antagonistic."

Rupert chuckled. "I'm not sure Miranda would agree with you. I wasn't entirely blame-free in our marriage falling apart. Anyway, we're straying from the original subject. This guy, you said, became paranoid and possessive."

Regretfully Jennifer tore herself away from Rupert's much more interesting relationship to hers, which had produced very few good memories. "I used to dread going home – to my own apartment. I never knew what was going to

198

greet me."

"Did he ever hurt you?" Rupert's voice was gentle and Jennifer felt a quiver of pleasure. He did care for her, surely, to be so concerned?

"No. But we'd row, or rather he'd shout and I'd try and calm him down before the neighbours complained again. And the more agitated he became the more aroused he got and he'd want us to perform all these weird sexual moves that I didn't feel comfortable with."

"Did you tell him?"

Jennifer shrugged. "He wouldn't listen. Or he'd say that I was a frigid bitch, so I felt I had to prove I wasn't."

"Did he ever force you?"

Jennifer paused for a minute to think. "Only mentally, I suppose, not physically. It's not like it was rape or anything."

"I'd say that was a pretty thin line. So what happened in the end?"

"Eventually I told him he had to go and he seemed OK about it. But when I got back after the play I was doing at that time, he'd trashed my apartment. Broken everything he knew I cared about, painted all over the walls and even wrote 'You Bitch' in blood, which I presumed was his." She picked up her tea, finding to her surprise that the cup was shaking.

Rupert removed the cup and held her shaking hands in his. "I can understand why you're celibate considering what you've been through, but I wouldn't give up on all men quite yet, unless you're thinking of becoming a nun!"

"You don't think I'd look good in a habit?"

"I'm sure you could carry it off, but it would

199

be a waste for us hot blooded males to have you hiding your loveliness." He gave her hands a squeeze and Jennifer let out an involuntary gasp of pain.

Rupert frowned. "What's wrong?"

"Nothing."

Rupert turned over her hands, studying them. He held up her right wrist and she winced. "That's swollen to almost double its size," he said. "No wonder you're so pale, it must hurt like hell. Why didn't you tell anybody? Wesley was quite prepared to get a doctor."

"I felt stupid enough without making any more fuss. And I can flex it so it's not broken, right?"

"Let's see." Rupert tested it gently. "I don't think it's anything very serious; just a nasty sprain. I had a couple of those when I played tennis. You were lucky you didn't break it; you went down pretty heavily."

Jennifer sighed ruefully. "Tell me about it. Hoffman the Heffalump."

"Have you got a bandage?"

Jennifer found one in a first aid kit she'd bought years ago for emergencies but never opened, while cursing the fact her damn wrist had stopped the romantic mood she felt had been building up. Rupert packed her wrist with ice and then tied the bandage tightly round. "Keep that on tonight and try to avoid using it. Now, I ought to make a move."

Jennifer thought quickly, determined to re-capture the earlier atmosphere. "Since I'm banned from using my wrist, could you possibly help me make up my bed?"

"Sure." Rupert glanced around her studio apartment with its very simple furnishings cramming the small space. "Um, where is it?"Jennifer pointed to a cupboard door which, on Rupert opening it, revealed a bed inside. "I've never seen a proper pull-out before," Rupert exclaimed with a note of excitement as he yanked it down and placed the duvet and pillows on it. "I never quite understand how they don't suddenly shoot back upwards in the middle of the night, with the occupants' legs flaying over the edge." He leapt on and off it a few times, experimenting with interest.

"It's never happened to me yet," Jennifer said, sitting down next to him. "Maybe I've never used it energetically enough." She blushed, realizing how obvious she sounded.

Rupert got up and stretched. "Right, I really am going now. It's getting late and you should get some sleep after your shock."

"I'm not tired. Besides after all you've done the least I can do is offer you a bed for the night to save you having to find a cab at this time." She paused and then added. "I could sleep on the couch."

"In an apartment this size, I don't think I'd be accountable for my actions."

Did he think she had a problem with that? Jennifer closed her eyes and tilted her head back, praying she wasn't making a complete fool of herself. As she felt his lips on hers, she was hugely relieved on two fronts: the first that he had kissed her, and the second that she was wearing her decent Victoria's Secret's underwear, especially as Rupert's hand was slipping

201

up inside her T-shirt where, with an obviously practiced move, he undid her bra one handed. As he started to run his hand over her breasts Jennifer felt a thrill she'd forgotten existed. She gave a gasp of pleasure as Rupert, pushed her back on the bed, pulled up her T-shirt and started kissing her chest. But within seconds he stopped, and with a curse pulled her T-shirt back down, leaving her breasts dangling under it.

"What's the matter?" Jennifer opened her eyes and sat up, close to tears with disappointment. Were her breasts that awful?

Rupert sighed and cupped her face in his hands. "I'm the matter, Jennifer. I'm sorry. I should never have started this and I have to stop now before I totally mess up."

"Why? Did I do something wrong?"

"Oh Christ, you sound just like..." He stopped and started again. "No, you did nothing wrong. You're a lovely, attractive woman and under different circumstances I would have had sex with you with the greatest pleasure. But I'm involved with somebody and I'm trying not to screw up another relationship."

Jennifer's initial dismay that Rupert was involved with somebody was replaced by desperation. "They wouldn't have to know. I promise I'd be very discreet." Jennifer blushed as the needy sounding words came out.

Rupert kissed her gently on her forehead. "I'd know and I can't hurt her. She's very like you in many ways." He got to his feet and pulled on his coat. "I'm truly sorry. And I know it's a terrible cliché, but I honestly mean this: please can we still be good friends?"

"Of course." Jennifer gave what she hoped was a convincing smile.

"Good. Now, take care of that wrist and I'll re-bandage it tomorrow. I'll sort you out a sling too. I wore one for a play once, so I'm quite good at them."

Jennifer nodded eagerly. "*Blithe Spirit*, wasn't it? When Elvira is trying to kill Charles."

Rupert chuckled. "If I ever need a biographer I'll know where to come!"

"Sorry, I'm such a groupie. I won't have to wear a sling for the play, will I? Judith would go nuts."

"Technically you should, though I see it could be rather a disadvantage. However, you will need to keep it bandaged, so I'll unearth a flesh coloured one which will be less obvious."

Jennifer sighed. "Judith's not going to be happy."

"Judith is rarely happy so don't take it personally! Besides, she'd rather have you bandaged than perform with your understudy. Now I really am going. Good night, beautiful."

Jennifer waited until she reckoned he'd have left her building and let out a wail. How could she have been so stupid? If her pride had been hurt by her fall it was nothing to how it felt now. The phone rang, jolting her. Praying it would be Rupert, she answered on the second ring only to find it was Alyce, checking on her before she went to bed.

Jennifer tried to sound light hearted, talking initially only about her wrist, but ultimately telling Alyce the entire story. "Please don't say I told you so," Jennifer pleaded.

"Hon, you've only done what we've all done in our time. Bloody actors are a lousy lot."

"But Rupert's so nice."

"It doesn't stop him being a louse in the sex department."

"But he stopped before we'd even got past second base. Doesn't that show he has some sense of decency?"

"It sounds more like he's worried about getting caught and losing this woman he's with. Maybe she's the jealous type who'd have him tailed."

"He said I was a lot like her."

"Oh right. Like men haven't used that line before. Hon, do you wanna come stay over? We've got a comfortable couch you could use."

Jennifer felt she might burst into tears. "No, I'm good. Thanks Auntie Alyce."

"OK. But tomorrow we meet for coffee before rehearsals and go in together. No arguments. And the couch offer is always open."

Rupert walked the thirty or so blocks back to the hotel, trying to clear his head. Not that he was drunk, in fact very far from it. He'd known exactly what he'd been doing and furthermore enjoyed it far too much. There was something exhilarating about seducing a woman for the first time. Not that he'd exactly instigated the seducing, but he'd hardly discouraged it. Perhaps Judith was right and he wasn't capable of changing. He had, admittedly, stopped himself before he'd gone too far, although that was little consolation to Jennifer who'd looked utterly bereft at his sudden about turn. After her disastrous last relationship she didn't deserve to be hurt anymore, yet it was that vulnerability which attracted him. He was a total sod. He'd send her some flowers in the morning, or, since this was New York, he could most likely do it now. Failing flowers he could send her a dozen bagels.

Hearing about Jennifer's wrist, Wesley insisted she have it professionally checked out and X-rayed which confirmed Rupert's diagnosis. For the next five shows she performed with her wrist strapped up, wearing a sling whilst not on stage. It was almost worth the pain and inconvenience to have Rupert ministering to her as he bandaged it each day. He'd insisted on her switching hands for carrying and holding props during the play which she did warily, dreading an outpouring of rage from Judith that her precious direction was being altered because some ungainly actress was incapable of staying upright. On the contrary, to Jennifer's great relief, Judith saw her performing with a bandaged wrist as irksome, but overall a good example of struggling through adversity.

In spite of Judith's moaning that Broadway had a ridiculous amount of previews, three weeks in all, she managed to fill them with rehearsals and notes. Two nights before the press night, when Rupert was alone with her, he put his foot down over a proposed six hour rehearsal for the following day. "Judith, we're all exhausted. If you insist on this call tomorrow nobody is going to be capable of performing properly for the opening."

Judith crossed her arms in preparation for battle. "There are still things which need work."

"No, there aren't. This play is as close to perfection as it's ever going to be. You've done an amazing job. Don't make us so tired we can't prove that to the best of our ability."

"Fine, forget it, though honestly you're a feeble bunch. I'm older than any of you and do you see me complaining?"

"No, but I do see you stressed beyond belief and in need of a break yourself. You aren't indestructible remember."

Judith scowled. "One tiny bout of pneumonia and I'm never allowed to forget it."

Rupert gave an exasperated growl. "Tiny bout my foot. It nearly killed you and it could recur if you overdo it."

"You sound like fucking Victor."

"Talking of which, when's he arriving?"

"Not until the afternoon of press night. I didn't want him before that, and even then he's not allowed to see me until after the show."

"In which case tell him he's welcome to use my hotel room as a base."

Judith nodded as if she expected nothing less from Rupert. "It's a shame young Holly can't be here. She would adore this whole Broadway opening nonsense."

"Yes," Rupert said carefully. He was still feeling guilty about the whole Jennifer situation, even though Jennifer had conducted herself impeccably since that rather disastrous evening, and they'd stayed friends.

"Mind you," Judith continued with her train of thought, "her enthusiasm might be rather nauseating."

Rupert pulled a face at her. "It's not nauseating, it's charming. Not a subject you'd know much about."

"Fucking cheek. I'm going home. I suppose you're staying to ingratiate yourself with the fans by signing, so I won't wait. You'd think your ego was big enough without wallowing in all that groupie bullshit."

Rupert could tell Judith wasn't in the kind of mood to hold a debate on the subject, so he bade her good night and went outside brandishing his Sharpie pen to scribble something, which approximated his signature, for the waiting crowds.

Judith, walking passed the hoards as she got into her car, caught sight of Rupert, his arm around the shoulders of some hideous girl who was grinning like a baboon as an elderly woman, no doubt the girl's mother, took a photograph of them together. She could never understand why people believed they had a right to treat actors like public property.

Arriving at the hotel, she ignored the greeting from the concierge, stroked the resident cat, and got into the elevator, neatly pushing the button so the door shut in the face of a man who'd been gesturing at her to hold it. The last thing she wanted was anyone talking to her. If she'd waited for Rupert and Richard at least they could have done the social chit-chat nonsense. At the recollection that Rupert was moving out at the end of the week she gave the lift a frustrated kick.

Reaching her room she inserted the key card. As the door swung open she let out a shriek. Steadying herself on the doorway she caught her breath. "What the fuck do you think you are doing?"

CHAPTER THIRTEEN

Mindy swung around, holding a black skirt and sweater of Judith's. Before Judith had made her presence known she'd been holding them up against herself and admiring the look in the full length mirror.

"Well?" Judith demanded.

Mindy hung her head to symbolize Eve's apparent humility. "I'm sorry; I thought you were still at the theatre."

"And that gives you the right to come into my room and go through my wardrobe? How the hell did you get in anyway? Did the front desk give you entry because in that case I'm going to give the manager hell?"

"No. I let myself in."

A sudden realization struck Judith. "My God, the key card I lost. You took it. Jesus, I thought I was going fucking senile."

Mindy had the grace to look slightly shame-faced. "I didn't intend to cause you mental anguish, but it seemed essential that I could get into your apartment should you need me to do anything for you." Judith stared at her, uncomprehending. "As your assistant," Mindy explained. "Eve is Margo's assistant, right? I'm sorry if I startled you. Your clothes are so stylish that I felt impelled to admire them. I aspire to dress like you."

"Bollocks." It wasn't the most eloquent response but Judith was beyond caring. "Firstly, you're not my assistant, you're my fellow actress, God help me. Secondly, I'm not interested in clothes unless they're costume so don't give me any crap about style. They're serviceable; that's all. And thirdly you have no right to come into my room uninvited whatever your excuse."

Mindy crossed the room until she was standing right in front of Judith; a brave, if foolhardy, move considering Judith's mood. "I had to experience the emotion of holding Margo's clothes and to imagine wearing them, or I couldn't correctly emulate it for the scene where Eve does that. There's something so personal about clothes." She ran her hands up and down the skirt again in a way which gave Judith the shivers.

Grabbing the skirt and sweater, Judith threw them on the bed making a mental note to give them to a charity shop at the first opportunity. Then she seized Mindy by the arms and shook her, hard. Mindy's eyes opened wide, but she didn't try and escape Judith's clutches, which further frustrated the older woman. "For fuck's sake, these are my clothes. If you must feel Margo's then do so with my costumes at the theatre."

"I did," Mindy said, "but your dresser made me quit."

Judith made a mental note to give Tim a bigger tip, because now she came to think of it she'd rather Mindy didn't touch anything she had to wear, it was too creepy. "Just use the ones you actually hold in the show," Judith stated, and with a final shake she released Mindy and moved away to sit down on the chair, exhaling deeply. "You took my gloves, didn't you? I knew I'd seen you wearing them the other night."

"I borrowed them so I had something of yours to work with. I would have given them back." Mindy's expression showed no sign of contrition. "I'm not a thief."

"And the notes I lost?"

"I wanted a sample of your writing. And as your understudy I required your concepts of the play."

Judith gritted her teeth but refrained from comment over the understudy remark. She was more interested in recalling the day the notes had gone missing. "But weren't you helping me to look for them?" she asked. The relief of knowing she wasn't losing her mind didn't stop her fury at Mindy's behaviour. "How could you do that when you'd taken them?"

Mindy looked surprised. "Because that's what Eve would have done."

Judith stared at Mindy unable, for once, to think of what to say. There was something incredibly unnerving about these method convictions. "Stay here," she snapped eventually, and pointed to the chair as she got up from it. Mindy obediently obeyed as Judith left the room and walked along the corridor to Rupert's. There was no reply to her knock. Praying that he and Richard hadn't gone out, she sank down on the floor outside to wait, uncaring as to how strange she must appear.

As she waited Judith beat her hands on the floor either side of her. It would be just her luck if Rupert had chosen tonight to fuck some stage door groupie; probably the girl with the baboon

211

grin – and her mother to boot. To her great relief he arrived back within ten minutes. Taking one look at her expression, he helped her to her feet and into his room. Pouring them both a large glass of whisky he listened as Judith filled him in.

"Jesus," he said. "That's one crazy girl."

"Crazy? She's certifiable. I'm never working with method actors ever again."

"I don't think all method actors are like Mindy. Maybe only the ones who work with that awful Krystal; or maybe Mindy merely has a naturally obsessive personality." He sighed and rubbed his eyes. "I'll go and talk to her, though God knows if I'll make any more headway than you did. Why don't you stay here?"

Mindy listened attentively as Rupert explained that taking, or even borrowing, other people's items was not acceptable, even for character research, and neither was breaking into hotel rooms. Although Mindy appeared to be nodding in agreement, Rupert felt his remarks weren't hitting home.

"You're a very powerful man, aren't you?" Mindy said as he finished. Rupert frowned, wondering if she meant that he had influence over Judith. He couldn't think of anything else in which he wielded much power – certainly not one to concern or interest Mindy. "I understand what you want from me," Mindy continued.

"Good." Rupert stood up to leave.

"And I shall understand if you want to be brutal with me. I'm sure a man with your personality must have certain deviant ways in that department."

212

"What?" Rupert swung round, wondered what Mindy had heard about him – and from whom.

"Just don't leave any visible marks." Mindy slipped off her shoes, lay down on the bed, pulling up her skirt to reveal the smallest thong and closing her eyes as if in revulsion. "I'm ready, Addison. Do with me whatever you wish. It's all in the cause of my career."

"Jesus Christ, Mindy!" Rupert pulled her skirt back over her knees and yanked her into a sitting position. "Have you been listening to a word I've said?"

"Don't you want me, Addison? I thought this was what you would expect now you've made me such a success. Don't you want to take your pound of flesh?"

Rupert gave a growl of frustration and hoped Mindy wasn't going to stray into *The Merchant of Venice*. The way Judith felt about her at present she might be tempted to perform such surgery. He sat down on the bed and took hold of Mindy's shoulders, turning them until she was facing him. "Mindy..."

"Eve."

"No, Mindy. You are an actress playing a role and while I realize you need to become more engrossed in your character than most of us, you cannot take it to such extremes. You must be able to differentiate between reality and fiction. You are Mindy Blue, actress, Judith is Judith Gold, actress and I'm Rupert Blake, actor."

"So you don't want me?"

Rupert felt like shouting, an unusual emotion for him. What would it take to get through to her? "No, I don't want you."

"But you fancy me, right? That's why you do what you do to make me a success."

"In the play, Mindy, I fancy you in the play; on stage every night and twice on matinee days."

"Oh." Mindy nodded slowly. "OK."

Rupert still wasn't convinced she understood, but he'd had enough of banging his head against a brick wall for one night. He insisted she hand over the key card, accompanied her down to the street and put her into a cab. It was interesting, he thought, that Mindy's offer, unlike Jennifer's, hadn't tempted him in the least. But then Mindy hadn't wanted him, she'd wanted Addison DeWitt to do God knows what to her. Getting the elevator back to his room he reported the events to Judith.

"Goodness, a girl with her legs open, all ready for the taking and you turned her down," she said.

Rupert raised his eyes to the ceiling. "I wish I hadn't told you that bit now."

"It was the best part. Mind you, if you had fucked her on my bed I would have insisted on changing rooms – or even changing hotels. Actually, I'm going to phone housekeeping and demand clean sheets anyway."

"Goodnight, Judith."

Judith looked at her empty glass and then at the door. "I'm not sure I can face going back to my room yet. The image of that girl splayed on my bed is too unpleasant."

"Well, if you stay here you'll have to share my bed and I warn you I practice my backhand in my sleep."

214

Judith left with bad grace. Once in her room she picked up the phone and rang her landline in London, waking Victor.

"I'm phoning to tell you I'm not going senile, after all. That's it." And she put the phone down. It rang a few seconds later.

"I never thought you were," Victor said, and he too hung up.

"Don't you dare hang up on me like that," Judith said, having redialled immediately.

Victor chuckled. "I give as good as I get, Judy. You should realize that by now. So what momentous event has brought about this new-found confidence in your mental stability, or have you decided to go into therapy and discover your inner self?"

"Don't be stupid. This isn't the time to talk, though. Surely it's the middle of the night there?"

"Oh, now you think of that!" Judith gave a derisive sniff to show she didn't appreciate his sarcasm. "Still, I'm always happy to hear from you, Judy – whatever the time." Judith made a gagging noise and Victor chuckled again. "Sorry, I slipped into sentiment there. I'll endeavour not to let it occur again. Anyway I'm awake now, so tell me everything."

Attempting to sound as if she were doing him the favour by unburdening herself, Judith told Victor the whole story, embroidering the fear she'd felt on finding Mindy in her room.

Once she'd finished Victor let out a low whistle, causing Judith to inquire if he was attempting to deafen her down the earpiece. "Now that is a girl who seriously needs therapy," he said.

"She needs therapy? Have you any idea how terrified I was?"

"I'm sure it gave you a real scare, Judy, but somehow I can't see you being terrified. You could eat her for breakfast."

Judith tried to sound outraged but it was pointless; bloody Victor knew her too well. "All right, maybe not terrified, but it was unnerving." She scowled; a futile exercise since Victor couldn't see her. "Honestly," she snapped, "why do I bother confiding in you when you're completely unsympathetic?"

"Judy, I am sympathetic and I'm sure you're badly shaken, and I hate the fact that I'm three thousand miles away and can't physically do anything to help. Why don't I fly out later today instead of tomorrow? Then I could act as your personal bodyguard or defend your room from intruders – whichever you preferred."

"Christ no, I don't need any further distractions. I'm going to sleep. Goodnight." She slammed the phone down before the temptation to accept Victor's offer was too great. She refused to become one of those weak women who needed a man for protection. As she phoned the front desk to demand clean sheets she told herself she was only feeling jumpy because it was late; an hour when everything seemed stranger and more frightening. But in truth, being a theatre creature, night was her natural habitat. It was mornings she couldn't cope with.

Mindy went home frustrated by the lack of understanding as to her way of working. On stage she felt so at one with Eve that the performance flowed out of her. It was living Eve's life off-stage which was proving difficult. Something as routine as shopping became a struggle while attempting it in the correct 1950s manner. Her research into the period had shown shopkeepers to be polite and helpful, not shouting "next in line," as at her local food market. There was no doubt that living in twenty first century Manhattan was testing her character assimilation to its limits. Without her nightly conversations with Krystal in LA she might have lost her battle.

Last night Krystal had asked how Eve's interaction with her fellow cast members was progressing. Mindy considered them varied and not without their excitement or their tensions. Margo was furious with her, which was in keeping with their relationship later in the play, as was her rejection by Bill, though oddly he'd looked more terrified than offended. But tonight Addison had spurned her advances, which was surely an incorrect response. And she'd offered him carte blanche. Sure, there was a part of her which was relieved that he hadn't taken her up on her offer. Sexual deviancy wasn't Mindy's thing, but Eve would accept it to forward her career and therefore so would Mindy. She'd even studied certain sexual fetishes which Addison might demand. It was beyond her why a woman would enjoy being put across a man's knee and spanked, yet she understood a man like Addison, who was all about power, might enjoy performing such an act.

Her adventure earlier tonight though was her greatest achievement in developing Eve's persona. The thrill of being illicitly in Margo's private space was an emotion she could use on stage. Press night would hold no fears for her now. That and the two hours prior to that show which Krystal had agreed to spend talking to her on the phone. It was a shame her mentor couldn't be in the audience, but there were actors in LA needing her expertise and Mindy knew she was privileged to even be permitted those two hours.

Opening her bag she carefully removed a blouse she'd taken from Margo's closet while she was out of the room, and hung it so she could see it from her bed. She'd taken this before Addison had told her not to remove any more of Margo's things, so it didn't count. That was what Eve would think. "Move over Margo Channing," she said out loud. "Here comes Eve Harrington."

CHAPTER FOURTEEN

On the afternoon of *All About Eve's* opening night, one of the most hotly anticipated
on Broadway, Judith, miraculously, heeded
Rupert's advice and only called the cast in for
an hour's pep-talk at 4pm. Technically it was
Aubrey's pep-talk, but he'd been thoroughly
briefed by Judith so no one was fooled. Since
the curtain was to go up early at 7pm that night
to enable the critics to meet their deadlines, this
left the cast a couple of hours to sort through
the gifts and flowers which had flooded in to the
stage door.

There was one bunch of huge tropical flowers, taking up half the entrance, which turned
out to be for Judith. As Tim carried them into
her dressing room Judith's mouth fell open.
"Jesus, they're fucking triffids. Get rid of them,
Tim. I don't want to come back in the interval
and find they've eradicated your personality.
I'm surrounded by enough zombies as it is."

Mindy was carefully removing all carnations
from her bouquets, recalling Krystal's admon-
ishments about their being unlucky.

Rupert was inspecting some excellent bottles
of wine sent by his agent when the stage door
keeper informed him there was a Victor Lewis
to see him.

"Victor, it's good to see you." Rupert shook
hands and ushered him into his dressing room.

"I'm not stopping because Judy will kill me if

she finds me in her personal territory, but I have a delivery from Holly." He dug into his pocket and brought out a small wrapped object. "She gave me a gift for Judy too but I'll leave that at stage door." Victor paused, unconsciously examining his hand. "How is she?"

"Busy giving notes."

Victor laughed. "That's OK then. I worry too much."

"With good reason and I will go and check on her in a minute. But I think we'll all be glad when tonight is over. Are you coming to the party?"

"I doubt it because I don't suppose Judy will. On the other hand if she merely wants to go home and sleep I might sneak out and gate-crash."

"Come as my guest, I'm not taking anyone." Rupert fingered Holly's parcel.

"I might take you up on that. Have a great show."

After Victor had left, Rupert tore open the paper and slipped the catch of the box beneath. Inside was a fob watch and on the back was engraved: R. Love H. An enclosed piece of paper informed him the watch was a genuine 1950s article. He was tempted to put it in his show jacket, but if it should fall out or even be seen, Judith would be furious.

Judith, attempting to concentrate on her role, was being increasingly frustrated by members of the company bringing presents and good wishes. Eventually she sent Tim to stand guard outside with instructions to admit no one. It was ridiculous to be this terrified yet, however many opening nights she'd experienced, it never got easier. She strode up and down the dressing room performing her breathing exercises. In spite of what she said about critics not mattering to her, they did. Any attack on either her or the play would be soul-destroying.

To keep herself occupied, Judith started opening the pile of cards and presents stacked up on her dressing table. Jesus, an *All About Eve* baseball cap and knapsack from the producers; did they seriously envisage her hiking around New York, her bobbed hair protruding from the cap and a tent, sleeping bag and gas stove on her back? If Wesley had anything to do with these so-called gifts she'd tell him exactly what she thought. But there was a separate one from him: a framed photograph of the front of the St James Theatre with a queue of people waiting for returned tickets. Carefully she placed that on her dressing table. Holly's gift was also a frame, with a photograph of Judith in costume. Engraved on top of the frame was, 'Judith Gold is', and at the bottom, 'Margo Channing'.

She was still clasping Holly's photograph when Tim came in to get her dressed. He studied the frames. "I'd better get some silver polish," he said. "With the dirt in these old buildings they'll tarnish quicker than I can get a tall skinny latte in Starbucks."

Once she was in costume and Tim had returned to guard duty, Judith opened her final two gifts. Victor's was a pair of beautiful antique earrings, which, knowing his obsession with accuracy, were sure to be authentic for the period, and certainly be to Margo's taste.

Whatever Rupert had given her, was contained in an envelope. As she tore it open a key fell out. Frowning, she read the accompanying note.

Dear Judith,

What can you give somebody who has everything and has given me the chance to perform on Broadway? I hired a personal shopper in Bloomingdales to help me find something perfect, but she was so sexy I forgot about the shopping. (And yes I am kidding before you bollock me!). Instead here is a spare key to my new apartment so you can feel you're always welcome.

All my love and admiration for your wonderful Margo Channing.

Rupert.

Judith allowed herself a small smile and placed the key carefully in her bag. She didn't envisage turning up unannounced, but she had to admit, grudgingly, that the gesture had touched her. She wished she'd made more of an effort with Rupert's present, yet she always did the same for opening nights: bottles of good champagne for everybody backstage, from actors to stage management to dressers. Anyway, as he'd said, it was thanks to her that he was on Broadway.

Rupert was doing up the cufflinks in his shirt when there was a knock on the door. "Hang on, I'll put on some trousers," he called out, grabbing them from a hanger.

"Don't bother on my behalf."

Rupert froze at the familiar tones. The door opened and in walked a glamorous woman with auburn hair, wearing a low cut white dress which clung to every curve, finishing with a large slit up the side, revealing a lot of leg and a tiny bit of lacy underwear. "Surprised?" she asked.

"You could say. How did you get down here? Stage Door are usually strict about visitors."

"I told them I was your wife and they let me straight through."

"Ex-wife, Miranda."

"Don't niggle, darling. Most people still think we're married."

"I don't."

Miranda pouted. "You don't have to be such a brute. I thought it would be nice to come to your first night. I was trying to be supportive."

Rupert sighed. "I'm sorry." He moved towards Miranda and kissed her on the cheek. "That's very sweet of you." He had little doubt that the lure of a Broadway first night had more to do with Miranda's presence than providing him with support.

Miranda sat on Rupert's dressing table and crossed her legs, thereby revealing even more of her anatomy through the slit.

"Jesus, Miranda, if you sit like that in the theatre nobody will even be watching the play. In fact, you may be arrested for indecent exposure."

Miranda smirked. "Thank you, darling. Don't worry I'll keep my legs demurely together in the auditorium." She fluttered her eyelids at him.

"What do you want?" Rupert asked, finally pulling on his trousers and starting to fasten his bow tie in the mirror.

"What do you mean?"

"You only flutter your eyelids like that when you're after something."

"Oh. Well, Mike managed to get me a ticket for the play tonight, which wasn't easy."

"What a dedicated agent he is." Rupert looked at the bow tie and decided to re-do it. Even divorced Miranda was demanding his full concentration.

"Yes." Miranda was using her most cajoling tones. "Yet he completely failed to get me an invitation for the party after."

"What a shame."

"Rupert!"

"Sorry, your timing is off. Only a few minutes ago I asked Victor to come as my guest if Judith doesn't go."

"Victor? That funny journalist man who's obsessed with Judith? What's he doing here?"

"He's Judith other half, as you know perfectly well."

"I keep forgetting; it's so extraordinary."

"It's not in the least extraordinary. Victor is a very special man."

"Apparently so, since you're taking him to the party."

"For God's sake, Miranda." Rupert sighed again, wondering why he always gave in to her. "All right, I'll see if I can swing another guest ticket to the party for you. However, if Victor does come you'd better be polite."

Miranda smirked. "I'm sure I can utterly charm him."

"I wouldn't suggest that unless you want Judith to lynch you."

"Is she actually serious about him?"

"I'm not going to deign to answer that question. Now, do you promise to behave if I do this?"

"Yes! Thank you, darling." Miranda slinked her way to standing and kissed Rupert fully on the mouth.

Rupert glanced in the mirror. "Wonderful, Addison is now wearing a very vibrant shade of lipstick."

Miranda gave a sexy chuckle. "Shall I wipe it off?"

"No, I'll do it. Just leave me to get ready in peace, please."

"If you insist. The last thing I want to do is distract you." Miranda went to the door and as she opened it found Jennifer outside about to knock. "Look, darling, you've got another visitor."

"I'm sorry," Jennifer said. "I didn't mean to interrupt; I brought you something." She thrust a brightly coloured gift bag into Rupert's hands, noticing his lipstick covered mouth. "I'll go now."

"Don't worry, I'm leaving," Miranda said. "Rupert says I'm far too distracting. I'm Miranda Flynn, Rupert's wife."

"Jennifer Hoffman." Jennifer stuck her hand out, which to her annoyance she found was shaking. "I recognize you of course. I love English TV and I've seen you on stage when I've been to London. You're wonderful."

"How adorable you are. You must make Rupert feel right at home. That's why I'm here tonight, to provide wifely support." She gave Jennifer a look which left her in no doubt that she was totally de trop in this dressing room.

Red faced, Jennifer virtually ran back upstairs.

"Miranda, that was bloody rude," Rupert said.

"What do you mean? I was charming."

"You were condescending. And stop telling everyone we're still married."

"Married, divorced, what the difference?"

"A lot of alimony, although on the up side my credit card no longer goes into cardiac arrest when you go shopping." He opened the gift bag to find a book on Manhattan's secret haunts. Inside Jennifer had written:

I thought you might like to see a less tourist-side to our city. I'd be happy to show you some of them – or not – whichever. Anyway it's wonderful working with you and I know the next six months are going to be phenomenal.

"How sweet," Miranda commented, reading over Rupert's shoulder. "She has a serious crush on you. Are you screwing her?"

"No, I'm not. And will you please go away."

Miranda gave Rupert another kiss before he could stop her, this time on his cheek, leaving a perfect lip outline. "Since you're wearing more of my lipstick than I am I'd better touch up," Miranda said, using Rupert's mirror to do so. Unable to clean his face or even check his bow tie Rupert resigned himself to putting on his shoes and socks.

Jennifer sat in her room feeling an unmitigated idiot. No wonder Rupert wasn't interested in her when he was obviously back with Miranda Flynn – Miranda had said as much by introducing herself as his wife. Plus Rupert had her lipstick all over his face. And who could blame him? Miranda was so glamorous, especially in that stunning outfit, the split of which seemed to virtually reach her waist. Jennifer looked sadly at the black dress with the low cut back she'd been thrilled with when she'd bought it yesterday. She might as well wear a caftan and turban for all anyone would notice next to Miranda.

Angry with herself for caring so much, Jennifer started to put on her show underwear, pulling her tights up with such ferocity they laddered and she had to ask the wardrobe department to provide her with a new pair. As her dresser fastened her opening frock, Rupert popped in and she felt her heart leap.

"Thank you for the fascinating book," he said. "I'd be delighted to take you up on your offer to play intrepid city explorers. I'll bring a compass and emergency rations." He pointed to Jennifer's *All About Eve* knapsack. "Our producers have even provided us with the appropriate gear."

Jennifer beamed with relief. "Great. Whenever you want, I have no life as you know."

Rupert grinned. "Then we'll have to get you one. And I'm sorry about Miranda's behaviour."

Jennifer pretended to look mystified. "Behaviour?"

"She can be a little condescending on occasions."

"I didn't notice."

"Hmm," Rupert said, with total disbelief. "It's nice of you to say so." He put his arms around Jennifer and gave her a hug. "Have a great show. It's wonderful working with you too. Now

I must go and check on Judith."

Jennifer felt much happier as he winked at her and left. As long as his relationship with Miranda wasn't going to spoil their friendship then she'd have to be content with that.

Tim was still on guard outside Judith's door, sitting on the stairs. He looked up as Rupert approached. "You are the only person I'm permitted to allow in. Only I'm afraid I might've got you into a little trouble with her." He gestured with his head into Judith's dressing room.

"That'd be nothing new," Rupert said. Before Tim could elaborate further Judith's voice demanded Rupert's presence.

Judith was still marching around both rooms, fully dressed in her opening outfit for the play within the play, comprising of a crinoline style dress and a wig of ringlets.

Rupert took hold of her arms to keep her still. "It's going to be fine, really."

Judith scowled. "What makes you the oracle of all knowledge?"

"Didn't you know I had an 'O' level in Oracle-isms?"

"Don't you mean in orgasms?"

Rupert grinned. "I have a Master's degree in those."

Judith snorted, pulled away from him and started marching again. As she reached the far side of her dressing room she swung round. "Tim told me there was a woman at stage door declaring she was your wife. I wasn't aware you were married at present."

"Neither was I."

"I take it from Tim's description that it was

Miranda."

"Yes, and before you ask, no I didn't know she was coming. And yes she is coming to the after-show party."

"That doesn't bother me since I won't be. Still, she'd better not distract you."

"The play has my full attention, I promise."

"Good, now go away and leave me to pace."

"Oh fuck," Judith muttered five minutes later when the beginners' call for Act One came over the show relay system. "I am never doing this again." She stuck her head outside the dressing room. "Tim! Get me out of this bloody outfit. I'm going to be sick."

"No you're not," Tim said. "Apart from anything else I'm not cleaning vomit out of those ringlets. Now, get on stage and make that audience forget Bette Davis ever existed."

Judith stared at Tim for a minute, before giving a slight smile. "Bette who?" she said. Taking a deep breath she began walking down to the stage. "Remind me to fire you later for insubordination," she called over her shoulder.

"Again?"

Judith swung around. "Cheeky fucker!" In spite of her best efforts there was no hiding the smile on her face. Thank God for Tim, and for Rupert. With them she could feel confident on and off stage. If only she could feel as confident about the audience, particularly those with pens, paper and torches, searching for flaws to enliven their reviews. Sod them. There were no flaws in her performance. And anyone who dared to disagree would be very sorry.

CHAPTER FIFTEEN

As the curtain finally came down, after tumultuous applause, the cast hugged each other with relief, with the exception of Judith who went straight to her dressing room and knocked back a glass of whisky. The performance had gone perfectly, but she was longing to return to the hotel and go to sleep. The company manager arrived a few minutes later to explain about the VIP room allocated at Tavern on the Green, the venue for the first-night party, for cast, VIPS and important backers only.

Judith shrugged. "I don't care since I have no intention of going."

The company manager's face fell. "You'll be expected."

"Then un-expect me. I'm shan't be a trophy for the money men to pose with."

"You don't have to stay. Be seen arriving, have your photograph taken, drink a glass of champagne and you can leave. You're the leading lady; you have to go to your own party." The company manager was getting desperate.

"No, I don't. As the leading lady I can do whatever the fuck I want."

"Five minutes?"

"You may as well give up, you won't win," Victor said from the doorway, where he'd been quietly standing, listening to the conversation.

"But..." the company manager stopped in mid-beg as Victor gently shook his head. Admitting defeat, the man sloped away to break the news to the producers.

"You're scandalizing Broadway, Judy." Victor crossed to where Judith sat at her dressing table and kissed her lightly on the top of her head. "But you were truly wonderful tonight. The entire audience were blown away."

"What an interesting sight. Did they inflate first?"

Victor laughed. "Touché, that was an appallingly clichéd remark, especially from a writer. So I take it we're not joining the celebrity gathering tonight?"

"You can, but I'm certainly not. Actually, you should go and get out of my hair." She passed him an envelope. "Here, have both my party tickets and take somebody else."

"Rupert's offered to take me as his guest."

"Now he's taking Miranda."

Victor was surprised by few things in life, but this news took even him aback. He looked at Judith quizzically, but Judith had lost interest. "You can take me home and then carry on to the party. On second thoughts, get me something to eat first. I suddenly feel hungry. And maybe a bottle of champagne; that's the least I deserve."

In the end Victor never made it back to the party – and he wasn't bothered in the least.

The rest of the cast arrived at Tavern on the Green dressed up to the nines and smiling through the endless photographers stationed outside. Miranda was in her element and Rupert had to virtually drag her inside to allow other people to receive the press's attention.

"I love the fact you can see Central Park from

231

the restaurant," Jennifer said, as she and Alyce arrived together and posed for photographs. Hoping she'd be able to spend the evening with Rupert – as a friend – she hadn't brought a guest. "Where's this famous Nate of yours, Alyce? I thought he was coming."

"He should be inside; his carer brought him here straight after the play finished." She took Jennifer's arm as they started to walk into the restaurant. "You see, if he'd arrived with me we'd have been pictured together and they'd run some story about a Broadway actress with a physically challenged husband. Even if they merely printed the photo he'd hate it. Plus he didn't want to detract from me. He's a good man. Come meet him."

Jennifer was charmed by Nate. In spite of being mostly paralyzed below the neck, with a little movement in his arms, he used his head and face to express and gesture and his smile was engaging.

"So, Jennifer, you're the one to whom my wife has been playing agony aunt. Don't let her get too bossy. She can be insufferable when she's doing her Mother Teresa act." He gave Alyce a wink.

"Cheek!" Alyce retorted. "If you slander me like that I shall refuse to fetch you any food."

Nate gave a roguish grin. "You do and I'll phone my lawyer and divorce you immediately."

"Promises, promises!"

Jennifer saw a look of such affection pass between them, she felt almost jealous. She watched as Alyce collected a plate of food and helped Nate to eat.

"Hey guys," Kyle, said, as he, Lauren and Richard joined them, and introductions were made.

"Where's Paige?" Jennifer asked, scanning the room.

"In the VIP room," Kyle said. "She wanted us to join her but I'd rather stay with everybody else. I hate this segregation crap, while Paige is young and inexperienced enough to find it exciting that people want to schmooze with her."

"I imagine half of them will want to schmooze with her date," Richard said. "He's utterly gorgeous and I could be wrong but I think he may bat for my side."

"Who's Rupert with?" Kyle asked. "She looks familiar."

"His wife, the actress Miranda Flynn," Jennifer said.

"Christ, is he?" Richard said, glancing horrified in the direction Kyle was looking.

"It's a stunning outfit," Jennifer said.

"Only if you want to resemble an upmarket tart," Richard retorted. "Damn, they've seen us."

Rupert came over, followed by Miranda wearing her most seductive smile. "Hello, I'm Miranda Flynn. It's heavenly to meet you all. I've heard so much about everyone from Rupert."

Rupert knew he'd told Miranda absolutely nothing about anyone for the very good reason that she wouldn't have been interested.

"Richard, it's delightful to see you again," Miranda continued, giving Richard two quick kisses, having reminded herself of his name in the *All About Eve* playbill. "How lucky you are, being under Judith's patronage."

Richard gave her a forced smile. The woman was pure poison; what was Rupert doing bringing her tonight?

"You must be Lauren," Rupert said, breaking in before Miranda could continue winding up his fellow cast members. "I'm glad you could find another babysitter. Kyle said the one you'd booked was ill."

"Thank you. It was rather a last minute panic. I'd have been so pissed to miss tonight."

"Pissed over here means the same as pissed-off in English, not that you're drunk," Jennifer translated.

Rupert, even though he hadn't needed the translation, gave her a nod of thanks. "Your husband is a mine of information on American sports," he said to Lauren. "He's kindly invited me to join your family at a Mets game this summer which he informs me is <u>the</u> team to support. I'm going to buy the appropriate baseball cap so I fit right in."

Lauren smiled at him. "I shall look forward to that, though I warn you the children get very overexcited."

"And I should warn you, so do I! On the positive side, I always sleep through the night, unless otherwise occupied, and am fairly well potty trained."

"Rupert, don't be vulgar," Miranda complained. "I'm sorry, he only has to have one drink and he becomes a lager lout."

Rupert rolled his eyes. "It's always nice to have one's reputation destroyed in a single sentence," he said. "And if I'm going to be any kind of lout tonight it's going to be a champagne one." To prove his point he swapped his empty glass for a full one from a passing tray. Then he turned to Nate. "You must be Nate. I have to thank you for having such a charming wife. Alyce is the mother hen to the company and we'd be lost without her."

Nate's eyes lit up and he nodded with alacrity. "She sure is special."

Rupert crouched down so he was level with Nate. "You have a lousy view here with all these people blocking you. How do you fancy a male promenade? I promise Alyce we won't look up too many skirts, although some of the girls hardly have a skirt worth mentioning. I'll go first like those men who used to walk in front of cars in Victorian times." Rupert grabbed a white napkin off a passing waiter and, waving it, he started making honking noises to clear the route for Nate to come through in his electric wheelchair.

Miranda scowled after him. "Honestly, he can be so embarrassing."

"Rubbish," Richard said tersely, having had enough of Miranda already.

Alyce looked after her husband who was laughing and calling things to Rupert as Rupert hooted loudly at a pompous man to clear the way so Nate could reach the table of desserts. The pompous man gave a loud tut and then put on a false smile as he realized he'd just tutted at one of Broadway's hottest actors. "Miranda, I may have misjudged your husband," Alyce said.

Miranda gave a saccharine smile. "How sweet of you to say so."

Paige dashed over. "There you guys are! I was

looking for you in the VIP room. There are some real cool celebrities there."

"None of whom have anything to do with *All About Eve*," Kyle pointed out.

"Where's your hunky date?" Richard asked.

Paige frowned. "When I left the VIP room he seemed to be chatting up one of our backers."

"I'm sure she wasn't as pretty as you," Alyce said.

"It wasn't a she."

Richard gave a shout of laughter. "Sorry Paige," he said, seeing her wounded expression. "It's only I had a hunch he was that way inclined."

Paige exhaled crossly. "It proves there are no decent straight men in Manhattan."

On their last lap of the room, Rupert and Nate, scattering guests and waiting staff as they went, nearly ran into Mindy who was leaving.

"You're going early," Rupert said.

"I have to, in order to concentrate on my role. Parties are a distraction."

"Mindy, we're doing this show for six months. You've got to have some fun."

"Fun? Eve is totally focused. That consumes my energy."

Rupert glanced around. "Are you on your own? Didn't your boyfriend fly over for the opening?"

Mindy regarded him puzzled. "Eve doesn't have a boyfriend."

Rupert sighed. "Doesn't she even have any friends to ask to her opening?"

Mindy looked rather sad. "I don't think so." Then she shrugged. "Anyway, I gotta go. Goodnight, Addison. Goodnight, Addison's friend." She tripped off towards the exit.

Nate gawped up at Rupert with an expression of astonishment. "And I thought Alyce was exaggerating. She actually called you Addison."

"Oh yes!"

"And Mindy has a boyfriend who she won't acknowledge since Eve doesn't have one."

"Apparently so; he's a movie director based in LA."

"Man, are you guys in for an interesting time."

Rupert and Nate rejoined Alyce and the other actors. Even from the other side of the room, Rupert could see Miranda had been flirting with Kyle and was now giving Paige tips on how to improve her style. He gripped his ex-wife firmly by the arm and moved her away under the guise of getting something to eat. They nearly kicked somebody wearing a tux sitting on the floor calmly eating a plate of food.

"Tim?" Rupert queried.

Tim lifted his eyes to them. "It's always the same with these parties: so many people and so little room. What can you do?" With an air of resignation he went back to eating.

Miranda grabbed another couple of glasses of champagne and passed one to Rupert. He was going to be drunk soon, but what the hell. He didn't open on Broadway very often.

Paige glanced at her watch. "When do the reviews come out?"

Alyce, having attended more Broadway first night parties than anyone else, indicated the party still in full swing. "The papers don't come out for a while, but the online reviews will be appearing already. If they'd hated us the champagne would've stopped flowing and the room rapidly have emptied. I think we could be a hit."

"Cool," said Paige, getting another drink. "If no one minds I might go back into the VIP room and see if I can find any celebrities to flirt with since my date is a dead loss."

"I'll come with you," Richard said. "If your date is out of the closet I want to introduce myself!"

"OK," Paige giggled. "Let's see who can pull first."

Miranda, seeing a famous face not in the VIP room, disappeared in pursuit. Rupert wandered back to the lessening group of his co-stars. Kyle and Lauren had found chairs and were sitting either side of Nate, chatting to him.

"Cheers," Rupert said, clinking Alyce's glass.

"Thank you." She glanced at her husband. "You gave Nate a great time tonight. He thinks you're terrific."

"Have you disillusioned him?"

"No." Alyce studied him. "It bothers you to be less than popular with someone, doesn't it?"

Rupert raised his eyebrows. "You're being very insightful, Miss Gilmore." He thought for a second. "I suppose I don't relish the idea of people not liking me. But surely that's a universal emotion?"

"Not everyone's so bothered. There are always gonna be personality conflicts – some folks thrive on them – but you're so used to charming everyone it must throw you when someone doesn't fall for it."

Rupert frowned. "Do you think I was playing wheelchair grand prix simply to charm Nate, and therefore you?"

"No, of course not. I'm not saying your charm is an act because if it was I'd have no time for you at all, while actually I think it's as natural to you as breathing."

"I always believed if people didn't like me it was because I'd unintentionally upset them in some way, while you seem to be saying it's my ego. Am I really that shallow?"

Alyce smiled. "I doubt you do upset many people – perhaps just the odd angry partner of women you've slept with, or possibly the women themselves if they wanted a more permanent commitment."

"Ouch. You really don't think much of me."

Alyce crossed her arms and screwed up her face as she considered the question. "Actually, I do in most ways and I think you're very far from shallow. But I recognize a philanderer and I don't want Jennifer hurt. I'm very fond of her."

"So am I. I don't intend to hurt her." He grabbed two more glasses of champagne and offered one to Alyce with a bow.

Alyce took one and laughed.

"What?" Rupert asked. "Too charming?"

"Too charming, and way too gentlemanly. See, Jennifer is crazy about anything English and that includes charming English gentlemen."

Rupert squeezed her arm. "I'll behave, I promise." He glanced over to the other side of the room. "Oh Lord, Miranda's trying to chat up Alec Baldwin. I'd better go and rescue him."

*   *   *

Alyce's deduction proved correct and the internet reviews filtering through were hugely favourable to *All About Eve* and its entire company. As a result the party continued into the early hours, although by then only Paige, Richard and Rupert remained from the cast plus Miranda, and none of them were especially sober. Rupert's provided car, waiting outside, obligingly took Paige home once it had dropped the other three at the hotel, Miranda having booked a room there too.

"Shhh," Richard said, as he nearly fell into the hotel. "We mustn't wake Judith."

"Even with her hearing I doubt we'd be audible in the lobby from the twelfth floor," Rupert pointed out, a remark which seemed rather funny for some reason. At least Richard and Miranda seemed to think so. The night staff smiled at them politely as they wended their way to the lift.

"What floor are you on, Miranda?" Richard asked.

Miranda studied the buttons with interest. "I can't remember." She gave a husky laugh. "Let's push them all and see which one looks familiar when we stop."

This seemed like a good idea to Richard and the two of them did just that, in spite of Rupert's protestations. Unfortunately, each floor looked identical and finally they had to return to the front desk and ask which room Miranda was booked into. Turning out to be two floors below Rupert's, Miranda got out of the lift and then sank down directly outside. Rupert, who was marginally more sober than his ex-wife, decided he'd better go with her and ensure she arrived safely.

Miranda threw herself on to the bed and kicked off her shoes. She certainly was drunk, Rupert thought, to treat her designer shoes in that manner. "That was a wonderful party," she said. Producing a piece of paper from her bag she waved it in Rupert's face. "I've got lots of movie stars' numbers. They thought I was sexy." She put one finger to her lips as if to impart a great secret and another pointing to the paper. "This one said he had a huge project which would be perfect for me."

"I hate to disillusion you, Miranda, but he's the receptionist at the office of one of our producers."

"How do you know? You weren't there."

"Actually, I was. Right after I stopped you from trying to snog Alec Baldwin."

"Oh." Miranda's face fell. She studied the paper again. "Well somebody here could be useful. Let's celebrate some more. Raid the mini-bar, Rupert."

"No, I'm going to bed. So should you."

"Please don't go." Miranda's voice was tremulous.

Rupert sighed. "Don't give me that dramatic act, Miranda. Save it for your TV show. It would be perfect for Nurse Cathy to employ over some dying patient."

He'd reached the door when Miranda spoke again. "There's not going to be any more Nurse Cathy. I've been fired."

Rupert spun round. "What?"

Miranda sat huddled on the bed, her whole demeanour changed in an instant. "The pro-

241

ducers of *NHS: The National Hope Service* fired
me because I complained about their scripts."
Miranda gave a half sob. "All I wanted was good
writing." She dug into her suitcase and produced a page of crumpled script. "Read that."

Rupert read the beginning:

DOCTOR CHRISTOPHER:

But Nurse Cathy, you are the only nurse I
can work with. You understand me in the
way no one else ever has. You anticipate
my every need in the operating theatre.

NURSE CATHY:

I can anticipate your every need in other
departments too, Doctor Christopher.
(*Slowly she starts to undo her nurse's
uniform and puts Doctor Christopher's
hand on her breast.*) I know exactly what
you need and I can give it to you.

Rupert raised his eyebrows. "Well," he said
carefully, "it's not exactly Shakespeare."

"It's crap. You can recognize that. *NHS: The
National Hope Service* started as cutting edge
television and it's turning into a soap opera and
a bad one at that. Even *Casualty* has less embarrassing story lines. I called Mike to tell him I
wouldn't do it and the idiot had the nerve to tell
me I didn't have script approval. What kind of
an agent is he?"

"Very few actors get script approval and as
far as I recall he did get you a better dressing

242

room, an on-call car and wardrobe consultations, not to mention a decent pay increase. Script approval might have been pushing it."

"Whose side are you on?"

"Actually, I'm on yours. I'm not sure I've ever been as proud of you as I am tonight. You're making an artistic stand, not one based on vanity."

"Thank you, darling. It's nice to have support, unlike that miserable little weasel, Rob."

Rupert's heart sank. If Miranda split up with Rob it would make his life a lot harder. "What did Rob do?"

"He agreed to go on strike with me, but as soon as the producers became nasty he turned tail and went running back to work."

Rupert held up his hands to stop her. "Back up a minute, darling. What strike?"

"Obviously, when Mike wouldn't help and the producers wouldn't change the writers I had to do something. So we went on strike. We refused to shoot a single scene."

"Bloody hell, I never saw you as the militant type. What happened?"

"They agreed to a meeting at which those brainless producers stated that the young writers they'd brought in would appeal to the youth audience and spice up the series. I told them that since the series wasn't an Indian curry it didn't need spices. And if by youth audiences they meant some hooded yobs that get their kicks by watching talented actors performing banal sex scenes then they could look elsewhere for a Nurse Cathy. And we walked out. The next day Mike phoned to say I'd been fired – or to be precise they were terminating my contract. A minute later Rob was on the phone to his agent begging to be kept in the show. And to think I'd let him strip me the night before as a reward for his support."

"Is that a special privilege? As far as I recall you rather enjoyed such an act."

"Yes." Miranda sounded doubtful. "You were so careful though, even when you were being forceful." Miranda squirmed with pleasure at the memory. Sex after rowing with Rupert had always been amazing. "Rob always seems to rip something. I had brand new La Perla underwear on that night too, which will never be the same again. I've tried to explain about designer labels, yet he claims that act is the only time he feels masterful in the bed department." She shook her head in incomprehension. "He makes it sound as if I'm domineering."

Rupert, feeling almost sorry for the wretched Rob, turned away to hide a smile, but Miranda was far too busy with her grievances to notice. "And I had to pleasure him, in the early evening in the sitting room and with the lights on, to convince him to join me in the first place."

"You certainly were determined to enlist his help," Rupert said, unable, in spite of his best efforts, to stop from picturing the scene. Much as Miranda enjoyed sex in a variety of ways, she was strangely old fashioned about keeping it in the bedroom.

"We could've started an entire walkout at the BBC." Miranda's eyes shone as she remembered the picket line she'd envisioned. It would have been a stylish one, very media friendly, with actresses in short skirts and high heels.

Rupert watched her face. "And you visualized them eventually making a movie about you: the actress who stood up for good writing."

"Fuck off, Rupert," snapped Miranda, who'd visualized precisely that. It was one of Rupert's more annoying traits that he was so good at second guessing her. "Do you want to hear the rest of the story?"

"There's more?"

Miranda thought for a moment. There wasn't much, but she was enjoying wallowing in her misery and not yet ready to finish. "So Rob went rushing back to work and I was left on my own with no job, no money coming in, and the degradation of being fired. That's partly why I came tonight. I knew you'd be supportive."

Rupert wondered whether she meant emotionally supportive or financially. Knowing Miranda, it was probably both.

Miranda rolled shakily off the bed and took some miniatures out of the fridge. She gave one to Rupert and drank the other straight down, without even noticing what it was.

"Miranda, that isn't going to help."

"You're quite wrong. I feel much better already," Miranda said, waving the empty bottle.

Rupert sighed, opened his bottle, poured it into a glass and added a mixer. "Here's to a very brave actress," he said, raising his glass to Miranda. He picked up the page of script and read it again. It really was appallingly bad. He squinted at a scrawl at the bottom of the page. "What's this?" he asked.

Miranda glanced over. "I was trying to rewrite

it. I thought anyone could do a better job. But I'm not certain I'm cut out to be a writer."

Rupert grinned. "I don't know; you could probably write for Mills and Boon." He held the paper up and declaimed Miranda's rewrite. "God, Nurse Cathy you are the sexiest woman I have ever seen, come here and let me screw you."

"It doesn't sound as bad when you say it," Miranda said. "You always were a good actor. You could make any line believable. Maybe if I'd been a better actress I could've made those other lines work."

Rupert looked at Miranda's despondent face. He moved closer and put his arms around her. "You are a good actress, darling. Nobody could make that script sound believable. And once the news is out that you're available you'll be inundated with offers. After all, you've got all those movie stars to visit."

Miranda cuddled up to him. "Yes, you're right. I could make it as a movie actress, couldn't I?"

"You could certainly give it a shot."

"I'm not too old, am I?"

"They must need actresses of all ages," Rupert lied, knowing full well that few actresses around the forty age mark stood much chance in LA. But tonight wasn't the time to humiliate Miranda any further. "I'm going back to my room now. I'll see you in the morning."

"Pass me one more drink before you go." Rupert did so and Miranda took it, opened it, dropped it, spilling it down the front of her dress, and promptly burst into tears. Swiftly Rupert pulled the dress off, helped her into the hotel's bathrobe, dabbed at the stain with a towel and promised he'd get the dress cleaned tomorrow.

"Thank you, darling," Miranda sniffed. "And for your support tonight, it makes me realize our marriage wasn't all bad, was it?"

"It was very far from all bad." Rupert leant over to kiss her before he left. This was certainly one opening night he wasn't going to forget.

CHAPTER SIXTEEN

Rupert woke up the next morning with a vile hangover. He hadn't even closed the curtains last night and the light was shining right in his eyes. In point of fact the curtains appeared to have moved – or rather the window had. The room's furnishings were the same but the lay-out was different. Gingerly he turned over and realized his hangover wasn't his biggest predicament. Miranda lay beside him and both of them were naked.

"Oh, fuck, fuck, fuck," he muttered under his breath, throwing on his clothes. He wished he could pretend he'd been so drunk he couldn't recall what had happened, but that wasn't the case, although he'd been far from sober. He'd got as far as the door when Miranda had called his name, and he'd turned around to find her lying there wearing nothing but her underwear, and... well he didn't want to remember his actions after that. He supposed it was ironic that, after years of cheating on Miranda while being married to her, he was now cheating with Miranda while living with somebody else.

The phone rang. Miranda stirred, leant over and answered it, shielding her eyes from the light. "Hello. Yes, he's here. Hold on." She held out the phone to Rupert who'd been gesticulating for her to deny his presence. "Darling, it's for you. God, I feel awful." She lay back down and shut her eyes as Rupert took the phone from her.

"Hello? Christ, Judith, please can you speak a little quieter." He held on to his head with his other hand as Judith continued to scream at him down the line. After about a minute the phone was slammed down and Rupert slowly got back to his feet and finished getting dressed.

"Rupert, I need Alka Seltzer," said Miranda, her voice muffled under the bedclothes.

"I'll go and get some." Rupert struggled to the nearest drugstore, aware how he must appear in his ruffled party outfit, although being New York no one batted an eyelid. He bought two packets, dropped off one with Miranda and then opted to climb the two flights of stairs to his room where he found Victor standing outside his door, holding a coffee cup. "Don't shout at me too before I've taken some of these," Rupert said, waving his purchase. "Otherwise my head may explode."

"I wasn't going to shout. I'm merely the messenger." Rupert gestured Victor inside where he added the Alka Seltzer to a glass of water and swallowed it in one go. "Here's a chaser." Victor passed him the coffee. "I bought it for myself, but I'd say you needed it more."

Rupert sipped it gratefully. It'd been a long time since he'd drunk that much and he had no intention of ever repeating the experience. Eventually he looked over at Victor who was leaning against the wall. "Of what are you the messenger? Does Judith want a public flogging or a day in the stocks?"

"Actually she wants you to retrieve a missing blouse which she's convinced Mindy took."

"Oh, God." Rupert drained the last drop of coffee. "That's the last thing I need."

"Is it? I thought you might have bigger problems," Victor said, dryly. A second later there was a banging on the door.

"You were supposed to bring him back," Judith snapped at Victor as he let her in.

"He was being compassionate and allowing me a last coffee before my execution," Rupert said. "I'm sorry about your blouse. She must've taken it before I got there."

Judith sniffed. "And that makes a difference?"

"It would do in her head. I didn't tell her to stop taking things until she'd already done the act, so it doesn't count." Rupert was impressed how well his brain was functioning. He massaged his temples. "Do you want to wear it today or could it wait until tomorrow?"

"Wear it?" Judith virtually spat. "Are you a complete idiot? I'm never wearing it again. I shall destroy it. I merely don't want to think of her doing... God knows what with it."

"Right, I'll shower, change and then sort it out." Rupert started to get to his feet.

"Sit down, I haven't even begun yet," Judith hissed. Rupert did so. This must be the way virtually every actor Judith had worked with had felt at one time or another. Until now he'd personally never fully experienced it. He'd certainly been on the receiving end of her rage on the odd occasion, but he'd never felt like a schoolboy about to be punished and it brought back unpleasant memories. Judith stood over him, arms crossed. "I phoned you here several times late this morning when I'd discovered my blouse was missing. Then I phoned Richard, who said the last time he'd seen you was escorting Miranda back to her room. So I tried there and guess what? You were still there – the morning after."

"Yes," Rupert hedged. "Miranda was drunker than I was, so I thought I ought to make sure she was OK and we ended up raiding the mini bar, in fact I've a feeling we emptied it, and before I knew it I was waking up to find it was morning."

"Really? You simply fell asleep?"

"Passed out is more the expression."

"Humph." Cynicism oozed from Judith's every pore. "Fine, it's none of my business."

"That's funny, I thought that's what I told you earlier," Victor commented.

"Shut up!" Judith marched to the door and then swung around to glare at Rupert. "And don't bother retrieving my blouse. I'd intended to ask you because I trusted you, but I'm not sure I do anymore." She opened the door and disappeared into the corridor. A second later her voice floated back, "Victor!"

Victor pushed himself away from the wall and walked across the room. "By the way, your reviews are great," he said to Rupert. "I sneaked out and read them since Judy not only refuses to look at them but won't even have them in the vicinity in case they contaminate her. In truth I think she's terrified they'll say something negative, but they're incredibly good. They all rave about Judy and the play and they're pretty keen on you too. One of them calls you 'mesmerizing'

251

and a 'great stage actor.'"

"Bloody hell, are you sure they have the right Rupert Blake?"

"I don't know. Are you sure you are the right Rupert Blake?"

"I rather wish I wasn't, at the moment."

"Yes, I can imagine." Rupert caught Victor's cool gaze and quickly returned to the original subject. "Are you going to tell Judith we're an official hit?"

"I might leave the papers lying around – by mistake of course. I've a feeling she'll be too tempted to ignore them. There isn't a hint of negativity or criticism in them and she deserves some praise for her hard work."

"What would you have done if there had been bad reviews? News gets around, however hard you try not to listen."

"I'd have stood guard so no one could talk to her, unless I'd briefed them first. I couldn't bear to see her hurt."

"You're a good man, Victor."

"If you love someone you don't want anyone or anything to cause them pain. Do you?"

Rupert tried to hold his gaze. "No."

"Right, I'd better go before Judy screams the hotel down."

In spite of the rave reviews, which she'd found lying in her room marked in hi-lighter pen – a temptation impossible to ignore – Judith was far from happy. Victor had refused point blank to retrieve her blouse from Mindy since he barely knew the girl, as did Richard who wasn't risking being alone in Mindy's apartment without a chaperone. As a last resort Judith phoned Wesley, who was reading the reviews with great pleasure, and demanded he do it, thereby instantly spoiling his enjoyment.

Mindy had readily given up the blouse to her producer, explaining, as Rupert had surmised, that she would no longer take anything of Margo's since Addison had forbidden it.

"And you believed her?" Judith demanded of Wesley, as she hacked the blouse into tiny pieces with nails scissors in her dressing room.

"Yes." Wesley watched her, finding her rage unnerving, even by Judith's standards. "I don't think she's a liar, only very odd."

Judith rolled her eyes. "Odd – she's fucking certifiable!"

The stress over Mindy, on top of her frostiness with Rupert, meant Judith wasn't in the best mood for that night's show even though her fellow actors were ecstatic about their reviews. All of them had been singled out for praise in one medium or another, although Judith, Rupert and Mindy had received the highest accolades.

Aubrey, whose direction had been acclaimed in the *New York Post*, was strolling around the theatre hugging a copy to him and beaming at everyone he met, making Judith feel quite murderous. "It's my direction which makes the play work," she said, trying to set fire to the pieces of her blouse with a cigarette lighter.

"Which is why you should be pleased it got so well received," Wesley replied, firmly removing the lighter before the smoke alarms went off.

"If he wasn't so smug and even half admitted my input I wouldn't care so much."

"We all know," Wesley said, grateful that from next week he wouldn't have to deal with such problems, at least not face to face, since he was returning permanently to London. The Americans could earn their percentage of the show he'd built up, by dealing with any crisis. He wasn't comfortable sharing the role of producer anyway, and was longing to return to his wife and daughter.

Leaving Judith still sulking, Wesley went around the other dressing rooms to be greeted by a company in high spirits, other than Rupert who seemed unusually low and admitted to being hung-over.

"You must be thrilled by your reviews," Wesley said to him.

"Yes. They're great."

"Judith doesn't seem happy."

"What else is new?" Rupert rubbed his chin. "Plus I don't think she's having a very good day."

Judith's day didn't improve. Fifteen minutes after the show had gone up, two late audience members with front row seats were hastily seated during the second scene change. Removing their coats and scarves, the latecomers placed them on the stage in front of them as if it were a clothes rail. As Judith entered with Mindy and Alyce to play the next scene, she was greeted by a variety of outer garments in what was supposed to be Margo Channing's apartment. Tempted as she was to demand the cretins remove their clothing, or even kick the items back at them, this would mean breaking out of character which was completely against Judith's theatrical principles. Yet neither could she leave them sitting on the set. She'd have to do something in character.

Turning to Alyce she said, "Birdie, some of those tiresome visitors last night appear to have left their attire behind. Perhaps you could be so kind as to hang them in the closet."

"Sure." Alyce grabbed the offending articles, much to the astonishment of their owners who sat transfixed in their seats, and took them into the wings dumping them unceremoniously on the floor before returning on stage to continue the scene.

"Dear me, heads are going to roll," Richard commented from the wings where he was waiting to go on stage. He examined the clothes with his foot. "Good quality – shame the same can't be said for their owners." He turned to Rupert who was creased up with laughter beside him. "That's the most cheerful I've seen you all day."

"It's the most cheerful I've felt all day. There is something truly magnificent about that woman. By the way, isn't that your cue?"

Richard shot on stage, leaving Rupert laughing even harder.

When Judith came off in the interval she discovered the stage manager about to go through the pass door into the auditorium with the offending garments. "Don't even think about it," she snapped.

"But it's their property."

"Then they can come to the stage door at the end where I will personally return the items to them."

"You will?"

"Oh yes." Judith was already planning her

255

lecture on theatre etiquette. "Tim, take them to my dressing room."

"Where do you think this spine-tingling exchange will take place?" Richard asked Rupert. "I want to film the event for posterity."

"I think you'll find that won't be happening," Judith's tones thundered down the corridor.

"Damn!" Richard lowered his voice. "I always forget about her incredible hearing. Sometimes I believe she's got superwoman powers, like the Bionic Woman when she flicked back that hair and her ear would flash."

"I think it beeped not flashed," said Rupert.

Richard clapped his hands in delight. "Goody, another closet Bionic Woman fan."

"Merely in the cause of research; she was a tennis player if you recall and I needed to watch her for inspiration."

"I see."

"And I loved the way she looked when she ran in slow motion. It was very sexy. What's your excuse?"

"Programme quality, of course."

"Of course."

"Do you think Judith is going to slaughter those people?"

"No," said Wesley, who'd come through the pass door. "I'll return the bloody things quickly and quietly at the end. Where are they?"

"In her room," Richard said, disappointed there wasn't to be a showdown: a sort of Clothes-fight at the 44th Street Corral.

"I'll collect them while she's on stage."

"Judith will kill you."

"Probably, but as of next week I don't care."

*　　*　　*

A good hour after that evening's performance had come down, Miranda was waiting at the hotel for Rupert's return and wondering what was taking him so long. She'd tried phoning his room, banging on his door and ringing his mobile which went to voice mail. Where was he?

Rupert was actually in the hotel, but in Judith's room, where he'd resolved to come clean with her and Victor regarding his activities last night. It was obvious that neither of them had believed his story, so why keep up the façade? More importantly, and to his surprise, he found he wanted to tell them, which was an entirely new experience for him.

If he'd expected or even wanted chastisement from Judith, the ferocity of her attack took even him aback. It was the biggest bollocking he'd ever had in his adult life. After she'd finished she slammed into the bathroom.

"I'm not sure if she's angrier because she's disappointed in me, or because she's fond of Holly," Rupert said to Victor, still rather shaken.

"A bit of both I'd imagine."

"And you?" Rupert almost held his breath, waiting for Victor's response. It was odd how much he minded about this man's opinion.

Victor was silent for a while. "Being separated from one's other half for months on end like you are so often in your business, and to a degree in mine when we're reporting away from home, it's very easy to fall into bed with someone else. It's a combination of temptation and loneliness. Having said that though, Holly is one of the nicest people I know and I'd hate to see her hurt."

"So would I."

"Then are you going to tell her?" Judith demanded, re-emerging from the bathroom.

"I keep asking myself that. I hate the idea of lying to her, but she'd be devastated if she knew."

"Then don't tell her. What about Miranda? Will she keep her mouth shut?"

"Lord knows. She's awfully bitter at the moment because she's lost her job and possibly her boyfriend."

Judith gave a horrified gasp. "Tell me she doesn't want you two to get back together."

Rupert scowled. "If she does then it's entirely one sided. I'm hoping she's merely furious with Rob for letting her down, because otherwise he's perfect for her. He's everything she wanted me to be but wasn't." He ignored his ringing mobile which displayed yet another call from his ex-wife.

Judith was nodding slowly, her face a picture of contemplation. Victor and Rupert exchanged glances. "Judy, are you scheming?" Victor asked.

"Mind your own business. Think carefully though, Rupert, before you unburden yourself to Holly. There are occasions when ignorance and not honesty is the best policy."

"I'm glad you care for her so much," Rupert said.

"Care be damned. I simply can't face the notion of you being utterly miserable and walking around with a face like a wet weekend if you and Holly split up or, even worse, the prospect of you and Miranda back together." She picked up the phone.

"Who are you calling?" Victor asked.

"Wesley."

"It's awfully late."

Judith gave a satisfied smile. "That's the idea. He spoilt my fun by returning those morons' coats to them and I'm going to make him suffer. Sleep deprivation is only the beginning." There was a click as the phone was answered. "Wesley, I'm sorry to disturb you, but there's an emergency here at the hotel and you need to come right over." She hung up and then rang down to the front desk. "Yes, you can help me. There's a man called Wesley Bartlett arriving shortly. Please tell him it's far too late to receive any visitors and he's not to disturb me. Thank you."

"Judy, that's pure evil." Victor frowned at her.

"You know I don't like to be crossed. Those people deserved a proper admonishment which I'm certain Wesley didn't deliver, and I won't tolerate it. And if you don't wish to sleep in the corridor I suggest you keep your opinions to yourself." Rupert stood up and Judith swung round to him. "And if you imagine I'm letting you leave and warn Wesley then you have another think coming. Sit down." She glanced at her watch. "We've time for another drink. That should take long enough for Wesley to get here, receive my message, return to his hotel and go back to sleep. Then I'll call him again – perhaps a rumour about the theatre being on fire. Ah, revenge is sweet."

CHAPTER SEVENTEEN

The incident with the coats was quickly picked up by the media, and as she arrived at the theatre the following evening Judith was surrounded by reporters, hoping for comments or a statement.

"I don't give interviews for money so I am hardly going to give any for free," Judith remarked as she swept inside. As soon as she'd passed through the stage door she stopped dead, and then started to laugh. Every conceivable space backstage was covered with coats and scarves: hanging from doors, draped over furniture and dangling from ceilings. Even the set was adorned with them. The stage management and wardrobe departments, having raided every thrift store in the city to produce this décor, were greatly relieved at Judith's positive reaction.

In her dressing room she was greeted by a pile of hand-delivered letters, full of admiration, from other Broadway performers who had suffered similar conduct from their audiences, without dealing with it so stylishly.

"Why do I bother sweating my guts out every night to give a performance when I could merely become a cloakroom attendant?" Judith commented to Tim as she leafed through them. "Christ, there's some actor here wanting to organize an evening in my honour at the top of the Marriott Marquis after Sunday's matinee. How truly ghastly. Be a dear, Tim; phone and tell them I suffer from vertigo."

"They may suggest some place else."

"Then tell then I suffer from Actor-tigo – a phobia of a surfeit of actors in a social setting."

Even aside from Judith's hatred of such events, she was otherwise engaged on Sunday evening. On Monday Rupert was moving to his new apartment while Victor was returning to London, so she had invited both men out for dinner, in spite of Rupert's initial reluctance to play gooseberry on Judith and Victor's last night together.

Miranda had also been angling for a dinner invitation. Having failed to meet Judith in the hotel, even though she'd hung around endlessly in the lobby, she'd finally managed to 'accidentally' bump in to her at the theatre. This hadn't been an easy accident to engineer and Miranda's rehearsed excuse of looking for the Ladies didn't sound very convincing when actually uttered. Judith had merely acknowledged her and pointedly wished her a pleasant flight home. It wasn't fair. She'd worked with Judith and believed Judith had liked her and yet now she was left out in the cold.

Miranda had no more success in trying to get an invitation to Rupert's new apartment. When Rupert had finally got back to his room, following his confession to Judith and Victor, she'd been up the two floors in no time, clad only in a new set of sexy underwear – with a coat over the top. When he'd opened the door, she'd walked in and dropped the coat.

"Rupert darling, I thought you'd never come back."

"Miranda, please go back to your room. Preferably having replaced the coat or we'll have hotel security up here." He picked it off the floor and held it out to her.

"What do you mean? After last night you can't pretend we're not meant to be together."

"Pretending has nothing to do with it; we're not. Full stop," Rupert said, bluntly. "We were both very drunk and fell into a familiar routine. That's all. I love Holly, and while you're angry with Rob at present you're perfect for each other. The best idea would be if we forgot last night happened. That means we mention it to nobody. Do you understand?"

"No I don't. What has Miss Goody Two-Shoes got that I haven't? I bet she's not nearly such a good fuck."

"Miranda, I am not holding this conversation with you."

"Perhaps I should hold it with Holly then."

"Don't you dare."

"Why not? Wouldn't it be ironic if she knew how it felt to be the cuckolded one?"

"I'm warning you, if you contact Holly under any pretence then you'll find any support from me will disappear, physically and financially. Whatever you do or say is not going to get us back together, so you'll only alienate yourself. And I don't see Rob being thrilled if he discovers you've been unfaithful to him."

"I don't care, I hate him."

"No you don't. Think about it. Goodnight." And he firmly shut the door in her face.

Miranda had thought about it. She knew Rupert well enough to know she'd never win him round if she pissed him off, so she'd play nice – for the moment. In this vein she slinked her way into his dressing room on Saturday night waving a white paper tissue. "I come in peace," she said. Rupert regarded her dubiously. "Please don't look so stony faced," Miranda pleaded. "I'm trying here." Rupert gave a half smile. "Thank you. I wanted to say I was sorry about my threat. I wouldn't have told Holly, honestly. I'm not that vile."

"I'm glad."

"I'm only hurt because you treat Holly like a goddess and me like the devil incarnate."

"If I'd treated Holly like a goddess, I wouldn't have slept with you."

Miranda gave a wounded sniff. "That's charming; now I feel like a prostitute. As I recall I didn't exactly force you."

"No, you didn't. I'm totally to blame."

"And was it that awful?"

"Miranda, sex with you has always been fantastic, and this time was no exception, believe me."

Miranda grabbed at this. "So, since we're alone in New York and no one would ever be the wiser why can't we continue... enjoying each other." She took a step closer to him.

"Absolutely not!"

"But..."

"I messed up big time, and however enjoyable it was it's not happening again."

Miranda's placatory manner disappeared in a flash. "Well don't come crawling to me when Holly discovers what a louse you are and dumps you, or you want to have sex with a real adult."

263

Miranda slammed out of the dressing room with a frustrated shriek at such volume that it could be heard several floors away.

'Operation Miranda,' Judith's scheme, came into force on the same Sunday of her meal with Rupert and Victor. It involved sending a car to the airport to pick up a passenger off a flight from London and drive them to the hotel, under strict instructions that they should claim their visit was entirely off their own bat.

Miranda was sitting, bored, in her room. She'd had to stop after five hours of retail therapy when it occurred to her that she no longer had any income with which to pay off her already overstretched credit cards. Perhaps she could persuade Rupert to help out, but since sex, her normal bargaining tool, was obviously no longer an option she wasn't sure how to approach him. She had bought him a huge scented candle for his new apartment (candles weren't exactly his thing but it was the thought that counted), so maybe she'd give him that and then ask. She tried to remember what else gave Rupert pleasure and drew a blank. Most mutual activities during their marriage had been of her choosing. There was tennis of course, but how could she use that? Dress up in a tiny white dress and frilly knickers and offer to play with his balls.

She flipped through the TV channels, all of which appeared to be showing commercials or programmes starring nobody over the age of twenty five. Did she really stand a chance of getting work in LA?

There was a tentative knock on the door and

Miranda jumped, wondering if her credit card had been refused and it was the hotel manager demanding she vacate the room immediately. Nervously she peered through the spy hole and then flung open the door in surprise.

"Rob!"

"Hello, Miranda." Miranda's former co-star in *NHS: The National Hope Service* and lover, status to be confirmed, handed her a huge bunch of flowers. Miranda couldn't decide whether to accept them or throw them back in his face.

"What on earth are you doing here?"

"I've come to see you. Could I come in?" Rob asked.

"Why?"

"I wondered if we could talk." His voice held a note of hope if not conviction.

"I've made it quite clear what I think of you, Robert Collins. I don't ever want you to darken my door again."

"I love the way you say that line."

"Are you insinuating I'm acting?" Miranda screeched.

"No! But you make it sound so dramatic. You're such a wonderful actress. Even if you never want to see me again I shall never get bored of watching you perform."

"Oh." Miranda was vaguely mollified. "I suppose we could talk, since you've come all this way. However, that's not to say I forgive you."

"I don't blame you. I have been telling the other cast of *NHS: The National Hope Service* how badly you've been treated, though. But you see I needed to keep the job and the money because I'm in the middle of paying off a loan for us to have a holiday in Mustique for Christmas. It was going to be a surprise."

"Mustique?" Miranda's eyes lit up and then grew hard again. "Bloody Rupert promised we could go to Mustique before he left me for that pathetic Holly."

"I wouldn't leave you, if you'd consider forgiving me. The idea of you being with anyone else makes me feel quite ill. When I heard you'd gone to New York I was terrified you were going back to your ex-husband. Please tell me I'm wrong."

Miranda shook her head dismissively. She was still thinking about Mustique. "First class flights?"

"Absolutely: only the best for you."

"You'd better come in. We can't talk on the doorstep. But don't expect sex. I'm still very angry with you."

"Yes, Miranda. But your anger is getting me terribly aroused."

"For God's sake," said Miranda, hiding a smile of pleasure.

"How long before you're back?" Rupert asked Victor over dinner at the River Café in Brooklyn. The combined fame of Judith and Rupert guaranteed them a prime table by the window, overlooking the illuminated lower skyline of Manhattan.

"I don't know. I want to do a series of articles on our troops in Afghanistan. More and more soldiers are being killed there and it's got to the stage where all they say on the news is: 'Another two soldiers were killed today in Afghanistan. Their families have been informed. And now on to sport...' I want to put faces and personalities to these youngsters and show the conditions they're living under."

"Are you going out there?"

"At some point, but I'm researching from this end first. There are some fairly disillusioned army officials who I'm hoping will give me interviews, if I don't reveal them as my sources." He smiled across the table at Judith. "I keep telling Judy that it's getting safer over there for non-military personnel, demonstrated by the fact they're trying to rebuild their tourist industry – albeit not very successfully."

"Suicide bombers and landmines aren't much of a selling point," Judith snapped, stabbing the table with her fork.

"I'll be careful and not take any risks, I promise."

"Do what you like as long as you don't expect me to leave the show to come and collect your dead body."

Victor laid his hand over Judith's, halting her table stabbing. "I'll ensure that's clear to everybody concerned. And I'll be back so soon you'll barely notice I've gone. I may even come back here first."

"Jesus, will I never get any peace?" Judith pulled her hand free and signalled at the waiter to bring another bottle of wine. "How many times do I have to tell you that you're distracting?"

Victor smiled. "You're merely my cover, Judy. I actually only come to see Rupert."

"I'm sure you'll be very happy together."

Rupert blew Victor a kiss, causing their waiter

to wonder if it was worth offering this handsome movie star his phone number.

Rupert left Judith and Victor alone at the restaurant once he'd eaten, and was packing up his hotel room when there was a wild knocking on the door.

"Thank God you're here," Miranda said, pushing her way past him into the room. "I need to ask you a small favour."

"Yes?" Rupert's tone wasn't encouraging.

Miranda paused, while she considered her best approach. "The good news is that Rob's here and suitably apologetic, and he's going to take me to Mustique, which you never bloody did." Rupert opened his mouth to say something congratulatory, but Miranda jumped in. "Our predicament is that his savings are going towards that and so he has no ready cash to spend here. And I've rather depleted mine. He's flown all this way especially and has to go back tomorrow, and we can't even afford a cab between us, let alone a celebratory meal." Miranda sighed dramatically.

Rupert gave a half smile at her performance and got out the wad of notes he usually kept on him; a habit left over from their marriage. "Here, go and have fun."

Miranda reached up and kissed him. "Thank you." She tucked the money into her bag while wondering if she could go any further. What the hell, she decided, in for a penny in for a lot of dollars. "Rupert, I was terribly depressed when you'd spurned me after our little encounter." Rupert raised his eyes to the ceiling.

Miranda sounded like a character from a terrible old play. "And that rejection came on top of my career rejection when my contract was not renewed," Miranda continued, so caught up in her role as the wronged woman that she didn't notice Rupert's sardonic facial reactions. "So I did a little shopping to cheer myself up. And I'm not sure I have quite enough funds to pay for everything, and the interest rates on credit cards are so high and I couldn't bear it if I had to go through the disgrace of bankruptcy..."

"How much?"

"I'm not exactly sure, I'm terrible with figures." Miranda fluttered her eyelids at him.

"You're only terrible with figures when it suits you. Still, if you don't know, I'm not sure what I'm meant to do."

Quickly Miranda produced all her card receipts and put them on the bed. Rupert took the pen and paper from beside the hotel phone, added them up, converted them into pounds, and wrote her an English cheque for the full amount, wondering how she'd already managed to spend the large lump sum he'd given her in alimony.

Miranda gave a little squeal of pleasure as she took one side of the precious cheque, although Rupert still held on to the other. "This is it, Miranda. Anything else you spend is your problem. Don't suddenly call me from jail because you couldn't pay some restaurant bill, or because your furniture is being repossessed, and expect me to bail you out, OK?" Miranda nodded and Rupert released his side.

"Isn't it wonderful how Rob flew all this way

to see me?" Miranda said. "You never made such romantic gestures."

While Rupert could, in fact, recall a quantity of occasions where he'd travelled huge distances to see Miranda when one or other of them had been working away, he certainly wasn't arguing if it meant Miranda getting back with Rob.

Miranda waved the cheque absently. "I wonder how he knew I was here. I didn't tell him." She looked at Rupert. "Did you, to get me off your back?"

"No." Miranda eyed him, suspiciously. "I swear," Rupert added, holding up his fingers in a salute Baden-Powell would have been proud of. "Scout's honour."

"You weren't ever a scout. You'd have been thrown out for unsuitable behaviour with the girl guides."

"Good point. However, I swear I didn't tell Rob you were here. I expect he saw you at the first night party on the internet – he'd hardly miss you in that outfit."

"Really?" Miranda simpered.

"Yes. On all the best porn sites."

"You bastard!" Rupert laughed at her outraged expression. "Well, I've got your cheque now, so I don't have to stay here and be insulted." She marched towards the door.

"Remember I can always cancel it," Rupert called after her.

Miranda swung back, clasping the cheque to her chest. "You wouldn't?" Rupert's eyes twinkled at her mischievously. "Ooh, you make me so mad." Miranda stormed out.

That, Rupert mused, was a great deal better

than making her amorous.

He debated Rob's opportune arrival for a moment, and then scribbled a mock telegram which he slipped under Judith's door.

OPERATION ROBERT COLLINS BIG SUCCESS. STOP. MISSION ACCOMPLISHED. STOP. BELIEVE GENERAL GOLD RESPONSIBLE. STOP. MUCH RELIEVED. STOP. BLAKE. STOP.

If his hunch was incorrect Judith would think him crazy but he was fairly sure it wasn't.

Judith and Victor took longer to leave the restaurant than they'd anticipated when Judith's car failed to turn up. When Victor rang the car service they insisted it'd been cancelled.

"It's that bloody Mindy," Judith said. "In the play Eve organizes for Karen to drain the car of petrol so she can play Margo's role and this is no doubt her equivalent."

Victor laid his hand on her arm. "I expect it's simply a mistake. They're sending a car now so let's have a nightcap while we wait."

Judith scowled at him. "You don't know Mindy. We'll go over to her apartment right away and have it out with her."

"No." Victor's voice was firm. "Tonight's my last night and I'm not sharing you with Mindy or Eve or whoever she thinks she is."

Judith started to protest, but then shrugged. When Victor was being resolute there was nothing in the world she could do to change that – besides, she rather enjoyed it.

CHAPTER EIGHTEEN

"No, I didn't, I swear," Mindy insisted, having been summoned to Judith's dressing room after Tuesday's performance with regard to the cancelled car.

Judith glared at her. "I don't believe you."

"It's true. You could check my phone records. There wouldn't be a call to the car company on them." Mindy was proud of that idea. Checking phone records was what happened in the movies to solve murders and find missing people.

"What about a payphone?"

Mindy stared at Judith in amazement. "A payphone?" She'd never consider using one of those.

"Oh, get out," Judith snapped. "And keep out of my way except on stage."

Mindy got out, running into Kyle who was about to leave the theatre. "Hey, are you OK?" he asked, having seen her expression.

"Not really." Some impressive tears poured down Mindy's face. "Margo hates me."

Kyle glanced around at the deserted theatre; he was only still there because he'd been entertaining friends who'd been to the show. "Come on," he said leading her into the dressing room he'd just vacated. "Tell me what happened."

The timing and situation couldn't have been better for Mindy. Lloyd was a man with whom Eve had an undeniable affair in the play and she had, as yet, failed to get the opportunity to experience it. Now, unexpectedly, she had her chance. She told Kyle about Judith's car accusation, embellishing the story for dramatic effect and making her look very much the victim, while conveniently forgetting to mention such incidents as her entering Judith's hotel room and taking personal items.

This had the desired effect of making Kyle sympathetic, if puzzled. He'd never seen Judith as the kind of actress to live her role, the way Mindy did. He gave the slightly sobbing Mindy a friendly hug, and was thrown when she returned the hug with a great deal more fervour. "Mindy, we should go." Kyle tried to release her grip.

"Lloyd, you've been so kind. I'd like to thank you properly." There was no doubt to the meaning behind the words.

"Are you crazy?" Kyle pushed her away with more force.

"You and me. Eve and Lloyd. Having sex would bring genuine passion to our roles."

"No!" Kyle's head was swimming. "I love my wife and I don't have affairs."

"Lloyd is in love with Karen but he still sleeps with Eve. I won't screw up your marriage. Eve doesn't screw up Lloyd and Karen's."

"Doesn't she? It certainly isn't the same afterwards. And besides, we're not Eve and Lloyd." He slapped his hand against his forehead as a thought came to him. "Was this a set up? Did Judith actually upset you?"

Mindy looked at him innocently. "She was real mad."

"Jesus, I'm outta here."

273

Mindy watched him virtually sprint out of the theatre leaving her in his dressing room. She was utterly mystified. What was wrong with these actors? Of course Lloyd had an affair with Eve; it was there in the play. She must call Krystal when she got home and see what was going wrong. Slowly she wandered around the room, running her hands along Kyle's costumes and personal effects trying to soak up emotions from those. On the dressing table was a photograph of two young children, which didn't fit into her Lloyd/Eve scenario. She turned the frame face down. That was better, much better.

Kyle barely stopped running, other than on the subway, until he'd reached home. Lauren was sitting up in bed reading, and smiled as he came in. "Hey, what's up?" she asked at the expression on his face.

Kyle was about to feign ignorance of what she meant, but in the end he told her. "Are you laughing?" he demanded as Lauren's face twitched.

"Not exactly, but you have to admit it is kinda funny."

"It wasn't at the time."

Lauren pulled him down beside her. "I'm sorry. Still, I'm very flattered that you turned her down. Weren't you even a little bit tempted?"

"No." Kyle stroked his wife's face. "Not only is she eccentric, to the extent of being creepy, but I prefer my women..."

"Yes, I know, with stretch marks."

"I was going to say normal and with a sense of humour but stretch marks works too."

*   *   *

Before the matinee the following day Kyle related his encounter to Rupert, only to find his co-star had previously undergone the Mindy experience. And not only Rupert, but Richard too. "You might have warned me," Kyle protested.

Rupert sighed. "I'm sorry, that was a definite error in judgement on my part. I thought I'd convinced her to stop living as Eve after I'd turned down her offer to let me do God knows what to her, but patently not. Maybe Judith was right and Mindy did cancel her car. Damn it."

"Incidentally, how did Richard take Mindy's advances? I can't quite visualize it."

"Apparently it killed his libido stone dead – for either sex!"

Richard's libido had returned to life following the first night party, where Paige's date had shown far more interest in her co-star, a sentiment which Richard reciprocated. Tom was a theatre dancer who, after appearing in two short-lived Broadway musicals, was now waiting tables at Joe Allen's. There was a twenty year age gap between him and Richard, and Richard wasn't so naïve as to believe this was going to be the great love of his life – he'd already found that in his beloved Scott and nobody could replace him. But Scott had been dead for four years, and Richard had finally moved from the mourning stage to the lonely stage. Tom was great company, charismatic, and adored Richard's English accent and manner. Furthermore, unlike many of the men Richard had half-heartedly dated, Tom hadn't immediately expected sex, happy to wait until Richard felt ready, which to Richard's surprise hadn't been long.

Both Rupert and Judith were apprehensive over this relationship, hoping Tom wasn't using Richard as a trophy boyfriend. Richard, touched by their concern, hastened to introduce them over a post-show meal at Tom's tiny apartment, where Richard was spending an increasing amount of time. The dinner took place only two weeks after press night, but Richard felt an intimacy with Tom which made their time together seem far longer.

"What's your justification for escorting Paige to the party and leaving with Richard?" Judith demanded, almost as soon as she'd walked through the door. Having been pre-warned about Judith's manner, Tom gave her his most pleasant smile, which earned him a "Don't tell me you want to screw me too – are there no limitations to your sexual preferences?"

This remark confounded even the well-prepared Tom. "No, of course not."

Rupert surreptitiously made a reproachful face at Judith as he handed over the two bottles of decent wine they'd brought. Judith ignored the look and continued with her interrogation

"So you suddenly changed your sexual orientation halfway through the evening?"

"Judith, stop it," Rupert said, giving up on the subtle approach.

"That's OK," Tom said. "It's a fair enough question. I never told Paige I was straight. We met at a dance studio and hit if off, so when she asked me to accompany her to the first night party of such a prestigious event, I jumped at the chance."

"So you used her?"

"No. I only thought of her as a friend. I never misled her."

"Are you sure you're not misleading Richard instead?"

Richard shot Rupert a despairing glance, wishing he'd never suggested this evening.

Rupert took Judith firmly by the elbow. "Come on, I want to look at Tom's bathroom."

"Why?"

"I'm considering retraining as a plumber." Rupert marched her from the room.

"Delightful if you're a midget," Judith commented in the tiny bathroom where she and Rupert barely fitted. "And don't start pointing out stopcocks or washers, because I don't care."

"Well, please care about Richard and stop being vile to Tom."

"Do you want some unemployed dancer taking him for a ride? I don't trust him. Do you?"

"You don't trust anybody. And I can't make a decision with you giving him the third degree. Besides, Richard is a grown man; we can't nanny him."

Judith picked up two bright pink towels which read 'his' and 'his' and held them at arm's length, whilst making vomiting noises.

Rupert removed them from her and replaced them on the rail. "If you're going to continue like this you might as well go back to the hotel and the rest of us can have a pleasant evening," he said.

Richard meanwhile was abjectly apologizing to Tom who was in the process of putting the finishing touches to dinner. He'd even borrowed a table and chairs from friends so Judith and Rupert wouldn't have to eat squashed up on the pull-out breakfast bar sharing the two stools.

"It's no problem," Tom replied, neatly chopping chives and basil to sprinkle on top of the side salad. "I'm glad she cares enough for you to make such a fuss." He drained a big pan of spaghetti and stirred in a homemade sauce, gesturing towards the bathroom. "Do you think they'll be long in there? Everything's ready."

Richard was poised to fetch them when they emerged with Rupert full of compliments for the smell of supper and Judith silent, patently making a point. It wasn't until they'd eaten their main course that she deigned to join in the conversation, and then left straight after dessert and coffee. Once Rupert returned from putting her in a cab the atmosphere became conspicuously more relaxed.

"I think it's real nice how much Judith must care for Paige to be so defensive on her behalf," Tom commented as they analyzed the evening over the second bottle of wine.

Richard and Rupert both laughed. "She doesn't," Richard explained. "It's merely an excuse to be horrid to you. I am so sorry." He leant over and kissed Tom on the cheek and then looked rather embarrassed at doing so in front of Rupert.

"That's fine," Tom said. "She's quite a character."

"She's certainly that," Rupert said. "Tom, did you make these chocolate truffles?"

"Yes, are they OK?"

"They're delicious. I never knew people made

them. I thought they only came in boxes from Fortnum and Mason's. Richard, this one's a keeper!"

Richard smiled affectionately at Tom. "I think so."

Rupert cleared his throat theatrically. "I recognize that look and I don't want to be a voyeur, so I shall take this as my cue to leave." He stood up and shook hands. "Thank you for a delightful evening. It was lovely to meet you properly, Tom."

"Thank you for undertaking this evening," Richard said to Tom after Rupert had left.

"No problem. Rupert's great and Judith is... a character."

"What can I do to make it up to you tomorrow?"

"I have a tap class. There's an open audition for *42nd Street* next week and our teacher's running over the routines. Do you want to join me?"

"Good Lord, I haven't taken tap classes since they were compulsory at drama school. Can I come and watch?"

"Only if you promise you won't have eyes for anybody else. There will be a lot of Lycra clad pretty boys there who make me look as old as the hills."

"Lycra is so yesterday." Richard took Tom's hand. In spite of Judith's less than desirable behaviour, the evening had given him a new found confidence and appreciation of his relationship. He very much doubted that had been her intention.

CHAPTER NINETEEN

Aubrey, having insisted on remaining in New York for the entire run of *All About Eve* (in a luxury apartment paid for by the producers), was revelling in the glory this production had brought him. To justify his huge fee, and apartment, Aubrey wandered the St James Theatre giving notes to his actors, which they knew better than to take if they were contrary to Judith's. Aubrey barely noticed; he was performing his job and if the cast paid him no heed it wasn't his problem.

Paige, being the youngest and least experienced of the company, made the mistake of playing one of his notes during a performance, in direct contrast to Judith's concept. Having been summoned to Judith's dressing room after that show, she emerged ten minutes later shaken and tearful. The following day an enraged Aubrey discovered he'd been banned from the theatre. A security guard, temporarily employed by the producers on Judith's insistence, was stationed at the stage door to implement this exile. There were times, Aubrey thought, when it was difficult to ignore such affronts.

Resolving to show Judith he was capable of more than simply being her 'Yes Man,' to be expelled from the theatre on her merest whim, Aubrey accepted another directing job, with an Off-Off Broadway theatre company. The play entitled *Life...?* was written by a student from

NYU who, it was implied, was the next Edward Albee, a writer Aubrey much admired and had previously directed to great acclaim. In spite of it offering a profits-only deal, with limited expenses (which in exchange for providing his genius for free, Aubrey insisted included free food, coffee and wine throughout the rehearsal period), Aubrey accepted the assignment with alacrity in the hope it would garner him praise from a more diverse crowd.

"Where's my cigarette case?" Judith demanded, staring at the props table before one show, a week after Aubrey's banishment. The props man pointed at a silver case sitting on the table. "That is not the one I've always had before, so don't try and tell me it is."

"It's similar," said the luckless man.

"I don't care if it's solid silver from Tiffany's. Where's mine?"

"I don't know. It kinda disappeared."

"Kinda?" Only Judith could endow the word with such meaning.

"It was there last night and today when we did our check it wasn't, so we're using the spare."

Judith's eyes narrowed. "Search Mindy's dressing room."

The props man's mouth almost fell open at the prospect. "We can't. That's a violation of her privacy."

"Oh, for fuck's sake."

Judith stormed into Mindy's room where the younger actress allowed her to search without protest, while denying all knowledge of the whereabouts of the case.

"You probably removed it last night and it's doubtless on its way to California by now for your collection," Judith snapped as she left the room and returned to the stage. "From now on I want all my props locked away at the end of the show," she told the props man. "I don't care if you have to buy a special safe, just do it."

Even though no one else would agree, Judith considered she gave a sub-standard perform-ance that night because of the replacement cigarette case. She didn't consider herself par-ticularly superstitious, but there were certain theatrical traditions she did believe in, one of which was keeping the exact same props and costumes for the entire run (unless something actually fell to pieces). Then there was not quot-ing from Macbeth or whistling backstage; no one realized how stressful it was being an ac-tress. One day she really must retire. Strangely, whenever she mentioned this intent to anyone - Rupert, Alan East her agent, Wesley, Victor - they laughed. Especially bloody Victor.

Rupert had been an acceptable escort since Victor's departure, and at least she got more sleep and didn't get dragged around New York playing at being a tourist. Most Sunday nights they'd go out for dinner after the matinee and end up at Rupert's apartment talking or playing backgammon over several drinks.

Two months into the run there was one Sun-day evening which Judith would have to fill on her own. A movie which Rupert had made the previous year was opening in LA and, to ensure their star could attend to promote the movie, the studio had arranged the premiere for a Monday night, flying Rupert out after the Sunday matinee and back very early on the Tuesday.

"You'd better not be late back for the show," Judith warned. "Remember France?"

Rupert remembered France very well, when a wildcat airport strike had grounded all flights when he'd been filming on location in the French Riviera and he'd had to use a private plane, courtesy of George Clooney, to get him back in time for a performance of *All About Eve* in London. Even though he'd made it by the skin of his teeth, Judith had been livid.

"If it appears there's any chance of delay I'll take over the cockpit and fly the plane myself," Rupert promised.

"Don't be facetious."

Rupert normally quite enjoyed premieres, yet having to fly six thousand miles round trip for this one merely to walk down a red carpet and be photographed was too much of an effort. It wasn't even a movie he felt passionate about: a romantic comedy in which he played a suave English aristocrat at odds with a scatty American girl from the wrong side of the tracks with whom he eventually falls in love.

"I bet they only want me because Hugh Grant isn't available," Rupert had told Holly when he'd been offered the role. Still, he'd enjoyed working with the film's highly-respected director and the location work in Boston. And the fee that his agent, Jane English, negotiated with the Hollywood film studio was enough for her to buy a French holiday home on her fifteen percent commission alone.

Although Rupert was staying at a hotel only a

five minute walk to Grauman's Chinese Theatre, the premiere's venue, a car was sent to collect him. The Studio had intended for him and his female co-star to arrive together until his co-star insisted on being escorted by a woman with whom she'd recently started a passionate and public affair. So Rupert arrived alone.

Dutifully he smiled at endless cameras, did a series of brief interviews and then worked his way around the crowd held back from the red carpet.

"Could you say hello to my Mom?" one girl asked, holding out her mobile phone.

"Hello, Mom," Rupert obliged down the mouthpiece.

"Rupert, Rupert!" Rupert turned towards the voice, expecting another autograph or photographic request; it was odd how strangers used actors' Christian names as if they were old friends. "Rupert!" The voice was almost desperate – and also slightly familiar. A beautiful blonde was jumping up and down and waving with such fervour she was in danger of concussing her neighbours.

"Good God, Echo!" Rupert leant across the barrier, to ensure he wasn't imagining things. It was indeed his *Blithe Spirit* co-star from a few years back. An American ex-beauty pageant queen with no acting talent whatsoever, but a truly ghastly stage mother who thought otherwise. Rupert gestured to a security man that Echo was with him and she was allowed through, where she proceeded to throw her arms around Rupert, much to the annoyance and curiosity of the fans. Several press cameras clicked furiously.

"Let's get inside before we're on the cover of every Hollywood gossip magazine," Rupert said, taking Echo's arm and leading her into the cinema. She looked every bit as beautiful, in fact the same in every way – except there was no dreadful mother as chaperone. "What on earth are you doing here?" Rupert asked.

Echo took a deep breath. "I saw your movie was premiering tonight and I hoped real bad that you'd be here and I've been waiting all afternoon so I was at the front of the line, so you wouldn't miss me if you were coming, and you did come and you did see me and it's like so cool." She beamed at him, displaying her perfect bleached white teeth.

Rupert smiled back. "I'm highly flattered you went to all that effort. It's lovely to see you. But what are you doing in LA? You wrote me a letter a while ago saying you were now living with your Dad in Alabama and had gone back to school."

"Yeah. And I graduated."

"That's great news. Well done. You didn't come all the way to LA to see me though, did you?"

"No, though I would've if necessary. I live here now."

Before Rupert could ask her anything more it was announced the movie would be commencing directly, and with a quick seating adjustment, and to her great excitement, Echo got to watch it sitting beside Rupert. Rupert, glancing sideways at her as she laughed constantly, concluded he couldn't have asked for a more appreciative companion.

At the post premiere party Rupert merely showed his face before giving Echo the option of staying there alone or joining him for a quick bite to eat.

"Eat with you," Echo replied, before he'd barely finished the question.

"So what are you doing in LA?" Rupert asked, as they ate at a local Mexican restaurant. "If you graduated high school have you gone on to college?"

Echo shook her head. "Nah, I didn't get real good grades and everyone else was smarter than me and the only thing I was real good at was doing people's make-up and telling them what to wear, cos I knowed all that from when I was a beauty pageant queen. So I'm at beauty college here and then when I'm done, which is real soon, I'm gonna open my own saloon."

Rupert tried to hide a smile. "I think that's salon, Echo. Saloons are usually some kind of bar, like in cowboy movies where people rush in and shoot each other."

"Shucks, I'm still so dumb. No wonder everyone at beauty school laughed at me when I told them I wanted a saloon."

"You're not dumb. Lots of people get words muddled. It's much more important that you're good at what you want to do. And I'm sure you are."

Echo gave him a dazzling white smile. "Yeah. I'm gonna be the best make-up person ever. Then maybe I can go back to London and work there for while. I was gonna go after I graduated and I called your house to see if I could come stay, but Miranda got real mad when I asked

286

to speak to you and hung up. I didn't dare call again."

"I'm sorry about that, I didn't know. But I imagine it was me she was mad at and not you. You see, we're divorced."

Echo's mouth fell open. "You're kidding."

"No, I'm not kidding. I have a decree absolute to prove it."

"Huh?"

"A piece of paper to say I'm divorced."

"Oh." Echo looked hopeful. "Are you living on your own now?"

"No. I'm living with Holly."

"You mean Holly who fed me my lines?"

Another obstacle to Echo's acting career was her inability to learn lines. Holly had been brought in to *Blithe Spirit* to feed them to her via an earpiece. For introducing Holly into the company, and hence into his life, Rupert would always be grateful for this impediment of Echo's.

"Yes, Holly who fed you your lines."

"She was real nice. So she's like your roommate?"

"No, she's nothing like my roommate. More like my bed-mate."

There was a silence as Echo's brain grasped the notion. "Oh, right. Gee." There was no mistaking her disappointment.

"What about this guy you told me about in your letter? The one you were dating from a pizza place, wasn't it? Did that work out?"

Echo screwed up her face, and then remembering her mother's warning about wrinkles instantly relaxed it. "No it didn't. We had sex in this cheap motel and it was horrid. He had this big ugly thing which he kept pushing and pushing between my legs and inside me and grunting and that was it. And it hurt. And it was real messy after; I dunno what the maid would have thought. So I don't wanna do it again. It was gross. Why do people think it's nice?"

Rupert was biting his lip trying not to laugh, at the same time feeling sorry for this childlike woman. That mother had a lot to answer for. "I'm sorry it was awful, Echo, but don't let it put you off. The first time is often painful for girls, I believe. And he obviously wasn't a very considerate lover. You'll find someone better and start to enjoy it."

Echo looked doubtful and then thoughtful, two expressions which usually blended together when she attempted to act. "Rupert, do you remember when we had foreplay in Judith's dressing room?" She announced 'foreplay' as if it were something sacred.

"Yes." How could he ever forget Judith's insistence that he get Echo aroused enough for her to be able to emulate the feeling on stage? Even Miranda had permitted the undertaking for the good of the production, on condition it went no further than foreplay. It had worked, only Echo had pined hopelessly for him ever since.

"Well, Kevin, this guy, didn't do any of those cool things you did," Echo continued. "So maybe it'd be different with you. Would you show me how it's done proper? I'm sure you'd make it nice and it wouldn't hurt so bad. And I wouldn't expect it to be a real relationship 'cos you've gotten Holly, but I wanna know how it's supposed to be."

Rupert almost choked on his tortilla. "That's a very charming invitation, Echo, but I'm afraid I can't. I love Holly and when you feel that way about someone you can't go around having sex with other people." There was a brief pause, before he added, "At least you shouldn't."

"Oh." Echo gave a quiet sigh of disappointment. "You're not mad at me for asking?"

"No, I'm hugely flattered." He gestured for their waitress to bring the bill. "But I do have to go back to the hotel now and get some sleep. If I'm too tired and mess anything up on *All About Eve* tomorrow night then Judith will kill me."

Echo, having been on the wrong side of Judith's tongue on numerous occasions, nodded sympathetically. She couldn't understand why Rupert would ever want to work with that terrifying woman again. "I wish you could stay longer," she said.

She looked so sad that Rupert found a piece of paper and scribbled two numbers on it. "That's Holly's mobile and our landline in London. If you need any advice or help give her a call. I know she'd love to hear from you."

Echo's face immediately lit up. "You think she'd like to talk? I'd like that lots. I had friends in school, but not so many here."

"So call her. Only remember the time difference. London is eight hours behind LA."

Echo started counting on her fingers while mouthing each number. "So if I call tonight it would be like afternoon there, right? Would that be good?"

"That would be good."

"Thanks, Rupert. You're real swell."

Switching on his mobile as he alighted from the plane in New York the following day, Rupert received three voice mails from Judith insisting he come to the theatre immediately. Barely had he walked into her dressing room when she thrust an object into his hand. It was the framed photograph of Judith as Margo Channing which Holly had given her for opening night, but the word 'bitch' had been scrawled in black pen several times over the photograph.

"Jesus," Rupert swore.

"I found it when I came in. It's horrible." Rupert could only agree with her. "Somebody has been in my dressing room and I'm sure it was that fucking Mindy."

"But that's not an Eve action. I see no reason why she'd do that."

"Because she's crazy."

"No, I don't think she is. Not in that way."

"Will you ask her?"

"I suppose so." He glanced at his watch. "It's only four thirty so I doubt she'll be in for a while. Why are you here so early?"

"I wanted some peace on stage before the hoards got in." Judith was staring at her defaced photo again.

"I'll ask Holly to get you a replacement from wherever she got it," Rupert promised. "Then maybe we should get the locks changed on your room and ensure only essential people have keys. OK?"

Judith nodded, Rupert's calm manner soothing her. "All right. So how was Hollywood?"

"Interesting. You'll never guess who I found hanging around outside the cinema."

"Please don't say Miranda."

"No, Echo. Remember her?"

"How could I ever forget? The dreadful American girl, with no talent and a lobotomy."

"Judith, that's cruel."

"I consider that's generous."

"She tried very hard."

"She was certainly very trying. Tell me she hasn't got some starring movie role?"

"No, she's at beauty school."

"Good. Long may she stay there. Rupert, will you get rid of that photo? I want to go on stage by myself for a while."

"Of course."

At the door Judith turned back. "You didn't sleep with Miss Lobotomy, did you?"

"No, I didn't! I can restrain myself occasionally."

"Humph." She disappeared in the direction of the stage.

Rupert carefully removed the photograph from the frame with a tissue. No doubt he'd been watching too many CSI episodes, but he wouldn't get his fingerprints over it – just in case.

Mindy, as with the cancelled cab, denied all knowledge of Judith's photo defacement, and had the alibi of being in her apartment all day, a fact which could be backed up by her doorman. When Rupert broke this news to Judith she scowled. "There's doubtless a fire escape she climbed down." Rupert just looked at her.

"Fine, so I'm paranoid – but with good cause. Oh, for God's sake let's get on with this damn show. There's an audience out there who think actors are wonderful magical people, not fucking lunatics with marker pens."

Rupert, shattered from his LA trip, was fast asleep when the phone rang at 3am. "If it wasn't Mindy, I bet it was Aubrey," Judith said, as he reluctantly picked up the receiver. "He hates me because I've banned him from the theatre."

"If you've banned him from the theatre how did he get in to deface your photo?" Rupert enquired, failing to stifle a yawn.

"Fuck off," Judith retorted, slamming down her receiver.

"With pleasure," Rupert muttered to the silent phone, wondering when he'd strayed into an Agatha Christie whodunit.

Aubrey was in his element on *Life...?*, directing actors who were thrilled to be working with a celebrated West End legend. Admittedly, he found the play fairly incomprehensible but opted to treat it as if it were a classic, thereby convincing his cast that they were creating something very special. In turn the actors considered it refreshing to find a director who allowed them the freedom to do what they felt, emotionally. They even put Aubrey's less than clean clothes, slight smell and ability to eat and drink nonstop, down to English eccentricity and genius.

In order that his *All About Eve* cast could attend the first night of *Life...?* Aubrey requested a Monday evening press night when most of

Broadway didn't perform. Judith, Rupert and Kyle refused to spend their night off on what sounded a dire project, so it was left to Mindy, Jennifer, Alyce, Paige and Richard, accompanied by Tom, to dutifully attend. After Act One Mindy and Alyce left, Mindy citing a lack of concentration on her Eve role, and Alyce a threat to her sanity. The others stood around gloomily awaiting Act Two.

"It's pretty awful, isn't it?" Paige said. "Still, I guess we've all done something worse."

"No," Richard replied. "Maybe almost as bad, but I have never done anything worse than this. I'm not sure it would be possible."

"I don't understand the play," Jennifer said. "The actors seem lost too. And the direction doesn't make it any clearer. Do you think it's meant to puzzle and consequently force us to discover the message ourselves?"

"No, it's just appallingly badly written," Richard said. "I would imagine Aubrey didn't understand it either, so he left it to the actors and there wasn't a Judith among them to help him."

"But he's directed so many wonderful plays," Paige insisted. "His résumé is amazing."

Richard pulled a face. "Yes, but it's a résumé of classic plays where you can't go very wrong if you've got a good cast. Failing a good cast you can always find essays or annotated notes. All Aubrey has to do is regurgitate other people's ideas. He's been doing it for years."

"I love that you're so cynical; it's quaint," Tom said, putting his arm around Richard's waist, causing Richard to half push him away, secretly delighted.

"What are we going to say to Aubrey at the end?" Paige asked.

"Tell him you've never seen anything like it." Richard advised. "After all, it's the truth."

"Yeah, that's good."

"And that you don't want to see anything like it ever, ever again."

CHAPTER TWENTY

While *All About Eve* settled into a comparatively stress free run, relationships and friendships amongst the cast developed. Richard left the hotel and moved into Tom's tiny apartment, while Jennifer spent less time at her own apartment and more at Alyce's where she grew as fond of Nate as of his wife. He was funny and smart and never bitter about his disability. Also, to her great relief, she and Rupert continued to hang out together as friends, although she couldn't help but mind how little Rupert must fancy her to find it so easy.

Rupert also struck up a more unusual friendship with Alyce. Having discovered that her passion for tennis extended to physically playing, he offered to coach her whilst assuring her he would genuinely take pleasure in doing so. Initially wary at playing an ex-professional, Alyce enjoyed these sessions enormously. Once the weather grew warm enough to play outside, Jennifer came with Nate and they would cheer Alyce on as if she stood a chance of winning, even with Rupert playing at a fraction of his ability.

In turn Rupert was inducted into the world of baseball, attending Mets games with Kyle, Lauren and their two children, to whom he became known as Uncle Wupert.

Even Paige was finally dating a man who had proved himself not to be gay on their first night together. "Thank the Lord," Richard said, the following evening. "Somebody has finally had sex." Paige stared at him amazed, wondering how he knew. "You have that look, a sort of rampant glow," Richard clarified. "It's about time. Tom and I were about to sign you up to a dating agency."

"Well, you can't steal this one. He's definitely straight!"

Richard regarded her wickedly. "Ah, but they say there's a homosexual streak in everybody. It merely takes the right person to unlock it."

"No!" Paige wailed. "Tell me that's not true."

Richard chuckled. "Don't worry. I have enough on my plate with the one I did steal. I swear I'll keep my hands off this one."

Mindy, in contrast, continued to connect only with her fellow cast on stage. Judith was convinced that the disappearance of another couple of items, a scarf and her signing pen, were down to her co-star, while general opinion was she had merely mislaid them. Even Rupert was dubious about the loss of the signing pen since he'd lost two of his. Besides, as he pointed out to her, she never signed anything so what did it matter?

"It matters because I don't lose things," Judith snapped. "And my stage champagne glass was smashed yesterday too."

"Glasses get smashed," Rupert said. "I expect the props guys washed it up too roughly." Judith gave him such a look of total scepticism that Rupert gave up trying to be logical.

After disastrous reviews and the instant

closure of Aubrey's Off-Off Broadway show, Judith relented and allowed him back into the theatre, on the proviso he didn't interfere with her play. Instead, Aubrey used the dressing room he'd commandeered as his base, inviting anyone in the least influential to visit. He even held weekly soirées for the company, serving drinks and light snacks. Judith never attended these, but the other cast dutifully turned up most weeks, although after Aubrey took a photo of one of these events and sold it to a magazine, Rupert refused to attend another.

One Thursday evening, nearly three months into the run of *All About Eve,* the packed house took their seats after the intermission, buzzing with anticipation for Act Two. The curtain rose, the lights came up, Judith and Richard spoke the first two lines and suddenly the entire theatre was plunged into darkness. Judith, Richard, Kyle, Jennifer and Alyce froze on stage but under a "keep talking" hiss from Judith continued with their lines.

After a while they were cut off by the deputy stage manager announcing, in the darkness, "Ladies and gentlemen, we appear to be having some difficulty with our power supply. Please remain in your seats for the present while the problem is rectified. Thank you."

"What the hell is going on?" Judith said, as the curtain came down, a rather pointless exercise in the blackness.

The stage manager rushed on stage bearing a huge torch. "It's a complete power cut, the whole grid's out," he explained. "Manhattan is black."

There were gasps from the majority of the cast, and even an "Oh, my God," from Paige who, along with Rupert and Mindy, had felt her way to the stage from her dressing room.

Judith was having none of it. "Big fucking deal," she said. "We had power cuts all the time during the 1970s miners' strikes. And in the war we had blackouts every night, no street lamps, nothing. I can't believe you stopped the show like that."

The stage manager made a sort of squeak, but in the dark it was hard to tell what emotions he was displaying in response to Judith's criticism. "We can't do a show without lights," he said. "We'll have to cancel."

"Cancel?" Judith's tone left no one in doubt as to how she felt about that notion. "How many torches do you have in the theatre?"

"Huh?" the stage manager asked.

"Flashlights," Jennifer translated.

"Find out and bring them here," Judith ordered. It wasn't an easy task without light, but eventually fifteen assorted torches were amassed.

Judith grabbed one of the larger ones and passed it to Rupert. "Light me," she told him. "And for God's sake somebody bring up the curtain before the audience think we've died and go home."

"Ladies and gentlemen," Judith announced, as the curtain rose and Rupert shone his torch on her. "It appears that this city which never sleeps has temporarily hibernated and furnished us with a complete blackout. Obviously we can't perform the play with the correct lighting state so if you feel strongly about that I suggest you leave and ask for a refund at the box office."

"Not now," hissed the rather desperate stage manager. "It's all computerized. It won't work without electricity."

"Apparently you may only receive a refund at a later date, because no one can work manually anymore," Judith amended. "However, if you are willing to stay and watch a performance by flashlight we will be commencing shortly. Those who wish to leave please make your way towards your nearest exit which will be illuminated now by our front of house staff." There was an arc of lights as ushers waved their torches around the auditorium, but not one person moved. "Thank you. Give us a couple of minutes to set up." Judith gestured for Rupert to shine the torch off her.

"I'm sure this is against safety rules," the stage manager muttered, huddled in the darkened wings with the rest of the company.

"And it's safer if our entire audience stampede outside into a blackout along with thousands of other theatre goers?" Judith retorted. "It'll be Slaughter on 8th Avenue. Right, I want anyone backstage ready with a torch, stage management, crew, wardrobe, wigs, if you've got a hand which doesn't shake you're temporarily hired as members of the lighting department. We need some of you torching from the side and some from the front. Try not to light our faces from directly below or it looks horrifying. And ensure the actor who is speaking is illuminated. Actors, keep movement to a minimum and only when it's necessary for the narrative. It's too dangerous to do set or costume changes so we'll work on this sitting room set, using the sofa for a bed when appropriate and setting a table and chairs downstage for restaurant scenes. Jennifer, we'll talk about the car running out of petrol as if it's out of view rather than sitting in it." She exhaled, thoughtfully. "Yes, I think I've covered everything. What are you waiting for? Let's go."

The torched performance was surprisingly successful. There were a few occasions when an actor moved and their light didn't, but the torch operators always caught up before too long. It certainly added a very sinister air to the play. In a scene where Eve realizes the hold Addison has over her, Judith took a torch and, contrary to her own instructions, lit Rupert's face from directly below which gave him suitably menacing air.

During the final moments of the play, as Phoebe imagines herself becoming another Eve Harrington and curtsies towards an imaginary audience, Judith instructed the other actors, bar Mindy, to hold torches above Paige's head, while Mindy was lit gently by only one in the background. This scene was powerful at the best of times, but lit like this it was so impressive that there was a gasp from the audience before they broke into tumultuous applause. The response at the end was unsurpassed, outdoing the first preview, the press night, or the visit by the Bette Davis fan club who had been most vociferous in their approval.

"That was awesome," Paige summed up as

the curtain came down, and the audience carefully made their way out into the dark streets outside.

"It certainly was," Rupert said. "Judith, that was an inspirational idea, perfectly implemented."

"Don't be ridiculous," Judith retorted, as the company gave her a round of applause. "I was merely ensuring the show wasn't cancelled. Now how the hell are we going to get home? Is my car here?"

The stage manager shook his head. "The streets are like a parking lot because the traffic lights are out. Even if it made it here I'm not sure you'd get home. And the subways are out too."

"I suppose I'll walk then. Can you spare one of those torches? Will there be enough to go round?"

"I'll walk you back," Rupert said. "We can share a torch and you can keep it. I've got this huge perfumed candle which Miranda bought me for a house-warming present. I've been wondering what to do with it."

Most people left in groups to share torches. Out of the cast Kyle had the longest walk, which was going to take him up to two hours. Rupert offered him the use of his sofa bed, but Kyle was keen to get back to his family so they weren't alone in the dark all night.

As Rupert and Judith left the theatre they found it was surprisingly light outside. Not only was there a bright moon, but the car headlights, even in gridlock, shone out their beams. Many of the buildings and shops had candles in their windows and there were patches of brightness from those people lucky enough to have obtained torches.

As they walked through Times Square and along 42nd Street they found people sitting on pavements, talking on mobile phones or even to complete strangers. In Bryant Park, people were camping out using bags as pillows and jackets as blankets. Some had make-shift picnics. Pretzel and hotdog vendors were wheeling away empty carts.

"Why don't these people book hotels?" Judith said.

"I imagine they've all been taken – if, of course, they can book anyone in on computers with no electricity," Rupert replied. "It's lucky it's such a warm May night. If this was England they'd be suffering from hypothermia."

Several of the campers, recognizing the two actors as they walked past, smiled or waved. "It's like a different city," Judith commented. "There's a spirit of the blitz feel about it."

"I didn't know you were old enough to have been around in the war," Rupert teased her, knowing that if she really was the 55 she'd owned up to being since he'd known her, she wouldn't have been.

"Well, I might just have been," Judith conceded. "And it made a big impact, even as a tiny tot."

"No doubt even as a babe in arms you were performing down the air raid shelters."

"You mean you've never heard of Goo-Goo Gold, the infamous baby prodigy?" Rupert laughed. "Now do we go right or left here?"

302

Rupert shone his torch on to the street number. "Unless you want to go shopping at Macy's, I suggest left."

"Oh Christ," Judith said, as they reached the hotel, "I suppose the lifts aren't working. The twelfth floor seemed a good idea when I checked in."

"I'll push you," Rupert offered.

"You don't need to. You've got your own apartment block to scale."

"It'll keep me fit."

On the eighth floor Judith sank down on a stair, insisting she have a break. Rupert threw himself beside her. "Who says appearing on Broadway isn't glamorous?" he asked, shining their torch at the grey stairwell, intended for use in emergencies only. "This could be the perfect photo-shoot for *Hello* magazine: *All About Eve* star Judith Gold relaxes on her sweeping staircase after a normal evening at the theatre."

Judith rested her head against the wall. "Perhaps Broadway isn't all it's cut out to be."

Rupert frowned. "Are you sorry we're doing this?"

"No. But there are occasions I miss London."

"London? Or someone in London?"

"For fuck's sake, we're not all as love sick as you over Holly. And Victor has to be in London to look after my cats. I don't trust my housekeeper."

"You don't trust anyone."

"True. By the way, when is Holly getting here?"

"In two weeks. Her show closes on the Saturday night, she has an audition on Monday, and flies over on Tuesday."

"I can't see your face, but I'm sure you're grinning like the demented Cheshire cat you usually resemble, so stop it and let's finish our mountaineering expedition before I lose the will to live." She stood up and sighed. "You know what? I'm hungry. I normally eat after the show but with all the fuss I forgot."

Rupert looked down the eight flights of stairs trying not to show his lack of enthusiasm. "Do you want me to try and find something?"

"You truly are unbearably nice, Rupert. It's not normal."

"Judith, do you think I put it on – being nice and charming to make people like me?"

"Christ, we're staggering up Mount Everest in the middle of a city-wide blackout and you're asking for a personality analysis. What on earth brought that about?"

"Something Alyce said at the first night party."

"And you've been festering about it ever since? You shouldn't care, like I don't."

"Don't you?"

"This isn't about me. I suppose it's good to know that even the outwardly confident Rupert Blake is vulnerable. If you want my honest opinion, Rupert, I'm afraid you are genuinely nice, which is incredibly annoying for the rest of us mere selfish mortals. If you'd thought, 'If I offer to get Judith food that'll make her like me even more,' like your ex-wife would, that would be truly sycophantic, but I'm betting you didn't. However, I won't take you up on your offer anyway. I'll just have a drink and eat the ice."

304

"I imagine the ice machines aren't working either."

For the first time that day Judith sounded thoroughly put out. "Now that really is the fucking limit."

CHAPTER TWENTY ONE

On the Tuesday, two weeks after the city black-out, Judith called a notes session for the full cast on stage at 3.30pm. She considered bad habits were slipping into performances and intended to nip them in the bud. The main offender was Mindy whose perception of Eve didn't always agree with Judith's, and where it didn't there was complete stalemate.

"Where's Rupert?" Jennifer whispered to Alyce, as Judith and Mindy did battle. Or at least Judith did battle while Mindy remained unperturbed, but unmovable. "We may need him to arbitrate."

"He's obviously not fucking here," Judith snapped, causing Jennifer to nearly drop her bottle of water.

"Beware super-hearing-woman," Richard muttered directly into Jennifer's ear so even Judith couldn't hear. "I'm with you about Rupert though. If he doesn't join us soon I suppose I'll have to do the arbitrating and I'm far too young to die."

Jennifer giggled, earning Judith's wrath once again. "Is there something amusing you'd like to share with us?" she demanded.

"No. Sorry." Jennifer wished she could vanish.

"What the fuck is the matter with everybody? You're behaving like a bunch of amateurs, on and off stage, and no one appears to care. Do

I have to carry this show more than I am already? Or would you prefer to perform without me? You could all take a leaf out of the book of little Miss Method Actress here and go around in your own individual characters and to hell with what the playwright meant, or what works best." She swung around, her gaze resting on each one of the stunned and silent actors in turn. "Do any of you actually care?"

"Of course they do. We all do." Rupert had walked quietly on stage behind her.

Judith swung round. "Oh fan-bloody-tastic. Now you turn up after I've done the hard work. Do you think you're too good for rehearsals?"

"No." Rupert's voice was calm, but around him the other actors were exchanging glances. If Rupert was in trouble they stood no chance. "I was at the airport; I did tell you." He gestured behind him and for the first time the company realized Rupert wasn't alone. A young girl with dark curly hair, clinging to a rucksack and looking apprehensive, was standing half on stage and half in the wings.

Judith stared at the girl for a moment. "Well it was a lousy time to arrive." And she stalked off stage.

"Charming," Rupert remarked.

"Bad timing, I'm afraid," Richard said to the girl.

"That's OK. I'm used to it," she replied.

Rupert took her hand and pulled her into the centre of the group. "Everybody, this is Holly. Holly, this is Mindy, Kyle, Alyce, Jennifer, Paige, and you know Richard."

"Hello," Holly said. "I'm so pleased to finally meet everybody. Rupert's told me so much about you."

"Are you a relation?" Alyce enquired, who didn't recall hearing anything about her from Rupert.

"God, I hope not or what we've been doing would be highly incestuous." Rupert grinned as Holly blushed. "Holly's my girlfriend, or significant other, or whatever the PC expression is now. She's been in a play in London which closed on Saturday, so now she's able to join me here."

"You're Holly Brooks," said Jennifer. "You just won an Olivier Award for your role. And your reviews were wonderful. Didn't one of them say you could be the next Judi Dench?"

Holly face registered total astonishment. "Well, um, yes."

"Jennifer's our Anglophile," Rupert explained. "There isn't anything she doesn't know about England. I half expect her to acquire an honorary landed-gentry title by pure enthusiasm and knowledge, maybe Lady Jennifer of Jupping?"

"Is there a place called Jupping?" Jennifer asked quickly, to hide her embarrassment, combined with pleasure, at Rupert's teasing.

"You haven't heard of Jupping?" Rupert said. "What kind of an Anglophile are you?" Jennifer's face fell.

Holly dug Rupert in the ribs with her elbow. "Ignore him, Jennifer. As far as I'm aware there is no such place as Jupping."

As Rupert introduced Holly more fully to the other cast, Jennifer studied the newcomer. So Rupert wasn't getting back together with his ex-wife, rather it was Holly Brooks for whom he'd spurned her. She was a little surprised that Holly was Rupert's type; she was so different from Miranda Flynn, reserved, pretty but not in a glamorous or sexy way – and young. She barely looked out of her teens. And worst of all she was obviously arriving to stay, thereby putting an end to her and Rupert's excursions.

"Jennifer?" Rupert's voice broke into her thoughts.

"Sorry, I was miles away."

"Holly's been saying for ages that one of the first things she wants to do here is go on the Staten Island ferry and I told her you were the expert. How about on Thursday the three of us go and you can fill her in on the history and point out the interesting buildings? I've forgotten everything you told me."

Jennifer gasped. "Oh no, I'd feel a real gooseberry coming on the same boat as you guys."

"Well, you could come on the boat behind, but it would make it hard to hear you!"

"Surely I'd be intruding."

"No, you wouldn't," Holly broke in. "I've read every guide book I could find but it'd be tons better to learn about it from a native New Yorker. And I want to know what else I should see and where I should shop as a local as well as a tourist. So please come with us."

"OK, if you're certain." Jennifer hoped her eagerness didn't show too much.

Holly beamed. Rupert put his arm around her. "Since this rehearsal seems to have been aborted, let's get you back to the apartment and settled in." The other cast watched them as they walked off the stage.

"If I'd known he liked women so young I'd have made a real play for him," Paige said.

Richard shook his head. "Forget it. Rupert adores Holly. He's not interested in anyone else."

Ain't that the truth, Jennifer thought, catching Alyce's eyes on her and quickly looking away.

"She's kinda ordinary though."

"Paige, if you don't want to make an enemy of Rupert I wouldn't repeat that last remark." Richard's voice was unusually sharp. "Now since we appear to be liberated from our note session I'm going in search of a large piece of apple pie. Anybody fancy joining me?" Four hands went up – Mindy opting to stay and prepare for her role. "Oh goody, I hate to pie alone."

"That was a nice thing you said to Jennifer," Rupert remarked to Holly as they reached the stage door.

"I didn't say it to be nice. It would be fun to have a New Yorker to show me around, especially the shops because I know you hate shopping, and Jennifer seems lovely." Holly didn't add that she could also see Jennifer had a major crush on Rupert. It wasn't that she wasn't used to that or to the expressions of astonishment on girls' faces, as with Jennifer's just now, on realizing that he was dating her. It wasn't always easy to cope with; it could be hurtful and made her feel terribly insecure, though she'd never admit that to Rupert. Besides, it was hardly his fault if girls fell at his feet – after all, she had.

Rupert's mobile rang. He answered it, listened briefly and said, "OK, but you'd better be a lot politer," and hung up. "That was Judith wanting us to go to her dressing room," he said. "I'm hoping she's feeling guilty about her earlier rudeness. Can you face it?"

"Of course."

"Holly dear, it is good to see you even though your timing was terrible," Judith said, as they walked in.

"I'm sorry, I should have got a different flight."

"No you shouldn't," Rupert broke in. "Judith, I told you I was meeting Holly at three, so if you'd wanted me to attend your rehearsal you shouldn't have called it at three thirty. There isn't a landing strip bang in the middle of Broadway."

"Stop lecturing me." Judith was being particularly vile because she had totally forgotten about Holly's arrival and knew Rupert had told her. It was one step nearer to senile dementia and fear of that had made her lash out. She tried to make amends. "Do you want to go out for a coffee?"

"No thanks, I'm taking Holly back to the apartment. We can do coffee a lot of other times. Holly isn't going anywhere – I hope."

"Fine." Judith gave a dismissive wave, slightly disappointed which was ridiculous. She had work to do at the theatre and didn't have time to waste scouring Times Square for a Starbucks with spare seats.

"Wait," Holly said, putting down her rucksack, digging inside it and producing a plastic folder. "Here." She opened the folder and pulled out a copy of the photograph of Judith in the play, the original of which had been defaced.

"Rupert told me what had happened to yours. That's so horrible."

"Yes, it was, for all the sympathy I got." Judith glowered at Rupert.

Rupert raised his eyes upwards, not sure how else he could have sympathized short of throwing himself on the ground and wailing.

Judith pointed at Holly's rucksack. "Is that all the luggage you've brought?"

"Oh no, I left my suitcase at the stage door. It's rather heavy because I didn't know what clothes I'd need and I didn't want to embarrass Rupert by not having the right thing for the right occasion, and then I worried that it would be overweight for the plane, but they didn't care, because when I got to the airport Rupert had been very naughty and upgraded me to Upper Class. It was incredibly luxurious, but I'm sure it was horribly expensive."

Judith regarded her with amusement. "You certainly don't have to worry about your girlfriend having grand expectations, Rupert."

Rupert grinned. "No. It's most refreshing. If I didn't take Miranda Upper Class she'd have strung me out on the wing!"

Holly was utterly enchanted by the apartment, especially the small fire escape with a view of Central Park on which she could sit by climbing out of the bedroom window. "Oh, I shall feel just like Francie in *A Tree Grows in Brooklyn*," she exclaimed, that being one of her favourite novels.

"Well, make yourself at home. There's food in the fridge, delis on every corner, or a twenty four hour diner about two blocks west. I've left you some money." Rupert pointed to a pile of dollars on the coffee table.

"I've got my own dollars. I'm not having you pay for everything."

"Fair enough, but I insist you let me spoil you a little. I've been looking forward to doing so for the last three months. Now I ought to get back to the theatre. Judith gets most disgruntled if I'm not there an hour before the show and as you noticed she's already not in the best of moods today. I only hope she hasn't committed Mindy-cide while we've been gone." He leant over and kissed her. "I'll see you when I get back, presuming you're still awake."

"Oh, I will be. I'm far too excited to sleep. And besides, don't you want to... you know..."

Rupert raised his eyebrows in a cavalier fashion. "I do indeed." He ran a finger down her body, watching her squirm with pleasure. "In fact I'm exceedingly tempted to ravish you right here and now, but then I'd never make it for the show."

Holly wrinkled up her face. "That's probably as well. I feel pretty dirty after that flight. Even going Upper Class," she added in case she should sound ungrateful. "I can have a shower and change and be prepared for your return."

"I can't wait. I'll be trampling over the fans in my rush."

When Rupert did get back he found Holly fast asleep on the sofa, wearing a dress Rupert didn't recognize – presumably bought especial-ly. He fetched the spare duvet and put it over her. Strangely, he was rather relieved that there

313

would be no sex tonight, in spite of the fact he'd been craving it since he'd got to New York. It was that bloody guilt thing about Miranda. He'd have to get over that and damn soon. He scribbled a note and left it on the coffee table.

Dear Sleeping Beauty,

Have retired to the royal bedroom to a mattress under which lies a pea. If you wish to join me at any point, please instruct my flunkeys to allow you to pass. I did consider waking you with a princely kiss, but my frog lips kept getting in the way. With love and deep affection

Prince Charming.

PS I feel I may have got my fairy stories somewhat mixed up. Or is there one called Narcoleptic Cinderella and the Frog Pea?

CHAPTER TWENTY TWO

Once Rupert had gone to his matinee the following day, leaving Holly with a map and promises of what he was going to do to her later, Holly spent a blissful day exploring and preparing for his return. Tonight she had every intention of staying awake.

A few blocks away she discovered Fairway's, an impressive food market, where she bought quantities of delicacies which she laid out on the table, along with an enormous bunch of flowers. When she heard Rupert's key in the door she couldn't decide whether to greet him reclining on the sofa, lying in bed, sitting at the table or leaning seductively against the wall. As a result Rupert was greeted by the sight of Holly hurling herself from the wall on to the sofa.

"Is sofa-diving a new Olympic sport?" he enquired, as Holly emerged from the depths of the cushions.

Holly sighed. "I was being indecisive," she explained.

"Ah." Knowing Holly, this made total sense to Rupert. "I like the choice you made. And everything looks great – as do you." He surveyed the table. "Are you intending to feed the entire Broadway contingent?"

Holly giggled. "I got carried away; everything looked so good. I hope you're hungry."

"Absolutely; although what I'm really looking forward to is dessert." He wiggled his eyebrows at her.

Holly crossed her arms. "Do you think you can pull with a line like that?"

Rupert laughed. "Sorry, it is a bit of a cliché, though I was rather hoping you were a sure thing, which was very presumptuous of me." He put his arms around her and kissed her.

Two hours later Holly, still on London time, fell fast asleep, but Rupert lay awake, silently cursing himself. In spite of his best efforts, sex with Holly hadn't been good. Every time he caught sight of her trusting, loving face, he felt incredibly guilty. He hoped Holly hadn't noticed, and that if she had she'd put it down to tiredness or their long separation.

Holly had indeed noticed a difference but, as Rupert had hoped, she put it down to their enforced absence and, being Holly, blamed herself. She was obviously jet lagged and lacking some basic vitality. Or perhaps she'd got out of practice in three months. She mustn't panic, it would work out. Thankfully, with Jennifer as chaperone on their Staten Island Ferry trip later, she and Rupert could pretend nothing was amiss. It was a hot June day and it was a relief to escape from the city's heat on to the water. Rupert watched Holly nod with comprehension as Jennifer confessed how she'd imagine herself as an immigrant arriving at Ellis Island.

"Can you imagine thinking you were finally going to be starting a new life in a new country and they sent you back with all your dreams shattered, simply because you might be weak or sickly?" Holly said. "I was terrified they were going to send me back at airport immigration because I wasn't the right kind of person."

Rupert put his arm around her. "Then I would have been on the next plane out to join you, play or no play."

Holly smiled up at him and Jennifer watched them, trying not to feel too envious. Holly was so sweet it was hard to resent her – but not impossible.

Holly went into the theatre with Rupert and Jennifer that evening so she could watch the play in its Broadway reincarnation, and afterwards received a grilling from Judith wanting to know how the two casts compared.

"They're different," Holly said, carefully. "Yet every bit as good. Mindy is more subtle as Eve than Abigail was, but it works. Jennifer and Kyle have a good onstage chemistry; you believe they're a married couple. Alyce is more outrageous as Birdie, whereas Janet was quieter but still funny, and I think Paige is slightly stronger as Miss Caswell than she is as Phoebe, but that's a more important role."

Judith made a noise of annoyance. "I knew we should have got two different actresses. Paige is obviously useless as Phoebe."

"No," Holly cried. "That isn't what I meant. She's great as both. Oh dear, I shouldn't have said anything."

Rupert laughed. "Come on, sweetheart, let's leave Miss Contrary here and go home."

Judith frowned. "But I have lots more questions for Holly. I want to know whether the dynamics have altered in a different theatre and if the audience response is what I want it to be.

317

It's the first time I've had anyone out front who I can trust since that bloody deserter Wesley went back to London."

"What about Aubrey?" Holly asked, puzzled, if thrilled, by the compliment.

"Don't be stupid, Holly dear. You'll spoil my confidence in you. Why don't we go out for dinner?"

"No, thank you," Rupert broke in. "Holly is trying to stifle a yawn as it is." Holly blushed at the truth of that. "Good night, Judith."

"Fine, go and have passionate sex then. I realize it's all you're interested in."

"How well you know me. Come along, Holly, we have our instructions!"

Tonight it was Holly's turn not to sleep, in spite of her jet lag. There was something horribly amiss; Rupert no longer seemed interested in her sexually. Was she doing something wrong, or had he found somebody else? Perhaps Jennifer's crush had led to other things and Rupert hadn't told her yet. She lay in bed watching Rupert sleep. Perhaps in a few days time Jennifer, or some other New York woman, would be here in her place while she sat on a plane back to London.

The next few nights were no better, though neither Rupert nor Holly made any reference to it. Finally on Sunday Holly resolved to take action. While Rupert was doing his matinee she found a hairdresser where they straightened her curly hair so it hung seductively over her face, and bought a sexy set of underwear and negligee from Victoria's Secret.

In the apartment she discovered a partially

used perfumed candle in a cupboard, placed it in the bedroom and drew the curtains, since it would still be light when Rupert got back around 6pm. Next she laid a trail of rose petals from the front door to the bedroom, virtually mutilating her hands while pulling them from their thorny stems. A few minutes before she expected him she lit the candle, put on some romantic music and lay on top of the bed in what she hoped was a sexy pose, the negligee slightly open to show glimpses of the underwear.

She heard Rupert come through the front door, call out and stop as he obviously spotted the rose petals. As he came into the bedroom she ran her tongue over her lips. "Hi," she said, praying she sounded like Lauren Bacall and not Minnie Mouse.

Rupert stared at her. "What the hell are you doing?" He turned and walked out of the room. Holly could hear him in the kitchen slamming things around. She pulled her knees to her chest and sat in the corner of the bed trying not to cry. She was obviously so unattractive Rupert couldn't even face seeing her in a sexy outfit. Quickly she ripped off the offending articles and pulled on a simple sundress. Taking a deep breath she crept into the kitchen. Rupert was sitting at the table, his head in his hands and a full pot of coffee, untouched, beside him.

"Rupert?"

Rupert sat up with a jolt and turned towards her. "Holly, I'm so terribly sorry."

"It's OK. I understand." Holly swallowed. "Um, should I pack and go now? I could stay in a hotel if there isn't a flight tonight."

Rupert's face was a picture of anguish. "I know I deserve it, but please don't go."

"But I thought... Aren't you breaking up with me? You looked like you hated me just now."

Rupert groaned. "Holly, no, I don't hate you; I hate me." He took her hands and pulled her into the chair beside him. "I have to tell you something and then you can decide whether you want to go back to London. I certainly wouldn't blame you." He picked up the coffee pot and poured them both a cup, adding milk to Holly's. Then, for the first time in his life, Rupert told his current partner that he'd cheated on her. "And seeing you lying there in the way Miranda used to when she wanted something, even with the bloody candle she gave me beside you, I totally lost it," he finished off.

Holly didn't say anything. She merely got up, took her un-drunk coffee to the sink and threw it away. Then she started washing up the coffee machine and wiping down the kitchen surfaces with a dishcloth.

Used to Miranda's tirades when she'd suspected his affairs, Rupert found Holly's silence far worse. "Sweetheart, please speak to me, even to tell me I'm a total bastard."

"It's OK. You were elated from press night and Miranda's very sexy and you know each other so well. It was completely understandable. It's fine."

"Holly..."

"It's fine," Holly repeated. "Only I might go out for a little."

"Of course." Rupert looked around trying to think of anything he could offer her. "Have you got your map?"

"Yes, in my bag. I'll go and get it." Holly went into the bedroom, still carrying the dish cloth which she absent-mindedly threw into her bag. In spite of it being another hot day she found she was shivering and put on a jumper.

Rupert was hovering outside. "You're as white as a sheet," he said, looking at her ashen face. "You should stay here. I'll go out."

"No," Holly almost snapped. "I want the air."

Rupert watched Holly walk shakily down the corridor towards the elevator, using all his self-control to stop himself running after her.

When his phone rang at 9pm Rupert grabbed it only to hear Judith's tones. "I'm bored. Can you and Holly come over for a drink?"

"No."

"Why not?" Rupert was silent. "Why not?"

Rupert sighed. "Because Holly isn't here."

"So tell her where you are and she can join us later."

"I don't know where she is."

"Christ, she hasn't even been here a week and you've lost her. That seems terribly clumsy. But haven't you heard of these gadgets called mobile phones? You ring them, the person answers and they tell you where they are – an impressive if often annoying invention."

"She's not answering. I've phoned about five times in the last hour."

Judith's voice changed from mocking to harsh. "What the fuck have you done?"

Rupert took a deep breath. "I told her about Miranda and me."

321

Judith gave an exasperated sigh, rather than the curse he'd expected. "You certainly pick your time to start being honest. Really, Rupert, you are bloody stupid sometimes." There was a click and Judith had hung up.

By midnight Rupert was seriously concerned. He'd left so many messages on Holly's voice mail, sounding increasingly frantic with each one, that if anyone monitored them he'd sound like a desperate stalker.

It was 2am when he heard the front door quietly open and he practically leapt towards it, making Holly jump as she crept in. "Thank God! I've been worried sick. Are you OK? Where have you been?" He gently took her by the hand, led her into the living room, and as she sank on to the sofa he crouched beside her, studying her face. She was still deathly pale and her eyes were red and swollen. "You're not hurt are you?"

Holly smiled, faintly. "No, I'm fine, although a bit bushed. I walked for miles and miles, I don't even know where. Then about 9 o'clock Judith rang and asked me to go over to her place, but when I finally found where I was on the map, it was way downtown and I'm not confident about the subway system yet and I didn't know if I had enough money for a cab, so I walked and didn't get there until nearly 11 o'clock."

"Sweetheart, I'm so, so sorry." Rupert rubbed her hands. "Judith would have paid for the cab."

"Yes, that's exactly what she said, but I didn't like to ask."

"Oh, Holly." Rupert ached to hold her, but wasn't sure of the reception he'd receive.

"Anyway, it doesn't matter. It was very good

exercise and I've seen tons of New York. And when I got to her hotel Judith was terribly kind. I wish other people, like your cast, could see her when she's like that. I hate the fact that people believe she's heartless."

"I rather think she prefers it that way."

"Yes, maybe. It's odd, isn't it?"

Rupert smiled and squeezed her hands. "So have you been at Judith's since then?"

"Yes. I was going to call and tell you, but Judith wouldn't let me. She said you should suffer a bit longer. She wasn't awfully nice about you."

Rupert pulled a wry face. "I can imagine. Still, it was entirely justified."

"But you're her friend, much more than I am, and you're wonderful to her, so she shouldn't be so rotten. And I told her that." Rupert chuckled at the picture of Holly berating Judith. "She wanted to book me a room there for the night, but I knew you'd worry, so I came back."

"I'm incredibly glad you did." He frowned. "You didn't walk?"

"No, Judith ordered me a car and said it can go on Wesley's account. I must pay him back."

"I doubt he'd want you to." He released her hands and stood up. "You look completely shattered, you should go to bed. I can sleep on the sofa bed if you'd rather."

Holly put her arms around her body, hugging herself. "No, I'd like to talk."

"Of course. Do you want something to eat or drink? Have you had anything?"

Holly shook her head. "I wasn't very hungry. Judith kept trying to give me whisky..."

"But you don't really like it," Rupert finished. "An aversion Judith can never entirely understand! It was probably as well if you hadn't eaten. How about a cheese omelette? We still have about eight different varieties of cheese from your foray into Fairway's."

"No." Holly sounded almost cross. "Rupert, will you just let me ask you something?"

"Sorry." Rupert sat down beside her. "Go ahead."

Holly took a deep breath. "Why did you tell me? I can't stop thinking about that. You never used to tell Miranda, so why me? I never would've known. Is it because I'm less likely to hit you with a candlestick, like Miranda did?"

Rupert scanned her confused and hurt face. "No, that's definitely not it – in fact if you want to hit me with a candlestick, please feel free. The only answer I can give you is that I know you trust me and that made me feel guilty beyond belief. Miranda never trusted me – rightfully I suppose – which made me feel less guilty somehow. It doesn't make sense, yet it's the only way I can explain it."

Holly nodded slowly for a while as if taking everything in. Then she said, "Thank you for being so honest." She got up. "I might have something to eat now."

"I'll make it."

"No, I'll do it. You go to bed. I'm going to stay up for a while."

"I'll stay up with you."

"No!" The vehemence in Holly's voice startled Rupert. "Please, let me be alone."

"All right; whatever you want." He watched

her heading towards the kitchen. "Holly?" She turned back to him. "Will you still be here in the morning? You won't be on a plane back to London?"

Holly gave him a watery smile. "I haven't been up the Empire State Building yet. I can't possibly go home until I've done that." She disappeared out of the room.

Rupert went to bed, but he couldn't sleep. Eventually he heard a slight noise. "Holly?"

"Go back to sleep."

"I wasn't asleep." He sat up and reached over to turn on the lamp, but Holly put her hand over his to stop him.

"You shouldn't see me in the light; I've got a huge cheese belly," she said. "I feel like cows must before they've been milked." She sat on the edge of the bed.

Rupert ran his hand down to her stomach. "I can't feel any udders."

"Wait until I start mooing."

"God, I love you, Holly." Tentatively Rupert held out his arms. Holly stared at them for a moment before she snuggled into them. "You are an amazing person."

"No, I'm not. You see, in a funny way, after the initial shock it was a relief that you'd only had a one night stand with Miranda. I thought you were dumping me and although I've always half expected that..."

"What?" Rupert released Holly from his arms and leant up on his elbow, staring at her. "Holly, do you really think I'm going to eventually dump you, as you so elegantly put it?" Holly bit her lip and looked away. "Sweetheart, why would I

325

want to dump you?"

Holly turned back to him. "Because I'm gauche and unglamorous and a bit mousy and not terribly sexually experienced and I see stunning girls stare at me in amazement when they realize we're together. Why wouldn't you be tempted to swap me for one of those?"

"Because I want to be with someone who isn't over-confident and doesn't believe the world revolves around them, and who isn't utterly obsessed with sex – which is not a statement I ever expected to hear myself say – and who gets lost in books and movies and sobs when Bambi's mother dies."

"Everybody cries when Bambi's mother dies. Don't they?"

Rupert chuckled. "For two hours?"

"But it's so sad! It was like losing one's own mother."

"Maybe that's why I didn't cry," Rupert's voice was cold.

"You wouldn't wish your mother dead, would you?" Holly asked, half curious and half shocked.

Rupert shrugged. "I wouldn't wish death on anyone, but I can't say it would affect me. Anyway, I don't want to get on to the subject of my mother tonight, although we do need to straighten something out right now: I don't intend ever leaving you." He frowned at Holly. "I wish I could think of a way to prove that."

"You don't have to. I believe you and I'm awfully, awfully glad." She yawned. "However, I'm terribly tired and I think I would like you to sleep on the sofa bed."

"Oh, right." Rupert was taken aback, but really it was the least he deserved. He got out of the bed and started towards the door, then stopped at a giggle. He regarded Holly uncertainly.

"Well, you can't begrudge me a little bit of revenge." She gave a wicked smile and held the duvet open. An hour later they finally fell, exceedingly contentedly, asleep.

CHAPTER TWENTY THREE

The following morning Rupert, bearing a bag of doughnuts and two coffees, hailed a cab and asked the driver to take him and Holly to 5th Avenue and 57th Street.

"Tiffany's?" Holly asked, as they arrived. Rupert waved the bag at her. "*Breakfast at Tiffany's*," Holly said, with sudden understanding.

"I personally think they should have a Holly Golightly café in the shop; it's a totally wasted merchandizing opportunity," Rupert said. "But we'll have to make do with eating out here, only hurry up because there's something I'm rather nervous about doing afterwards."

Curious, Holly ate her doughnut so fast she choked on the crumbs. "OK, I'm done," she said, washing it down with the coffee and following Rupert down 57th Street where, to her total astonishment, in a small alcove he suddenly dropped on to one knee.

"Holly Brooks, will you do me the honour of becoming my wife?"

"Are you serious?"

"I'm on one knee in the middle of a busy street in Manhattan – believe me, I'm serious."

"You're not just being kind-hearted and asking to stop my paranoia?"

"I'm not that kind–hearted."

"Then yes. Yes please."

Rupert stood back up, dusting off his

trousers, and kissed Holly. "Come on, Audrey Hepburn, let's go and buy you an engagement ring," he said, steering her through the door into Tiffany's.

Inside Holly took a sharp intake of breath and stopped still. "It's amazing," she said, "only perhaps we should go somewhere smaller."

"Why?"

"Because these salespeople will be used to smart New Yorkers who know exactly what they want while I'll probably choose something totally inappropriate and they'll look at me grandly and say: 'Of course if that's what Madame really wants...' and then they'll laugh at me when I've gone and that'll be so embarrassing for you, because they'll know exactly who you are. Maybe they'd even leak it to the papers that the Broadway star's fiancée has no taste."

"Bollocks."

"You can't say that here; this is Tiffany's," Holly said, scandalized.

"Holly, nobody is going to laugh at you and you can't make an inappropriate choice. You choose exactly what you like. Come on."

To Holly's relief the staff couldn't have been more delightful or helpful and nobody was patronizing or objected when she turned down ring after ring until eventually her eye was caught by one holding a small sapphire surrounded by diamonds.

"Do you like it, Rupert?" Holly asked.

"It's beautiful, yet unostentatious, like its future owner." Holly blushed. "See what it looks like on." Carefully he slid it on to Holly's engagement finger.

329

"It's perfect," Holly said, waving her hand around. A few minutes later she gasped in horror as the saleswoman punched up an amount on her till. "Rupert, you can't spend that much on a ring. I'll choose another one. They must have something cheaper."

"I'm buying you the ring you love," Rupert said. "If I wanted to do it on the cheap I'd have waited until we got home and gone to Argos."

"We could still do that."

"No we couldn't. Stop arguing." He handed over his credit card and the woman swiped it through.

"What if I lose it?"

Rupert ruffled her hair. "Try not to."

"Or if we get mugged in Central Park?"

"Then I'll tell the mugger to take you and leave me the ring." He grinned at her before leaning over to sign the sales slip.

"You've got your fucking Cheshire Cat expression on again," Judith said, as Rupert came into her dressing room the next evening, following their Monday night off. "I take it you and Holly have made up, though God knows why she should have forgiven you so easily. I wouldn't."

"No. You'd expect self-flagellation, sackcloth and ashes and lying prostrate at your feet."

Judith's mouth twitched. "And that would be for starters."

"Thankfully, even without performing such acts, Holly has agreed to marry me."

Judith stopped twisting her hair into pin curls to go under her wig and gave Rupert her full attention. "I have to say I'm sadly disap-

pointed in Holly's resolve, although hardly surprised. She's a hopeless case. You should have
heard her berating me on Sunday night over
my less than complimentary remarks concern-
ing your conduct, while I was attempting to be
supportive. Still, I suppose it's about time you
did the honourable thing, if that's what appeals.
Now go away and let me concentrate. With the
amount of sentiment oozing around here I'll
never make Margo cynical enough."

At the end of the show the full company were
invited to Rupert's dressing room for a drink,
where he announced the engagement. Holly
blushed scarlet as everyone congratulated her
and toasted her and Rupert with champagne.

"Where's Judith?" Alyce asked.

"Judith isn't one for company events," Rupert
explained. "And I told her the news earlier."

"And she still didn't turn up?" Paige said.
"That's awful impolite."

Rupert shrugged. "That's Judith." He held
up the magnum of champagne, the contents of
which were rapidly dwindling. "She did provide
this."

"It's perfect actually," Richard said. "This way
we can enjoy a smooth drink without the acid-
ity Judith could provide by her very presence.
And I say that with the deepest fondness for the
woman – and with the deepest wish for a fill-
up." He held out his empty glass to Rupert.

Jennifer swallowed her champagne with difficulty, wishing it were her in Holly's position.
Quietly she slipped away and climbed to her
own dressing room, where she realized she'd left
her key at stage door. She couldn't be bothered

331

to fetch it and sank down on the stairs instead, putting her head in her hands.

"Jennifer?"

Jennifer jumped at the voice and found Holly standing a few steps below.

"I wanted to see if you were all right," Holly said. "I saw you leave the party."

"I'm sorry. I didn't feel too good. I think it was a bit stuffy and crowded in there and I needed some air. But I'm OK now. You should go back."

"To tell you the truth, even though it's my party, I found it a bit over-awing too. I quite liked an excuse to escape for a minute."

"Right." Jennifer knew she sounded rude, but she didn't want Holly hanging around her.

Holly got the hint and started to walk back down the stairs. Then she stopped. "I may be totally wrong and even if I'm not it's actually none of my business, but you and Rupert..."

"There's nothing between me and Rupert," Jennifer broke in quickly.

"I know."

"Oh." Jennifer wondered if it was possible to feel more unattractive. Holly evidently didn't consider her any kind of threat.

Holly played with her hair, nervously. "It's only that I know you're good friends but sometimes it's easy to misinterpret Rupert's manner. He has a way of making a woman feel they're the most important person in the world to him. And when they realize he's merely being friendly it can hurt a lot."

"Are you warning me off?" Jennifer was defensive.

"No. No, I'm so sorry. I didn't mean that

at all." Holly sat down beside Jennifer. "All I meant was that I saw your expression when I arrived last week and you looked so shocked. Rupert obviously hadn't told you he was seeing me, which was very naughty of him and... Oh dear I'm making this worse. Talk about foot in mouth."

Jennifer shook her head. "No, it's OK. I'm sorry I snapped at you." But it wasn't OK. This virtual teenager was playing agony aunt to her, a woman almost twice as old. It was embarrassing – and yet the desire to talk about Rupert with anybody, even Holly, was too tempting. "How would you know about women only being a bit of fun to Rupert when you're his girlfriend?" she asked, trying to keep any bitterness out of her voice. "He's obviously serious about you."

"I wasn't his girlfriend, not for ages. He was just charming and flirtatious to me like he is with everyone." Holly omitted to mention their one night stand, since it might only make Jennifer feel more rejected. "I knew him for nearly two years before we became a couple and it was torture watching him and Miranda together during that time. I still can't believe we're truly together. I keep imagining I'll wake up one morning and find Miranda standing over me brandishing a killer stiletto and ordering me out of her bed."

"But now you're engaged to prove it's real."

Holly's face lit up. "Yes, I'm incredibly lucky." She leant over and took Jennifer's hands. "And you will be too. You're so lovely any man would be fortunate to have you. And since you adore England then you must come and stay with us.

That would be so much fun. Perhaps we'll even find the perfect Englishman for you. Do say you will."

"I'd love that," Jennifer said, sincerely, her resentment for Holly slowly abating. "Only, don't you feel threatened hanging with someone who kinda likes your boyfriend?"

Holly shrugged. "If you date somebody like Rupert you get used to it. My best friend, and ex-flatmate, makes passes at him whenever the chance arises. Yet I'd hate to lose our friendship over it."

"She makes passes in front of you?" Jennifer was horrified.

"No. Even Scarlett isn't that obvious. But Rupert tells me. He's keeping a tally. When she reaches one hundred he's going to give her a medal for resistance in the face of futility."

"I'm sorry if I'm insulting your friend, but that's an awful thing to do to you."

Holly shook her head. "Scarlett isn't being malicious. To her Rupert is a challenge. You see, she's gorgeous and can't understand why Rupert chose me over her."

Jennifer thought she could see exactly why. "Doesn't it upset you knowing things like that?"

Holly was taken aback by Jennifer's perception, yet was saved from answering by footsteps on the stairs and Rupert appearing.

"There you are, sweetheart," he said. "I thought I'd been jilted before I even got to the altar. Everyone else has gone except Alyce who's been searching for you, Jennifer." Jennifer scrambled to her feet and went to find her friend, wondering what Alyce would make of her exchange with Holly.

"What were you two talking about?" Rupert asked Holly as they prepared to leave the theatre and face the fans still faithfully standing outside.

Holly smiled up at him. "You."

"Ah." Rupert had the grace to look slightly uncomfortable. "Sweetheart, I swear I didn't..."

"Yes, I know."

When they reached their apartment block the doorman produced the most enormous bunch of flowers either of them had ever seen.

"Good God, somebody has sent us half of Central Park," Rupert commented.

Holly read out the card.

Marriage is an unnatural state in my opinion, but I suppose one has to say congratulations.

Judith

"Who says romance is dead?" Rupert said. "Quick, let's take it upstairs before the park police come looking for their missing foliage!"

CHAPTER TWENTY FOUR

The annual Tonys, Broadway's most prestigious awards and a major event in New York's theatrical calendar, was to be held on the second Sunday in June. The nominations had been announced some weeks before, and though *All About Eve* had picked up a generous number no one dared mention them for fear of incurring Judith's wrath.

"I dunno why she won't talk about them when she's been nominated," Paige said, having brought up the subject one night after the curtain call, with the result Judith had stormed off. Rupert raising his eyes upwards had gone after her. "If it was me I'd wanna tell everyone."

"I think Judith disapproves of anything which takes her away from acting and that includes such frivolity as awards," Richard explained.

"But she's gonna go, right?"

"Let's say Rupert's working on it. The producers tried and failed."

"It would be like so rude if she won and wasn't there."

"Does Judith strike you as someone who would care?" Richard gave a dramatic sigh. "If it had been me nominated I'd be bribing every one of the voters: chocolates, alcohol, money, sex."

"You should be nominated for best person coming in to save a show," Jennifer offered.

"Or best musical performance in a straight play," Alyce added, thinking of Richard's piano playing.

"You're all wrong," Kyle broke in. "Richard should get the award for best upstaging on David Letterman's show. All those in favour raise their hands." Everyone raised their hands. "Richard, you are officially the winner."

Richard bowed. "I would like to thank my mother and father and the hundreds of queens in London who would kill to be in my position."

Paige turned to Mindy who was watching the proceedings with a vague expression. "You're gonna go to the awards, right?"

Mindy nodded. "Sure. It's kinda weird though because Margo and Eve are up for the same award. Maybe that's why Margo doesn't wanna go, because Eve wins."

"She wins a Sarah Siddons Award in the play," Kyle jumped in quickly. "That's a fictional award, Mindy. It doesn't mean you are going to win a Tony."

Mindy smiled. "Whatever." She wandered upstairs to her dressing room.

"Lord," Kyle said. "If she honestly believes she'll win because Eve does, what happens if she doesn't? Will she insist on going up to collect it anyway?"

"If she does we'll hold her down," Richard said. "My money's on Judith winning."

"What about Rupert?" Jennifer asked, slightly too eagerly.

"He's unlikely to win best actress," Richard replied.

Jennifer hit him playfully. "You are so quaint. But honestly, do you think he can win best actor?"

Richard shrugged. "I'm afraid I'm not an expert on Broadway actors."

"The competition is pretty tough," Kyle said. "It's been a strong season for straight plays for once, with some first-rate performances. Whatever the outcome, it's great we're all invited and I intend to thoroughly enjoy the evening. Lauren has booked two babysitters in case one gets sick, and the kids have been dragged into so many dress shops looking for her perfect outfit I expect to come home one night and find them both dressed in Prada. Is Nate coming, Alyce?"

"Yes. I've sorted wheelchair access. It means I won't be sitting with the rest of you guys, but I'll be rooting from behind. I'm sure we don't need to ask if you're bringing Tom, Richard."

Richard looked coy. "We've already got him a tux specially."

"And I guess you're bringing your new guy, Paige," Jennifer said. Paige nodded. "And Rupert will be bringing Holly, and Mindy doesn't count, so I'll be the only sad loser with no date."

"Judith won't have one if she goes," Richard said, mischievously. "You could escort each other. We could even dress you up in a suit, slick your hair back and give you a moustache."

Jennifer gave a horrified gasp. "Am I that manly?"

"Of course you're not, hon," Alyce said. "You're lovely. And please join me and Nate for the evening. He'd love the idea of accompanying two women."

Judith eventually agreed to attend the awards, but steadfastly refused to allow an excerpt of the play to be pre-recorded, or, even worse, perform live on the night. "We're a straight play, not a fucking musical," she snapped at the company manager who had been sent to her dressing room with the request. "Perhaps you'd like Mindy and myself to perform a duet? Or why not turn the end into a song and dance finale, with a five minute tap routine à la *42ⁿᵈ Street,* or a *Full Monty* strip number?"

"We could combine the two and perform a tap dancing strip routine," Rupert commented from the corner of the room.

Judith glared at him. "I appreciate that would be your fantasy. However, there isn't enough money in the world to make me perform for these bloody awards, with or without clothes. I'll turn up, sit through the damn things and go home. And I'm only doing that under sufferance. Now go away." She glared at the company manager who was considering whether his medical insurance included actress-induced nervous breakdowns and was more than happy to make his escape. "I wish people would let me simply act without the rest of this paraphernalia," she said to Rupert.

"What? Oh sorry, I was miles away visualizing you in tap shoes and tassels."

"Get out!"

Judith's anti-awards stance was, in truth, mainly built on a dread of not winning. She hated not to be deemed the best and most successful at her job, and would rather not be present if she was to be humiliated by failure on that front. She could more or less cope with losing to the other nominees, but it would be unbearable to lose to Mindy, an inexperienced theatre actress whose performance owed everything to Judith.

With this scenario hanging over her it was a huge relief to Judith when, following the matinee on the day before the Tony Awards, there was a perfunctory knock on the dressing room door and Victor strolled in. Judith, being determined not to display any sentiment, merely demanded, "Did you tell me you were coming back today?"

"No, it was meant to be a pleasant surprise." Victor crossed the room, took Judith's hands, put them to his lips and kissed them. "You didn't think I'd miss these awards, did you?"

"These fucking awards are all anyone can talk about. Don't you have an important war to cover?"

"I'm only here for a few days to offer my support. If you'd rather I didn't escort you I can stay in the hotel and watch them on TV instead."

Judith pulled her hands away and started to remove her make-up. "Since you're here you may as well come," she said. "However, if anyone, especially reporters, should ask who you are, we're old friends. Nothing more."

"An old friend. Got it. An old friend who keeps a toothbrush at your house."

"You dare mention a toothbrush or any other item at my house and I shall personally tell immigration that you're an illegal alien and should be deported from the country immediately."

"Yes dear."

There was a tentative knock and at Judith's command to enter Holly came in, her face lighting up as she took in the room's other occupant.

340

"Victor!" She ran across the room and hugged him. "What a wonderful surprise."

"It's nice someone thinks so," Victor said, looking pointedly at Judith, who scowled at him before continuing with her face cleaning ritual. Turning back to Holly, Victor caught sight of her left hand. "Hello, what's this?" He pointed at the ring, which Holly had finally agreed to wear once Rupert had assured her he'd added it to their insurance policy. "Is there something I should know?"

Holly gasped. "I'm so terribly sorry. I should've phoned you. I thought Judith... sorry, that was very presumptuous of me."

Judith glanced up. "Ah yes, it sort of slipped my mind. Rupert and Holly are engaged, they'll get married, live happily ever after, blah, blah, blah. Anyway, I sent them flowers."

"From both of us?" Victor enquired.

Judith frowned. "I can't remember – maybe."

"Which patently means no. Holly and Rupert must have thought I was incredibly rude making no acknowledgement of their news. Holly, many congratulations; I am so pleased for you both. And that's a beautiful ring."

"Thank you. It's from Tiffany's." Holly sounded like a five year old with a new toy and Victor smiled at her enthusiasm and pride.

"I wouldn't expect Rupert to buy it from anywhere else. I must congratulate him too."

"I'll tell him you're here." Holly started towards the door.

"Holly?" Judith called after her. "Did you come in here originally for a reason or were you merely wandering through every dressing room

341

to flaunt your ring?"

"Oh yes, sorry. Rupert and I are going out for food and we wondered if you wanted anything brought back."

"Tim's getting me something. I can't imagine why Rupert doesn't have food brought in after matinees too; this way he has to deal with those fans at stage door twice."

Holly frowned. "I didn't think of that. He's probably only going out because I love exploring."

"Then I would imagine he gets enormous pleasure from that," Victor said. "Ignore Judy's cynicism, she's basically bitter and twisted."

"Get out," Judith screamed, throwing a lipstick at him.

"No." Victor flung himself in a chair, neatly catching the powder compact which followed the lipstick. Holly took this as her cue to leave.

Rupert was delighted to hear of Victor's arrival. If nothing else Judith would have someone to fall back on if perchance she didn't win the next night. As he and Holly were about to leave the theatre, Holly pulled on a pair of gloves. "Sweetheart, it's around eighty five degrees out there," he said. "I don't think you'll need those."

Holly blushed and looked down at the floor. "I like them," she muttered.

Rupert pulled her head up so he was looking into her eyes. "And?"

"And nobody will be able to see my ring and try to steal it."

Rupert shook his head in despair. "All right, if you're really that worried, let's at least buy you an elegant, cooler pair. There's something rather incongruous about a summer dress, sandals and thick woolly gloves!"

The Tony Awards started shortly after the Broadway matinees finished. Coaches ferried casts from shows across to Radio City Music Hall for last minute rehearsals and seat allocation. Judith and Rupert were seated one behind the other near the front of the auditorium with their guests beside them. Aubrey, nominated for best director, was on the other side of the aisle with Mindy beside him since neither of them had guests. Wesley, who had flown over especially, was sitting several rows further back with the other producers. The un-nominated cast members were far enough away not to be in view of any camera recording the event live for television.

The evening seemed never-ending to Judith. Interminable excerpts from musicals, all appearing to have derived from the Andrew Lloyd-Webber school of musicals – not a good thing in Judith's book – were interspersed with lengthy speeches from recipients of various awards in other categories.

"Is it obligatory to cry and thank one's parents?" Judith grumbled to Victor, after another winner wept while declaring her love for her mother. "It's utterly nauseating. I may actually be sick."

"That'll endear you to the audience." Victor was staring, fascinated, at the stage. "Do you know that presenter's dress is totally see-through?"

"For fuck's sake, you've been spending too

much time around Rupert."

Victor chuckled and turned around to look at Rupert whose grin told him he had indeed noticed the same thing.

Two hours into the ceremony the non-musical acting awards were announced. Judith leaned nonchalantly back in her chair and fixed a smile on her face; nobody would be able to say she minded about the outcome. Victor slipped his hand into hers and found it firmly gripped.

Christopher Plummer walked on to the stage to present the best actress award. "Christ, it's Captain Von Trapp," Judith muttered, her mouth carefully averted from the cameras in case of lip readers. "I should have come as a singing nun to win."

"Nun, maybe." Victor had heard Judith sing and it certainly wouldn't help win any award.

Singing nun or not, Christopher Plummer opened the envelope and proclaimed Judith the winner. Richard and Kyle sat on the edge of their seats prepared to sprint forward and tackle Mindy if necessary. To their great relief she made no attempt to collect the award, merely appearing puzzled at the outcome.

Judith rose slowly to her feet. Nominees had been warned there was a time limit to their acceptance speeches, after which the band would strike up and they would be forced to finish. This melodic cut-off resulted in winners racing up to the stage so as to not waste precious speaking time. Judith, however, refused to sprint up the aisle like a geriatric athlete. Besides, she had prepared no speech, which she considered the height of bad luck, and didn't intend spending ages thanking producers and directors when she'd done all the work. She accepted the statue with an inclination of her head and ignored Christopher Plummer's attempts to kiss air with her.

"Thank you so much," she said to the audience, holding the award up with what appeared to be genuine emotion. Then with a mischievous smile she added, "You wouldn't believe how much I needed a doorstop for my dressing room. The fucking bathroom door is always slamming shut." And she walked off stage to a combination of laughter and shock, crossing over with Sarah Jessica Parker who was preparing to present the best actor award. CBS, who were broadcasting the ceremony live to the whole of America, were having fits over Judith's profanity. Swearing on the main networks was taboo.

In the wings Judith waved aside a Tony Award press agent, so she could watch the result of the next award, for which Sarah Jessica Parker was opening the envelope. "And the award for best actor goes to Rupert Blake."

"Good," Judith said, as if she'd expected no other outcome.

In his seat Rupert leant over and kissed a radiant Holly. Behind him he could hear the whoops from his fellow cast. He collected his award from the woman Miranda would have killed to have met; gosh, she was tiny. If she hadn't been wearing such high heels he would have had to collect it on his knees.

Like Judith he hadn't prepared a speech, and it was a fairly safe bet he wasn't going to thank his mother. "My fiancée," he smiled at Holly who nearly fell out of her seat at this public announcement of their engagement, "recently won a Laurence Olivier theatre award in London. Her initial reaction was that her name had been wrongly read out and at any moment she'd have to return it to its rightful owner. Tonight I feel the same about this award. However, before anyone can rectify the mistake I'm taking this, leaving the stage and only the most successful rugby tackle will manage to relieve me of it. Before I do that, I must briefly thank my wonderful co-cast, our English producer Wesley Bartlett who has been to hell and back with us, and especially Judith Gold, without whom none of us would be here tonight." And with that he sauntered into the wings to join Judith.

"You sloppy thing," she said, privately pleased.

"Christ, if I hadn't said anything about you I never would have heard the last of it."

"True. All right," she snapped at the press agent still trying to get a photograph of her with her Tony. "Come on, Rupert, let's get this over with or we'll miss the directing award."

Much to Judith's dismay, not to mention Aubrey's, *All About Eve* failed to win in the best director category. "How could we not?" Judith raged. "Everybody's waxed lyrical about the production."

"At least you didn't have to listen to Aubrey making his acceptance speech for your work," Rupert tried to calm her.

"Fuck that. It's my direction and I want to know why they didn't choose it." She glared around as if to locate the perpetrator of this miscarriage of justice.

In spite of not winning best director, *All About Eve* won best new play and Wesley collected the award on behalf of the producers and Owen Brady, the author, who was now living in a commune in Wales with his girlfriend and had given up on showbiz events.

"How could we win new play and not direction?" Judith wasn't dropping the subject, continuing to complain throughout the announcement of the final award for best musical.

Rupert steered her away from the stage area. "Let's find the others."

Wesley, Victor, Holly and the other cast, less Mindy, were waiting outside and gave Judith and Rupert a cheer when they emerged. "Where's Aubrey?" Rupert asked, as Holly nestled proudly up to him.

"He went straight off to the Tony Ball as soon as the ceremony finished, taking a puzzled Mindy with him," Wesley said. "I suppose he wants to network there, but he wasn't happy."

"He wasn't happy," Judith snapped. "How do you think I feel?"

"But you won," Paige said.

"Only for acting."

Victor laughed. "Come on Joseph Mankiewicz, let's go back to the hotel." He put his arm around Judith's shoulders, but she shook it off. Victor hailed a cab and opened the door. "Well, I'm going." He climbed in and leant over to close the door, but Judith grabbed it and climbed in after him. The cab drove off into the night.

"Why did he call her Joseph Mankiwich?"

Paige asked.

"Mankiewicz," Richard corrected. "He was the director of the original movie."

"Oh yeah, duh," said Paige, feeling stupid for forgetting that, but still not understanding why Judith wasn't happy.

"I take it Judith isn't going to the Tony Ball then," Wesley observed. "Are you, Rupert?"

Rupert shook his head. "No. Holly and I decided that since only nominees are invited we'd rather go to our producers' party as that's for the full company."

This statement was greeted by a cheer from the rest of the cast as they wended their way through the streets to start their celebrations.

In the cab Judith sat stiff backed and silent and it wasn't until they'd reached her hotel room that she let out a shriek and threw her award on the bed. Victor picked it up and put it on the table. Then he sat Judith down on the bed, holding her there and ignoring her struggle. "Judy, you've just won the most important accolade Broadway has to offer for acting, so stop sulking."

"I should've got best director, even if I had to pretend it was Aubrey's award."

Victor took her chin so she couldn't help but look straight into his face. "Your direction is fantastic, but Broadway is a tight-knit community from what I hear, so perhaps it got around that you had more to do with the staging than Aubrey. If that were the case the voting panel might have been hesitant about giving the award to a director who hadn't really directed. Have you thought of it that way?"

"I don't care."

"Don't you?"

"No. I'm tired. I'm going to bed." She pulled away from him and stormed into the bathroom. Victor sighed and lay back on the bed. Sometimes it was impossible to console Judith.

Five minutes later Judith emerged again. "Do you really think that's why I didn't get it?"

"I think it's a very strong possibility, yes."

"Humph." Judith put up a bit of a fight as Victor pulled her down on to the bed – but only a very little.

Mindy sat in her apartment attempting to call Krystal yet again. Even though call waiting told her the person knew she was on hold, Krystal didn't cancel her other call. Mindy felt she was cracking up. Living two lives for such a long period was beginning to take its toll and there were times she didn't know who she was anymore. The Tony result only added to her confusion.

Furthermore her boyfriend had recently informed her that he'd found somebody else, somebody who would acknowledge his existence even when they were working. Mindy couldn't understand his attitude. He was a director and should empathize with her acting methods.

Eventually she gave up trying to get hold of Krystal. Perhaps Krystal wouldn't bother with her now she was a loser – Eve wasn't a loser, so maybe in some way she'd failed to live up to Krystal's teachings.

It didn't occur to Mindy that although Eve achieves her objectives it is Margo who is the winner, discovering true happiness, while Eve has nothing but her career. Mindy was becoming more like Eve than she realized.

CHAPTER TWENTY FIVE

The day after the Tony Awards, with no performance and Victor around to keep Judith occupied, Rupert and Holly took a picnic into Central Park. Hiring a rowing boat, Holly proved herself a better oarsperson than Rupert, who'd never rowed before and had the habit of going round in circles since his tennis playing arm was more powerful than the other. Having nearly hit two other boats, including a gondola which looked strangely incongruous in Manhattan, Holly insisted on taking over and rowing them safely to shore where they sat on a rock overlooking the boating lake to eat their picnic.

"Now I've announced our engagement to the whole of Radio City Music Hall and on national television," Rupert said, "perhaps we ought to think about the wedding."

"It's so beautiful here," Holly said, loving the fact that while they were sitting surrounded by trees and lakes and general serenity, above them loomed these huge skyscrapers. "I half wish we could get married here and now." She looked down at the ring on her finger, which she'd agreed to wear without gloves – if Rupert was there as bodyguard.

"Don't you want a big wedding with hundreds of friends and relations and you walking down the aisle in a massive white frock?" Rupert asked.

"I suppose so. Certainly my parents would be

gutted if I didn't. What about you? Did you have that with Miranda?"

"Yes, accompanied by *Hello* magazine. Miranda was half an hour late to the church because *Hello* didn't like the way her hair was styled and insisted on having it redone. Hardly the most romantic start to a marriage, although in retrospect it was an indication of how our relationship was going to work." He smiled down at Holly who was lying with her head in his lap. "I'll get married any way you want me to, sweetheart, as long as we don't sell the pictures to a magazine, and I don't have to dress up in something embarrassing – I have to do enough of that in our business anyway."

"So a medieval wedding with me in a pointed hat and you as a knight on a charger with a lance being pursued by the *National Enquirer* is out of the question?"

"Lances are a bugger to get round those narrow London streets," Rupert commented, "although I'd happily stick one into any photographer or reporter working for the *National Enquirer*."

Holly paused, wondering if she should ask this, but in the end her curiosity got too much for her. "Did your mother come to your wedding to Miranda?"

"Yes." Rupert's reply was cautious.

"Are you going to ask her to ours?"

"Not if we're going to hold it on this rock; we'll never all fit." Holly reached out and playfully hit him. "Does it really matter to you whether she comes or not?" he asked.

"I'm just a little curious. You never talk about

her and I've never met her, while you've met my parents."

"Who thoroughly disapprove of me."

"No they don't," Holly protested, untruthfully. When she'd broken the news of their engagement to them over the phone she could hear the horror in their voices. It wasn't that they didn't like Rupert, he'd charmed them within five minutes of being introduced, but he was so much older than their beloved daughter and already had one failed marriage behind him. Besides, they'd heard rumours that he'd been frequently unfaithful to that wife.

"They believe I'm an old letch who's out to corrupt their daughter before leaving her destitute in the gutter," Rupert said. "Can't say I blame them – I haven't done very well proving myself honourable so far."

"Stop it. That subject is closed and besides you're evading the question. What about your mother?"

"We don't get on. That's all."

"When did that happen? You must have got on when you were little though? Even if she didn't teach you Pooh-sticks and left you hiding without bothering to seek." Holly couldn't forget those two things which were almost sacrilege to her.

Rupert stared out at the lake, not speaking. Holly tilted her head back to look up at him. "Why do you want to know so badly?" he asked.

"Because I want to know everything about you, and parents have so much to do with the way you turn out, don't they?"

"Christ, I hope not."

Holly winced. "Was it that bad?"

"It rather depended on which step-father she was with at the time, all of whom I had to call Daddy even though, since she only married three of them, most weren't legally step-fathers. I will forever be in debt to the one who taught me to play tennis when I was seven, because at thirteen I got into a residential training scheme and left home for good. Mostly her taste in men was truly dire – I have no idea whether that included my father since even she didn't know who that was." Holly didn't say anything; just continued watching him. "I guess I never forgave my mother for not standing up for me against them."

"Standing up over what?" There was another long silence. Holly sat up. "Rupert, you always listen to everyone else and never talk about yourself. That's got to be bad for you."

"Doctor Holly to my rescue, eh?"

Holly scowled. "Stop laughing at me. I'm a good listener."

"I know, sweetheart, but I'm a lousy talker."

Holly played with her ring. "That's not fair. Marriage is supposed to be about trust, isn't it? It's not good to start off with secrets."

"They're not secrets." Rupert's tone was almost harsh. "They're things I'd rather forget, OK?"

"But you haven't forgotten. I can see that in your face. What was it your step-fathers did that was so awful?"

"They locked me in the cellar so I couldn't go to the ball and sent me out into the woods where a witch tried to turn me into gingerbread."

"Honestly, Rupert, sometimes you are infuriating."

"You sound like Miranda."

"Well, perhaps she had a point." Holly glared at him, refusing to drop the subject.

"You're getting quite obstinate, aren't you?" Rupert grinned at her. "I blame Judith's influence."

"I try to stick up for things when they're important, and I think this is." Holly was struggling to explain. "It's so frustrating when you always seem to understand me and know what I'm thinking and yet you're such an enigma. Please tell me."

Rupert made a gesture of surrender. "All right, you win. Which of my delightful stepfathers would you like to hear about first? The one who used to creep into my room at night, pull down my pyjama bottoms and play with my private parts. Or the drunk or the politician who it turned out had several other mistresses. Then there was the con-man who took my mother's every penny which meant she had to find someone very rich so we could actually afford to eat and ended up hooking a merchant banker. Actually, the banker was one of my favourites since he further encouraged my tennis, paying for the best equipment and for extra lessons. Sadly my mother got bored with him once we were solvent and dropped him – poor guy had left his wife and kids for her so he ended up with nobody. My mother was very sensuous and men fell at her feet. Instead of him, just as I started at a very strict secondary school, she moved in this guy who'd destroy my homework

355

for fun as I was leaving in the morning, so that I'd have to go in and say I hadn't done it, which meant I was regularly caned for laziness. Is that what you wanted to know?"

Holly's eyes were wide open in dismay. "Didn't you tell them at school what had happened?"

"Once, and I was told it was a worse excuse than the dog ate it and given an extra two strokes for lying. It wasn't so much the injustice or that it hurt like hell, but I was terrified it would damage my hands for tennis playing. I must have been the only boy to ask if they'd cane my behind rather than my hand; more humiliating but less damaging."

"And did they?"

"Oh yes. I'm sure I made that sadistic headmaster's year. I only had to walk into his office and he'd be clearing a space on his desk for me to bend over. He must've been at a loss when caning was banned. Holly, are you OK? You've gone awfully white."

Holly nodded. "And your mother did nothing?" she virtually whispered. "Did you tell her about the one who was... you know?" Holly gestured towards Rupert's crotch.

"Yes, eventually, because..." Rupert stopped.

"Go on."

Rupert was staring into the distance, where a small dog was trying to jump out of a rowing boat. He felt Holly's hand over his. He continued to stare at the dog while he spoke.

"One night he came into my room when my mother was out, sat me down, told me to shut my eyes and open my mouth and I'd get a big surprise. And I did, but not the sweet I was hoping for. Instead he shoved his dick in and told me to suck it. I was only six and I thought I was going to choke. When he stopped I threw up over my bed, but I was too frightened to do anything so I had to sleep in vomit covered sheets. The next day when I got back from school my mother was waiting for me with the dirty sheets and I explained what had happened. She told me I was a filthy lying little bastard, dragged me into the bathroom and made me scrub the sheets in the bath. Then she locked me in my room until my step-father came home. She obviously told him what I'd said because he came in, threw me down on my bed and beat me with his belt – the buckle end, until I started to bleed. You asked me once what that scar was on my back; now you know. So you see I have no great love for my mother."

Rupert stopped, dreading an outpouring of horror and sympathy from Holly. Instead she merely said quietly, but with determination, "Your mother is not coming to our wedding."

"I don't have a problem with that." Holly lay back against his chest and he put his arms around her. "So am I less of an enigma now?"

Holly gazed, unseeing, at the trees above her "I think it explains a lot. I'm sure you hide your real emotions under humour so you don't get hurt again, and you play peacemaker so brilliantly because you lived in a permanent battle zone, and watching your mother sleeping around must have had a terribly detrimental effect..."

"Ah, so my inability to remain faithful is my mother's fault?"

"I didn't mean... I don't know...."

"Maybe you're right. I'm sure a psychologist would have a field day with me, but it was a long time ago and I'm over it, so please don't start analyzing me, sweetheart. Honestly, you ask a girl to marry you and she turns into Sigmund Freud!"

Later that night, when Rupert was asleep, Holly moved around the other side of the bed so she was facing his naked back. Cautiously, she opened the curtains a crack, producing a chink of light, and examined the scar of which she now knew the history. How could anybody do such a brutal thing to a six year old child? Gently Holly ran her finger along it, shuddering as she envisioned the belt buckle descending. In her mind the step-father bore a strong resemblance to the brutish Wackford Squeers in *Nicholas Nickleby*, a book that was rather on her mind at the moment. Rupert stirred. "What are you doing?" he murmured.

"Nothing." Holly quickly took her hand away and sat on it.

He rolled over and regarded her with a sigh. "I knew I shouldn't have told you. Let it go, sweetheart. I'm fine, or I will be if you don't start playing social worker in the middle of the night."

Holly rolled over him to her side of the bed. "Did you ever tell Miranda about your step-fathers?"

"No."

"Why?"

"Well, even apart from the fact I prefer not to talk about it, I don't suppose she'd have been especially interested." Holly tried not to feel too pleased. "I take it that was the answer you wanted?" Rupert asked, raising his eyebrows. "Yes, you are the only person I have ever told."

Holly blushed. "Am I so easy to read?"

"Yes." Rupert smiled.

"You aren't really sorry you told me, are you?"

"No," he said truthfully after thinking about it for a minute. "No, actually I'm not. But I would like to drop the subject now, OK?" He gave a huge yawn and pulled Holly down beside him. "Now, go to sleep young lady." Holly shut her eyes, but it was a long time before she fell asleep.

CHAPTER TWENTY SIX

Wesley had opted to leave the Tony Award for best play at the theatre, hoping it might appease Judith for failing to win best director. He'd dropped it there after the awards on Sunday night, and placed it on a shelf in the wings so the entire company could see it.

On the Tuesday evening, the first show after the ceremony, Judith arrived at the theatre at her usual early hour to spend time alone on stage and found the Tony with a printed sign stuck on it which read: JUDITH GOLD IS A BITCH. Since Judith's own award was safely in her now highly secure hotel room, she decided this was obviously the nearest way Mindy could strike out for not winning.

Judith's first response, to literally strike out herself by physically hitting Mindy with the award, was replaced by a more subtle approach. She'd merely show Mindy why she was the better actress. During the show that night Eve Harrington wasn't going to stand a chance with Margo Channing. She was going to wipe the floor with her.

As the curtain came down on Act One the cast staggered off stage utterly stunned. Judith immediately shot back to her dressing room, while Mindy returned more slowly and pensively to hers.

"What on earth is going on?" Richard asked.

"It's like acting with Cruella De Vil, Lucrezia Borgia and that awful teacher in Harry Potter who burns the lines in Harry's hand."

"Dolores Umbridge," Jennifer supplied.

"Judith Umbridge," Richard retorted. "Yes, most appropriate. The look in her eyes today would terrify any young wizard – or any actor!"

"She sure scared me," Paige said. "I know Margo is supposed to be snooty to Miss Caswell at the party, but I thought she was gonna eat me alive."

"There was no subtlety at all," Alyce said.

"Any ideas?" Kyle asked Rupert.

Rupert shook his head. "She was behaving strangely when I went in before the show, but wouldn't say why."

There was the sound of footsteps and Victor, who'd been watching from out front, appeared. "What's going on? Why is Judy performing Margo like a demented banshee?"

"We're not sure," Rupert said. "I suppose I should go and see what's wrong."

"No," Victor said. "Allow me." He disappeared in the direction of Judith's room and within seconds they could hear shouting.

Rupert sighed. "I'm going to get ready for Act Two," he said, pointedly.

"Absolutely," Alyce said, marching up the stairs with Jennifer at her heels and Kyle shortly behind.

"Rupert is too damned honourable on occasions," Richard commented to Paige. "I'm dying to eavesdrop. Aren't you?"

Paige giggled. "Yes."

Richard grabbed Paige's hand and pulled her

up the stairs, where they stood a couple of steps up from the dressing room door trying to look as if they always hung around on stairwells to chat. Much to their disappointment the shouting had stopped and short of standing directly outside the door and putting their ears to it, at which even Richard drew the line, they couldn't hear a thing.

The reason for this ceasing of vocal confrontation was that Judith, having failed to throw Victor out and discovering that screaming at him to mind his own business also had no effect, was now refusing to speak.

Victor stood over her, his arms crossed, and spoke quietly. "Judy, I don't know why you're behaving this way, although I imagine you have a reason. However, one of the things I've always admired and loved about you, yes loved," he repeated as Judith gave a derisive snort, "is your professionalism. You never give less than one hundred percent."

This was too much for Judith's self-imposed silence. "And I didn't this afternoon. In fact I believe I gave over a hundred percent."

"Yes, I agree, which could also be known as hamming."

Judith stared at him open-mouthed. "You're accusing me of being a ham?"

"Yes. That Margo Channing was a caricature. There was no truth in her and you've always been such a truthful actress."

"You're daring to tell me how to act?"

"No, I'm telling you how not to act."

"What makes you think you know what the fuck you're talking about?"

"I may not be a star on Broadway, but I can tell the difference between good and bad acting and this was bad. You're so busy trying to upstage everybody that you're ruining your own performance and theirs too because they play off you. Rupert's the only one who is managing to salvage anything, which is doubtless only because he's so used to you he can cope better. The rest of the cast look like they're on the proverbial ship without a paddle, while Mindy is hardly noticeable, which is ironic in a play called *All About Eve*."

Judith gave a slight smirk, which Victor spotted. "Is that what this is about?" he demanded. "Trying to upstage Mindy?"

Judith shrugged. "I could do that without trying."

"Yes, you could, but then you lose the point of the play and I thought you cared about that. Or do I have it wrong? Are you merely concerned about proving you're the star? You were almost performing a one woman show out there – and not a very good one at that."

"How dare you! You have no right to pretend you know me so well because you don't."

Victor stared at her for a moment before he spoke. "You're wrong. I know you very well, and this behaviour is totally out of character. That's why it's so disappointing."

"Get out of my dressing room. In fact, get out of my entire life, you bastard. I don't need some ex bit-part actor telling me I'm a ham. If you could genuinely recognize good acting you wouldn't have attempted to become an actor in the first place. You never had what it took."

Victor nodded slowly. "All right, I'm going. Heaven forbid you should be forced to share your life with an ex bit-part actor with no talent." He turned and left the room, nearly bumping into Tim who was preparing to get Judith ready for Act Two. He gave the dresser a curt nod before heading to the stage door and out into the street.

Judith stormed back on to the stage for the second act. If Mindy defacing the Tony Award wasn't enough, now she had that fucking Victor daring to tell her, Judith Gold, how to act. Well, she'd show him and the cast. If they thought Act One was aggressive wait until they saw Act Two. Yet, to her great annoyance, her heart was no longer in it. Why, she couldn't understand. Still, she could hardly change her performance half way through, so Margo Channing continued in the Machiavellian vein. At the curtain call her applause was rapturous, while everyone else's was comparatively muted.

"I doubt the audience noticed there were any other actors on stage except Judith," Kyle remarked at the end. "If it wasn't at the cost of the rest of us and the play I'd say she was magnificent."

"My Mom and Dad were in watching for the first time tonight," said Paige. "They've come all the way from Colorado. I was so insignificant, they probably thought I was lying and wasn't even in the play."

"Paige, I'm terribly sorry," Rupert said. "Actually, on behalf of the English contingent of this play I wholeheartedly apologize for Judith's on-stage conduct. If there's anything I can do to make up for it..."

"Would you say hi to my parents?" Paige jumped in. "They'd be real excited by that. We're gonna eat right next door. Would you come join us?"

"I'd be delighted." Rupert didn't feel delighted. He wanted nothing more than to go home and forget about this disastrous evening. Still, Paige's parents were thrilled to meet him and hadn't noticed anything odd about that night's performance.

"We thought Judith Gold was swell," Paige's mother said, biting into a piece of bread. "I don't suppose she wanted to come eat with us too? I'd love to meet her."

"Judith doesn't socialize much," Rupert said.

"I guess she gets kinda tired," Paige's mother said. "She works real hard. Paige honey, you must learn so much, acting with her."

"Yeah, it's a real learning curve, Mom."

"Paige is a big asset to the company too," Rupert said, earning a grateful look from Paige.

"Isn't that nice; you hear that, Pop?" Paige's mother said to her husband, "Paige is an asset."

"Sure she is." Paige's father patted his daughter's arm. "She's gonna be a star like Judith Gold one day, right?"

"Pop!" Paige exclaimed, blushing. "I could never be like Judith."

"Don't be modest, pumpkin. Whaddya say, Rupert?"

Rupert smiled. "I agree with Paige, she'll never be like Judith, but that's not necessarily a bad thing. Judith is a one off – which is also no bad thing. Paige has to be an actress in her own right. And I certainly believe she has the talent

365

to succeed, although sadly in this business that isn't always relevant."

The waiter brought over appetizers for Paige and her parents and Rupert seized this opportunity to make his excuses and leave.

"Wouldn't you even like dessert?" Paige's mother asked, upset that their distinguished guest was about to depart.

"Thank you, but no," Rupert replied. "My girlfriend will be waiting for me."

"You have a girlfriend?" Paige's mother regarded Rupert with obvious disappointment.

"Yes."

"Are you serious about her?"

"Mom!" Paige shot her mother a look of horror.

Rupert hid a smile. "Yes, I'm very serious about her. Thank you very much for the drink and it was delightful to meet you both." Feeling that this couple would expect some special English leave-taking, he kissed Paige's mother's hand and shook Paige's father's. "See you tomorrow, Paige." He winked at her as he left.

"What a nice man," Paige's mother said dreamily. "And cute. Have you met this girlfriend of his, Paige honey?"

"Yes."

"You think it is serious, because he seemed real keen on you?"

Paige shook her head fervently, "No, he's not, believe me."

"But you like him, right?"

"Sure. But I'm dating someone now. You're gonna meet him tomorrow."

Paige's mother wasn't prepared to let the subject drop yet. "But you'd look great with a big star like Rupert, and it wouldn't do your career any harm either. And relationships in your business are always breaking up; I read about them in magazines."

"Mom, stop it! Besides, Holly's not just his girlfriend, they're engaged and he bought her a ring from Tiffany's, and you don't do that unless you're serious." Paige quickly changed tack before her mother could offer any other arguments. "Will you come see the show again while you're here? Hopefully it might be a little different."

"Different?" her mother asked. "Judith Gold will still be in it, right?"

Paige sighed. "Sure, she'll still be in it. Only you might notice me more next time – or maybe not."

Judith returned to her hotel in a vile mood. Bloody Victor had better be prepared to apologize for his accusations or he'd be sleeping in the lobby tonight. Ham indeed.

Her room was in darkness. When she switched on the light it illuminated a note on the bed.

Judy,

Since you have made it clear you don't want me around, I'm catching a flight home tonight and not waiting until Thursday.

Victor

"Fuck!" Judith rolled the note into a ball and threw it across the room. Then for good measure she retrieved it, put it in the basin and set fire to it with her lighter. She didn't need anyone in her life – especially those who were going to criticize her acting. No one did that, whoever they were.

CHAPTER TWENTY SEVEN

The following day's matinee was almost unbearably tense with nobody certain what to expect. Mindy had spent much of the night before attempting to comprehend the situation and adopting her own strategy: if Margo was going to upstage Eve, then Eve was fighting back. As a result the audience were treated to a full scale onstage battle by the two leading ladies.

The other cast were singularly unimpressed. At the end of the play Rupert marched into Judith's room, slamming the door behind him. Judith opened her mouth to say something, but for once she wasn't quick enough.

"Be quiet and listen!" Rupert said. "I don't know why you're behaving like this, but you have to stop. It's not fair on any of us, or on the audience. Yes, they're responding to you and Mindy acting like spoilt school girls, but only because they don't know the original concept of this play. If we had the critics in today you'd be crucified."

"Fuck off," Judith managed to break in.

"No I won't. How many times have I heard you lecture about professionalism on stage? It's what I admire most about you, and what makes you a pleasure to act with. Yet these last two shows have been an embarrassment and I don't want to be associated with them, so if you don't stop what you're doing you can find another Addison DeWitt."

"Are you going to walk out on me too then? Go back to England?" Judith's voice was almost trembling with rage. "Fine, see if I care. This is my play and no one has the right to tell me how to perform it. Besides, Mindy was altering things this afternoon and she certainly has no right to do that."

"I imagine that's only because you rendered her virtually invisible on stage last night. No doubt she was attempting to find a way around that."

Judith gave a screech of frustration. "Then she shouldn't have vandalized the bloody Tony."

Rupert halted in his reprimand. "What?"

Judith opened her mouth in preparation for telling him to forget what she'd said, but instead found herself telling him her discovery.

When she'd finished, Rupert sat down and exhaled slowly. "That's awful; it must have shaken you terribly. I wish you'd told me. Still, even if that was Mindy..."

"Who else would it be?"

Rupert didn't point out that several people backstage, whom Judith had berated at some point, might have been tempted to perform such an act. "OK, say it was Mindy, then you would have every right to be upset with her, but the stage is not the place to take your revenge, and so unlike you."

Judith shrugged. She knew Rupert was right, although had no intention of admitting it.

"Did you tell Victor this?" Rupert asked.

"No."

"Why not?"

Judith narrowed her eyes at him. "I'm hardly

going to confide in a man who tells me I'm a ham."

"Ah." Victor was a braver man than him, Rupert mused. Telling Judith she was a ham was tantamount to committing theatrical suicide. "Why don't you talk to him now? He'll be a lot more sympathetic if he knows the reason."

"I can't, even if I wanted to – which I don't."

"Why not?"

"He's gone back to England."

Rupert looked surprised. "I thought he wasn't going until tomorrow."

"He left early." Judith gave an impatient shake of her head. "We're finished."

"You're what?" Rupert's voice mirrored the shock and horror he felt.

"Honestly, Rupert, you'd think finishing relationships is something you were an expert on. Surely I don't have to explain."

"But..."

"I thought you were lecturing me on my performance, not my love life. And I'm certainly not stopping that while Mindy is attempting to upstage me."

Rupert held up his hands in surrender. "If she agrees to return to what we originally rehearsed will you do the same?"

"I want an apology for what she did to the Tony first."

Rupert sighed. "I can try, but what if it wasn't her?"

"How dare you doubt me?" Judith shrieked. "You're as bad as the rest of them."

Rupert was debating whether to ask who the rest of them were, but was saved by a knock on

371

the door.

"What?" Judith screamed out.

The door opened rather hesitantly, and Holly put her head round it. "Judith, I'm sorry, is this a bad time?"

"Yes!"

"Oh, right." Holly gulped, but persevered. "It's just I need to ask Rupert something rather urgent. It's about Echo."

"Echo!" Judith stared at Holly as if she were insane. "For fuck's sake we've got more important things to discuss than that moronic beauty queen."

Holly fiddled nervously with the door handle. "It's only that I think she might be in trouble."

"Don't tell me she's accepted another theatre role and has recalled she can't actually act, or learn lines?"

"Not exactly a theatre role, but she just phoned to tell me that she's making a movie in LA. Apparently she was talent spotted somewhere and asked to go for a screen test."

"Hollywood has even less artistic judgement than I believed," Judith commented.

"Why do you think she's in trouble?" Rupert asked, ignoring Judith's exasperated sigh.

Holly grimaced as she attempted to explain her gut feeling. "Echo said it was a run down building, not like a proper studio. Then they cast her straight away without any kind of audition – and she was so proud of learning that monologue I gave her when we were doing *Blithe Spirit*."

"Wonderful, now it discovers it can learn lines," Judith remarked acidly.

"It did take her a very long time and it was only a short piece," Holly said quickly, not wanting to get Echo into trouble.

"And involved a lot of work from Holly," Rupert added. "Go on, sweetheart."

"And her costume is a short frilly dress with ankle socks and patent leather strapped shoes and ribbons for her hair."

"Isn't that the perfect costume for child beauty pageant queens?" Judith said. "I would have thought she'd feel right at home." Rupert frowned at her and she gave a dismissive wave. "Fine, go ahead, Holly."

"When she asked if there was a script they told her it was improvised and that she should watch the scene they were shooting before hers to get an idea of what they wanted. Apparently this scene was a big black guy, wearing only a thong, smearing something on two girls lying on a double bed. Now, I know I don't know much about LA, but…."

"Oh, Christ." Rupert covered his face with his hands for a moment. "OK, have you got her number?" Holly brought up Echo's number on her phone and passed it to Rupert.

Echo answered almost immediately. "Rupert!" There was no mistaking the pleasure in her voice when he'd identified himself. "I was speaking to Holly before."

"I know, which is why I'm phoning. We need to talk about this movie you're making."

"Yeah, it's kinda weird. These guys just came past with a wind machine, and I asked if were we gonna have a storm in the movie, which would have been so cool, but they said it was

373

to make us girls real cold. And I said, 'like air conditioning' and they laughed and said no one was that dumb. What does that mean?"

"It means you need to get out of there. Do you have your stuff with you?"

"It's in the restroom. I had to change there – they don't have no dressing rooms."

"Go and get it and leave."

"But it's a movie."

"Not the kind of movie you want to be in."

"Huh?"

"Echo, it's a porn movie."

"Porn?" Rupert could almost hear Echo's mind slowly ticking over, no doubt the expression sounded familiar, but she couldn't quite put her finger on why. "That's bad, right?"

"I certainly don't think it's what you want to appear in, especially since, from the way Holly says they've dressed you, I'd say you're being used to appeal to the child pornography audience."

"Oh." Echo had finally understood. Child pornography had been a serious issue on the beauty pageant circuit and her mother had taught Echo to constantly watch out for suspicious looking men. "Oh, gee. Whadda I do? Whadda I do?" Her voice was filled with panic.

Rupert kept his voice calm. "Go into the restroom, Echo, and collect your stuff." Rupert could hear Echo moving and a clunk where she'd obviously bent down to pick up her clothes. "Now go back the way you came and leave the building."

"What if they try to stop me?"

"Just keep going. They're not going to hurt

you. It's a porn movie, not a snuff movie."

"A what?"

"Echo, just go. And call Holly when you get safely home, OK?"

"OK."

Rupert hung up and looked at Holly and Judith speechlessly. Much to his and Holly's amazement there was a snort of laughter from Judith, a snort which turned into several snorts and something which could be considered an actual laugh. "My God, Echo was making a porn movie," she gasped out. "Can you imagine her ghastly mother's reaction to that? I wonder if the movie's producers checked that Echo wasn't wearing an impenetrable chastity belt before they cast her." Tears were running down Judith's cheeks.

"Poor Echo," Holly said. "She was so excited about doing a movie. Do you think she'll be OK?"

"Yes, I do." Rupert replied. "Her simplicity means she bounces back easily. Tomorrow she'll be as excited about another project."

Judith threw herself down on the bed exhausted with all her laughter. "I must get some sleep before tonight's show or I'll be useless." She looked at Rupert. "If you can get Mindy to agree to a truce then I suppose I can tone down my performance a little."

Rupert smiled at her. "Thank you." As Rupert and Holly left the room, Judith was still quietly chuckling.

Rupert resolved to make Aubrey earn his retainer fee and be the one to talk to Mindy. She was the only member of the cast to take any notice of their director, so it might have an impact. Aubrey was ecstatic to be asked to deal with a situation which didn't involve crossing Judith. Within seconds of Rupert's request he was out of his dressing room and on his way to Mindy's, bearing the pizza he was in the process of eating.

"I felt it was how Eve would behave when challenged by Margo in such a manner," Mindy explained, as Aubrey attempted to settle into one of the beanbags which comprised Mindy's chosen furniture. He wasn't exactly a beanbag man.

"I hear you, Eve." Aubrey was the only person who recognized Mindy's desire to be addressed by her character's name. "And I feel for you. Margo is a demanding woman, but we can't let her get to us and to the play. Eve would never let Margo get to her. I know you can rise above it."

Mindy smiled at him, feeling a weight taken off her shoulders. This was a man who understood. "Sure."

Aubrey proffered the pizza box and was relieved when she declined. There were only three slices left. He took one himself and bit into it, squirting his shirt with cheese and tomato, while a piece of pepperoni nestled into a crease in his trousers.

Mindy barely noticed; her mind was jumping ahead. Krystal had finally returned one of Mindy's many calls but had explained how busy she was with new clients and therefore felt unable to give Mindy guidance at the present time. Maybe this man would help her instead. "Would you like to go some place tomorrow and talk more?" she asked Aubrey, whose efforts to sit higher on the beanbag had resulted in his sliding to the floor.

"That would be super." Aubrey remained sitting on the floor, using the beanbag as a backrest and attempting to look as if that had been his intention.

"There's this cute English tea shop near me, based on *Alice in Wonderland*, which has these pots of different teas. We could go there."

"OK." There was a note of disappointment in Aubrey's voice. "Do they also do food by any chance?"

"I believe they do sandwiches and cakes."

"Cakes," Aubrey said, perking up. "What time shall we meet?"

At the end of that night's show, with Judith and Mindy's ceasing of onstage hostilities, Rupert popped into Judith's room. "You were fantastic tonight. I loved every moment of working with you."

Judith gave a brief nod. "I don't suppose Mindy admitted to defacing the Tony Award?"

Rupert shook his head. He hadn't entrusted Aubrey with that undertaking and had discreetly asked Mindy himself. She'd convincingly denied it, so either she was innocent or a very good actress. Besides, if he'd read her correctly she would have labelled the award 'Margo Channing is a bitch' and not Judith Gold.

Judith looked mutinous at Mindy's denial, so Rupert quickly added, "Holly heard from Echo who got home safely, although in such a rush to leave the 'porno building', as apparently she calls it, she didn't stop to change and travelled back still wearing the complete child's outfit. I understand she got some fairly strange looks and several invitations! Invitations which I think Holly persuaded her not to accept."

Judith smiled and Rupert grasped this opportunity to return to an earlier conversation. "Judith, when you said you and Victor were finished, you didn't actually mean it, did you?"

Judith's smile vanished. "Mind your own business."

"It is my business. You're both my friends."

"Well, your friend Victor left me a note saying he was going back to England. He didn't even have the nerve to tell me to my face."

"What did you say to him?"

"What the fuck makes you think it was my fault?"

"Because it would take a hell of a lot to make him leave you."

"Well he got 'a hell of a lot'. All right? He won't want to come back. End of conversation."

At 1am, as Rupert and Holly were about to go to bed, the phone rang. It was Judith, sounding far from sober. "Rupert, do you remember I told you why Victor and I split up originally?"

"Yes." Rupert wasn't likely to forget that Victor had asked Judith to marry him when they were both young actors, and she'd told him she couldn't possibly be involved long term with a mere understudy. They hadn't seen each other again for nearly forty years.

"I might have made a similar remark yesterday when he told me I was a ham," Judith continued. "Maybe I shouldn't have."

Rupert laid his head back against the chair and sighed. "It possibly wasn't the most tactful thing to say, but we all say things in anger we don't really mean. And besides, you're both older and wiser now so perhaps it'll blow over more easily."

"I don't think so." There was a click and Judith had hung up.

"Poor Victor," Holly said, after Rupert filled her in. "Do you think we should phone him?"

Rupert pulled her down on to his lap and put his arms around her. "They're grown up people. They must do things their way."

Three hours later, while Rupert slept, Holly crept up and dialled Victor in London, figuring that was a civilized time to call there. She might be doing the wrong thing but she had to enlighten him over the vandalized Tony. She couldn't bear it if Judith and Victor split up because of a misunderstanding.

When she'd finished there was silence from Victor's end of the line. "Victor? Are you still there?"

"Yes. I was thinking. It explains a great deal; Judy must have been incredibly upset. Even if she doesn't care what people think of her, and I believe underneath she does, that's downright malicious."

"So you'll make it up with her?" Holly's optimism echoed down the phone line.

"The thing is, Holly, why didn't she confide in me? That's what couples are supposed to do. Why did it end up being Rupert she told? That's what makes it so hard sometimes."

Holly gave an involuntary gasp. She hadn't thought of that. Maybe that's why Rupert had told her to leave it alone. She'd ended up hurting Victor more. She tried to dig herself out of the hole into which she was rapidly sinking. "I don't think she intended to tell Rupert. She sort of blurted it out in a state." She had a brainwave. "And she was only in the state because you'd left."

Victor laughed. "Nice try!"

"Honestly, Victor, she really is upset. Please talk to her."

"Look, I'm flying to Afghanistan next week, which should provide me with a sobering experience. I'll be so glad to get back to normality after that I'll be begging Judy to insult me. But for now I need my own space, although I greatly appreciate your concern, and whatever happens I certainly intend staying friends with you and Rupert. As soon as I get back I'll give you both a ring."

"Please be careful out there."

"I'm a cat with nine lives."

"How many have you used up?"

Victor laughed again. "I'm not certain, but I'm sure I have some left! Now you should go to bed, it must be the middle of the night there."

"It's gone 4am, but I'm not terribly tired. Maybe I'll go and watch the sun rise over Central Park."

"I wouldn't unless you want to give Rupert heart failure. New York is a pretty safe city now, but possibly not Central Park in the middle of the night. I certainly wouldn't allow Judy out there, however full scale a battle that might involve."

"You see, you do still love her!" Holly's voice was triumphant.

"I never said that I didn't. Goodnight, Miss Relationship Counsellor."

Holly curled up on the sofa staring out of the window. Talking of confiding in partners had reminded her she hadn't broken the news to Rupert that she had to go home.

CHAPTER TWENTY EIGHT

Jennifer's phone rang at lunch time one day, and she felt the usual thrill of excitement on answering and discovering it was Rupert.

"Do you want to go and play," he said. "We still have several places in your book to explore."

"Sure. Is there anything you and Holly want to see especially?"

"Holly's deserted me and gone back to England."

"Oh." Jennifer's heart was beating like crazy, but she tried not to sound too pleased. "I'm sorry, did something happen?"

Rupert's laugh didn't sound like he was heartbroken. "Lord, no. She got a recall for an audition she had before she came over. She'll be back in a couple of days, but meanwhile I'm in need of companionship."

"I'm an expert in companionship." Jennifer could have kicked herself for continuing to imagine anything would happen between her and Rupert. Still, at least they could have the day together.

"Wonderful. In fact, I told Richard what a brilliant guide you were and he wants to join our outing, if that's OK. Tom's doing a double shift at Joe Allen's so I think he's at rather a loose end too."

Jennifer's ocean-sized fantasies were shrinking into small puddles. "OK," she mustered, "Manhattan Sightseeing Tours for Englishmen times two."

"Jennifer, is something wrong?"

"No. It sounds great. You know how much I love to show off my insider knowledge."

"I tell you what. Why don't you and I have coffee first?"

"You don't have to."

"I'd like to. I enjoy our conversations enormously. Besides, it does my reputation no end of good to be seen alone with a beautiful woman."

Holly had been spot on with her analysis of Rupert, Jennifer thought as she hung up. He had the knack of making a woman feel completely special.

He was waiting in Starbucks when she arrived, with her favourite Frappuccino and a choice of muffins lined up on the table. He stood up and kissed her. "Thanks for keeping a homesick Englishman company."

"You know us Americans, we're very hospitable however arduous that might be!" She looked down at the muffins. "Are you trying to stop me fitting into my costumes?"

Rupert wagged his finger. "Ah-ah, this afternoon is about enjoying ourselves – no guilt trips. Besides, you have a perfect figure."

Jennifer blushed and quickly changed the subject. "So what's Holly's audition for?"

Watching Rupert's face light up, Jennifer wondered why she was torturing herself like this. "It's for a new movie version of *Nicholas Nickleby*. She's up for the role of Kate Nickleby, Nicholas's sister."

"She'd be perfect for that," Jennifer said.

"She's got exactly the right innocence, purity and loyalty."

"Yes, I agree. And thank you for recognizing that." Rupert leant over the table and touched Jennifer's hand. "I'm glad you two get along. You know, it's a whole new experience for me having a partner whom people like."

"Surely Miranda was popular? She's totally glamorous and vivacious."

"And she considers every other woman as competition, especially other actresses, which tends not to endear her to people. Right, enough about me; tell me something I don't know about you."

"I'm so boring. There's nothing to tell."

"Rubbish. Let's see. If you could be anywhere in the world at this moment, doing anything you wanted, what would it be?"

"I'm rather afraid I'd choose to be here."

Rupert sighed. "That wasn't quite the reply I was hoping for."

"Sorry." Jennifer tried to recall her daydreams before she'd met Rupert. "OK, I'd like to be in an English country pub eating roast beef and Yorkshire pudding and treacle tart, with the perfect Englishman and lots of dogs, wearing wellington boots."

"You or the dogs?"

"Me, idiot!" Jennifer gave a girlish giggle, which really was most unsuitable for her age.

If Rupert was of the same opinion he showed no sign of it. "That sounds idyllic," he said, and then added rather sheepishly, "and I'm glad you mentioned dogs because there might be a slight change of plan this afternoon involving animals."

"Does it involve having to ride one, clean one out, or merely admire from a distance?"

"Admire from behind a fence I hope. After I'd spoken to you, Kyle phoned to say he and Lauren were taking their children to Central Park Zoo and that the children wanted me to join them – for some reason I've become an adopted uncle. When he heard I had plans with you and Richard he extended the invitation to you both. Richard said as long as he's allowed ice cream then he's happy. Is that OK?"

Jennifer tilted her head on one side. "Do you know I've never been to Central Park Zoo in all the time I've lived here?"

"Good, it'll be a mutually new experience. Do you have any animal preferences?"

"I don't like ones that could eat me."

"Take the spare muffins to use as a decoy, just in case."

In the end it developed into a fairly large outing after Jennifer suggested they also ask Alyce and Nate. It also turned out to be a great success. The children adored getting so much attention from so many adults, and the fact that they had both Kyle and Rupert's shoulders to alternate sitting on.

"Can I have a turn too?" Richard asked Rupert. "My feet hurt."

"No, you certainly cannot," Rupert retorted. "I'm only a mule for people under the age of five and weighing less than 50lbs."

Richard sat down and kicked his feet in a pretend tantrum. Kyle's children stared at him in astonishment. "Want more ice-cream," he demanded.

"Richard, you are a terrible role model," Kyle complained as the cry for more ice-cream was taken up by his young family. "You've all had one already."

"More!" screamed Richard.

"More," screamed the children.

"I'll get them," Jennifer said, enjoying the afternoon more than she could have imagined. "Who else wants another?" When there were no other takers she added, "Just the children then," and laughed as Richard stuck his tongue out at her.

"I've always had an affinity with penguins," Richard commented as he licked his ice cream. "I'm sure it's because of all those butler roles I played in bow ties and tails."

"I bet you were real cute," Jennifer said.

"Cute wasn't exactly the look I was going for. I doubt the great butlers of literature and celluloid would thank you for such an observation." He gave Jennifer a playful nudge. "But ta anyway."

"Ta – I love that expression. It's so English." Jennifer sighed. "It sounds silly when I say it though. But I've always wondered why 'ta' means thank you, but 'ta-ta' means goodbye."

"Lord, I don't know. The English language is a mystery to me. Rupert, any ideas?"

"What? Sorry, I was attempting to figure out why you were discussing penguins."

"We're in a zoo," Richard pointed out.

"Yes, only we're looking at the monkeys."

"I don't have an affinity with monkeys. And don't you dare comment on that," he added as

Rupert opened his mouth and shut it again, chuckling. Richard finished his ice cream with an elegance which Kyle's children failed to emulate. "Where are the penguins? I want penguins," he demanded

"Penguins, penguins," the children screamed, as Lauren wiped them down with wet wipes.

"Shall I take him home?" Rupert enquired of Kyle.

"No, don't," Jennifer begged. "He's so funny. And I love penguins too."

"It seems the penguins have it," Nate commented. "Lead on, woman."

"Don't you woman me," Alyce said, "or I'll feed you to the polar bears."

Kyle's children stared at Alyce opened mouthed and moved closer to their parents.

Nate laughed. "Don't worry, kids. Alyce is only messing, aren't you honey?"

"Don't be so sure!" But Alyce was smiling. "So which way are the penguins?"

At that moment Rupert's phone rang. He moved away from the group to talk.

"Look at the way his face lit up; it must be Holly," Jennifer said.

"Young love," Lauren commented. "I remember when Kyle used to look at me that way when we were first married."

"I still do," Kyle protested. "It's only that you don't always notice over the heads of our attention-seeking children." To prove his point Kyle leant over and kissed Lauren on the mouth.

"Gross," said their daughter.

"Gross," Richard repeated.

"Gross, gross, gross," shouted the children,

jumping up and down.

"Honestly, Richard," Kyle, said, "I'm going to take Rupert up on his offer to take you home in a minute!"

Richard smiled, enjoying the banter and the day generally. He wasn't sure he'd been as happy as he was now since his beloved Scott had died. Tom, of course, was one reason, but it was equally the whole Broadway experience. He glanced over to where Jennifer was standing a little way off, intently watching Rupert talking on the phone. "You know, if we put him in a cage you could stare at him for hours without arousing suspicion," he muttered in her ear, making her jump. "Mind you, that might baffle the children."

"I don't know what you mean. Suspicion about what?" Jennifer almost stammered. She glanced around at the rest of their group who thankfully were otherwise occupied watching Kyle's children doing monkey impressions. "I was only wondering how long Rupert was going to be before the children get bored."

"Jennifer, just because I'm gay doesn't mean I don't understand or know about heterosexual relationships or desires. It's been questionable this afternoon whether you've been studying the animals or Rupert more."

"That's ridiculous, I..." She caught Richard's eye and he winked at her. She couldn't help but smile at him, if somewhat shamefacedly. Richard was so nice, and English, and at least with him she wouldn't make a fool of herself since she drew the line at making passes at gay guys. "I wish this job could go on forever," she said, determined to change the subject. "Not only because the role is the best I've ever had on Broadway, but also it's such a special company."

"I'd like that too," Richard replied, "although for different reasons. Yes, I love the play and the role, but it's more that I desperately want to stay here. I feel this is where I'm meant to live and work, as if it's my spiritual home. Ooh, that sounds terribly new age, doesn't it? Perhaps I should become a moonie, or are they the sect that wears nappies? But I digress. I only got this job by default, for which I often say a prayer to Saint Digby." Jennifer laughed at the very notion of the dreadful Digby with a halo. "And I'm not going to be offered another."

"Surely now everyone's seen how fabulous you are you'll have offers flooding in."

"But I don't have a green card or international star status like Judith and Rupert. The only way I could get a work permit would be to marry an American, and sadly gay marriages aren't legal in New York. Alternatively I'd need a skill that no one else in this great country has, and I don't think misbehaving on David Letterman's show counts. I must simply appreciate every moment."

"You can always come visit. You will, won't you?" Richard's gentle smile told her what she already knew: visiting a city was totally different from working and living in one. She'd visited London countless times but her dream was to work there. Jennifer watched Alyce carefully adjust Nate's headrest and a thought occurred to her. "What about Tom?"

For a brief moment she glimpsed an expression of sadness on Richard's face. "This conversation is getting far too sentimental," he said. "I want to know why Kyle's children aren't adopting me as an uncle as well as Rupert." He put his bottom lip over his top in a perfect childlike pout. "It's not FAIR!"

Jennifer crossed her arms. "Judging by your behaviour today they're more likely to consider you their younger brother!" Richard blew a raspberry at her. "Point proven," Jennifer said, laughing. Then she lowered her voice. "But seriously, what are you going to do about Tom?"

"What are you going to do about Rupert?"

Jennifer frowned. "That's totally different."

"Is it? Whether or not you slept with him..."

"I didn't," she said quickly.

Richard nodded. "Sensible girl."

Jennifer hung her head. "It wasn't exactly my choice."

"Ah." He patted her arm. "Anyway, my point is whatever did or didn't happen, it would finish at the end of this job. Show romances rarely last, especially if the couple concerned are on opposite sides of the Atlantic. Tom has been a fun interlude. That's all."

"No!" Jennifer protested. "I won't believe that. I've seen you guys together. You give me hope that there's always a chance."

"You mean for us oldies."

"No. Well yes, but older not old." Jennifer was floundering. "Just not Paige's age."

"It should be illegal to be Paige's age. Do you know she's not aware that Jude Law's version of *Alfie* is a remake? Perhaps that's why I hang around with her in the hope that some of that

390

youth might rub off and I could be eternally young."

Jennifer considered his remark. "Would you actually want eternal youth?"

"Not the mind of a youth, but I'd certainly adore the body of one. No more wrinkles or everything creaking when you stand up – heaven." Richard slipped his arm through Jennifer's and squeezed it. Then he gestured towards Kyle's children who were investigating the workings of Nate's wheelchair under Alyce's careful supervision. "If Rupert doesn't get off the phone soon the children are going to get fractious."

"They are, or you are?" Jennifer teased.

As if on cue, Rupert wandered back over, slipping the phone into his pocket. "Sorry," he said. "Penguins, right?"

"You look like the cat that got the cream," Richard said. He lowered his voice so the children couldn't hear. "Have you been having phone sex?"

"No!" Rupert couldn't imagine Holly doing such a thing. She was an old-fashioned romantic and would be uncomfortable with such an act – especially when she knew he was in a public place.

"No," Richard said, considering the matter more loudly, "I suppose you wouldn't want to frighten the horses."

"Can I ride horses?" Kyle's daughter asked.

"There aren't any horses, honey," said Lauren. "Richard's talking metaphorically."

Her daughter nodded seriously, having no idea what that word meant, but not wanting to ask in front of all these grown ups.

"Is there good news?" Jennifer asked Rupert.

"Holly's had a final recall for *Nicholas Nickleby* and it sounds very promising, although Holly's so unconfident it's hard to tell. She'd always be convinced they hated her."

"Like most actors," Jennifer observed.

"Hear, hear," said Richard. "However, I'm sure Holly will wow them. Now can we please go and see the penguins?"

"Christ, that's my idea of hell," Judith said that evening, when Rupert told her about their afternoon.

Rupert chuckled. "You might've been surprised if you'd tried it. Richard was a different man."

Judith wiped a smear off her make-up mirror, thoughtfully. "Yes, he's changed here, hasn't he? Young love I suppose. It's utterly nauseating."

"Don't be such a cynic!"

Judith raised a half made-up eyebrow at him. "Why not? I'm exceedingly good at it."

"True."

"When will Holly know about the role?"

"According to our agent, it's between her and two other actresses, all of whose screen tests are being sent to LA for the bigwigs to look at. It doesn't start shooting for a while so at least she can fly back here while she waits to hear."

"I'm sure she'll get it. In my opinion Holly's an excellent actress, and perfect for Kate Nickleby, and I'm never wrong." Judith gave a sniff and continued with her make-up. Rupert got up to leave, but Judith's voice stopped him as he reached the door. "Are you free for dinner after the show or do you have a hot date with a polar bear?"

Judith suddenly seemed terribly alone, Rupert thought, huddled over her dressing table. He wondered whether they should have invited her to join them at the zoo. Somehow he couldn't envisage her screaming for ice creams and doing penguin impressions. "You're in luck," he told her. "The polar bear turned me down flat."

"That must be a new experience for you."

"Apparently they never date actors."

CHAPTER TWENTY NINE

"My God, did you hear what Judith said?" Paige shrieked, as she came off in the interval of the Friday show the following week.

"We could hardly miss it," Jennifer replied.

The scene they had just finished contained Margo's line regarding the substantial business her plays always did at the box-office. But tonight Judith had unmistakably proclaimed that her plays did substantial business at the war-office. There had been a stunned silence on stage before Rupert had ad-libbed, "What an appropriate allegory for your off stage behaviour, Margo. I for one feel I am constantly at war with you."

Judith had grasped at the life-line she'd been thrown and got back on track, but she came off in the interval, cutting everyone dead, and slammed into her dressing room banishing even Tim.

"I've never known Judith go wrong before," Richard said. "That's doubtless why she's in such a vile mood. She'll hate herself for making a mistake."

"Every actor makes a mistake occasionally," Kyle said. "We're only human and surely the training we do in improvisation is there to help us deal with it."

"That was a great save, Rupert," said Jennifer, as he joined them after failing to gain entry to Judith's room.

"Thanks." Rupert gave a brief nod and went down to his dressing room. It wasn't so much Judith slipping-up which was worrying him, but the expression of terror and confusion he'd seen on her face. Judith was quick-witted and more than capable of ad-libbing her way out of the situation without help. Rupert had often seen her do it when other actors or something technical had gone awry, whereas tonight she looked like the proverbial rabbit caught in headlights, unable to move or think. That's why he'd jumped in so quickly with his improvised line, which thankfully she'd responded to.

In Act Two Judith appeared edgy, which the other actors put down to her error in Act One, but Richard was astonished to feel her physically shaking as Margo and Bill are reunited and embrace. As if that wasn't strange enough, she knocked over a glass during the restaurant scene and the ginger ale, representing champagne, splashed out and seeped into the table cloth. Rupert, sitting with Mindy at another table, again saw the look of panic and fear in Judith's eyes. At the curtain call she barely acknowledged the audience and refused to take her solo bow.

Rupert quickly changed and dashed to Judith's room determined to find out what was going on. He met Tim coming out with the laundry and costumes to press for the next day's show.

"I'm supposed to take the key out of the door so she isn't disturbed," Tim told him.

"I'll take full responsibility."

"We'll all chip in for your funeral."

Rupert grinned and gave Tim a wave as the dresser disappeared down to the wardrobe department. Rupert's immediate greeting on entering the room was to 'get the fuck out' but he ignored that. Judith was sitting in her theatre dressing gown trying to take her make-up off with a hand trembling so badly Rupert was amazed the cleanser wasn't splattered around the walls. The other hand, clasping a lit cigarette, was similarly trembling and flicking ash on to the carpet.

Rupert removed the cleanser and cigarette, taking no notice of Judith's cursing and efforts to stop him. "What the hell's going on?" he demanded.

"Mind your own fucking business and give me back my cigarette."

"No. You'll set off the smoke alarms if you're not careful." He stubbed it out in the basin. "We're not going anywhere until you tell me what's wrong."

"I fucked up, OK? I'm not fucking immortal. We all make mistakes."

"You don't. You never even made a mistake when you played a whole show with chronic pneumonia."

"I've told you it's none of your business. I'm perfectly capable of sorting out my own life. I'm not your responsibility."

"Actually, without Victor here I consider you are to some degree."

A strange sound erupted from Judith's throat, which if it had come from anyone else might have been considered a sob. But Judith didn't do crying. In her opinion this was a slightly unusual hiccup and she tried, unsuccessfully, to hold back another one.

Rupert was growing increasingly alarmed. "Judith? Please talk to me. Is it Victor? Have you two rowed again?"

Judith shook her head and yet another unusual sounding hiccup emanated from her. She stood up, preparing to change into her clothes to go home, but as she did so she swayed. Rupert grabbed her arm, led her across to the bed and sat down beside her. "Has something happened to Victor?"

Judith's mouth twitched as if she wanted to speak but couldn't quite. Eventually she managed, "He's missing."

Rupert took a sharp intake of breath. "Oh Christ. In Afghanistan?"

"No, in fucking Fulham, that hot bed of terrorist hijacks and kidnapping. Where else would he go missing?"

"Sorry, that was a stupid question. I'm just trying to get my head around it." He ran his hand through his hair. "How do you know? I thought you two weren't speaking. Perhaps it's merely that he hasn't updated you on his whereabouts."

"I'm not that obtuse, Rupert. I know because the newspaper he was writing the piece for phoned me. It seems Victor put me down as his emergency contact. They told me he went out with another reporter and an interpreter to visit some army base at which they never arrived. They haven't been heard from since, over forty eight hours ago. Bastard – I told him I wasn't going to Afghanistan to pick up his dead body."

"You're not going to have to go anywhere. It'll be fine. Victor knows what he's doing. There're a million places he could be and I would imagine communications there are limited. Doubtless he's got some scoop, but can't get in touch with his paper to tell them. I'm sure he'll ring you soon to fill you in."

Judith shook her head slowly. "No, I don't suppose he will. He made me his emergency contact before I told him he was a lousy actor and to get out of my life." There was an expression of anguish on her face which Rupert had never seen before. "God, Rupert, if he's been killed those would have been the last words I said to him."

"He's not going to have been killed," Rupert said, with a lot more conviction than he felt. "Now finish getting dressed while I go and sign autographs and cancel your car."

"Why?"

"Because you can share mine since you're coming back to our apartment."

"No. I want to go home."

"You're not going back to a solitary hotel room." Judith started to protest but Rupert cut her off. "It's not negotiable."

Holly, having returned from her screen-test in London a couple of days ago, had been preparing supper when she heard the front door of the apartment open and two voices. Rupert came into the room with a pale faced Judith, and briefly filled Holly in.

Holly gasped and flew across the room to try and throw her arms around Judith, but Judith immediately held up a hand to stop her. "I don't do sentiment," she snapped.

Holly looked at Rupert helplessly. Judith wasn't the easiest person to comfort. "I'll make you a hot drink," she said, heading towards the kitchen.

"I don't want a fucking hot drink," Judith complained. "I want something stronger."

"That wouldn't be good for you if you're in shock." Judith glared at her. Holly gulped; Judith's looks were not easy to ignore, but she stood her ground. "If Victor's in trouble, it's not going to help if you're in an alcoholic stupor."

Judith continued to glare at her for a few seconds before giving an indifferent shrug. Holly took this as acquiescence and busied herself in the kitchen creating a mug of her speciality, extra sweet because she'd read that sugar was good for shock. Judith drank it, huddled on the sofa, refusing any offer of food but insisting that Holly and Rupert ate their supper. "It's a lovely cup of tea though, Holly," she said, putting down the empty mug.

"Um, thank you," Holly said, not pointing out that it had been hot chocolate.

By 4am, having had the news on constantly for any reports from Afghanistan, Judith eventually agreed to try to sleep. Holly insisted on her having the bedroom while she and Rupert slept on the sofa bed. Judith protested but Holly was already changing the sheets and laying out a pair of her pyjamas and the toothbrush from her Virgin Upper Class goody bag.

"Do you really think Victor is OK?" Holly whispered to Rupert as they climbed into the sofa bed.

"Well, he's smart and he's experienced."

"But you hear reports of journalists being kidnapped and tortured and then executed."

Rupert put his arms around Holly and hugged her tightly. "Yes, I know."

Rupert woke a couple of hours later to find an empty space beside him and a noise emanating from the bedroom. Going to investigate, he stopped dead in the doorway. Holly was sitting on Judith's bed, her arms around the older woman whose entire body was convulsed with sobs. Aware how mortified Judith would be if she knew that in addition to breaking down in front of Holly her frailty had furthermore been witnessed by him, Rupert crept back to the sitting room. He switched on the computer and checked the internet for any news of Victor, but still there was nothing. Climbing back into the sofa bed he lay there listening to Judith's muffled sobs. It was nearly an hour before Holly tip-toed into the room.

"How is she?" Rupert asked, making Holly jump.

"Asleep, finally; I didn't want to leave her until I knew she was. You heard?"

"Yes, but I thought it was better she didn't know. You were the perfect person for the job. Thank you."

"I was merely in the right place at the right time."

"Don't underestimate yourself, sweetheart. Judith would rather slit her wrists than break down in front of most people."

Holly smiled at the compliment and then felt bad because of the circumstances. "I wish

I could do more. Do you think she'll continue doing the show?"

"Knowing Judith I'd say it's pretty likely, as long as she's not too distraught to concentrate. I can't visualize her sitting in her hotel while the play goes on without her. Besides, it'll be healthier for her to have an occupation."

Holly stared up at the ceiling, her face screwed-up in thought. "If he has been kidnapped, will they demand a ransom? And if so, can Judith pay it? I mean, if she can't afford all of it we could help too, couldn't we? I've got a bit saved up."

Rupert sighed. "There's no point in speculating until we know what's happened."

"But we could?" Holly insisted.

"Of course, only it might not help."

"Why not?"

"Afghanistan does have a high percentage of finance based kidnappings, but a fair share are carried out by political extremists, usually members of the Taliban, for whom holding Western journalists hostage is first rate publicity." He ran his hand down Holly's worried face. "So the chances are if he had been snatched we'd have heard something by now. It's more likely they had a burst tyre and are having to walk for miles to get assistance. You can't phone the AA in the middle of the desert. Let's try and get some sleep so we can be optimistic for Judith tomorrow."

"OK." There was a few minutes silence before Holly said, "Wouldn't they carry a spare tyre?"

CHAPTER THIRTY

The next morning when Rupert and Holly surfaced Judith had gone, leaving the bed made up and Holly's pyjamas neatly folded on top. There was no note, and they received no reply on her hotel phone or mobile. Since it was a matinee day Rupert resolved to go straight into the theatre and hope Judith would turn up there, while Holly would wait at the apartment and keep phoning.

When Judith wasn't at the theatre her usual one and a half hours before curtain up, Rupert stationed himself outside her dressing room, filled with a deep unease. When it came to work Judith was never late. As the other actors trudged passed him on their way to their dressing rooms, regarding his position with puzzlement, he gave them a cheerful wave as if sitting on the stairs outside the leading lady's room was quite usual. Richard was the only one who enquired if he'd been banished and offered to bring him a cushion and coffee.

As the half hour call was announced over the relay system, Rupert heard a familiar step on the stairs and Judith appeared. "Is there any particular reason you're camped outside my dressing room?" she enquired. "You look like one of those poor homeless buggers. If I give you a dollar will you go away so I can get in?"

Rupert slowly stood up and followed Judith into the room, trying to keep his tone light. "You are an hour later than usual, so, strangely, under the circumstances, I was a little concerned as to your whereabouts."

Judith gave him a contemptuous look. "Why? Did you think I was going to hijack a plane to Afghanistan and interrogate the Taliban until I found the stupid sod?"

"It had crossed my mind."

Judith produced a fleeting smile. "My hijacking licence has expired – and I gave my thumbscrews to Oxfam."

"So where have you been? We've been trying to call."

"I know. I have something like fifty missed calls from Holly. She's most persistent, your fiancée."

"She was extremely worried. And you haven't answered my question."

Judith gave a dismissive wave. "I've simply been walking around thinking. I wasn't aware I needed your permission. Now I need to get ready, so fuck off and leave me alone."

"Are you sure you'll be OK to do the show?"

Judith regarded him as if he were insane. "Of course: I don't miss shows. And anyway I'm sure you're correct and the bloody man will be perfectly all right. Besides, since we're finished why should I care?"

Rupert gave up. Every time he thought he was coming close to understanding Judith she'd surprise him.

The performance Judith gave that afternoon was perfect, as if nothing had happened. She even gave Rupert a surreptitious wink when she got the box office line correct. Rupert was beginning to wonder if she'd privately received news of Victor. That notion vanished when Richard burst into his dressing room between shows to tell him that Janet Williams, the actress who'd played Birdie in London, had just phoned him from England to say it had been on the BBC news that a journalist called Victor Lewis was missing in Afghanistan. She'd wanted to know if they'd heard and whether it was true. Rupert had no choice but to confirm Janet's report whilst being aware how much Judith would hate everyone knowing.

"Lordy, poor Judith," Richard said. "No wonder she was all over the place last night. Yet she seems fine today."

"I know." Rupert frowned. "That's what concerns me."

Judith steadfastly refused to stay at Rupert and Holly's apartment that night, declaring she'd sleep better in the bed she was used to and muttering about the hotel's three hundred and fifty thread Egyptian cotton sheets until Rupert threatened to break into the by then closed Bloomingdale's and buy some if that would change her mind. In the end he gave up, merely making her promise to phone if she needed anything.

Much to his surprise she did just that at 8am the following morning. When Rupert sleepily picked up he could barely hear anything through the noise. It sounded as if Judith was in the middle of a train station or.... "Judith," Rupert shouted down the mouthpiece in sudden panic.

"I'm not fucking deaf," Judith snapped.

"Sorry, but there's so much noise. Where are you?"

"JFK. I'm about to board a plane to fucking Dubai."

"Dubai?"

"Don't tell me your tennis playing education didn't run to geography. It's a port in the United Arab Emirates."

"I know where Dubai is. What I don't know is why the hell you're flying there."

"Apparently you have to fly via there to get to Afghanistan. It's a nightmare. Why don't they have direct flights?"

"Because it's hardly a holiday destination," Rupert growled at her. "It's bloody dangerous out there. Don't board that plane. I'm getting a cab to the airport now."

"It's too late, the flight leaves in half an hour. That's why I'm phoning now because I knew you'd try and stop me. But I decided I'd better let you know where I was before you started haunting my dressing room again."

Rupert clasped at the only straw he could think of. "Judith, you'll miss performances. You don't do that."

There was a brief silence on the other end of the line. "Yes, I know. Believe me I haven't made this decision lightly. But there's only the matinee today, then tomorrow we have off and by Tuesday I might be back." Even Judith's acting skills didn't make that sound believable; hardly surprising since the flight to Dubai alone was fourteen hours, making a return within two days a distinctly unfeasible scenario.

Rupert wasn't even clasping at straws now,

405

more like cocktail sticks. "Judith, I understand why you're going, but by flying out there you could create a much worse situation."

"How kind of you to have such confidence in me."

"Seriously, what do you think you'll achieve? All you're going to do is make yourself an exceedingly high profile target." Rupert had a sudden idea. "Your being there could detract from the search operation for Victor."

"Rubbish." But there was a note of doubt in Judith's voice.

"There's only a certain amount of army and ambassadorial help available to English citizens in Afghanistan. If they're too busy protecting you, because it's going to look very bad for the country if you're hurt in any way, then they're not going to be out hunting for Victor."

"How do you know all this?"

"I've been up half the night talking to the Foreign Office." Rupert was improvising madly. "I actually suggested that you and I both fly over to help and they explained how damaging that could be." There was silence from Judith's end of the phone. "Look, give it another few days anyway. We'll probably have heard something by then." There was another long silence. Rupert prayed that meant she was at least considering it. "I'm leaving the apartment now so wait for me. Please."

"You'll probably have a wasted trip."

"Where on earth did you come up with that stuff you told Judith?" Holly asked as their cab raced towards the airport, under the promise of double the fare if they made record time.

Rupert gave a tired smile. "The whole thing about being a high profile target came from an army thing I did on telly once. The rest of it was pure bollocks."

"It was very believable bollocks." Holly stared out of the window at the early morning light. "Do you think she would be a high profile target if she does insist on going?"

Rupert shrugged. "I suppose it would depend on how the Afghans feel about classical English actresses with attitude. I imagine it would be worse if she was someone political, but kidnapping any celebrity would be excellent publicity." He gave a rueful smile. "I don't know what we're worrying about. If the Taliban capture Judith there'd probably be a mass surrender to the allied forces within two hours!"

Boarding for the Dubai flight had closed by the time Rupert and Holly reached the airport and the woman on the airline desk refused to reveal whether or not there was a Judith Gold on board. It was a security ruling, she explained rather reluctantly to Rupert. She'd have been more than happy to reveal virtually anything to this gorgeous actor. Eventually she did agree to have Judith paged, requesting her to come to the airline desk if she was in the airport.

Rupert and Holly later decided it was amongst the longest ten minutes of their lives standing there waiting until they saw Judith striding towards them across the concourse.

"I'm not the most popular person in this airport at present," Judith commented as she reached them, with no allusion to their rescue mission. "When I refused to board the flight they had to locate my luggage in the hold which severely delayed them. I thought at any moment they were going to bodily thrust me onboard the plane and strap me into my seat."

"Nobody would be that brave," Rupert commented.

Judith glared at him. "I'm tempted to inform them it was your fault and they can lynch you." She glanced at her watch. "If you drop me at the hotel I can get a couple of hours sleep before the matinee."

"You can sleep at our place," Rupert said, tossing Judith's case into the cab which he'd asked to wait. "I'm not risking you going AWOL again."

Judith started to say something, but then stopped, shrugged, put her head against the window as the cab moved off and didn't say another word as they drove back into Manhattan.

Since the news of Victor's disappearance was now general knowledge, the *All About Eve* Company were amazed at Judith's presence for each performance, and how, after that Friday night show when she'd almost gone to pieces, she displayed no sign that anything was amiss.

"How can she behave like nothing's wrong?" Paige asked Richard after the Sunday matinee, a week after Judith's aborted trip to Afghanistan. It was impossible at the moment to ask Rupert anything privately since he barely left Judith's side.

"She's good at hiding what she feels," Richard said. "Though God knows how. I'd be a total wreck."

"Maybe she doesn't care for him so much," Paige continued. "I never saw her be nice to him."

"I honestly don't know, Paige, but I'd imagine it's her way of coping."

"Is it an English way of behaving? We Americans talk about our emotions. It's not good to repress feelings."

"I'm not certain I completely agree. Sometimes a stiff upper lip and getting on with things has its advantages." He pulled his best stiff-upper-lipped face, one he'd perfected with his years of playing butlers, making Paige giggle. "Besides, it saves us a fortune on psychiatrists' fees."

"I don't see a shrink anymore."

Richard gazed at her. "Why did you see one in the first place? You seem pretty together to me."

"I was kinda low when I moved here on account of not getting work. So I saw one who helped me accept my audition rejections and regain my confidence as a performer."

"That's what's called being an actor, Paige. Unemployment is part of the package. It's not a personal slight. I could have told you that for free."

Jennifer came running down the stairs, her face pale. "Have you seen Judith?"

"She and Rupert just left," Richard said. "What's wrong?"

"I found this stuck on the door to the stage." Jennifer held up a piece of cardboard. Pasted on it was a photograph of Victor, taken from the BBC website, and around his neck somebody had drawn a noose and scrawled 'suffer bitch'. "Whoever could have done such a thing?" Jennifer was almost in tears.

"Do you think she saw it?" Paige asked.

Richard shook his head, even his normal sangfroid shaken. "I'm sure we'd have heard about it if she had. Whoever did this obviously knew her routine was to go on stage at the end of the evening. What they didn't know was that she's been foregoing that routine since she's been staying with Rupert."

Jennifer held it at arm's length. "What should I do with it? Should we tell her?"

"No."

"What about Rupert?"

"He has enough on his hands at the moment. Give it to me and I'll keep it somewhere safe. Maybe we could find a fingerprint kit and test everyone in the building – I've always wanted to play detective! Meanwhile, do you want to go for a drink? You look like you could do with one."

"Oh yes, please."

"Paige?" Richard asked.

"No thanks, I've got a date."

Jennifer caught Richard's eye which told her he'd seen her look of relief that it would just be the two of them.

While Judith regularly protested over Rupert's insistence that she stay with him, in truth she was grateful. As the days rolled by and there was no news on Victor she found she was becoming more reliant on Rupert and Holly than she cared to admit. Their company and performing the play each night kept her mind engaged.

410

Her reason for agreeing to stay, as she informed Rupert, was the necessity of having the BBC and other news websites set up on his laptop which she demanded be constantly monitored.

If Judith had more knowledge of computers it would have made Rupert and Holly's lives easier, but her one foray into that world consisted of becoming so annoyed with the frequent appearance of the squirming paperclip when attempting to write her autobiography that she'd kicked the machine to such a degree it had never fully recovered.

The autobiography had not, as yet, progressed past page two. Judith had decided that in the writing she'd incomprehensibly come across as dominating and demanding, which she considered an overly-harsh view.

If Rupert and Holly, even after having Judith as a house guest, didn't totally agree with such an analysis then the Afghan Embassy, whose number Judith had on speed dial, most certainly would.

CHAPTER THIRTY ONE

"What the hell was Mindy playing at?" Judith demanded, following the Sunday matinee performance two weeks after Victor's disappearance. "She's started putting in these ideas which we tried in London and didn't work. Surely she hasn't been talking to that ghastly girl who played Eve there?"

Rupert was sitting in Judith's dressing room, waiting for her to get ready before they went back to his apartment. "Ah, that might be Aubrey. If you recall they were his original ideas in London, before you quashed them."

"You make it sound as if I never let him have a say."

Rupert raised his eyebrows "Do I? I can't imagine why."

"Piss off. Anyway, if that's the case why is Mindy suddenly using them? Who let him get at her?"

Rupert cleared his throat. "That's probably my fault. I suggested Aubrey talk to Mindy when you two were onstage feuding, and since then they've become rather inseparable."

"Well, un-inseparate them immediately. You can't let directors near actors, it causes chaos."

"What do you want me to do? Physically handcuff them to their individual dressing rooms?"

Judith gave Rupert a look which left him in no doubt how much she'd relish such a notion. "Tell Aubrey I want to see him immediately," she ordered.

"You'll be lucky. It's Sunday evening; he's doubtless cadged an invitation to spend the weekend in the Hamptons."

"Try. Otherwise I'll be fretting about it until Tuesday."

Rupert got up muttering about being too old to play messenger boy, but thinking that at least moaning at Aubrey might prove a temporary distraction for Judith. The past fortnight hadn't been easy for any of them and *All About Eve* was the only thing, other than searching for news of Victor, in which Judith showed much interest.

Left alone in the dressing room, Judith stared at herself in the mirror. She was certain she looked ten years older than two week ago and definitely felt it. At least she'd lost a few pounds because she simply wasn't hungry, in spite of Holly's best efforts to cook food which might tempt their guest. She'd better be careful though or her Margo Channing would end up resembling an old hag.

"You look beautiful to me."

Judith swung around at the sound of the voice. She hadn't even heard the door open. For a moment everything seemed to spin around her then, as it stopped, she charged into the ante-room launching herself at Victor and beating him with her fists. "You fucking bastard," she shrieked. "Have you any idea what you've put me through? I screwed up a whole performance because of you. I've never done that before. You selfish, selfish man."

Victor caught her hands and, pulling them

413

down to her sides, he enveloped her in a huge hug. "It's OK, Judy, it's OK."

"Don't you 'OK' me." Judith was furious that she appeared to be shaking. She made a half-hearted attempt to pull away, whilst revelling in the sensation of being enfolded in his arms. "Don't you ever, ever do that to me again. I thought you were fucking dead. I don't care if you have to report on local school fetes or mind-numbing parliamentary debates, you are never to go back into another bloody war zone."

Victor smiled down at her. "No, I rather think I won't. Still, it was almost worth it to receive such a tender greeting. Ouch," he added, as Judith elbowed him hard in the chest, while standing on his foot and taking advantage of this to pull free. "That's no way to treat a war hero."

"It's the perfect way to treat a war idiot; somebody who should know better at his age than to play at some young man's game."

"Ouch," Victor said again. "You know how to wound me physically and mentally. Besides, I'm probably better equipped to deal with it than younger men since I've had more experience. Still, since there's a fair chance this may have been the last of my nine lives, something Holly was asking about before I left, maybe it is time to stop."

Much as she tried to control it, Judith felt the relief show on her face. She was almost tempted to check the expression in the mirror so she could use it if needed in some future role. Instead, with an effort, she wiped the expression off – allowing Victor to glimpse any further display of emotion would never do. Instead she snapped, "I hope that doesn't mean you're going to be under my feet the entire time."

Victor laughed. "That would not be good for either of us. I don't intend retiring any more than you do. I'll merely work in safer areas."

"That's all right then. How long are you going to stay in New York?"

"I thought until *All About Eve* finishes its run. I can work from here, maybe cover some debates at the UN, and I'd like to write a series of short articles on the average American's view of the Afghanistan and Iraq wars."

"And where do you intend residing?"

"If you want your own space I'll get a separate room at the hotel to which you can banish me when you feel the need. Alternatively, we could look into getting a short-lease apartment together."

Judith gave a sniff. "Obviously Afghanistan wasn't that horrific since you've evidently had ample opportunity to contemplate work and accommodation scenarios. Why was I was even mildly concerned about your welfare? And I don't want to move out of the hotel." She paused before adding, "I suppose we could get a larger suite there though."

"Whatever you want, Judy darling." He grabbed Judith's hands, held them to his lips and said in his best melodramatic manner, "As long as we're together."

"You keep that up and you'll be staying in a different hotel. In a different city. The sentiment factor is far too high." Victor grinned; he'd have been disappointed by any other response.

There was a brief knock on the door and Rupert came in. "I can't locate Aubrey... Victor!" Rupert was across the room in a second and shaking Victor's hand. "I've rarely been so relieved to see anyone in my life."

"Thank you. It's great to be here. How's Holly?"

"Worried stiff about you. She's making a full Sunday roast dinner at the apartment, so please come and join us. I'd love to see her face when you walk in. Judith will have to collect her stuff from there anyway."

"Oh?" Victor regarded Judith with crossed arms. "Don't tell me they threw you out of the hotel. I told you about propositioning the lift boy."

Judith snorted. "Lift boy indeed – as if there was even room for one in that lift." Victor chuckled, and Rupert took this as his cue to leave. "Actually, I was only staying with Rupert because he has the BBC news on his computer."

"I see."

"Why the hell didn't they announce that you'd turned up like a bad penny? Then you wouldn't have given me such a fucking shock."

"It's complicated, and involved the safety of other people," Victor explained. "But I imagine it will be broadcast soon – if anyone else is especially interested." He put his arm around Judith and hugged her. "Besides, I rather liked the idea of surprising you; it must be that tiny bit of actor still in me – lousy though I was."

Judith took a deep breath. "You weren't that bad an actor. I would never have dated you if you had been. You simply didn't have the drive."

"No, not in the way you have. Still, I'm honoured by the sort of compliment."

"Humph."

Holly's display of joy at Victor's appearance far outdid anyone else's. She threw herself into his arms without using him as a punching bag, as Judith had done, and it took Rupert's remark that he could smell food burning to persuade her to release him. She insisted on serving his dinner first and hovered over him with second helpings before he'd barely finished what was on his plate.

"So are you going to relate what you've been doing while we've been searching for your whereabouts?" Judith enquired, after they'd eaten and were relaxing on the sofas drinking coffee.

"There's not much to tell," Victor said lightly. "We got caught up in an ambush and no one knew where we were for a while and panicked. But, as you can see, you can't keep a good reporter down."

"Couldn't you at least have found a phone or computer to let us know you were all right?"

"Not really; believe me, if I could've I would've." Victor had his arm around Judith whose head was lying on his shoulder. It wasn't a sight Rupert and Holly had ever expected to see.

Rupert offered their guests nightcaps but they declined, stating their intention to head home. Judith went to use their bathroom before they left, while Holly disappeared into the kitchen to make them a food and drink parcel, knowing that since Judith hadn't been back to the hotel for a week there'd be nothing there.

"Thank you both so much for looking after Judy," Victor said to Rupert.

"Our pleasure."

"Really? I wasn't aware you were both masochists!"

"It was preferable to having her boarding a plane to find you."

Victor chuckled and then stopped at Rupert's expression. "Oh my God, she didn't?"

Rupert gave him a brief version of Judith's airport excursion. Victor put his head in his hands. "Bloody woman, has she any idea how dangerous it is out there? It's a total war zone; she could have been killed."

"I rather think those were her sentiments about you."

Victor smiled wryly. "Touché! I can't believe she was willing to do that for me."

Rupert regarded him with surprise. "Can't you?"

"Yes," Victor said, slowly, "I suppose I can. She's one hell of a woman."

Rupert held up his coffee cup in agreement. "Victor, I don't want to sound rude, but you look pretty rough. Was it really as simple as you made out?"

Victor sighed. "I did play it down slightly. Pas devant les dames and all that."

"How very gentlemanly. However, the last time I looked I wasn't une dame."

"True." Victor nodded slowly as if wondering how much to say. "OK, we were ambushed, although I'm fairly sure it was to order rather than by chance. They grabbed both myself and

418

an American journalist whilst leaving our interpreter, which made for interesting conversations with our captors. My knowledge of the Afghan language is inadequate to say the least." Victor stopped.

"They've been holding you hostage all this time?"

"I was released first, after ten days, since it seems they hate Americans more than the English. However, the negotiators wanted to maintain a news blackout until they could obtain the American's release too. That happened early yesterday, so then I was free to leave the country and I've been travelling to get here ever since. I haven't been able to discover whether there was a ransom paid or we were part of a diplomatic exchange, but at that point I wasn't hanging around to find out. In a couple of weeks I might start probing – we journalists can never let a story drop with questions unanswered."

"It must have been hell."

Victor stroked his beard. "It's astonishing how people who are held captive for months or even years don't go completely crazy. I've certainly never been so glad to see daylight, or be able to move and sleep unshackled."

"Jesus Christ. I can't even begin to imagine it."

Victor shrugged. "It's not the only near miss I've had, but it was probably the worst, if only because there was so much time to ponder the situation. Whenever our captors pointed a gun at us we'd wonder if it was to threaten or to kill. For the only time in my life, that I recall, my carefree disposition utterly deserted me." Victor paused for a moment and Rupert didn't think he'd ever seen him look so sombre. But then he shook his head as if to clear the image and smiled. "Still, there's always a risk in my line of work."

"That's one way of putting it," Rupert said, amazed at Victor's stoicism.

"Victor, are you coming?" Judith called from the front door. "I'm tired."

"I'm waiting for Holly's Red Cross package," Victor called back.

"Are you going to write about it?" Rupert asked.

"I'm not certain. My reporter's instinct says yes, but I'm not sure how traumatic it would be for people I know, like Holly, to read."

"And Judith."

"I don't know about that. She might enjoy an account of someone putting a sack over my head and terrifying the life out of me; it's doubtless one of her greatest fantasies."

"I can't agree there. She was a total mess you know."

Victor was immediately serious. "Yes. It's funny how events can change one's perspective." Holly came in carrying two bags which she handed to Victor. "Thank you, Holly, that's terribly kind, and thank you both for everything you've done. Yes, I'm coming," he added, in reply to Judith's demand that he get a bloody move on.

After Victor and Judith had left, Rupert went to get a beer from the fridge. "Holly," he called, "I may be hallucinating, or perhaps we have very fat alcoholic mice, but wasn't this fridge full earlier, including some bottles of wine and beer?"

Holly came running in, with an apologetic expression. "I'm sorry. I thought Victor needed feeding up and they both needed a drink. I can go to the twenty four hour deli if you want anything."

"No, don't worry. After all this excitement maybe I'll just have a cup of tea."

"I'm afraid I gave them the milk too."

CHAPTER THIRTY TWO

Rupert arrived at the theatre one night the following week to discover members of the cast huddled around the stage door. From there Judith's voice could be clearly heard screaming from her dressing room. "What's going on?" he asked.

"It's awful," Paige told him, wide eyed. "Somebody cut up one of Judith's costumes."

Rupert stared at her speechless for a second before dashing up the stairs. Tim was sitting on the floor in the dressing room with a needle and thread attempting to mend a gash in Judith's green party costume. It wasn't a question of it having been torn by accident, but rather slashed twice from the bodice to the bottom of the skirt at the back so one piece of the material hung away like a train.

Judith meanwhile was cursing every person in the theatre, in New York and in America, and demanding action. The stage manager was huddled in the corner, whilst a hastily summoned American producer was attempting to get a word in between Judith's tirades.

Rupert left Judith berating the producer and crouched down by Tim. "What happened?" he asked quietly.

"I'd pressed it in here earlier and it was fine," Tim replied, equally quietly. "When I came back to do my pre-show check it was like this and I didn't have time to do anything when Judith came in and... well, it's been like this ever since. She tried to call you, but apparently your cell phone was off." Tim glanced towards Judith and said in an even lower tone, "Not that I blame you."

"Jesus," Rupert swore. "How fixable is it?"

Tim considered the start of his handiwork. "It might not show from the front. The skirt is so full the way the material falls should hide the worst of it, but basically it's ruined. And it's her favourite costume too. Do you think whoever did this knew that?"

Rupert shrugged, hoping that wasn't the case. "Tim, is it possible for me and Judith to have this room to ourselves?"

"No problem, I'll go work in wardrobe." Tim slowly stood up and left the room bearing the frock in his arms as if carrying a loved one. The room's other occupants were only too glad to make their escape at Rupert's request.

"What are you doing?" Judith demanded of Rupert. "I hadn't finished with them yet. This whole experience has turned into a total nightmare. If anyone ever mentions my working on Broadway again please shoot me. I'm surrounded by fucking morons, and now there's a scissor-wielding lunatic who I'm convinced is that bloody method actress. Imagine if we'd been performing a thriller - she'd have killed me on the first preview under the guise of realism." She covered her face with her hands. "God, I want to go home. I hate this bloody city."

"Sit down," Rupert said, gently. Judith sank down at her dressing table and Rupert pointed to her mobile. "Now phone Victor."

Judith stared at him. "Why? It has nothing to do with him."

"Of course it does. Phone him."

"You phone him if you're so concerned."

Rupert sighed. "There are occasions, Judith, when you can be amazingly dense." Judith glared at him, she'd been called a lot of things in her life, but nobody had ever accused her of being dense. "It needs to come from you," Rupert said, wondering how he could make it any clearer.

Judith continued to rant and rave for the next fifteen minutes until the door opened, Victor came in and knelt beside her, taking her hands in his. As Rupert quietly left the dressing room, he heard Judith saying to Victor, "It's my favourite costume."

"I know, Judy. I know. Don't worry, we'll get to the bottom of all this, I promise."

"And meanwhile am I supposed to go on naked?"

"Absolutely not! I would never permit that."

"Thank you."

"That's for my exclusive pleasure."

"Oh, honestly!"

Rupert grinned as he went back down the stairs. There was still a cluster of actors and stage management at the stage door, in addition to the producer who was nervously wondering if they'd have a leading lady that night. Having put their minds at rest with regards to Judith's intention of performing, Rupert went down to his own dressing room.

As he unlocked the door Richard came up

behind him holding something in his hand. "Can I come in?" he asked. "There's something you should see."

Five minutes later Richard left an appalled Rupert with the spitefully adapted picture of Victor with the noose around his neck. This was getting really vicious. Before he could decide when would be a good time to tell Victor without Judith knowing, his phone rang.

"Hi, sweetheart," he said as Holly's name came up on his display.

"Hi. I wondered what Judith said."

"Holly, I'm so sorry. I haven't had a chance to tell her yet."

"Oh, right, it doesn't matter."

"It does matter, only something came up." Quickly Rupert explained about the dress episode. Holly was appalled and prepared to dash to the theatre for moral support until Rupert told her that Victor was already there in that capacity.

"That's wonderful," Holly said. "Victor will be so happy she wanted him." Rupert said nothing. "Rupert, did Judith ask him to come?"

"Yes." Rupert said carefully.

"Did you suggest it?"

"I'm not answering that on the grounds it might incriminate me! So tell me, how is the soon to be Miss Kate Nickleby, star of *Nicholas Nickleby* the movie, feeling now the news has sunk in?"

"Unreal. I just want Jane to get my contract sorted before they decide I'm too old after all and change their minds."

"How on earth could you be too old?"

425

"I've been re-reading the book and at the start Kate is only fifteen."

"Sweetheart, you barely look older than that, and if you were actually fifteen I could be jailed for what I've been doing to you for the last year!"

Having expected Judith to demand a twenty four hour guard on her dressing room, and certainly an impenetrable lock, along with a personal bodyguard, Rupert was surprised when she announced she now wanted none of those. "It's his idea," she explained with a gesture towards Victor. "However, Tim's going to keep the costumes in wardrobe, and I'm taking everything of personal value back to the hotel." She held out her slashed frock with Tim's neat repair stitches. "What do you think?"

"Pretty impressive."

Judith snorted. "I'll look like I'm wearing Frankenstein's monster's face on my arse. Would you believe their other suggestion was to cover it with a large bow? Do I look like fucking Shirley Temple?"

"No!" Rupert and Victor said in unison.

Later at the hotel Judith curled up on the sofa in the large suite to which she and Victor had upgraded. Victor was serving Chinese food from boxes they'd bought on the way back.

"I'm going to hang around your dressing room during the shows for the moment until we've sorted this situation," Victor said, balancing a spring roll in his chopsticks.

Judith frowned, unsure of her reaction. Half of her wanted the security Victor's presence would provide; her rage today was partly disguising the horror she'd felt at this spiteful act. It was plain unnerving to have some unknown slasher loose in the theatre. Yet her other half hated people invading the sanctuary of her dressing room.

Victor watched her expression as she considered his proposal. "I know how you feel about your privacy, Judy, but you've got that anteroom as well as your actual dressing area, so I could sit there and close the door, which to all intents and purposes means you'd still be alone."

"Haven't you got better things to do?"

"No. Besides, I can take my laptop and work as well there as anywhere. I could do a series of articles: Notes from the ante-room of a Broadway actress."

Judith raised one eyebrow. "You do, and I'll retaliate with a series of monologues: Speeches from the hospital bed of a castrated reporter. And is there any chance of my getting even one spring roll before you demolish the lot? Honestly, I've been giving my all on stage under the most difficult circumstances and..." Judith's complaints came to an abrupt end as Victor neatly inserted a spring roll into her mouth.

Aubrey was woken in the middle of that night by a phone call from Mindy, who was evidently sitting in the middle of Times Square and needed to see him. Reluctantly relinquishing his hold on a delightful dream regarding future Broadway success, Aubrey got a cab the six blocks to reach Mindy – he'd make sure to charge it to the company since he was on company business.

Mindy was sitting on the large flight of red steps which rose above the half price theatre ticket booth, rocking back and forth, hugging her knees to her chest. Grateful that it was a hot August night, Aubrey sat down beside her. Mindy turned her face towards him and he saw she was crying. Inwardly he groaned; he wasn't a natural at dealing with emotions. Gently he patted her arm and when that didn't instantly stop her tears he reached inside his bag and produced a packet of Oreo cookies. Much to his astonishment Mindy gave a brief shake of her head.

"But they're Oreos," he said, unable to understand anyone turning down such delicacies. Mindy sobbed even louder. "You don't like Oreos?" Aubrey was completely bemused. He dug deeper into his bag and came up triumphantly with some Ruffles potato chips. They were rather crushed, but in Mindy's state he doubted she'd notice. Yet once again she declined. What on earth was wrong with the girl? He opened the Oreos and ate one to help soothe him. Sitting in Times Square in the middle of the night with a sobbing movie star was way out of his comfort zone.

"I can't do this anymore," Mindy eventually said, after Aubrey had demolished three cookies and was wondering where he could get a coffee to wash them down.

"Do what?" Aubrey asked, finding a crumb on his trouser leg and putting it in his mouth.

"The show; it's so hard. I love being Eve and I know she wouldn't feel alienated, but I do. I'm so lonely." She turned a tear stained face up to him. "Do you fancy me?"

"I er..." It had been so long since Aubrey had even contemplated sex with either man or woman that he was at a loss how to respond. The only constant relationship in his life was with food. "You're a very attractive, sexy woman."

Mindy smiled. "Thank you. Would you sleep with me?"

Aubrey grabbed another Oreo and shoved it in his mouth to give him time to think. As he chewed he came up with the perfect response and instantly voiced it, spitting out morsels of chocolate biscuit in the process. "I would of course, but I think inter-company relationships aren't a good idea. They complicate matters. Much as it's hard for me to turn you down, I must do so for the good of *All About Eve.*"

Mindy stared at him as if she'd received a revelation from on high. "You think that's why Addison, Bill and Lloyd all spurned me?"

Aubrey's mouth fell open in surprise. Good grief, he missed out on everything. "You asked them to sleep with you?"

"Sure; that's what Eve does."

"But Richard's gay."

Mindy shook her head. "Bill isn't." She regarded Aubrey in obvious disappointment. "I thought you understood."

Until now it hadn't occurred to Aubrey exactly how fanatical Mindy's method acting was.

Mindy suddenly leapt to her feet and threw out her arms as if she was about to take off. "I feel totally liberated now."

"Mindy, please be careful." Aubrey got up,

preparing to steady his leading lady if necessary before she nosedived to the pavement some distance below. As he did so his foot kicked a bag which had been sitting beside Mindy, producing an ominous clunk. On investigation it contained an empty bottle of wine which, since Mindy normally didn't touch alcohol, would explain her condition. "OK, we should get you home." Aubrey took hold of one of Mindy's arms, but she shook it off.

"Have you seen Titanic?" Mindy asked.

"The movie or the Broadway musical? I've seen both."

"The movie; I feel like when Rose stands on the prow of the boat as if she's about to fly. Only then the boat sinks and she has to swim." Mindy swung round to Aubrey with a gasp of excitement. "I wanna swim! I wanna swim as nature intended."

To Aubrey's horror Mindy stripped off her T-shirt revealing that she wasn't wearing a bra. A couple of passing late night revellers immediately got out a camera and started snapping. Aubrey grabbed the T-shirt and turned back to find Mindy lying on one of the steps doing backstroke.

"Mindy, do front stroke," Aubrey begged, and obligingly Mindy rolled over hiding her breasts from a small crowd gathering below. "Judith's going to kill me," Aubrey muttered. He must pull himself together. He was a director; a man in charge and he could deal with this situation. "Eve, this is not suitable behaviour for a woman of your status. If you continue in this vein you will not win the Sarah Siddons Award, and moreover you will lose the role in Lloyd Richard's new play. Margo Channing will play the part as was originally intended."

Mindy immediately sat up. Aubrey, using himself as a screen between her and their audience, managed to replace the T-shirt. "Now, Eve, we are going to get in a cab and return to your apartment." Slowly Mindy nodded, got to her feet and allowed Aubrey to lead her down the steps and deposit her into a cab where he instructed the driver to wait for him. Running back to the people with the camera, he grabbed it and with a polite, "Excuse me," he deleted all the photographs of Mindy.

"Hey, you can't do that," said its owner, trying to retrieve his camera from Aubrey, but Aubrey's fear of what Judith would do to him if such photos reached the press made him uncharacteristically speedy. Finally he returned it with a word of thanks, and for good measure passed over the squashed Ruffles potato chips as financial recompense.

He'd been amazing, he concluded, sitting back in the cab with Mindy. He, Aubrey Henson, had dealt with a potentially catastrophic situation and come up smelling of roses.

Unable to keep the story of his rescue mission to himself, Aubrey dropped enough hints the following day to guarantee news of his exploits reached the entire company. Summoned to Judith's dressing room, he expected to be praised for his actions, which showed how little he knew her.

"What the fuck were you doing letting Mindy parade topless in the middle of Times Square?"

was Judith's greeting.

"But I dealt with it," Aubrey bleated. "I stopped her and got her home and deleted the photographs."

"These photographs?" Judith pointed to some prints on her dressing table.

Aubrey peered in their direction. He wasn't able to see them clearly, and was unwilling to edge further into Judith's room, but he could make out the Times Square billboards. "But I did delete them."

"Was there only one person taking photographs?"

"I... I thought so." Judith gave a dismissive wave as if to say that he was a total moron. "Anyway I saved the situation."

"Did you hell. You couldn't save your own life if it required intellect."

"What do you suggest I should've done?"

"Phoned for somebody with an ounce of common sense, like Rupert; even our company manager might have had the odd idea."

Aubrey wondered if he'd ever felt so mutinous before – this simply wasn't fair. "Yes, but Mindy didn't call them, did she? She called me. She trusts me."

"Of course she does; she's the only person with a lesser IQ than yours."

"That's not true; Mindy is a very intelligent and sensitive performer. She merely works differently from you." Aubrey crossed his arms triumphantly, feeling he'd made an excellent point.

"Which is why I'm playing the leading role, with a Tony Award for my efforts, and Mindy is having a drunken breakdown in Times Square. Now go away, you odious little man, and let us professionals get on with it."

Aubrey went, mentally picturing various scenarios for Judith's future, none of which were terribly pleasant.

Victor, who'd been sitting in the ante-room during Aubrey's reprimand, stuck his head round the door. "You are completely unscrupulous, Judy. That poor man! He was virtually licking his wounds as he left. And from what I could gather he actually did do a fairly good job."

Judith's mouth twitched "Yes, he did, only we can't have him thinking that or he'll get over-confident and start giving notes and ruining the show. Besides, he needed to be brought down a peg or two before he blurted out the story to people outside this company. You can have your photos back now. As I surmised, he didn't dare doubt my word as to their authenticity."

Victor picked up some shots he'd taken of Judith around New York and put them in his bag. "Machiavelli had nothing on you, Judy."

"You do say the sweetest things. Now get back to your kennel. I must get ready. I've a feeling it's going to be an interesting show; Mindy must have the hangover from hell."

"And you're going to make her suffer, aren't you?"

Judith smiled in a way which left Victor in little doubt as to poor Mindy's fate.

Mindy, trying to put on her make-up with bleary eyes, swore she'd detox for the rest of her life – if she still had a life at the end of this show.

She was certainly never doing another play. It was movies from now on. Perhaps she could get Aubrey to direct her next project. He was so understanding about her way of working it would be a pleasure to see him in the directing chair every morning. She'd talk to her agent about him. She was certain he'd like LA.

CHAPTER THIRTY THREE

Miranda was certainly enjoying LA. Having put the humiliation of her firing from *NHS: The National Hope Service* behind her, she was preparing for an upcoming film role and staying in a delightful little bungalow. When Mike, her agent, had first conveyed the film company's offer she was less than happy that the role was that of a mother. Not the mother of a small child either, a notion she could tolerate even though she hadn't a maternal bone in her body, but the mother of two adults. While both these adult children fell in love and married in the course of the movie she was an irksome widow with no love interest of her own.

Keen to persuade his client to accept this lucrative role, Mike had pointed out that not only would it provide the break into movies which Miranda craved, but that she could flesh out this character with her own personality and talent. There was nothing, Mike assured her, to stop Miranda being an attractive mother. As a final incentive he reeled off a list of big Hollywood names lined up for other cameo roles. Miranda had signed the next day.

LA was Miranda's ideal city: the glamour, the weather, the beach and the shopping, with Rodeo Drive her fantasy street. Yet this elation was cut short when she first saw the designs for her costume: plain Victorian mourning clothes. Miranda hated black, unless it was very tight, very short and accessorized with killer heels and a designer evening bag. When discovering they also intended her to don a grey wig, Miranda was on the phone to Mike, screaming bloody murder.

"If they wanted a grey haired old lady why didn't they cast one?" Miranda demanded, and Mike could see her point. This widow was meant to be of a similar age to Miranda, and Miranda certainly wasn't grey – and frequent trips to the hairdressers guaranteed she never would be. After lengthy negotiations it was agreed Miranda's own auburn hair would be swept into a bun with a matching hairpiece added.

"But you cannot have a dress which displays your cleavage," Mike told her. "It simply wouldn't have been acceptable for a woman in mourning at that time. So don't even think about taking a pair of scissors on set and cutting a slit in your neckline."

Miranda had to laugh. Mike knew her too well. Still, she'd won over her hair, and when she'd had a costume fitting she'd insisted her corset was pulled in as tightly as possible to give her a tiny waist. This meant she could barely breathe, and certainly wouldn't be able to eat during shooting, but she didn't care. She was going to be a sexy widow and mother if it killed her.

As she was finally feeling happier Miranda received the revised script and full cast list. One glance and she was spitting with rage. This was not going to happen or her name wasn't Miranda Flynn.

* * *

436

Late one Sunday night, several days after she'd dealt with what Miranda hoped was the last of her problems, there was a thunderous knocking on her door. Miranda peered outside to discover, to her astonishment, that it was Rupert. Opening the door she was virtually knocked flying as Rupert pushed past and then swung back to face her.

"What the hell have you done?" he said. Miranda didn't think she'd ever seen him so angry, which was saying a lot after eleven years of marriage to her.

"I don't know what you're talking about," she hedged.

"Bollocks!" He took a step nearer to her and Miranda flinched. She couldn't imagine Rupert ever hitting a woman but then this was a whole new side to him.

"Aren't you supposed to be in New York?" she said, trying to throw him off track.

"I was, but I flew out straight after the matinee. I had to talk to you."

"That's sweet, but haven't you heard of this gadget called the telephone? I've heard they're all the rage."

Rupert ignored Miranda's attempts at humour. "I know how elusive you can be on the phone, not to mention hanging up if you don't like the way the conversation's going. I wanted to do this face to face."

Miranda fluttered her eyelids at him. "Darling, how very flattering, I didn't know you still cared so much. Is there anything special you want to talk about?"

"You tell me."

Miranda gave an innocent shrug. "Sorry, no idea. Can I get you a drink?"

Rupert shook his head. "But you can tell me why Holly is no longer playing Kate Nickleby in the *Nicholas Nickleby* movie."

Miranda opened her eyes wide to express her ignorance of Rupert's question. "Why would I know that?"

"Because she'd been offered the role and then the offer was withdrawn. Their explanation was a clash of personalities, but since I doubt Holly has ever clashed with anybody in her life I concluded there must be another reason. So I got Jane to do some digging."

"Jane, as in your agent?"

"She's Holly's agent too. And she wasn't happy that one of her clients had lost a hugely profitable job. And guess what she found out? There was one particular American producer who was against using Holly, claiming her employment would be detrimental to the film for reasons he wouldn't disclose. Strangely, it was the same American producer with whom you were seen dining out, two days before Holly lost the job. Christ, Miranda, if you're going to be malicious at least be subtle about it."

"I don't know what you're insinuating. We dined out to talk about my role in the movie." Miranda was giving the performance of a cruelly misjudged person – not something which came naturally to her. Rupert grabbed Miranda's wrists and threw her back on to the sofa. Miranda shrieked out, though with shock rather than pain. "I could have you up for GBH for this."

"And I could have you up for defamation of

Holly's character. Tell me what you did, now!" Rupert's face was close up against hers, and for the first time in her life Miranda felt afraid of him. Her brain, usually adept at convenient inventions, was a total blank.

"You don't understand," she almost sobbed. "I'm playing Mrs Nickleby."

"So?"

"I'd be playing Holly's mother. I can't play the mother of somebody who's screwing my husband. I'm not old enough."

"You did it for your vanity?" Rupert struck his forehead with the palm of his hand. "Why didn't I think of that? You got Holly fired because you won't admit to getting older. You selfish bitch."

"How dare you to talk to me like that," Miranda screamed, taken aback by the venom in his voice.

Rupert took a deep breath and clenched his fists. "Miranda, I've put up with a lot of things from you over the years, and I've always known you were totally self-centred, but I never realized before exactly how vindictive you were."

"It's all right for you; you're still playing romantic leads. Nobody's asking you to play fathers of grown up children."

"I wouldn't care if they did. I'm old enough – we both are."

"So you'd be okay if they asked you to play Holly's father?"

Rupert briefly considered the question. "That might be a little weird, but I'd play the father of one of Holly's contemporaries if the role was good enough."

"But this isn't a good role; it's lousy. Mrs

Nickleby is an irritating, wittering woman who doesn't get to be romantic or funny and has dowdy costumes. Would you believe they even wanted me to wear a grey wig?"

Used to Rupert's supportive comments when she complained about not looking the way she wanted, Miranda was shocked by his response that he didn't care if she had to wear a Yorkshire terrier on her head.

Grabbing Miranda's face in his hands, Rupert turned it so she had no choice but to look directly at him. "What did you tell that producer about Holly? I presume you didn't give him the real reason you wanted her off the picture?"

Miranda squirmed. "I can't exactly remember. I think I merely said she wasn't a very good company member. Yes, that was it, because she's so timid."

"Try again." Rupert's grip was tightening and struggle as she might Miranda couldn't loosen it.

"You're hurting me."

"Don't be so bloody dramatic. You'd know if I really wanted to hurt you. On the other hand, if you don't tell me the truth in the next few seconds I may lose control and press your face so hard you'll acquire a couple of very attractive bruises that the film company aren't going to like at all. Imagine – they might fire you."

"All right, just let go." Rupert released his pressure while continuing to hold Miranda facing him. "I might have mentioned something about her doing drugs when we were doing *Blithe Spirit*."

Rupert stared at her. "You what?"

"It was only meant as a joke." Miranda swallowed nervously. "I said I wasn't certain or anything."

Rupert scrutinized her. "No, you didn't. Let me guess: you said she was shooting up in the wings between giving Echo her lines?"

Miranda mistakenly let slip a small gasp. That was almost exactly what she'd told the producer, except it had been snorting cocaine in the Ladies – a more theatrical activity. She'd also 'hinted' that Holly was a dealer. She hoped Rupert would never find that out or she'd have to hire a bodyguard. "Rupert, I'm sorry, I wasn't thinking."

"Yes you were, Miranda, but only of yourself, as usual. I suppose it's partly my own fault you've become so spoilt. I always gave in to you because it was easier. Perhaps I should occasionally have put you across my knee and spanked you." He produced a brief smile.

Miranda took this as a ceasing of hostilities and gave a sexual simper. "Why, Rupert, I didn't know that kind of thing turned you on."

"It doesn't."

"But..."

"I meant as a punishment, like a parent to a naughty child, not a bondage fetish. I'd like to hope Rob would stand up to you, although somehow I can't picture that. It's a shame, Miranda, because there is a nice person down there somewhere; I used to see her when we were first married, only now she's in danger of completely disappearing." He let go of her, stood up and moved towards the front door.

Miranda followed him. "What are you going

to do?" she asked.

"Get Jane to talk to the *Nicholas Nickleby* film company about defamation of character and unfair dismissal, even if it means getting Holly to take a drugs test, though to be honest I'd rather she didn't know about that part. I'll merely tell her the true reason you begged the producer not to use her."

"Begged?" Miranda almost choked.

"Yes, begged," Rupert repeated, the chill in his voice silencing any further protest. "Unfortunately Holly hadn't signed a contract before your Lady Macbeth act and they've already offered the role to another actress, so I doubt there's much we can do. However, I'm not having her labelled as a drug addict because you can't cope with aging. And you can forget about receiving any further support from me; emotionally, physically or financially. You can be declared bankrupt, have a hundred disastrous relationships or never work again and I won't lift a finger to help you." He opened the door and the warmth of the Californian night air wafted in.

Miranda grabbed his arm. "Rupert, please wait. Can't we talk about this?"

"No." He shook her hand off him. "Frankly, Miranda, at the moment I don't feel I'll ever want to talk to you again." Miranda recoiled as if he had actually hit her. "If you'll excuse me, I'm going to meet Holly back at the hotel."

"You brought her with you?"

"I was hardly going to leave her alone after hearing such devastating news. Besides, we're treating it as a mini break. We aren't flying back

442

for the show until first thing Tuesday morning, so tomorrow we're going to Disneyland – a long-time dream of Holly's."

"I never visualized you as a Disney park man."

Rupert admitted the truth of that with a shrug. "It's the least I can do for her after my ex-wife has screwed up her career. I'd love it if one day Holly was in a position to lose you a job, but I can't imagine her doing such a thing."

"Oh yes, the world according to Saint Holly."

Rupert clenched his fists again then gave a brief shake of his head, turned and marched out of the front door, slamming it behind him.

Miranda slumped back on to the sofa, praying Rupert hadn't meant any of those things he'd said. She was used to leaning on him for everything, even after their divorce. It would all blow over, surely. Rupert never stayed cross for long – it wasn't in his nature. Perhaps she had gone a bit far, but how could anybody, even Rupert, expect her to play Holly's mother? It would be mortifying; she'd be a laughing stock. She'd give him a few days and maybe send some flowers to that ghastly Holly and things would be back to normal.

With that resolve she walked into her bedroom and peered in the mirror to check no bruises were developing. To her relief her face remained unblemished, although a little pink. She wondered if tomorrow was too soon to make amends. Then perhaps she and Rupert could go out to supper after his day in Giant Mouse land; he'd need some sensible adult company after that, even if Holly had to come too. Perhaps she could even offer to pay – and hope Rupert would refuse.

Picking up the phone she started ringing around the hotels where she considered Rupert might stay. Eventually she found his reservation at the Hollywood Roosevelt, no doubt chosen to keep that silly Holly happy. She wouldn't be seen dead there – it was so touristy. Anyone who was anyone knew THE place to stay was the Marmont.

In contrast to Miranda, Holly was thrilled by the Hollywood Roosevelt with its movie history and the fact that their room faced the famous Hollywood sign. Although hurt and bemused by the loss of her Kate Nickleby role, she was determined to enjoy this fleeting trip to LA – and especially Disneyland. She'd bought a guidebook at the airport and spent the time Rupert had been with Miranda making an itinerary and wondering whether Rupert could be persuaded to go on such childish rides as *It's a Small World*.

Rupert's rage with Miranda almost evaporated on seeing Holly sitting cross-legged on the bed in their hotel room surrounded by paper. She looked up at him radiantly. "This is going to be wonderful."

Rupert kissed her. "I do love you."

"Enough to go on a ride watching dolls singing and dancing?"

"Are they blow-up sex dolls?" Rupert raised an eyebrow.

"No!"

"Shame. But yes, I'll go on whatever you like."

"How did it go with Miranda?"

Rupert gave her a brief synopsis, carefully not mentioning the drug story, and informing her he was no longer going to be supporting Miranda in any way whatsoever. "And, Holly, that means you not falling for any sob story and convincing me I have to go and look after her."

Holly played with a piece of paper. "But it must be awfully hard for her. I don't know how I'd feel if you left me for a younger woman and I was asked to play her mother."

Rupert laughed. "If I left you for a younger woman I'd be dating a sixth-former!"

Holly frowned at him, trying to make her point. "Just try and see it from her point of view."

Rupert gave a half smile. "OK, maybe it was asking a lot of her, but if she was unhappy then she should have quit. There's no excuse for punishing you."

"Isn't there?"

Rupert gave a frustrated sigh. "I give up! You can forgive Miranda, I can't. Now I'm bushed, can we go to bed?"

"Sure." Holly leapt up and shot into the bathroom. "Do you think I'll be able to have a photo taken with Winnie-the-Pooh tomorrow?" she asked, sticking her head back out, waving her toothbrush.

"If you can't I'll hire a Winnie-the-Pooh costume when we get back to New York and you can have your picture taken with me in that!"

Holly giggled. "I'd love to see Judith's expression if you did."

"I'd love to see Judith wearing a Winnie-the-Pooh costume."

*   *   *

Miranda, having ensured that flowers and an expensive bottle of wine had been delivered at the Hollywood Roosevelt early the following morning, was greatly displeased to have them promptly returned with a note from Rupert.

Don't think you can bloody buy your way out.

Furiously, Miranda threw the flowers across the room and was about to send the wine to join them when it occurred to her that it would make an awful mess which she'd have to clean up. Besides, there was no point wasting good wine. By the time she'd finished the bottle she decided she didn't care about Rupert. Who needed him? What she needed was retail therapy. When, on her fifth designer purchase, her credit card was declined her first thought was to phone Rupert. The sinking realization that it would no longer do any good sent Miranda reeling back to her house in a state of total panic. What was she to do now? Shop at Oxfam? She hoped Rupert was having a bloody awful day at Disneyland. With any luck Holly would be mistaken for a one-dimensional cartoon character and never be allowed to leave the place.

Rupert was certainly having an interesting day. Theme parks weren't his thing, but Disneyland did have an oddly feel-good atmosphere. It was like walking on to the set of a perfect, squeaky-clean 1950s movie with its pastel coloured Main Street, canopied stores and ice-cream parlours. And Holly was in her element.

"I'm not sure I've ever seen you so happy," Rupert said, as they emerged from Space Mountain, Holly's hair flying everywhere with the speed of the ride and her eyes shining, while his stomach, not especially rollercoaster friendly, was gradually returning to normal. "Not even when I declared undying love for you."

"That's rubbish," Holly retorted. "I don't want to marry Mickey Mouse."

"You can't, unless he commits bigamy. What about Mrs Mouse?"

"Who?"

"Minnie Mouse." Rupert was rather proud of knowing this information.

"She's not his wife; she's his girlfriend."

Rupert feigned horror. "You don't mean they're living in sin? What kind of message does that give to the children here?"

"Oh honestly," Holly said, trying to look cross. "It's a platonic relationship."

"Lord, poor old Mickey; seventy odd years with no sex. He must be one horny mouse."

"I'm changing the subject before you get thrown out of the park for defamation of Disney characters," Holly said, looking at her schedule. "Do you want to go and shoot aliens with Buzz Lightyear?"

"I don't know; does Buzz Lightyear want to shoot aliens with me? And in fact, who is Buzz Lightyear?"

"You know, going to infinity and all that."

Rupert looked blank. "He's some relation to Captain Kirk?"

"No! *Toy Story*. Don't you ever take your god-children to see animated films?"

"I normally try and persuade them to go to retro movies at the NFT. Of course taking the

5 year old to *The Godfather* wasn't a huge success. His mother kept complaining he'd wake up screaming in the night about horse heads in his bed."

Holly gasped. "You didn't?"

Rupert chuckled. "Dearest Holly, you're wonderfully gullible."

"Right, for that we're jolly well going on Buzz Lightyear, and I shall shoot you instead of the aliens! Then we must find a good place to watch the parade."

Half an hour later, as the parade passed their viewing point, Holly turned to Rupert. "Doesn't Cinderella look a lot like Echo?"

Rupert looked vaguely into the group of singing and dancing Disney characters. "Which one's Cinderella?"

Holly stared at him askance. "Haven't you even seen *Cinderella*? It's ancient."

"Like me?"

"No, I didn't mean that, but everyone...." She stopped. "I suppose your mother never took you to Disney movies, right?"

"Right."

Holly squeezed his hand sympathetically. "Cinderella is the blonde in the big blue dress, blue hair band, blue gloves and a black choker. There."

Rupert peered in the direction Holly was pointing. She certainly did bear a very strong resemblance to Echo. At that point Cinderella started waving to some small children in front of them and beaming all over her face. "Good God, you're right, that's definitely Echo," Rupert said.

"How can you be that sure?"

"I'd recognize that wave anywhere. Do you remember in *Blithe Spirit* when Elvira had to give Ruth a dismissive wave and Judith told Echo she appeared to be about to launch a battleship?"

"How could I forget? I was the one reminding her every night, via her earpiece, that she was supposed to be waving."

"So you were. Well, it's the same gesture; hugely enthusiastic and totally unsubtle." He chuckled. "Only Echo could go from working on a porn movie to working on a Disney parade!" He watched as Echo virtually jumped off the float in her effort to communicate with the crowd. "It looks like she's finally found her niche. It's acting but involves no line learning or any great talent except enthusiasm. Let's phone her when she's disembarked from her float and arrange to meet for a drink."

"It'll have to be a soft drink. Disneyland's a dry park."

"If I'd known I'd have brought a hip flask," Rupert grumbled.

"I think it's nice. It means there's never going to be any drunkenness or rowdy behaviour in such a child-friendly place."

"I bet Winnie-the-Pooh likes a quick snifter in his honey," Rupert said. Holly dug her elbow into his side. "Ow!" he protested.

"Shh," said the woman beside him. "Some of us are trying to watch the parade." Then she realized who her neighbour was. "Oh my, you're Rupert Blake. Hey kids, it's Rupert Blake."

The group around Rupert instantly produced

their Disney autograph books and Rupert found himself signing on pages surrounded by scrawls from the likes of Mickey Mouse, Goofy and Peter Pan.

"I feel I should sign as Rupert Bear in keeping with the other signatories," Rupert whispered to Holly as he scribbled his name.

Half an hour later, Rupert and Holly were sitting in a cafe in Fantasyland, apparently Echo's favourite area of the park, when Echo rushed in, virtually squealing with excitement and threw her arms around Holly and then Rupert. "You saw me in the parade? Was I good? Did I look pretty? Isn't it a real cool job? I can't believe you're here. What are you doing in LA? Are you making a movie, Rupert? Will you come watch me again? If I know where you're standing I can wave right at you. I've never had anybody come see me specially before. Mommy's gonna come soon, but she's real busy with the beauty pageant stuff." Echo eventually ran out of steam – or out of breath – and sank down exhausted. Then she leapt up again to throw her arms around each of them once more.

"Echo, you look so happy," Holly said.

"I am. I'm real happy. You look happy too."

"I am." Holly stuck out her hand to show Echo her engagement ring.

"That's a real pretty ring," Echo said. Holly and Rupert waited for the penny to drop. It took nearly a minute of Echo staring at their expectant faces and the ring before she gave a little gasp. "Is it an engagement ring?"

"Top of the class, Echo," Rupert said. "I'm lucky enough to be marrying this gorgeous girl."

For a moment Echo's face fell, but then she leapt up to once again hug them both. "Congratulations; that's real cool. Can I be a bridesmaid? Gee Holly, you're gonna be Mrs Holly Blake."

"Yes, I am. I can't quite get used to it." Holly squeezed Echo's hand. "So how about you? Have you found anybody special in LA?"

Echo wrinkled her nose, before remembering about keeping her skin smooth. "I don't like men; at least not that way."

"Don't tell me you've become a lesbian," Rupert drawled. "That would be a waste for the male sex."

"Rupert!" Holly berated him.

Rupert grinned. "OK, I'll banish myself and get some drinks, shall I? What do you want, Echo?"

"Still water please; I have to keep my skin perfect to play Cinderella."

"Right, water it is." He disappeared off to the counter.

Echo regarded Holly anxiously. "Do you think Rupert's right and I am a lesbian because I don't like sex with men?"

"I doubt it, Echo. You haven't found the right man yet; that's all. Rupert told me you had a bad experience the first time, but you shouldn't let that put you off. My first time was a bit scary and painful too."

"Was that with Rupert?"

"No."

"I'm sure it would be good with Rupert, because when he had foreplay with me in Judith's dressing room on *Blithe Spirit* it was so cool. He

451

made me go all tingly and nothing hurt." Holly, who'd been entirely ignorant of this incident up until now, was too stunned to make any response. Unaware of the effect her remark had made, Echo continued with her train of thought. "Why didn't Kevin do what Rupert did? And why didn't Rupert do what Kevin did?" she asked.

Holly sighed, trying to clear her head of the image of Rupert and Echo doing God know what. "I'm not an expert, Echo. Rupert is only the second man I've slept with, but I know he was a hundred percent better than my first. I'd imagine he didn't go the whole way with you because it might've hurt you physically or emotionally, while it doesn't sound as if this Kevin was very considerate. And, although a lot of people enjoy sex for sex's sake and mightn't agree with me, I believe you have to be in love for it to be really good. So maybe when you fall in love it'll work out."

"But I'm in love with Rupert," Echo said sadly. "He's perfect."

"Nobody's perfect, including Rupert," Holly retorted, more harshly than she'd intended. Echo looked bewildered and Holly relented. "Well, I guess he's pretty special, but there are other special men in the world and you must meet so many people working here. Perhaps a gorgeous actor, filming in LA, will see you at the parade and be overcome with passion."

Echo's face lit up, visualizing a rich movie star sweeping her off her feet and carrying her to his Malibu mansion where he'd kiss her chastely and tell her how beautiful she was.

"Have you girls been putting the world to

rights?" Rupert asked, returning with their drinks.

Echo gazed at him adoringly. Holly watched her thoughtfully as she sipped her coke. They continued talking, mostly about *Blithe Spirit*, before Echo glanced at her watch and leapt up. "Gee, I gotta go get ready for the next parade. Will you come watch me? If I tell you where to stand I can wave at you. Oh boy, this is so cool."

"Of course we will," Holly said, producing her map of the park. Echo marked down a spot before dashing off.

"Two parades in one day," Rupert said. "You'd better cater to my every whim later." He waved his hand in front of Holly's vacant eyes. "Hello, anybody home?"

Holly swallowed. "Rupert?"

"Yes?"

Holly ran her tongue around her dry mouth, not sure why she was doing this. Was she trying to be kind to Echo or testing her own strength?

"Are you going to tell me or do I have to play twenty questions?" Rupert enquired.

Holly clenched her fists tightly under the table, so her nails cut into the palms of her hand. "I think you should sleep with Echo."

"What?" Rupert's face was a picture of astonishment.

"She adores you and that guy, Kevin, totally put her off sex, but you're sure to make her enjoy it and then she wouldn't have such a hang up about it and I wouldn't mind because I'd know you were only doing it to be kind and..."

"Holly, stop it," Rupert said, quite crossly. He picked up her left hand and ran his fingers over

453

her engagement ring. "I'm very fond of Echo, and I'm sorry she's got some kind of sexual repression, but I'm not willing to destroy my fiancée in order to help her."

"You wouldn't destroy me," Holly replied, hoping she sounded more believable than she felt.

Rupert shook his head at her. "Sweetheart, you have less confidence than virtually anyone I know, and marrying a reprobate like me is hardly going to help. I want to try and prove you can trust me, something at which, thanks to Miranda, I've already not been entirely successful. Besides, what makes you think I want to sleep with Echo?"

Holly gave a weak smile. "Well, I gather there was some stimulating foreplay – in Judith's dressing room too!"

"Ah." Rupert looked slightly uncomfortable. "I hadn't mentioned that before, had I?"

"It doesn't matter," Holly said, wondering why, actually, it did. "If anyone should have minded it would be Miranda."

"Actually, I had Miranda's permission." Holly stared at him in astonishment. Miranda had never struck her as a woman to willingly lend out her husband. Rupert laughed at her expression. "It's a bizarre story which I'll tell you later. But this general obsession with my sexually educating Echo is becoming too weird. There are sex therapists who are experts in this field, so maybe you could suggest Echo enlist their help. Meantime, I need food before this parade or I'm going to start eating Mickey Mouse."

"Mouse – ibal," Holly said, as Rupert pulled

her to her feet.

Sitting munching burgers on the sidewalk to ensure they'd get a decent view of the parade, Holly asked, "So if Miranda knew about you and Echo and gave her permission, why can't I?"

Rupert sighed. "For three reasons. One: Miranda only agreed because it was Judith's idea and she was utterly obsessed with pleasing Judith."

"Judith wanted you to sleep with Echo?" Holly said, utterly bemused.

"Merely for the good of the show – I told you it was a bizarre story. Number two: You're completely unlike Miranda and I feel very differently towards you, and three: it was only ever going to be foreplay and frankly Echo was so ripe for the picking I barely had to touch her and she was a quivering mass of hormones. That mother of hers has a lot to answer for. There should be a bloody exam for parents to stop them screwing up their children."

Holly, thinking of Rupert's mother, didn't feel hungry anymore. She put her burger down and looked at her watch. Another fifteen minutes until the parade and already the sidewalks were packed with people. Somebody moved behind Holly, stood on her burger and exclaimed in disgust as the ketchup leaked on to their shoes. Holly was about to apologize, but Rupert covered her mouth with his hand. "They'll never know it was yours," he whispered. "Besides, their shoes should be consigned to the bin; they're truly tasteless."

"I wonder Echo's arm doesn't fall off," Rupert

455

said shortly after, as Echo waved so hard at them she virtually knocked her Prince Charming off their float. "I think you can stop worrying about her," he added as the parade finished and they moved to Echo's designated meeting spot. "She's in her element."

"But she can't do this for ever, can she?"

"She's very young, especially mentally, and it'll do her no harm to play Cinderella for some time yet. And eventually she'll find her way in life, even if it's only to end up running the Disney parade. Either that or she'll suddenly meet the love of her life, settle down and have fifteen children, presuming she finally discovers the joy of sex."

"Shh," Holly said, horrified. "You can't talk loudly about, you know, in Disneyland."

"Sex? Why – don't cartoons have sex? However do they get baby cartoons then?"

Holly put her hands over her ears. "Stop it!"

Rupert pulled her hands away, laughing and assuring her he would stop. At that point Echo came bouncing up to them like a demented Tigger. "Did you see me wave at you? Wasn't that cool?"

"Yes we saw you," Holly said. "I've never had anyone wave straight at me in a parade before. It was very exciting."

Echo's elation was complete. "Really? I wish you could come again tomorrow."

"We have to go back to New York tomorrow," Rupert said. "If I missed a show Judith would kill me, and not even Victor would be able to stop her."

"Who's Victor?" Echo enquired.

456

"A saint."

Echo looked baffled, muddling saints with angels and visualizing a man sporting wings. Rupert briefly filled Echo in on Judith and Victor's history. Echo was stunned at the very notion of anyone being in love with Judith at all, let alone for most of their lives. "Do you think she has sex?" she asked. She couldn't visualize Judith lying back and letting men do (in Echo's opinion) unpleasant things to her.

Rupert regarded her very seriously. "You know, Echo, when you come to London for a visit you should ask her. I'm sure you're the one person she would confide in."

"Really?"

Holly nearly choked. "No, you most definitely should not." She glared at Rupert. "Behave." She turned back to Echo. "But please do come and stay with us in England when we get back."

Echo's eyes opened wide. "Honest? Because I have some vacation time soon and I can't think of anybody I'd rather spend it with than you guys."

"Honest, although I think Disneyland will lose their best Cinderella while you're gone." Holly gave Echo a long hug and then watched as Echo catapulted herself into Rupert's arms.

"Now let's get out of this park before there's a stampede at closing time," Rupert said.

"Aren't you gonna stay for the fireworks?" Echo asked in surprise. "They're swell and I know a real good place to watch from."

Rupert gave Holly an enquiring glance, but she shook her head; she didn't want to try his patience any further. Besides, fireworks were only fireworks. They said goodbye to a euphoric Echo and walked back along Main Street, Holly trying to soak in every last bit of atmosphere.

"You never met Winnie-the-Pooh," Rupert said, as they reached the exit. "How odd, I felt sure he'd be around here somewhere."

"Hmm, very odd," Holly replied vaguely, fully aware that the queues to meet the Disney characters had been horribly long, and she'd steered Rupert clear of them. She couldn't possibly make him wait all that time for some ridiculous childhood fantasy of hers.

Rupert had stopped and was looking back along Main Street. "Come on," he said, pulling her into a shop on the corner marked Emporium, where he picked up a large Winnie-the-Pooh. "Will this do? I know he's not life size, but you do get to take him home, something I doubt you could do with a Disney employee – with the possible exception of Echo."

Holly shook her head while looking wistfully at the bear. "I'm too old for that sort of thing."

Rupert laughed and took it over to the till. "Do you think he'll need his own seat on the plane?" he asked, as he passed over his credit card. "If he does he's going economy."

CHAPTER THIRTY FOUR

It was Tim who raised the alarm, on a Thursday afternoon a month before *All About Eve* was due to close. Within minutes of entering Judith's dressing room he was on the phone to her, while a nervous stage manager perused the room, dreading the tongue lashing he was sure to receive.

Fifteen minutes later Judith and Victor arrived to assess the damage. The floor was strewn with a mass of pearls, which had been ripped from their fastening. The box in which the string of pearls had previously been openly displayed had been torn apart while the card which read Darling J, A small token of my affection, Love V was covered in black scrawl.

"Christ," Judith said, sinking down on to the bed.

"Whoever it was certainly went the whole hog," Victor commented, "even though they can't tell fake pearls from real. At least I hope not since I'd be most put out if anyone considered I'd buy you fakes. Now let's see how Teddy here did." He lifted up a large teddy bear, which bore a label around his neck saying To Judith Gold, with great admiration from a fan, although actually purchased by Victor from a surveillance store, and from inside produced a tiny video camera.

"It will have recorded everything and not missed the vital area?" Judith asked. "I can't go through this whole set-up again; I'm not made to play Sherlock Holmes."

"Judy darling, you could play anything you put your mind to. And yes, the bear was set up at exactly the correct angle." He pushed a button to reset the tape from the beginning. "Are you ready?"

"No!"

Victor paused in his activities. "I can watch it alone if you'd rather. It must be upsetting for you."

"Rubbish," Judith said, having no intention of admitting that the prospect of finally discovering the identity of this stalker was rather alarming. "I meant we should wait for Rupert since he was in on this scheme."

As they waited Judith drummed her fingers on her legs and eventually banished the stage manager whose grovelling and hand-wringing were getting on her nerves. "If I wanted to be in a room with Uriah Heep I'd have chosen to appear in *David Copperfield*," she snapped at him. When Rupert eventually arrived he was greeted by, "Where the fuck have you come from, Outer Mongolia?"

"No, the Upper West Side, which I realize is the same thing in your book." He carefully stepped over the scattered beads to join Judith and Victor sitting on the bed.

"You didn't bring Holly?" Judith enquired.

"No, I thought she'd be distressed at the idea of innocent teddies being used as camera mules!" He laughed at Judith's disbelieving expression. "I'm only kidding! She and Jennifer have gone shopping this afternoon."

"That's probably as well. She'd no doubt find some mitigating circumstances for the perpetrator and plead for clemency. Right, let's go, Doctor Watson."

Victor ran the film. He'd been correct about the angle of the teddy which produced perfect shots of the pearl necklace being savagely pulled apart, the box ripped, the card of affection defaced – and a very clear picture of the culprit.

"That's not Mindy," Judith said, sounding slightly disappointed.

"Not unless she's wearing a very good disguise, and has changed sex," Victor commented. "Do you know who he is, Judy?"

"I haven't a fucking clue."

"It's Joe," Rupert said. "You must've noticed him, Judith. He's one of our stage crew."

"Stage crew?" Judith stared at him as if she couldn't possibly be expected to know everybody she came into contact with.

"What on earth did you do to the guy to piss him off so badly, Judy?" Victor asked.

"I haven't done anything. I told you, I don't even know him."

"Perhaps the fact that you don't, even after five months of working with him, annoyed him enough to carry out these acts," Victor said. "I suggest we find out."

Tim was dispatched to bring Joe to the dressing room, under the guise of a broken costume rail which needed fixing. As soon as Joe saw his reception committee, now sitting on three chairs in the ante-room like a jury, he started to back out, only to find Tim was standing between him and the door. Searching for another

461

exit he headed for the fire escape, but he'd bare-ly opened the window when he found himself firmly held by Victor.

"Gee Pops," he muttered, failing to get free, "You're strong for an old geezer."

"Thanks!" Victor glared at Rupert who was grinning at this observation. "Now you, sit down." He virtually threw Joe into a chair facing his 'jury' and returned to his own seat. "As well as being an 'old geezer', I am this lady's other half and I'm investigating certain attacks on her possessions; something on which I am hoping you can enlighten us."

"I dunno what you're talking about."

Victor picked up the camera and showed Joe the tape. "It's a good close up, don't you think? Gloria Swanson would be proud of it."

"Huh?"

"Gloria Swanson, you moron," Judith snapped. "She was a silent movie star, but in one of her few talkies she had the famous line, 'All right, Mr DeMille, I'm ready for my close up.' It was a movie called *Sunset Boulevard* – have you heard of it?"

"Sure, I crewed on that; it was at the Minskoff Theatre."

"That was the musical version written by that Cabbage Patch doll excuse-for-a-composer."

"It wasn't, it was written by Andrew Lloyd Webber," Joe sneered. "Now who's the moron?"

Judith turned to Victor. "We cannot have the right man; he's simply not bright enough to car-ry out such a carefully planned campaign."

"I think we have the man who carried out the campaign, only I'd say the planning wasn't his.

Am I correct, Joe?"

"I dunno what you're talking about," Joe repeated his earlier denial.

Victor leant closer to him. "Who put you up to this, Joe?"

"I dunno what you're talking about."

"For fuck's sake, the needle's stuck on the record," Judith said. "Can't you tie him to the chair and start with the red hot poker?"

Joe paled visibly. "You can't do that. I got my rights."

Judith got up and stood over him. "We're English though and therefore not covered by American law. In England we torture people incessantly. Have you heard of The Tower of London?" Joe nodded. "Have you ever been there?"

"No."

Judith gave an imperceptible smile; this was going to be easy. She leant over Joe. "In the dungeons there, we imprison those from whom we need information. If they do not give us what we want immediately we stretch them on the rack or chain them to the walls while we flay them with whips and other methods of torture." Judith slowly lit a cigarette.

"Hey, you can't smoke in here," Joe said.

"Who said I was going to smoke?" Judith said, moving her cigarette closer to Joe's arm.

Joe's eyes were almost out on stalks. "It wasn't my idea."

"We know that," Judith said, walking slowly to the other side of the room still holding her cigarette as if it were a weapon. "So give us a name. If we have a name we may go easy on you, although I can't guarantee anything. Victor may look old, but he's recently returned from live combat in Afghanistan. Me, I prefer the odd finger nail removal." She studied her own nails carefully. "Very painful, but less vulgar."

Joe looked at Rupert, hoping for assistance from someone who'd always been friendly in the past. "You can't let them do this."

Rupert held up his hands. "I'm sorry, Joe, I'm merely here as an observer. I have no influence with these people." Joe glanced at Tim, but he gave a brief shake of his head. He wasn't helping anyone who mutilated costumes. Besides, having several more brain cells than Joe, he was fully aware that torture had stopped being practiced at The Tower of London several hundred years ago.

Judith turned to Victor. "Shall we use your methods or mine?"

Joe gulped. "OK, don't hurt me. It was Digby Weston; it was all his idea."

"Digby Weston; that pathetic excuse for an actor we fired?" Judith enquired, as if there were a million Digby Westons with a Judith Gold vendetta.

"Yeah. See, he was real mad that you'd gotten him fired, so he asked me to do those things to you. I had to start small and get bigger so you'd get totally freaked. Cancelling your car one night was real easy, and hiding or breaking your props was kinda fun, oh and defacing the Tony. It was harder when you got your keys changed after I scrawled on your photo, but I managed to sneak a key off the new set and get it copied. And sticking up the picture of you, old geezer, with a noose around your neck, was one of my favourites."

"I didn't know about that." Judith said.

"No, you didn't," Rupert said. "So that back-fired, Joe, because Jennifer found it first and gave it to Richard who brought it to me."

Joe looked a tiny bit put out but then gave a careless shrug. "Well, I did good on everything else, didn't I?" There was a note of pride in his voice.

Judith sank back into her chair beside Rupert, stunned, temporarily, into silence.

"No, you did not 'do good'," Victor said, in a tone neither Rupert or Judith had heard before. "What you did was criminal and you could go to jail for it. How did Digby Weston persuade you to do such things? Is he paying you?"

"No. Well actually yeah, he's gonna pay for me to go back to college, because I never gradu-ated."

"Now there's a surprise," Judith commented.

"But that's not the reason," Joe continued.

"Are you his rent boy?" Judith enquired.

Joe stared at her open mouthed. "No! Gross! Digby's my uncle."

There was a brief silence as the other occu-pants of the room took in this information. "And did you happen to be working here by coinci-dence?" Victor asked.

"No," Tim spoke for the first time. "There was another guy here originally, but he left under suspicious circumstances. Joe was brought in to replace him. I'm guessing those suspicious circumstances might have to do with Joe here – or with his uncle."

"You've gotten no evidence that anything

except the pearls was me," Joe said. "And hiding cameras in teddy bears and setting up bait counts as... as... the thing where you lead people on so they look guilty."

"Entrapment," Victor said. "And you're wrong. It can be used."

"And I've got more evidence," Rupert said. "Judith's photograph which you defaced, I still have it. I'm sure we might find the odd fingerprint."

"I wiped the frame clean," Joe said, with a confident smile. "I've seen CSI."

"Did you wipe the photograph though?" Rupert asked.

"It's very hard to clean fingerprints off photographs," Victor added.

"I wanna lawyer," Joe said.

Judith frowned. "Tim, can you take this odious moron into the other room and keep an eye on him?"

After Tim had marched Joe next door, Judith, Victor and Rupert debated their next move. Judith was against involving the police because of the unwelcome publicity. Then again she wanted some reprisal, not necessarily on the hapless Joe, but on Digby Weston.

Victor was attempting to convince Judith that, no, they could not hire a professional thug to rough Digby up, when both became aware of Rupert chuckling.

"What?" Judith demanded.

"I can't get over that picture of you in full Gestapo mode, striding up and down the room waving your cigarette in a menacing manner and describing methods of torture. It was utterly brilliant, if slightly alarming."

"Honestly," Judith said, looking rather pleased.

"Which reminds me," Victor said. "Why exactly did you have a packet of cigarettes? I was under the impression you'd given up."

"I have. I merely keep a packet for use in torture sessions."

"A half empty one?" He held out his hand. "Pass them over."

Judith glowered at him. "Don't we have more important things to discuss?"

"Your health is the more important thing to me."

"Oh pe-lease," Judith said, but she got the packet out of her pocket and threw it at Victor. "If you hadn't done some disappearing act in Afghanistan I wouldn't have needed them. No, actually it was that fucking Digby Weston who started me back on them in the first place. So can we please return to that subject?"

"We must persuade Joe to sign a confession, which shouldn't be too hard thanks to your keeping that photograph, Rupert." Victor said. "That way Digby can't try and sue us for defamation of character, since I'm sure he has a barrage of attorneys on retainer."

"Do you think it can actually write?" Judith enquired. "Or should we compose the confession and it can put an X at the bottom?"

There was a shout from the other room. Victor and Rupert shot through to find Tim doubled over, pointing at a door the other end of the room from which a staircase led straight down into the wings. "I'm sorry, he jumped me.

I wasn't expecting it."

Rupert started down the stairs in pursuit, but Joe was far ahead of him and gaining speed. Below he saw Richard on stage sitting at the piano, practicing the music for later; something he liked to do every few days.

"Richard, stop him," Rupert yelled.

Richard looked up surprised. Normally nobody used those stairs. Rupert was gesticulating at a member of the crew who was running across the stage. Richard grabbed a props tray from on top of the piano and as Joe passed him he brought it down on the back of his head. While Joe reeled from the shock Richard threw his whole weight at him so Joe toppled over. Taking advantage of this, Richard sat down firmly on the prone body of his prisoner.

"Nice job," Rupert said, joining him with Victor not far behind.

"I do love working on Broadway, it's so exhilarating," Richard commented. "I feel like a secret agent." He inspected Joe's wriggling body. "Is he part of the Broadway mafia? Will I need to hire a bodyguard now I've thwarted some dastardly mission?"

Rupert grinned. "I think it's Joe who'll need the bodyguard." He gestured his head to where Judith was approaching, her expression less than happy.

"You winded my dresser," she said to Joe. "It is unacceptable to hurt my staff." Joe, faced once again with this terrifying woman, gave a whimper. Judith regarded him with contempt. "I now intend to press charges." She turned to Victor. "Get his confession. If he's stubborn use whatever methods are necessary to persuade him." Joe gave another whimper. "Then call the police or whoever deals with such matters. And get him off my stage – I don't want it contaminated." Richard reluctantly relinquished his role as captor and clambered to his feet. Rupert and Victor bent over to pick up his prisoner. As they did so Victor took a sharp intake of breath.

"Are you OK?" Rupert asked.

Victor nodded. "Just a twinge in my back; as Joe kindly pointed out earlier, I'm not as young as I was." He yanked at Joe's arm. "We're going to take a trip to the stage management office and deal with this situation from there."

"I'll help you," Richard said, unwilling to lose out on any of the drama.

"Good, then Rupert can check Tim is OK," Judith said. "I don't do nursing." Rupert was surprised; he'd expected Judith to demand involvement in Joe's interrogation. The reason became clear in the dressing room after Tim left, having confirmed that he was fine, merely mortified by his failure at guard duty. Judith sat down on the bed and patted the space beside her. Obediently Rupert sat there. "Rupert, I believe Victor isn't telling me the entire story about Afghanistan."

"Oh?" Rupert tried to sound as noncommittal as possible.

"Just then, for example, trying to pick up that idiot boy, he was obviously in pain. Yet he's never had back problems before."

"Backs can suddenly go out," Rupert hedged.

"There's more. For the first couple of weeks after his return he became ultra-modest. Never undressing in front of me; covering up totally even though it was fucking July in New York and about ninety degrees outside. Yet I still noticed red blisters on his wrists. And, even stranger, he's refusing to write about his experiences. What's the point in wasting an entire trip, not to mention the worry he put us through, for nothing? The least he could do is write something amazing and win the Pulitzer Prize."

"Did you ask him about this?"

Judith stared at him. "Of course not. It's his life."

"Of which you are a very important part. He might think you'd rather not know."

"Does he believe I'm so shallow that I'm not interested in what happens to him?"

"Not necessarily. Perhaps it's simply that he's worried it'll upset you."

"What will upset me?" Judith narrowed her eyes at him. "Did he tell you something he didn't tell me?"

"You need to talk to Victor, not me."

"He did, didn't he?"

Rupert sighed. "All right, he did, because I asked him directly."

"Wonderful," Judith snapped. "No doubt I'll be the last one to be told anything. I suppose Holly knows too."

"No. Victor didn't want to upset her either."

Judith slowly exhaled, her anger dissipating. "What the hell happened to him?"

Rupert was saved from reiterating that she needed to ask Victor by Tim's return, announcing that the police had arrived and did Judith want them to come there.

"No, I'll come to the office," Judith said, getting to her feet. "I don't want half the New York police department seeing the aids I need to look glamorous on stage."

Joe was charged with the damage he'd done to Judith's possessions and, with the prospect of a jail term or a hefty fine, quickly agreed to give evidence against his uncle.

Digby was duly questioned by the police, accompanied by several lawyers. Within an hour there were press outside both the police precinct and the stage door of the St James Theatre. Richard, in his element, took on the role of informant to the remaining cast as they arrived.

"I don't know why we didn't think of Digby before," Alyce said. "He was the most obvious candidate."

"Except he wasn't in the building," Kyle pointed out. "Using a substitute to carry out his dirty work was a smart, if sick, move. It'll be an interesting case to prove: nephew's word against uncle's."

"Why would Joe make it up?" Richard asked. "What would he have to gain by doing those things to Judith?"

"Nothing, it's only that the public still perceives Digby in his TV role as the perfect butler, incapable of doing anything underhand. In contrast Joe is merely a guy on the crew, slightly scruffy, and possibly not the brightest button. It's that fine line between fact and fiction."

"Only in this case the butler actually did it," Richard exclaimed, clapping his hands in glee. "I've always wanted to say that."

"You're so funny," Jennifer said fondly. "It

would be awful if you were right though, Kyle, and Digby got away with what he did. Don't you think so, Holly?"

She turned to where Holly had been standing beside her, an area which now only contained a couple of her own shopping bags. Holly had slipped away and was already in Judith's room checking on her friend.

"As soon as his lawyers get him out of there he'll be bitching about me on every medium available," Judith complained. "I don't care what people say when it's true, but I cannot abide slander. Can't you imagine what he'll say? 'I, Digby Weston, an actor whom you took to your hearts, have been wronged. I was the one fired by Judith Gold, a woman known to be cruel and sadistic. My nephew, sweet boy, took revenge on my behalf. It was a terrible misunderstanding; he mustn't be held responsible for his reckless if misguided actions'." Judith dropped her flawless impersonation of Digby to add, "And his adoring public will lap it up. It's enough to make you sick."

"Then you should beat him to it," Holly said. "I'm sure any TV channel would be thrilled to have you do an interview for them."

"I don't do interviews."

"Exactly; it would be a coup for them."

"Absolutely not."

"Wait a minute, Judy," Victor joined in. "Holly's got something."

"I trust it isn't catching."

Victor chuckled, relieved that Judith's sense of humour was still intact. "What if you make a very brief statement with the true version of

472

events? It would be simple and tasteful and make anything that Digby concocted appear tacky and bitchy in comparison."

"Do you think that's better than doing a chat show?" Rupert asked.

"It's more instant. If we organize it now it'll be on the nightly news. There are several stations that would kill for it."

"I'll talk to our producers."

"Good idea. I'll contact some of the stations. ABC, NBC, maybe Fox."

"There's NY1," Holly added. "It's a cable station, which has Broadway theatre segments, so they might be especially interested."

"OK, I'll get on to them too. Perhaps we could do a general press call."

"Excuse me," Judith broke in, "Am I allowed a say?"

"Of course you are, Judy darling."

"If I do this interview, press call or whatever you call it, can I be myself?"

Victor frowned. "Not really. If you don't tone down your language every other word will be bleeped out. Why don't you give the interview as if you are playing a role: that of a wronged woman with a terrifying stalker?"

Judith sighed. "Wronged women aren't exactly my forte; still, I can give it a shot I suppose. Holly dear, you'd better give me lessons on how to look vulnerable and a little pathetic."

"Judith!" Rupert protested, putting his arm protectively around Holly.

"What?"

CHAPTER THIRTY FIVE

As Judith had predicted, Digby denied any knowledge of his nephew's actions and produced an act of such innocence that his lawyers left him in little doubt that the charges against him would be dropped. They might even sue for defamation of character.

Digby's lawyers had, however, reckoned without one of England's finest actresses. Judith might have hated interviews and the press in general, but her performance for them, seated on the stage of the St James before that evening's show, could easily have won her an Oscar. From the moment the recording started she switched on the charm, virtually flirting with the cameras. Briefly she outlined the situation with Joe and then, in answer to a question from a reporter over Digby's sacking, gave a sigh of great distress and appeared to be searching for suitable words.

Finally she smiled sadly and said, "Of course I was devastated when the producers felt that Mr Weston had to leave the play. No one likes to see a fellow actor lose a role, but regrettably he wasn't equal to the task. It was clear from the start that he was struggling both with developing his character and learning his lines, an experience which strikes terror into the heart of every actor. While we tried to help and support him, ultimately there is little anyone else can do; an actor in that situation has an insurmountable problem. It is truly tragic." She gave a look of such grief towards the cameras that one cameraman all but offered her a tissue.

"Perhaps we might have persevered with Mr Weston if this had been the only dilemma, yet it was further felt, by every member of the *All About Eve* Company, that he considered theatre work demeaning. Even during rehearsals he was taking time off to audition for television work. For an actress like myself, who cares passionately for theatre, this was soul destroying. This play is so close to my heart that..." At this point Judith let a carefully prepared tear drop down her cheek, ensuring every camera got a close up.

"Christ, she's magnificent," Victor muttered to Rupert, from where they were watching in the auditorium.

Rupert grinned. "She certainly is. Look at that gesture." He motioned to where Judith had placed her hands on her heart. "On anyone else it would look melodramatic, yet she makes it look natural."

"Shh," Holly said, as Judith started to speak again.

"I am genuinely sorry that Mr Weston felt bitter enough to seek revenge in such a manner, but then I don't believe it is the sign of an entirely sane man to issue slights against me in the newspapers and to bribe his nephew to deface or destroy my personal items and costumes."

"Are you saying he needs psychiatric help?" asked one of the reporters.

"I couldn't possibly make such a judgement.

I would leave that for a professional. I'd merely suggest he sees one."

"How do you feel now the situation has been resolved?"

"Immensely relieved. I'm not a woman who is easily frightened, however this situation left me feeling vulnerable. Actors are highly exposed to the public and I never knew when I might come face to face with a deranged knifeman or knife-woman."

"Has this incident spoilt your experience on Broadway?"

Judith rewarded the cameras with an exceedingly rare smile. "Thankfully, it has not. Appearing on Broadway with *All About Eve* has been a dream fulfilled and I am grateful to our wonderful audiences and for the charming hospitality we have received. Missing out on such a phenomenal experience must make Mr Weston, nay, Digby, suffer the hurt of his departure even deeper and I feel for him."

"Nay?" Rupert chortled. "How very Shakespearean!"

Victor shook his head in admiration. "The TV stations are going to love her."

Judith stood up. "Now, I must prepare for this evening's performance. I'd like to thank you for attending this press call at such short notice, but I considered it imperative that poor Joe, a sweet lad merely misled by his uncle, not receive the blame for these harrowing acts. Thank you." Judith meekly bowed her head as the cameras stopped rolling.

"Was that fucking good enough? I felt like a fucking idiot with a fucking frog stuck in my throat trying to get that fucking nauseating stuff out," Judith said, as she marched back to her dressing room with Victor, Rupert and Holly at her heels. "And note I didn't swear once, though I seem to recall referring to Digby as a flounder – I was trying not to say fuckwit."

"I'm not sure being a flat fish is any more complimentary than being a fuckwit," Holly observed. "Still, it was a wonderful speech. The bit about caring for theatre so much made me quite tearful. And what you said about Joe was nice."

"I don't give a toss about Joe; I merely wanted to ensure Digby didn't get off scot-free."

"Well, you meant the bit about the theatre," Holly said. "I know you did, so don't deny it."

"Humph."

BROADWAY SCANDAL OVER SACKING: GOLD VS. WESTON. ACCUSATIONS FLY, screamed one headline the following day. Judith's photograph and a summary of her statement to the press made the front page of every New York paper, causing Judith to enquire whether she'd been made President of the United States without realizing.

Wesley, who'd intended to return to New York only for the final week of *All About Eve*, instead flew over immediately, bringing Henrietta and Blythe with him. Having established his wife and daughter in an apartment hotel, Wesley met his fellow producers to discuss the Digby situation. To his enormous relief the confidence of Digby's lawyers had waned in light of their formidable opponent. If there was a court case and Judith performed as she had for the press call, their client would stand little chance.

Over coffee and doughnuts, lawyers for both sides agreed that official charges would be dropped if Digby admitted his involvement on the grounds of diminished responsibility, brought on by pills he was taking for depression – a convenient if false pretext. In exchange Digby would pay to replace Judith's items and costumes plus a large donation to a charity of her choosing.

"Why did Judith let him off so easy?" Jennifer asked Rupert, after news of the settlement reached the theatre.

"The last thing Judith wants is a court case. She's received her apology and endeared herself to most of New York at the same time."

"I wonder what Digby will do now."

"Leave town if he has any sense. I don't see any Broadway producers employing him in the foreseeable future."

Digby was indeed leaving town and heading back to California where, under the misapprehension that all publicity was good publicity, he believed he'd be welcomed with open arms. Furthermore, he'd admitted to depression and drug taking which was virtually a pre-requisite for an acting job in LA. He'd briefly check into the Betty Ford Clinic for effect, and then call his agent. He might even try and get Krystal, Mindy's mentor, to take him on as a client.

Joe was now out of a job and had lost his chance of going to college. Even if he hadn't dropped his uncle in it, Digby was running low on funds, with no job prospects and having paid out a large sum to a cats' protection league, Judith's chosen charity. Under the watchful eye of the stage manager, Joe had been allowed back into the theatre to collect his things, and as he left he bumped into Holly who was coming to meet Rupert after the matinee.

"What are you going to do now?" Holly asked, feeling almost sorry for the boy.

"Dunno, I'm blacklisted on Broadway," Joe replied. "I guess I'll go back to my folks, only they're in Pittsburgh and I don't have enough money for the fare."

"Oh, that's awful." Holly glanced around, ensuring that Judith wasn't going to suddenly materialize and murder her for what she was about to do. She dug into her purse and brought out a $100 bill. "Will that be enough?"

"Sure, that's swell." He smiled at her. "You're kinda cute. Would you like to go get a coffee or something?"

"No!"

"Why not?"

"Because what you did to Judith was totally wrong, even if it wasn't your idea, and Judith's my friend. Besides, I hardly know you."

Joe smirked at her. "You still gave me a hundred bucks." He waved the note at her. "So you must like me."

"No, I felt sorry for you. I don't any more." Holly grabbed hold of the note and pulled so hard that Joe let go in surprise. "You can jolly well walk back to Pittsburgh." Holly marched through the stage door, furious that Joe had almost conned her and relieved he'd ultimately failed. The matinee was in progress so the only person not on stage was Wesley, who was de-

479

lighted to see Holly.

"I hear you're doing the *Nicholas Nickleby* movie," he said. "I've been meaning to get in touch to say congratulations."

Holly blushed. "Actually, I'm not anymore; it fell through."

It was Wesley's turn to look uncomfortable. "I'm sorry."

Holly shrugged. "At least this way I could stay here for longer, otherwise I'd have been doing pre-production stuff, and I'm having such a great time. I love New York."

"So you've got nothing lined up?" Holly shook her head. Wesley glanced at his watch. "I must get back to Henrietta and Blythe. Could you walk with me? I'd like to continue this conversation."

"Sure, I'd love to see them both anyway. If you like, I could babysit one evening so you and Henrietta could go out on your own."

Wesley's face broke into a broad smile. "Are you serious? That would be wonderful. And in turn I may have a proposition for you."

It was the half of the evening show and Rupert was in Judith's room discussing an end of run party, which Rupert was failing to convince Judith they ought to hold, when Holly burst in.

"You'll never guess what?" she stammered out.

Judith crossed her arms. "Let's see, the last time you burst into my dressing room it was because Echo was in a porn movie. Now perhaps you've come to announce that she's joined a dubious sect because they promised her pretty clothes, and has become the tenth wife of the sect leader and is bearing him multiple children."

"No! I went back with Wesley to see Henrietta and Blythe – oh, and I'm going to babysit tomorrow night."

"You came in here practically floating on air because you're going to babysit for my goddaughter?" Judith enquired. "My, you are easily pleased."

"If you'd stop interrupting the poor girl you might hear what she's trying to say," Victor said, wandering in from the ante-room. Even after Joe's removal from the theatre he'd continued coming in each day. It had become a habit and one with which both he and Judith seemed comfortable – as long as they kept to their own areas. Often Holly would also come in and the two of them would play Scrabble or backgammon while their partners were on stage.

"We're listening, sweetheart," said Rupert.

"OK. You know Michael Marston?" Everybody knew Michael Marston; he was the hottest young heartthrob in Hollywood. Even Judith, who feigned ignorance of adolescent movie stars, could hardly have failed to have heard of him. At the age of twenty eight he'd already received two Oscar nominations, dated every eligible actress under thirty and was in the process of starting his own film production company. "Well, he wants to do some theatre work."

"Why does every movie star think they can perform on stage?" Judith demanded. "They have no fucking idea how to do it."

"Judy, be quiet," Victor said, ignoring the

glare she gave him. "Go on, Holly."

"And he wants to do it in London."

Judith gave a squeal of annoyance. "What right do Americans have to use the West End as some kind of theatrical acting academy? Let them fuck up in their own country."

Rupert threw up his hands in frustration. "Judith, will you please let Holly finish?"

Judith gave a wave of her hand which Holly took as her cue. "So his agent approached Wesley as producer, because Wesley has a reputation for staging classy productions without cutting corners and Michael Marston wants to play Hamlet."

Judith let out a groan. "What has Shakespeare done to deserve this?"

Victor grabbed a handkerchief from his pocket and thrust it in Judith's mouth.

"And," Holly continued quickly, "Wesley's been looking for someone to play Ophelia with stage experience and apparently he immediately considered me, only he thought I was doing *Nicholas Nickleby*. When I told him today that I'm not, he phoned Michael Marston's agent straight away and the agent spoke to Michael Marston who said he was happy to go with whoever Wesley suggested, especially when Wesley told him I'd won an Olivier Award for my last play. So if I want the role it's mine. I'd be playing Ophelia in the West End. It's like a dream." She gave a beaming smile around the room.

"That's fantastic, lovely," Victor said. "You'll be a wonderful Ophelia."

"At least there'll be one person who can act on the stage," Judith commented. "Perhaps it should be re-titled, Ophelia, Princess of Denmark Hill."

Holly regarded the silent Rupert. "Aren't you pleased?"

"Of course I am; I'm so thrilled I'm speechless. It's a brilliant opportunity and I'll be in the audience virtually every night cheering you on, as proud as punch." He pulled her into his arms. "You really deserve this."

Judith gave a snort. "I don't see what the big deal is; Holly is the perfect person for the role and if I'd known Wesley was producing *Hamlet* I'd have told him to cast her."

"But you didn't and Holly got it entirely on her own merit," Victor said. "And possibly her enthusiasm for babysitting." He winked at Holly.

"Ensure you don't drop the child on its head or let it electrocute itself until you've signed a contract," Judith remarked.

Rupert grinned. "I don't think Holly needs to worry. Miranda told me she looked after Blythe for a few minutes once – a fairly terrifying prospect which Blythe appears to have survived unscathed – in comparison Holly's Mary Poppins."

"How about you and I go and have a drink to celebrate while our other halves give their all on stage?" Victor said to Holly. "We could go up to the Rainbow Room, bribe our way to a window table and watch the sun go down over Manhattan?"

"I'm not dressed for that."

"Then we'll swing by your apartment so you can change. You don't mind me stealing her, do you, Rupert?"

Rupert shook his head. "Only ensure she's

back here by the end of the show so I can celebrate with her myself, or I'll turn you into a pumpkin."

"If he keeps eating pancakes and burgers at our local diner he'll turn into a pumpkin without any help from you," Judith observed.

"And you, my darling Judy, can be my very own Cinderella."

"I don't do rags, crystal slippers – or for that matter fairy tales."

"You're very quiet, Blake," Judith said, at the end of the show while they sat in her dressing room waiting for Victor and Holly to return. "What's on your mind?"

"First you're concerned over Victor's Afghanistan experience and now you're attempting to probe my inner psyche," Rupert said. "It's unnerving."

"Fine, don't tell me then. I'm not actually interested."

"All right."

Judith eyed him with frustration. She hated not knowing everything. "You were exceedingly subdued when Holly announced her news. And I don't believe it was merely the thrill which rendered you speechless as you claimed; you're not that easily muted. Didn't you and Miranda meet when you were playing Hamlet and she Ophelia?"

"Yes."

"Ah."

"Ah what?"

"You're worried you might lose Holly to her leading man. After all, he is nearer to her in age

484

than you, and I believe exceedingly charismatic."

Rupert pulled a face. "Not every Hamlet ends up with his Ophelia."

"No, the gay ones usually end up with Laertes, or as a threesome with Rosencrantz and Guildenstern."

Rupert grinned and before he could make a retort Holly burst into the room, flew across it and into Rupert's arms. "We've had the best time. Victor told the waiters it was a special occasion and they made me feel like I was royalty – not that I know what royalty feels like - and Victor wouldn't let me pay for anything and I'm sure champagne and cocktails somewhere like the Rainbow Room is terribly expensive. Isn't Victor lovely? Everybody's lovely. And I love you so much." She giggled. "Oh dear, I think I'm a bit squiffy."

"A bit?" Rupert said, laughing. "Victor's a lousy influence! Come on, let's get some food down you before you pass out. I had booked a table at the revolving restaurant at the top of Marriott, but maybe you're not up to that."

"Yes, I am. It'll be lovely," Holly sighed, happily. "We can both go round and round together." She attempted a pirouette and landed up falling on to Judith's bed. "Oops, I don't think I'll ever make the Royal Ballet. Or even the Un-Royal Ballet." She went into peals of laughter.

Rupert glanced at himself in the mirror. "I don't know if there's a dress code for the restaurant, so can I borrow your tie, Victor?" Victor took it off and passed it over. Rupert studied it. "This looks familiar."

"It's yours," Holly called out from the bed.

"I lent it to him at our apartment when I was changing. That's so funny: two dates, two venues, one tie. Wouldn't that be a great title for a movie?"

"Alfred Hitchcock already made a movie about a tie," Judith said. "It was called *Frenzy* and the tie was used for murder, which I may very well commit if I don't get some rest soon. Does nobody realize how exhausting this role is?"

"I always like a subtle hint," Rupert said, pulling Holly off the bed and linking his arm through hers. "Goodnight you two, see you tomorrow."

"Goodnight," Holly sang out as they left. "It's been a wonderful evening."

"I don't think I've ever seen Holly so relaxed," Judith remarked to Victor.

"No. She's always too busy worrying. I'm glad she let her hair down tonight, although I hadn't anticipated how quickly alcohol went to her head. Do you want to go out and eat?"

"I'm not hungry. I want to talk to you."

Victor raised his eyes to the ceiling. "What have I done now?"

Judith tried to find the words to ask about Afghanistan, but instead she changed the subject.

"Rupert's worried about Holly playing opposite that movie star."

"Why? Is there something wrong with him?"

"He met Miranda when they were playing those roles and I believe he's worried Holly might fall for this Michael Marston."

Victor chucked. "It won't do Rupert any harm to experience an emotion of which I'm sure he's often been the cause for others. However, I think he's fairly safe; Holly's too besotted with him to notice anyone else. Is that really what you wanted to talk to me about?"

Judith took a deep breath. "No. I want to know exactly what happened in Afghanistan and I don't want the U-rated version."

Victor studied her for a minute and then nodded. "All right, but let's go back to the hotel. I don't want to be in mid-story and find the stage door guy rustling the keys outside your dressing room demanding to lock up."

Judith's eyes narrowed. "He'd never dare do that to me."

Two hours later Judith was lying on the sofa in their suite, her head on Victor's lap. "Why on earth would you choose to do something which involves such risks?" she asked. "What's the point?"

"The point is trying to make a difference. Telling people what's happening first hand, and ferreting out the actual truth. When I was acting I never felt fulfilled in the same way."

Judith sat bolt upright, nearly knocking her head on Victor's chin. "Are you saying that theatre is a superficial career? That it's not important? Because let me tell you you're entirely wrong. People need theatre to escape from reality by focusing on a different world which stops them going insane when somebody they care for has vanished in the fucking desert. Or... whatever their problem is."

"Hey." Victor put his arms around her and refused to be shaken off. "Darling Judy, of course what you do is as important, merely in a different way." He looked down at her. "Are you crying?"

"I most certainly am not."

"I see. Your whisky must have splashed on to your face then." He pulled out a handkerchief and carefully wiped some tears off her cheek.

Furious at this display of emotion Judith pushed him away. "If you're so obsessed with the truth why aren't you publishing your experiences? You're not the first journalist kidnapped and I doubt you'll be the last. People should be aware of what it's like. And frankly you ought to get some kind of recognition for what you endured."

"It might be too gruesome."

"That's never worried you before. People are always telling me what hard-hitting stuff you write." She glared at him. "You're worried that it might upset me, aren't you?"

Victor inclined his head. "Yes, to a degree."

"So now I know, and I demand you write the story."

Victor hesitated. "There's Holly too."

"Fuck Holly."

"I'm not sure Rupert would like that."

"Ha, bloody ha. Listen, Holly is absurdly oversensitive at times, but she will survive, and she'd hate to be the reason you lost this opportunity. If you're that worried tell her not to read it; she's so disgustingly obedient she'd probably do what you said."

"Whereas you, my darling Judy, would do the exact opposite."

"Absolutely. Victor, promise me you'll write

it."

"OK, I promise." Victor ran his hand down Judith's cheek. "Thank you, Judy darling."

"Don't get all sentimental on me. I have an ulterior motive. Once I finish this damn play I'm going to require a very long rest - I may even retire - therefore you'll need to earn a lot of money from your writing to support us."

"You'll never retire. Look at you, The Queen of Broadway: the one and only Margo Channing of the stage."

Judith snorted, yet, in truth, she was going to miss *All About Eve* terribly. It had been a part of her life for so long. Perhaps she should take it on a world tour and then back to London. Christ no, she'd be like Topol, still playing the same role in *Fiddler on the Roof* after fifty odd years.

"I don't want to be like Topol," she said.

Victor, who was rarely fazed by anything, merely enquired, "Shall I take out an advertisement in the *New York Times* to that effect?"

"Be serious."

"I am. I'm very relieved to hear that I won't have to go to bed with an elderly Jewish man who keeps singing *If I Were a Rich Man*."

"Honestly!" Judith stood up and stormed into the bedroom, from where Victor could hear stifled laughter. He turned on his laptop and started writing.

CHAPTER THIRTY SIX

The American producers of *All About Eve* had wanted to continue its run after the initial scheduled six months. The play was hugely profitable and it seemed absurd to close it. Since Judith, Rupert and Mindy wouldn't extend their contracts (which was judicious in Mindy's case as it was taking all Aubrey's efforts to keep her sane), the producers resolved to recast. When Judith heard this, and of some of the names suggested to replace her, she was adamant the play would not carry on without her.

Wesley was inclined to agree with Judith, even though he would lose the chance of further profit. It was better to quit while the product was quality rather than let it go downhill and cast God knows who in the roles. Since Wesley held the original rights, the Americans reluctantly agreed that the play would close as originally scheduled on September 20th.

While Alyce and Kyle accepted the play's imminent closure pragmatically (the fact that Rupert was taking Alyce to the US Open before the run finished, with a pass to the tennis players' area, was more exciting to her than any play extension) and Paige was happy since she'd landed a small role in a New York cop TV show, it was left to Jennifer and Richard to mourn the future loss of *All About Eve*. As they did this over many late nights in a variety of bars and restaurants, Jennifer wondered if she wasn't going to miss Richard even more than Rupert – though obviously for different reasons.

Strangely, Jennifer realized she was also going to miss Holly. Could she really go and stay with her and Rupert? Even though Holly had explained they lived in a three bedroom house in central London with a small garden, Jennifer still pictured a country mansion where she'd creep down long corridors to the west wing to discover Rupert waiting for her naked in a huge four poster bed. Maybe she shouldn't go. It might be too odd. She might be too odd. Perhaps she should take up Richard's offer of his sofa bed instead.

"You've still got me and Nate," Alyce told her, when Jennifer had poured out her heart to the older woman one night on the subway going home. "We're virtually neighbours and aren't gonna suddenly move to London. Hey, quit that," she added as a tear dropped down Jennifer's cheek.

"I hate it when shows close," Jennifer sniffed. "I know it's part of the business, but you get real close to everyone and then never see them again. It's like having a divorce in the family. I thought we might at least have a party or something, but I gather Judith doesn't want one."

"Yes, I was thinking about that, and I might have an idea."

"Christ, I'm shattered," Judith said, as she returned to the dressing room after the packed house on the final Sunday matinee had stood and cheered for curtain call after curtain call. One fan had even run forward and presented

491

her with a bunch of flowers. She glanced around at the bleak walls bereft of their good luck cards and other mementos which Tim had taken down during the second act. "Where's Victor? Typical, he's always hanging around and when he could finally be useful and help take my belonging back to the hotel he's done a vanishing act. Find him, Tim. Please."

"Sure." Tim disappeared off and didn't reappear.

"What is this, the Marie Celeste?" Judith muttered, putting the last few things in a bag and taking a final look around. Next week some other bugger would be sitting, staring at themselves in the mirror, preparing to go on stage.

"Saying goodbye?"

Judith spun round. "For fuck's sake, Rupert, you made me jump. And I was merely checking I hadn't forgotten anything. It's only a room, why would I be saying goodbye? I'm not emotional about inanimate objects. If I was I'd have been demonstrative with half the actors I've ever worked with. And where is everybody?"

"There's a meeting on stage; you're needed too."

"Forget it; the play's over, I don't have to do anything else about it."

"You might want to do something about this. The Americans have persuaded Wesley to recast after all and open again next month. Meryl Streep is on stage now considering the role."

"What!" Judith threw open the dressing room door, strode down to the stage where she stopped abruptly. "What the...?"

There was a general cry of "Surprise!" and

492

no sign of Meryl Streep. Instead the set was adorned with a huge banner which read:

THANK YOU JUDITH
A TRUE BROADWAY STAR

Under it stood the entire *All About Eve* acting, production, and backstage company, plus Holly and Victor. Streamers and party decorations were strewn around and there were plates of food on the props tables, which had been pushed on stage. On Margo Channing's apartment table sat a cake with the *All About Eve* poster iced on the top.

Jennifer pushed a glass of champagne into Judith's hand. "We wanted to do something special to thank you for giving us the chance to be involved in this play."

"We know you're not crazy about parties," Alyce explained, "so we thought we'd organize something on the set, as if it were almost part of the show."

"So there's no Meryl Streep?" Judith enquired of Rupert.

"You're so bloody obstinate I had to say something to get you down here. If I'd failed Victor was going to forcibly carry you. I wasn't that foolhardy!"

Victor grinned. "They asked me to be the one to convince you to come down, but I thought Rupert was the better actor."

"Yes, he is."

"Judith, that's cruel," Holly said, putting her arm through Victor's.

"It's OK, I'm getting used to it." Victor patted Holly's hand.

"We got you a present," Paige broke in, unable

493

to hold back her excitement any longer.

"For fuck's sake," Judith snapped. "We did first night presents, why on earth do we need to do last night ones too?"

"Because we wanted to," Alyce said. "Working with you has been an experience none of us will ever forget. You made the play what it was, and we wanted to give you something to remember us by."

"Admittedly after some of the less than good experiences you've undergone here you might prefer not to remember us," Kyle said, "but that's too bad. For once we're getting the last say."

There was general laughter, except from Judith. She folded her arms as she regarded Kyle. "I believe you'll find you're wrong young man: I always get the last say on my productions." The side of her mouth twitched slightly and the cast exhaled with relief. "So where is this offering? I should warn you, if you've bought me a Statue of Liberty headdress I will ensure none of you ever work again."

Jennifer carefully carried over a box and put it on the table from the last scene of the play. Judith pulled off the tape and stared inside in total silence.

"It's a model of the St James Theatre," Paige said.

Judith said nothing.

"You can take the roof off," Jennifer told her. Judith made no move so Jennifer did the honours. Underneath was a model of the *All About Eve* set, perfectly in proportion.

"That's incredible," said Holly, trying to make

up for Judith's silence. "Wherever did you get it made?"

"I have a nephew who builds exclusive doll-houses. I sent him photos of the theatre and the set and he copied them." Alyce said.

"He should go into making set models," Wesley contributed, examining it over Judith's head. "It's flawless."

"Do you like it, Judith?" Paige asked.

"I don't know how the hell I'm going to get it home," Judith finally spoke. "It's hardly practical."

"I'll carry it as my hand luggage," Victor said. "I'll sit with it on my lap the entire flight if necessary. Some things shouldn't be practical, and that is absolutely amazing."

Judith slugged back her champagne. "This is one lousy party; even I know they're supposed to have music."

Richard leapt over to the piano. "Please take your partners for a waltz," he called out as he started to play. Victor put the box and its precious contents out of harm's way in the wings and then held out his arms to Judith.

"Don't be silly, I'm not dancing."

"Yes, you are."

It was amazing how strong Victor's grip was, Judith thought, as he pulled her around the stage, to a round of applause from the onlookers.

Rupert took Holly's hand, but she shook her head. "Dance with Jennifer," she whispered, looking at Jennifer's bereft face. "I'm going to ask Wesley."

Jennifer buried her face in Rupert's shoulder

495

as they danced. "I'm gonna miss you so much." She took a deep breath, glad that she couldn't see his face. "You know I'm in love with you, don't you?" Jennifer felt rather than heard his sigh. "Sorry, have I embarrassed you?"

Rupert pulled away so he was looking at her. "Certainly not - there's nothing we men like better than a beautiful lady in love with us. But I'm not worth it, really. You can do a lot better."

"Why do men always use that as an excuse? Why don't they simply say, 'I don't fancy you'?"

"Well, in my case it isn't an excuse, it's the truth. You have no idea what a bastard I can be, and what Holly has to put up with. Believe me, when you're happily married to the perfect man you'll wonder what you ever saw in me. And FYI I do fancy you."

Jennifer tried to smile. "Is that the speech you give all your adoring females?"

"No. That's a Jennifer Hoffman, very dear friend, from the heart, special." He drew her closer and kissed her on the top of her head. At that point Richard increased the tempo of his playing and Rupert and Jennifer had to give their full attention to keeping up.

"Look at Aubrey and Mindy," Alyce panted as she and Kyle shot around the stage in something resembling a waltz. Aubrey didn't look as if he'd ever learnt to waltz and Mindy's dance experience appeared to consist of tai-chi, so the two of them were performing a strange arm-waving hop in the corner of the stage."

Judith and Victor left the party after an hour, so quietly that no one noticed immediately apart from Tim who had returned to the dressing room to wait for her. Judith shook his hand goodbye and palmed him five one hundred dollar bills. Then with a nod she was gone; goodbyes weren't her thing.

"Do you think she liked her present?" Jennifer asked Rupert as they cleared up later.

"I'd say she adored it."

"What about the party?" Alyce enquired. "She didn't mind, did she?"

Rupert shook his head. "I doubt anyone has ever thrown her a surprise party, or given her such a thoughtful present. That's why she was so quiet; Judith doesn't handle emotion very well or very vocally." He glanced over to Aubrey and Mindy, sitting huddled together on the on-stage sofa. "Should we tell them the party's almost over or leave them communing with each other?"

"Do you think it's a melding of great minds?" Jennifer asked.

Rupert raised his eyes upwards. "It certainly appears to be a melding of some kind of minds. I hope Hollywood is ready for Aubrey, if Mindy can swing him a job."

"I hope she can because I had a call from Michael Marston's agent wanting to know if Aubrey would be available to direct *Hamlet*," Wesley said. "He heard about the success of *All About Eve* and wants the same director."

"Then you'd better hire Judith," Rupert said.

"That's not a bad idea. But presuming Judith is not yet ready to admit to being a director, I would rather employ one for *Hamlet* who's really on the ball, since we have an actor new to the stage." He smiled at Holly. "Even though I have an experienced Ophelia."

Holly blushed. "Actually, I'm not that experienced at Shakespeare, I haven't done any since I was at drama school, so Judith's been giving me some advice."

"Some advice?" Rupert said to Wesley. "Holly's over at Judith's so often that Victor and I are officially declaring ourselves *Hamlet* widowers."

"Perhaps I <u>should</u> ask Judith if she'd like to direct it," Wesley said. "Although I doubt Michael Marston would survive the experience."

Kyle wandered over, carrying a handful of balloons. "Does anyone mind if I take these for my children?"

"Take some cakes too," Alyce said, piling some into a container.

From the piano came the sound of laughter. Jennifer had joined Richard and they were attempting to play chopsticks.

"I wish we could keep him," Alyce sighed. "He would be such an asset to Broadway."

"Yes, not many people can play chopsticks that badly," Rupert commented as a glaringly wrong note reached them. "Is there any champagne left?"

Kyle examined several empty bottles. "It doesn't look good."

"That could explain Jennifer and Richard's dubious piano playing," Rupert remarked.

"I suppose we should go soon and let them lock up the theatre," Alyce said with reluctance. "I expect Judith's already back at the hotel by now."

Judith had actually been driven off only a few minutes ago. Having loaded the provided car with Judith's possessions, Victor had returned to the stage door to collect her, expecting her to march through the huge crowd still loyally waiting outside. However, as Judith emerged the crowd broke into enthusiastic applause and after a couple of steps Judith stopped and turned to Victor. "I don't suppose you have a pen, do you? Tonight I believe I may stop and sign. Margo Channing is leaving the building in style." She lowered her voice. "Though if anyone should attempt to put their arm around me or touch me in any way I want you to inflict serious damage."

EPILOGUE

The wedding chapel on Las Vegas' famous Strip was packed with the acting company, late of the St James Theatre, New York. It was two weeks after *All About Eve* had closed, when the English contingent should have been on their way home and the Americans to find whatever work or unemployment benefits that they could. The invitation had been last-minute but universally accepted by the company and their families.

Outside, Holly nervously bit her fingers. "Do you think the arrangements are OK? It's so important that everything goes right."

Rupert put his arm around her shoulders. "It's going to be perfect."

Holly glanced at her watch. "Where are their cars? We can't afford to run late; we only have the chapel for half an hour. I don't want to have the next couple breathing down our necks. Maybe a Vegas wedding wasn't the best idea." She looked at Rupert, who was laughing at her. "You're not helping."

"It's the perfect idea and you're doing a marvellous job."

A white limousine rolled up disgorging Judith and Victor on to the pavement beside them.

"Sorry, we judged it rather close," Victor said.

"It was entirely Victor's fault," Judith broke in. "He was so busy gambling in the hotel he didn't bother telling me it was time to get ready."

"I sent you a text," Victor protested. "And I've

upgraded us to a suite on the proceeds of my winnings."

"How much did you win?" Holly asked.

"About two grand."

Rupert whistled. "If I come with you later can you give me some tips? That way I won't have to sell my future wife here into slavery if my career dies."

"Sure, only be careful no one thinks you're cheating or they'll take you into the back rooms and break your arms."

"Arms I could cope with as long as they didn't do any damage to my wedding tackle," Rupert retorted with a chuckle.

"That's not funny," Holly said.

Judith, who in spite of the intense heat was wearing a coat, finally threw it off and Holly gave a gasp. "Judith, you look beautiful. That dress is amazing on you."

Judith snorted. "I hardly consider it to be my colour, but since you bought it for me I felt obliged to wear it. Besides, Victor banned me from wearing black. He said it was inappropriate. I don't see why I can't wear what I want. It's hardly a traditional wedding."

Another limousine drew up; two passengers in its back seat. Holly smiled with relief. "Rupert and Victor, take your places in the chapel," she ordered. "We must start."

Rupert leant over and kissed her. "I'll see you in there."

Victor turned to Judith, obviously about to behave in a similar manner until Judith gave him a look to show exactly what she thought of that notion. He merely winked at Holly and followed Rupert inside.

"God knows why I agreed to do this," Judith complained. "I must be insane."

"Because you were asked," Holly said firmly, as the passengers alighted from the limousine.

The chapel doors opened and the congregation turned to watch the bride walk down the aisle. At the front her groom beamed at her with deep affection.

The vows were simple and within ten minutes Jennifer Hoffman and Richard Gresham were married. Rupert had acted as best man with Holly, Judith and Alyce as Jennifer's three attendants – the only title Judith would accept. If anyone had mentioned the words 'brides' and 'maid' she was getting straight on a plane.

As they walked back down the aisle Kyle's children, thrilled to be given official permission to make a mess, covered them with confetti.

"It's so romantic," Holly said outside, as Jennifer and Richard posed for photographs.

"Don't be ridiculous," Judith said. "They're marrying so Richard can get a green card to work here and Jennifer a reciprocal arrangement for England. They're hardly Romeo and Juliet."

"I think you're wrong," Holly said. "I mean, yes, that's part of the reason, but they're genuinely fond of each other."

"Holly dear, that may be true, but in case it's escaped your mind, Richard is gay. Unless he suddenly discovers some latent heterosexual tendencies, it's hardly a proper marriage."

"You can have a marriage built on affection." Holly wasn't giving up.

"Maybe, but, technically, unless it's consummated it's not a marriage. Tonight he should be fucking her until she can barely walk." Holly's mouth dropped open. There were times when, like Echo, she'd wondered about Judith's sex life. It was obviously quite animated.

After the entire wedding party had eaten at the Bellagio Hotel, with its view of the dancing fountains outside, Rupert, Holly, Paige, Mindy, Aubrey, Tom and the newlyweds took gondola rides inside the Venetian Hotel. Alyce, standing with Nate beside the fake canal, waved at them as they passed.

"I'm not sure if the gondolier should be serenading Richard and Jennifer or Richard and Tom," Rupert commented from one gondola, watching the unusual threesome on another.

"I wish Judith and Victor had joined us," Holly said.

Judith's precise words on being asked had been, "If I wanted to go on a fucking gondola on a fucking canal I'd go to fucking Venice."

As they alighted and ambled around the inside version of St Mark's Square, where the painted ceiling made it perpetual evening, Richard came up behind Holly and Rupert, putting his arms affectionately around their shoulders. "We're going back to the hotel so Jennifer and I can continue our personal research, because we don't know how soon the immigration people will begin their interrogation. Tom's started a dossier. We've already covered favourite movies, favourite books, desert island discs and most importantly favourite perfumes and aftershaves. It's like being on Mr and Mrs, only we

503

win a work permit and not a carriage clock. To-night we're covering childhoods. I don't suppose you have any tips about a heterosexual one, do you, Rupert?"

Holly glanced at Rupert anxiously, but he merely laughed and said, "Believe me, you wouldn't want my childhood."

"Fair enough. How about early sexual encounters with women? I need to convince these people that I'm straight – or at least bisexual."

"I'll make you some notes."

"Richard, are we going?" Tom called over.

Richard's face lit up. "Sure." He gave Rupert and Holly a quick peck each on the cheek and moved to join Tom.

Jennifer ran over to thank Holly again for her wedding organization and to give both of them a hug, holding on to Rupert for rather longer. "See you guys in England," she said. "I can't believe I'm gonna be able to live there if I want."

Rupert gently pushed her away from him. "So you'll finally be able to live your dream of sitting in an English country pub with dogs wearing wellington boots."

Jennifer blushed, half with embarrassment and half with pleasure. "I can't believe you remembered I said that."

Rupert grinned. "It was a memorable mental picture. I should warn you however, I can't visualize Richard marching through country fields in wellingtons or accompanying wellington wearing dogs."

"I don't care; I'll walk on my own. It'll work out, I know it will." Jennifer smiled and went off to join her husband and husband's boyfriend.

"I hope she's right," Holly said. "Marriage is such a big step, even in these circumstances."

Rupert took her hand. "Yes. And I can't wait until we get home and have ours."

Rupert had booked him and Holly into Caesar's Palace and after the exertions of the day Holly gratefully crawled into the massive bed, falling asleep within a few minutes and dreaming that Rupert was having his arms broken by casino employees for cheating at blackjack. She kept trying to tell them that he'd never cheat, but nobody would listen to her and in the end they nailed him to a giant roulette wheel and kept spinning him round and round, beating him with belt buckles, screaming that they were his stepfathers, while she begged them to stop, crying out Rupert's name. Then somebody was grabbing her; they going to nail her up there too. She tried to struggle but the grip was too tight, and she started screaming.

"Holly! Holly, wake up." Holly opened her eyes to find it was Rupert holding her. "It's OK, sweetheart, it's only a nightmare. What on earth was it about? You were shrieking out my name with such terror; I wasn't aware I frightened you so much."

Holly punched him lightly. "Idiot!" she said. "And it'll sound stupid."

"I promise not to laugh."

Rupert didn't laugh. Instead he wrapped Holly in his arms and lay with her like that until she fell asleep. Perhaps he shouldn't have shared his childhood with her if it was going to affect her so adversely, yet to his surprise it had felt good.

Rupert too drifted off, only to be woken shortly after by Holly shaking him because someone was knocking insistently on the door. It was amazing he hadn't heard it himself he thought, pulling on one of the hotel's dressing gowns, but then after years of living with Miranda he'd got used to sleeping through a lot.

Rubbing his eyes, Rupert peered blearily through the spy hole to discover Victor and Judith standing outside. He opened the door. "If it isn't fire, flood or earthquake I'm going back to bed."

"It's none of those," Judith said. "Only I've done something rather silly."

"No you haven't," Victor retorted. "Hello, Holly; nice toga - very in keeping with the hotel's theme."

"Thank you." Holly had joined them, with the bed sheet wrapped around her. "What did you do?" she asked Judith.

"Actually it's your fault," Judith said.

"It is?" Holly wondered what she could've done when she hadn't even seen Judith since the wedding meal at the Bellagio.

"You came up with this whole Las Vegas wedding notion. It puts stupid ideas into people's heads." She sighed. "You see, Victor and I appear to have got married."

Chewing the Scenery

Davina Elliott

"So," said Wesley, "Alexander has walked out again, Judith is re-directing the play and you suspect a major conspiracy. Anything else I should know before I swallow an entire bottle of Valium?"

Legendary leading lady Judith Gold is at loggerheads with avant-garde theatre director Alexander Columbus on a West End production of the ghostly comedy *Blithe Spirit.* Judith considers he is ruining an excellent play, an opinion shared by fellow cast members movie star Rupert Blake and his possessive real-life wife Miranda Flynn.

If Alexander doesn't ruin the play, his casting of a vacuous American ex-beauty queen with virtually no theatre experience and even less talent may.

For producer Wesley Bartlett, the perfect project has turned into a theatrical nightmare, complete with unexploded bombs and air raid sirens in a 1930s drawing room comedy.

ISBN 978-0-9560960-0-5

Climbing the Curtain

Davina Elliott

Janet sighed happily. "It's such a lovely company."

Rupert gave a short laugh. "You must be the only person to think that. We've got a notoriously difficult leading lady, an ex-Hollywood prima donna, a supporting actress who saves hedgehogs and wears no underwear, and an actor who's a drunk."

Judith Gold, grande dame of the British theatre, has chosen her latest venture – a stage version of the classic film *All About Eve*, written to her specifications. Resolving to have complete control, she informs producer Wesley Bartlett that she will select both creative team and cast. The result is a spineless director and the perfect acting ensemble, including movie star Rupert Blake.

Yet even Judith can't control her company's offstage lives, which threaten to cause onstage chaos. How fitting therefore that a respected war correspondent is taking an unusual interest in the play – and its leading lady.

ISBN 978-0-9560960-1-2